THE
BURNING
WITCH

Volume 2

Delemhach

To Robin Sullivan, who has been incredible with illuminating the ins an outs of the publishing world and offering her expertise, and to my highschool hero, Carolyn Martinelli. She was always in my corner even when the odds weren't in my favor and she deserves the world.

Cover design by Kate O'Hara

ISBN: 978-1-0394-4689-2

Published in 2024 by Podium Publishing, ULC
www.podiumentertainment.com

Podium

THE
BURNING
WITCH

Volume 2

CHAPTER 1

FLIPPING OUT

Katarina awoke the morning after rescuing Prince Eric Reyes feeling exhausted to her bones.

Despite not having used a significant amount of her magic, the strange man who had been the ringleader of the mercenaries keeping Eric hostage had performed something unlike anything she'd ever experienced before . . .

Slowly opening her eyes, Kat stared at the smooth, marble arched ceiling of her chamber and continued to lay still for several long moments.

Her index finger was tapping the crisp sheets beneath the blankets despite her weariness . . . which was abnormal. Usually, if she was tired, there wasn't any energy for her tics to show themselves.

Just what . . . is wrong with me . . . ?

Taking a slow, steady breath, Kat closed her eyes.

She searched her being for her magic, searched for the powerful burning hum that was always present whether she wanted it to be or not, and found—

She flinched.

Her magic was pouring through her like thick, searing molten steel.

Her heartbeat quickened.

Shifting her focus, Katarina switched her awareness to the aggressive swell of power in her chest that she had locked away a long time ago . . .

Her eyes snapped open, a cold sweat breaking out along her brow, and her aura already flickering wildly about herself.

"Gods. No, no, no!" Katarina sat upright, tears rising in her eyes as she jumped to her feet and began running around her chamber in her chemise.

She needed to burn it away quickly. Even though her body felt heavy, how was it possible her magic was *more* alive?!

As her fifth lap was ending, Pina appeared in Katarina's path, sitting primly as though she had been waiting there the entire time.

Skidding to a halt, Kat stared at her familiar, barely registering the calm, sweet gaze the feline bore as she reached down with trembling hands and plucked her up.

Pressing the kitten to her shoulder, Pina touched her soft cheek to her witch's and purred loudly.

With a shuddering breath, Kat closed her eyes. "It took me years to build up that defense . . . I just feel so . . . off balance. I don't know what that man did to me . . ." she whispered to her familiar as tears dampened her eyelashes.

Pina nuzzled Kat's cheek even more avidly, her whiskers brushing against the redhead's face, tickling her.

As Kat stood in place, clutching her familiar close, an ounce of calm reentered her being. She found her breaths were once again settling back down when a sharp knock interrupted the tentative stillness.

Giving a small start, Pina wasted no time in leaping down from Kat's arms.

"Who is it?" Kat called out, folding her empty arms over her middle protectively.

"It's me," Kezia's unmistakable voice called in hushed tones through the door. "Can I come in?"

Hastily wiping away her tears, Kat glanced at the full-length mirror in the corner of her room to confirm she didn't look weepy.

She grimaced.

While not weepy, she did look pale, and the deep, dark lines under her eyes appeared all the more dramatic.

Ah well . . . I'll blame it on the late night.

Crossing her chamber and opening her door, Kat gave a halfhearted smile at the Troivackian beauty whose left hand rested atop her growing belly.

"Gods, you look a fright. Come, let's get you fixed up." Kezia swished into the room, pressing the redhead back into the chamber gently before closing the door quietly behind herself.

"Do we need to prepare for the coronation?" Kat asked while rubbing her eyes to try and wake herself up and once again avoid worrisome thoughts about her unstable magic.

"You aren't doing *any* work today, *ryshka*."

"*Ryshka*?" Kat raised an eyebrow with a shadow of a smile. "Isn't that the old Troivackian tongue for *dear* or *darling*?"

Kezia grinned beautifully, her exquisite eyes dancing. "You know the old tongue?"

Kat nodded slowly. "My mother made sure my brother and I learned it from a young age, though we don't often get a chance to use it."

"The more I hear of your mother, the more interesting she seems." Kezia gave a tinkling laugh while pulling open the wardrobe containing Katarina's dresses.

The redhead didn't respond as her handmaiden hummed cheerily and began sifting through her clothes.

"What's going on?" Kat questioned, staring at Kezia's shining ebony locks that were half pinned back with crystals and gold chained adornments.

The handmaiden's hands that were fluttering like graceful doves over the dresses hesitated for a moment, but then continued their work as though nothing had interrupted them in the first place.

"You are to go to the kitchens. It is after the luncheon hour, so you must be hungry."

Kat sensed there was something else that Kezia wasn't telling her.

"So, all maids are banned from my room . . . I'm guessing because we are really leaning into that story about a flu, and that's why no one has seen me . . . ?"

"Something like that, *ryshka*."

Katarina could hear the smile in Kezia's response, and so she tried to force herself to calm down again, though it was proving difficult. "Is everyone else alright? Eric and Alina are reunited? Celeste and Mr. Kraft aren't in any trouble?"

"Yes, everyone is safe and sound here, and I'm given to understand it is in large part thanks to you, Lady Katarina." At last, Kezia turned around with the selected gown in her hand.

She had picked one of deep yellow and was holding it up between her and Kat with a satisfied glow in her cheeks.

"Here we are. This will match your eyes nicely."

When Kat didn't move a muscle and merely stared blankly at the dress, Kezia allowed her pleasant expression to change as her brows lowered and her mouth twisted in a small, worrisome knot.

"Everything will be alright," she attempted to soothe, but this only succeeded in making Kat jar out of her daze enough to take the dress and avoid her gaze.

"Thank you, Lady Kezia. I'll be sure to make my way down to the kitchen. Am I supposed to take the servants' stairwell?"

Kezia watched the redheaded witch as she walked over to the changing screen and began to undress.

"Yes. Everyone is preparing for the coronation tomorrow, so the far northeast stairwell will be empty, and it will let you out directly by the kitchens to your right."

"Alright. I guess I'll see you tomorrow then," Kat replied distantly.

She just needed to be alone . . .

Especially if she was to get her thoughts and feelings under control before whatever was about to happen, happened.

Kezia waited, staring at the wrought iron screen pensively. She was torn between wanting to console Katarina about whatever she had endured the previous night, or allowing her time and space to process whatever troubled her.

With a sigh, the expectant mother gave her belly a small rub before reaching a decision and taking her leave. She had decided that she could always try to speak more about it with the redhead later.

After pulling the deep yellow dress over her head and slipping her leather sandals on, Kat considered doing something with her hair, but the heaviness in her arms deterred any motivation to complete the task.

So after a quick brushing through of the coppery snarls, she set off to the kitchens.

The castle was eerily quiet as she traveled through its lonely corridors, but in a way, she was grateful for its chilly emptiness; it meant she didn't have to mask her true feelings.

She idly wondered what was awaiting her in the kitchens.

Perhaps Alina and her husband wanted a recounting of what had transpired the night before . . . or maybe it was just so she could eat in peace.

Katarina set foot at the bottom of the servants' stairwell and was again greeted with the same hush she had experienced the entire trip down.

She felt too tired for this new anxiety-inducing strangeness.

She faced the kitchen doors with her eyes fluttering.

I wish I could just stay in my chamber all day . . .

Pressing one of the doors open, Kat stepped inside, and she laid eyes on another person at last.

Frowning, she closed the door behind herself while gazing upon the person's back as they faced the fire; the repetitive clanking of steel against a porcelain bowl reached her ears.

"Eric?" she called out uncertainly.

Turning around, the prince of Daxaria held a pale green bowl filled with batter in his hands, his wavy blond hair pulled back in its ponytail, revealing he was dressed in a cream-colored peasant's tunic with an apron tied around his waist.

"Afternoon," he greeted with a small half smile and a nod of his head.

Kat moved farther into the room and peered around.

No one else was present . . .

"What's going on?" she asked while drawing closer to the cooking table.

"Ah, I asked Lady Kezia to help me arrange a meeting with you here," Eric explained while setting the bowl down and turning back to the clay oven with a grate over the flames. He reached to its side and plucked up a cast-iron pan that he then set over the heat before adding a dollop of butter and pushing it around the pan until it was thoroughly coated.

"That doesn't answer my question," Kat pointed out while gingerly reaching out to touch the table's worn top.

"Right, well I can elaborate in a bit. Been a while since I've cooked, and I don't think we want burned pancakes."

Kat blinked.

"Sit down." Eric looked over his shoulder at her, his hazel eyes unreadable. "You look tired."

Without even giving the time for Kat to react to his words, the prince returned his focus back to his task.

He proceeded to grab the green bowl and scoop out the batter into the pan, immediately filling the room with the very familiar smell of her father's special pancake recipe.

The smell of cinnamon and nutmeg . . . the faintly sweet aroma of the batter cooking . . .

Warmth and emotion overcame Kat as she sank into the chair at the table without a word.

"How . . ." She began to speak but didn't get the chance to finish before Eric proceeded to flip the breakfast pastry over once to reveal a perfectly golden, crispy circle.

So, she remained silent as he continued to cook pancake after pancake, until there was a stack of twelve that he carefully carried over to the table and set in front of her.

The steam, curling up and assaulting her senses in all the right ways, succeeded in relaxing Kat's nerves even further.

"Now, I think you were trying to ask me something?" Eric prompted while dunking his hands in a sudsy bucket, and then snagging a tea towel from the table and drying his hands.

"What are you doing . . . by making me pancakes and . . . and arranging a secret meeting?" Kat wondered aloud, her sluggish mind struggling with the sequence of peculiar events.

She tried to glean something from Eric's expression as she spoke, but aside from noticing he was pale and looked rather tired himself, learned nothing.

"Well, for one, you rescued me. Least I can do is make you a meal to say thanks," he began with a sincere smile.

Kat didn't smile back. She stared at him with a funny feeling brewing in her gut.

When he noticed her wariness, Eric let out a sigh and dropped his gaze to the table. There was no point in dragging things out.

"Kat, how much do you remember about when you rescued me?"

Her golden eyes snapped to his face.

She hadn't even started to try and piece together the chaos from the night before.

Blinking, Kat cast her mind back . . .

She knew the strange man had broken her defenses and forced her magic to the forefront, where it ruled her being . . . She remembered throwing some of the kidnappers around . . . She remembered the undying thirst . . . the *need* to end the man who had done that to her . . .

After that, things became hazy.

The foreign, violent urges had faded to something else though. Something gentler, and at the time, it had been a relief.

When she had opened her eyes and returned to full consciousness, she had found herself in Eric's arms on the broom, riding back to the castle, and shortly thereafter had the vague recollection of being escorted to bed.

"I think I recall most of it," Kat began while still feeling as though there was something else she may have been missing . . . "I remember chucking around a few men . . . One was a water witch, and the other . . . He . . . he did something that I—"

Eric placed the tea towel back on the table and stepped back awkwardly.

Kat frowned. "What is it? What happened?"

The prince bit down on his tongue, and his left hand gently clasped into a fist that he tapped his leg with.

It was something uncomfortable to talk about.

Kat realized this and stared at him in alarm. "What did I do?"

Wincing apologetically, Eric did his best to maintain eye contact with her when he said, "You kissed me, Kat."

The redhead's face grew slack, and her heart dropped to her stomach.

"I . . . what?"

"That's why I wanted to talk to you before we convened with Brendan Devark and my sister. I wasn't sure what you remembered and figured you might want to know everything before walking into that meeting."

Kat blinked at Eric.

The whistle of a kettle behind him made the prince turn. He once again seized the tea towel before hastily pouring the hot water into the awaiting rustic teapot.

Despite being several feet away, Kat could smell the familiar morning brew from where she sat. It was the special tea she drank every morning . . . How did Eric know what was in it?

"I think it has something to do with what the devil did to you magically. You went from, well . . . yourself to how you described yourself to me after being in the desert with the coyote," the prince's words barely reached Kat.

The redhead didn't move a muscle. In fact, she had become completely catatonic.

Eric was starting to debate poking her forehead to snap her out of it when she at long last spoke.

"Are you making me food and doing all this . . . because you pity me?" she asked with a note of trepidation.

It was Eric's turn to react in utter bafflement. "Why the hell would I pity you? I was the one who was kissed. Not to mention, I will remind you, I was *also* the one who was abducted and tortured."

"Right." Kat let out a breath of relief after hearing his glib response. "How are you feeling after that, by the way?"

"Oh, you know, right as bloody rain after meeting Satan himself."

Kat raised an eyebrow. "Hold on . . . Earlier you referenced the devil, and I thought you were giving your kidnapper a fun nickname, but . . . you mean to tell me you were taken by actual Satan?"

Eric nodded, his eyes becoming shuttered.

"So that's why it felt like he was . . . looking at my soul . . ." Kat sounded out, her realization bringing with it a spark of gladness.

Staring flatly at the noblewoman's odd reaction to the news, Eric couldn't help but comment.

"You know . . . I understand you are a little outside the standard of normal, but most people aren't happy about having their soul violated and meeting the figurehead of evil."

Kat waved him off with an easy smile while pulling the tower of pancakes closer. She suddenly was looking more like herself.

"I was scared that my magic had made me lose control and was making me do those horrible things, but if it was the devil making it happen? Pfft. Well, that's a load off my mind. Now we just need to avoid him . . . or maybe summon Kraken and my da . . . and everything will be fine!"

Eric opened and closed his mouth as Katarina tucked into her meal with renewed vigor.

Her knack for rebounding from bad times was impressive.

Even though he knew there was far more to be worried about than she seemed to believe, he didn't want to overwhelm her with bad tidings . . .

Not when she was clearly still feeling the effects of her confrontation the night before.

Shaking his head, Eric's mind nudged him closer to the other small detail of how the devil himself, after looking into the deepest recesses of his heart and soul, had informed the prince that he was in love with Katarina Ashowan.

The notion sent a fresh wave of panicked nausea through Eric, but he quickly pushed it away.

Whatever he was feeling toward the redhead wouldn't last.

There were far too many important things to attend to than something so futile.

No, Eric had simply made her breakfast using a recipe her father, Finlay Ashowan, had taught him many years ago in hopes of making her feel a bit better. She had saved him, and he was expressing gratitude and making sure she heard about their . . . *encounter* before the official meeting that was scheduled later to avoid surprising her.

It was just common decency.

Nothing else.

Nothing more meaningful . . .

Eric reached and grabbed a fork for himself with the intention of helping Katarina consume the pancakes, though he already knew it really wasn't a necessary aid.

Whatever strange kinship he had developed with Katarina Ashowan was from mere circumstances, and soon he would be too busy to spare a breath to think otherwise.

And even if he were in love with Katarina Ashowan?

There was no way in hell he would put her through the torture of being someone important to him.

CHAPTER 2

KARMIC CONSEQUENCES

I didn't know you cooked," Katarina mused casually while spearing the final forkful of pancake as Eric continued chewing his own bite.

"You think I could be friends with your father and not learn anything about making a meal?" he asked with a raised eyebrow.

"Fair, though the middle of these pancakes weren't fully cooked."

Eric's gaze moved to her face and regarded her flatly.

When Katarina finally noticed, she shot him a cheeky grin with food stuffed into the side of her cheek.

"I'm a mere mortal, not a house witch, you brat." Eric swiped up a dripping of butter and flicked it at the redhead.

Kat covered her mouth as she laughed, uncaring about the oily droplet that landed in her hair.

Smiling, Eric watched her as she struggled both to laugh and chew.

"Don't choke."

It took her a few moments to succeed in settling down and finishing her food, but when she had fully accomplished the task, she smiled at Eric.

"I have to admit . . . I'm glad you didn't give me any serious talk or sympathy . . ." Kat began carefully, sincerity bright in her eyes.

"Oh, I was going to coddle you of course, but that impulse was short-lived once I remembered what you're like."

"*You* were going to coddle me?" Kat gave a small snort.

"Fortunately, I came to my senses." Eric reached down and plucked up the plate from her and set to placing it in the wash basin.

"By the way," the prince began, crouching down near the basin, his back to the redhead as he proceeded to scrub the dishes clean. "Did the devil make you kiss me? Or was that your magic?"

Kat opened her mouth to respond, when she faltered.

Truthfully? She had no idea why she had kissed him . . . nor why she couldn't remember doing so . . .

"I'm not sure. Mr. Kraft was saying something about my magic controlling me, so that could be it . . ."

"I beg your pardon?" Eric turned around, for once his alarm pronounced in his features. "Your magic is controlling you? That sounds dangerous."

The redhead's brief reprieve from burdensome thoughts ended abruptly as her shoulders slumped forward and she avoided Eric's stare to face the table.

"I'll talk more with Mr. Kraft about it next time I see him."

Eric straightened from the floor and took a step closer to her. "Kat—"

The kitchen door swung open then, and in swept King Brendan Devark with his brother, Prince Henry Devark, and the king's assistant, Mr. Levin, on his heels.

When the ruler took stock of the scene before him, he lowered his dark brows.

"Your Highness, I was looking for you. Lady Katarina, what are you doing here?"

"I asked her to meet with me privately," Eric explained, his expression instantly transformed back to its usual neutral, unreadable one.

Brendan said nothing, but he did stare for a lengthy period of time at the prince before turning to Kat, who was watching the scene play out with only a bit of confusion.

"Very well. Both of you, come with me. We have much to discuss."

Kat rose from her chair and slowly followed after the king. The assistant bowed to her as she walked by, though there was a glint of interest in his eyes that didn't appear entirely friendly . . .

Distracted by this, the redhead didn't notice Prince Henry surveying Eric with a near glower. His face hardened, and a line between his eyebrows appeared.

Eric gazed back but didn't betray a single thought in his face.

The group made their way up to the king's office, and upon entering, it was revealed that Alina, Rebecca Devark, and Mr. Kraft were already there waiting for them.

"Found His Highness with Lady Katarina in the kitchen," Brendan announced briefly as he moved swiftly over to his wife, who didn't hide her look of surprise before she turned her questioning stare to her brother and friend.

"He made me food to say thanks for rescuing him," Kat clarified hastily, sensing Rebecca Devark's judging eyes on her.

"Interesting way of thanking her," Alina noted warily.

Kat was starting to feel a mite uncomfortable by the direction of the conversation, and so was incredibly relieved when the Troivackian king intervened.

"Suspicious meetings aside, we have far more important matters to discuss. Mr. Levin, you are dismissed."

The assistant clearly hadn't been anticipating his lack of inclusion, and so it took him a moment to gather his wits, bow to his sovereign, and depart from the small group.

Once he had left them, Brendan straightened and folded his arms while staring at Katarina.

"Faucher will be joining us shortly, but given that our absences are already noticed amongst the court, I believe we should commence this meeting. Lady Katarina, yesterday you battled with the devil himself, during which I'm told you nearly bested him."

Kat's gaze shifted to Eric uncomfortably.

"However, given the state in which you returned to the castle yesterday, would you say that you believe this was a fluke or that your abilities are indeed stronger than his own?"

Unsure of how to explain the fact that Kat had very little recollection of the event due to her magic consuming her consciousness, she was then also forced to admit to herself that she didn't particularly fancy letting everyone know about the new discoveries that were made regarding her magic. Especially before discussing things more with Mr. Kraft.

"Well . . . he . . . the devil . . . he did something. I didn't intend to use my magic quite like that, but . . . it's like he forced me to," she explained slowly. When she glanced around the room at the various faces listening pensively, she was startled to see Mr. Kraft's look of astonished awe, his eyes already glimmering.

"Your magic . . . I didn't notice yesterday because things were already chaotic, but . . ." He paused as he continued staring at Katarina and all around her flickering aura. "You built an emotional wall to safeguard your magic. He broke it down, didn't he?"

Everyone's attention snapped to the coven leader.

"What do you mean by that?" Brendan Devark demanded sharply.

"I was saying this the other day, but her magic is—"

"Shouldn't you be asking if I'm alright with this information being shared? It's about *my* magic," Katarina interrupted, a note of desperation entering her voice.

Mr. Kraft paused, momentarily taken aback by her outburst.

Brendan turned to face Katarina, his expression firm but not unkind.

"While I understand this might be a more private matter for you, Lady Katarina, this is a threat far larger than any of us."

"Maybe she doesn't need a crowd to know all about it before she does," Eric called out from his position at the back of the room, his arms crossed and his shoulder pressed against the wall as he stared coolly at Brendan.

"Yeah, that," Katarina confirmed, pointing her thumb over her shoulder in the prince's direction.

The king eyed the occupants of the room before facing Katarina wordlessly as he worked through his thoughts.

"Alright, I will insist on being present, Lady Katarina. But everyone aside from yourself and Mr. Kraft, you are excused. Stay outside the door for when we resume the meeting."

The redhead was opening her mouth to object to Brendan's presence, but before she could even make a sound, he gave his head a firm shake.

Alina watched the exchange, frowning, completely perplexed about what was going on, and it didn't help that for whatever reason, Kat wouldn't meet her gaze.

Once the specified people had filed out into the corridor and the door was shut, Alina instead turned on her brother.

"What is going on between you and Kat?"

The prince had been striding a few extra feet away from the group, his right hand already in his pocket, when his sister's words froze him.

No one moved a muscle as the question that had been on all their minds was finally said aloud.

Eric took his time turning around. When he regarded those behind him, the prince stared at the curious faces one by one, a strange coldness in his gaze that made it difficult to maintain eye contact with him. Even when he at long last locked eyes with Alina, his sister, this did not change.

"Kat is a good friend, and it's come to my attention that she is lacking those as of late."

Alina felt her cheeks flush. "What's that supposed to mean? She has me, Kezia—"

"You know, little sister, there were a few things about my rescue that were strange . . . and since last night, I've been doing some investigating . . ." Eric's eyes cut back to Rebecca Devark, the animosity in his expression fearsome.

"I've learned that no one has been serving Kat for the majority of the time she has been here, because everyone has received orders not to."

Alina stepped back in shock, then looked at Rebecca. "Is that true?"

The former queen didn't say anything.

"What's an even *graver* insult to Lady Katarina Ashowan, is that her own *personal* maid, Poppy, has been ordered away from her for weeks. Poppy is to obey one mistress, and yet, I'm given to understand if she were to fulfill her duties with regards to Lady Katarina, she would be bullied by the Troivackian maids here relentlessly." Eric's voice was deepening to a rumble.

Alina's fury was only outmatched by her brother's as she faced Rebecca. "You dared to insult . . . to harass . . . Lady Katarina to such lengths?" Her ire made it difficult to speak.

"Oh, the former queen here has done much more than that. She's even had people spying and reporting what Lady Katarina does," Eric added, and even Prince Henry couldn't disguise his own aghast reaction.

Alina was taking deep, slow breaths as she stared at her mother-in-law.

Despite this, when the princess slapped Rebecca's cheek, everyone was caught off guard.

The former queen raised an eyebrow in the moments after the blow and turned to stare down at Alina without a flicker of emotion. She then lifted her dark gaze to Eric.

"You've discovered quite a lot in a short amount of time, Your Highness. I'm surprised any of my loyal vassals would depart with such information." Her voice was calm and unwavering, despite the red mark from Alina's palm already blooming on her cheek.

Eric tilted his head over his shoulder, his expression never changing. "I can be resourceful when I need to be."

Alina rounded on her brother again, her hands clenched at her sides. "What was it about the rescue that made you suspect something . . . ?"

For a moment, Eric didn't move or say anything as he regarded his sister with the same iciness he'd had the entire conversation.

"Katarina went on an all-night search for me without any protection other than an air witch. Then I heard from Lady Kezia something about no one noticing her absence. Which one would imagine *should* be difficult."

"Why are you looking at me like that?" Alina asked after Eric's explanation still left her uncomfortable under his imposing attention.

"You haven't noticed any of these things, and running the staff is part of the duties you should be taking over. You don't even seem to be aware that Kat's been homesick but doing everything just to support you. You're supposed to be watching out for her; you're her best friend."

"*You* of all people have no right to lecture me on how to be good to my loved ones," Alina's voice rasped, tears in her eyes.

"Usually, you're right, but when I was gone, Lina, you still had our father. You were still doted on and taken care of as you should have been. Kat's here alone, and she's faced off against the origin of all evil. And now people are exposing personal things about her magic? Give the woman a damn break."

Alina glared at her brother, who didn't flinch or back down but held her stare with his own.

"I thought we were having a meeting. Why is everyone outside here?" The loud, gruff voice belonging to Faucher echoed up to the small group.

By the time the military man stood shoulder to shoulder with Eric, he had noted everyone's tense and angry auras before finding Prince Henry's gaze. The royal was the only one present who gave him any acknowledgement, though his silent message conveyed, *Whatever you do, don't ask what just happened.*

"Lady Katarina, the reason I am not allowing you to speak with Mr. Kraft on your own is that you have proved in several past instances to withhold information—and, yes, I know it is often out of concern for others rather than for duplicitous reasons, but for something as serious as this happening in my kingdom, I need to be aware."

Kat didn't look fully appeased but wasn't given much of a choice, when Brendan once again turned to Mr. Kraft. "What were you saying before about the devil breaking down her wall?"

"Lady Katarina's magic, I was informing the ladies yesterday, is too immense. It seeks to burn, to consume . . . It may even be too great for her to handle. I had no idea that you had already restrained it to such an extent." Mr. Kraft addressed the noblewoman, his concern no longer furious or condescending but more so . . . fearful.

Kat felt her lips remain firmly sealed. What was there to say?

"I thought her abilities were mutated, therefore, weaker. What do you mean it can consume?" Brendan prompted, his level tone helpful in restoring a small semblance of collectedness.

"Lady Katarina, your ability is rather remarkable now that I can see it more clearly—though no less terrifying. Your magic consumes any magic cast toward you, and it feeds on it, making both it and you stronger. What I think happens . . . is that when you are in a dangerous situation, your magic unleashes itself and feeds off either magic or intent to protect you."

"Feeds off intent? I don't understand." Kat shifted forward and stared earnestly at the coven leader.

"Well, if someone tries to kill you, it feeds off that and seeks to remove that threat."

Kat blinked. "Do you mean to say . . . I won't hurt someone unless it's in self-defense?" her voice warbled.

"If you don't grow to properly channel your abilities and learn to have an outlet for its hunger, then you still risk exploding and consuming everything. It could lead to a curse that could have unimaginable consequences, particularly if you consume another witch's abilities to the point of their death."

Kat's face paled.

"However, if you *do* learn to control it? Then you would be correct. You wouldn't hurt anyone unless they intended to hurt you as well. Though I am uncertain about just how much of an outlet you'll require, particularly as I mentioned before, your magic can feed off spells cast on you and grow stronger."

Hope filled Katarina's eyes as she stared with open desperation at the coven leader.

"How can I learn to control it?"

"That, I'm afraid, I do not know. It is not a normal ability, but . . . with His Majesty's permission, I would be happy to try and help you. Especially if it means better protecting ourselves from the devil." Mr. Kraft bowed to the king, who was listening intently.

Brendan looked from Katarina to Mr. Kraft, his reaction to the explanation unclear, until he finally opened his mouth.

"I believe, Mr. Kraft, that will be an excellent idea. Particularly as Lady Katarina is about to commence her swordsmanship training after the princess's coronation."

"Swordsmanship?!" Mr. Kraft spluttered, making Kat rediscover her smile.

"That's right. I'm going to be the first woman in all of Troivack to learn it, and with the blessings of two kings, no less."

The coven leader was rendered utterly speechless.

"Ah, by the way, Lady Katarina, there is one other piece of news I must relay to you before we invite the others back into the meeting." Brendan addressed the redhead, a weary resignation entering his eyes.

"I just received word this morning that your father, Viscount Finlay Ashowan, has finally accepted the title of duke."

It was Kat's turn to have her mouth fall open as she gaped at the king in disbelief.

"The meetings regarding this status elevation, according to the official notice I received, are already concluded. Meaning you are now one of the highest ranking noblewomen in all of Daxaria."

"Wh-What?! B-But my da said he'd *never* . . . W-Why is he . . . What?! Did Kraken do this?"

"What does a cat have to do with your father becoming a duke?" Brendan asked flatly.

Katarina wasn't able to answer, so she looked to Mr. Kraft, who was equally baffled by her reaction.

"Godsdamnit! I leave for a few months, and now this happens! Such a tragedy would've never happened if I'd been there . . ." Sighing and pinching the bridge of her nose, Kat made her way over to the door, her shoulders slumped.

The world was truly going mad.

CHAPTER 3

PLOTS AND PLANS

"Congratulations, Lady Katarina!" Prince Henry beamed at the redhead, even though she still appeared morose over the news of her father being awarded a dukedom.

Despite Kat's lackluster reaction to joining the upper crust of nobility, once the rest of the group had returned to his office, Brendan went ahead and informed everyone of the development.

"Kat, this has been such a long time coming for your family! I'm sure everything will proceed smoothly for your father." Alina clasped her friend's hands.

"Yeah, yeah . . ."

"Admittedly, this does make things difficult for us to summon Duke Ashowan to help us. However, I'm certain this will be deemed an emergency if we explain the actual child of the Gods is here and has an interest in Lady Katarina," Brendan affirmed from behind Alina.

"Absolutely. Now, we just need to figure out who in the court made a deal with the devil to kidnap my brother." Alina looked over her shoulder to her husband, whose eyes had already sought out Prince Henry's.

"We have a list of suspected courtiers. At the top, of course, is Duke Icarus, but he is the most difficult to find evidence against for a slew of reasons," Henry explained, his normally pleasant countenance darkened.

"His daughters are supposed to be joining him here in Vessa for the coronation. Perhaps I could try and glean something from them," Alina volunteered.

"His daughters won't know anything," Rebecca Devark informed her daughter-in-law without missing a beat.

"How can you be so certain? Even if their father doesn't tell them things, they may have noticed something strange happening at their home," Kat pointed out.

Prince Henry cleared his throat awkwardly while sharing a look with his mother, then his brother. "Duke Icarus's daughters are . . ."

"To call them half-wits would be accurate if the alleged half-wit was shared evenly amongst the four of them," Rebecca explained candidly while Henry winced at her bluntness.

"Or perhaps they are misunderstood! If their father is the villainous type, maybe they aren't all that bad, just beaten into submission," Katarina defended heartfully while looking to Alina for support.

"That's right, we can still try regardless . . . Oh . . ." The princess trailed off, a sudden thought pulling her in an entirely different direction. "I wonder if the devil is the one responsible for the sightings of the ancient creatures."

"He already has some that we can't see."

Everyone looked to Eric, who stood once again at the back of the group, his hazel eyes as shadowed and intent as ever.

"What do you mean—" Brendan asked while crossing his arms.

"Those aren't the same as the ancient creatures that are being spotted in Troivack," Mr. Kraft interrupted while eyeing Eric curiously. "If you are referring to the pixies, imps, and other small half fey, those are spirits that cannot directly touch anyone in this realm. They exist all around us but tend to flock to those tied to the ancient beings. Usually witches, or certain animals. How is it you were able to see them, Your Highness? Was this another ability that the devil possesses? To reveal such things to you?"

Eric stiffened, and his eyes drifted downward. "No. It was because when they took me, they dosed me with Witch's Brew."

Everyone stilled.

"Gods, how are you not more of a wreck after that?!" Prince Henry burst out frantically.

"Eric, you should have told us! You should see a physician!" Alina exclaimed, unable to stop herself from worrying for her brother's well-being, even if they had just fought moments before . . .

"I'm fine. It's already out of my system, but what is interesting is the devil . . . He said his name was Samuel, but he sounded as though he knew who had made Witch's Brew. He said it was a clever creation, and that it was a woman who'd made it. He then was asking if Lady Katarina was able to kill a deity like I mentioned before, though he hadn't wanted to interact with her. He said he didn't want to get 'entangled' with Lady Katarina, so I'm not sure if he's frightened of her, or interested for some other reason." The prince brushed off everyone's concern while pointedly avoiding Katarina's gaze and instead chose to direct his report toward Brendan.

"Mysterious creatures appearing, the son of the Gods amongst us, and someone concocting Witch's Brew that gives mortals the temporary gift of sight . . ." Mr. Kraft sounded out, the awe in his voice humbling them all. "It certainly seems as though it is all part of a grander picture we cannot see."

"We received the notes from the Coven of Wittica last year while I was in Daxaria regarding the dragon Mr. Aidan Helmer had as his familiar, however, any documentation about spirits, imps, pixies, or half fey weren't reliable. Their records only described such beings as figments of lore," Brendan recounted with a shake of his head. "More information would be helpful. Besides, I'm not even certain Duke Ashowan will be able to use any kind of magic here in Troivack."

Once again, everyone fell silent as they each tried to piece together the strange puzzle before them.

"Well, one thing is for certain, Alina getting crowned was a problem for them. So making sure everything runs smoothly tomorrow is of the utmost importance." Eric straightened himself, allowing his arms to fall to his sides.

Brendan faced Alina grimly. "There may be another attempt on your life beforehand."

"I'll make sure Captain Orion has every crack of the castle guarded." Faucher jumped in with an affirming nod toward the king.

"Yes. In the meantime, Mr. Kraft, perhaps try speaking with Mage Sebastian about any records the mages might have saved from their school." Brendan addressed the coven leader with a casual glance, though was forced to linger on the man when he noticed the witch cringe and subtly recoil.

"Oh, don't worry too much about Mage Sebbie. He's every bit as irritating and condescending as most mages, but at least you know what to expect," Katarina volunteered cheerfully.

Mr. Kraft closed his eyes and turned away from the group as though attempting to ignore something foul smelling.

Brendan decided not to chide the coven leader for his dated prejudice against mages, as he had more or less accepted the order.

"Tomorrow is to go off without a hitch. After that, Lady Katarina, you are relocating to Faucher's estate to begin your swordsmanship training. You will return here after you've mastered the basics. Understood?"

"I'm moving in with Faucher?" Katarina looked at the military man, who was making a face akin to someone who had just taken a mouthful of soured milk. "I mean don't get me wrong, you're a bag of laughs, but I'm not sure that is a wise decision for his sanity."

"Lady Katarina, you will reside there with Faucher's family, and I expect you to be respectful and grateful for their generous hospitality." Brendan's voice rose in warning.

Kat smiled innocently, then winked at Faucher, who was unable to stop himself from slipping into his new habit of looking to the ceiling and begging the Gods for divine intervention.

"Alright everyone, you are dismissed. Except for Prince Eric." The Troivackian king's sudden order caught everyone off guard, but they proceeded to do as they were commanded.

Once alone with his brother-in-law, Brendan let out an aggravated breath.

"While I am glad you are alive and seem to be taking something seriously at long last, your involvement with Lady Katarina is becoming far too dangerous. If you do not intend to marry her—"

"I do not." Eric interrupted firmly.

"Even if you are merely friends, things need to change. There is too much at stake now. I've already been getting reports from my assistant and mother that they have been intercepting rumors brewing here in the castle about you two. So, you are going to start courting some Troivackian ladies while you are here."

Eric stared blankly at the Troivackian king.

He had to have imagined what he'd just heard.

"Pardon?"

"I'm assuming you have no intentions to marry any Troivackian noblewomen, however, this will help distract the courtiers from Lady Katarina, and it will also place you near the daughters of powerful families. This might aid Alina's assimilation here as queen, and it could help us uncover information about who is pushing the rebellion to have her murdered."

"There would be fallout when I don't marry any of them. It's a risky idea, and I refuse to take part in it." Eric's voice was tight and his gaze resolute.

"All you would need to do is say His Majesty King Norman Reyes arranged a marriage for you back home when it becomes too problematic."

"Then I go home, and no news of my wedding comes, and then I've made powerful enemies here." Eric was starting to grow angry.

"You'll marry one day. Long betrothals happen when betrothal and marriage contracts get held up in negotiations."

"I'm not going to seduce women of your court, and that's final." The Daxarian prince turned his back on Brendan and proceeded to exit the office, slamming the door shut behind himself.

In the newfound quiet, the Troivackian king looked to the mountain of paperwork on his desk and closed his eyes in exhaustion. Despite outwardly remaining as in control, everything was becoming even more complicated and chaotic. He already felt as though there were fifty other tasks or questions he should be attending to or asking.

Alina needs to get crowned tomorrow no matter what. Ruling this kingdom when her brother and Lady Katarina are here is too much even for me.

For whatever reason, Katarina had reached her bedroom chamber after the meeting with the king with Alina glued to her side.

Her hazel eyes were cast to the ground, her brows furrowed deeply . . .

If they hadn't been in a hurry to get Kat back to her chamber sight unseen by anyone who believed her to be ill, the redhead would've asked what was bothering her friend. Though she did suppose that there was a good amount to be bothered about.

"Kat, could I speak to you alone?" the princess asked as Kat reached for the door handle.

Shooting Alina a look of concern, she nodded and proceeded to free the latch, then gestured for her friend to enter. Once inside, Kat followed, and after hearing the door clack shut behind them, stood with her head tilted and her eyebrow raised while the princess stood with her back to her, facing the window.

"Everything alright? I mean I understand you have to be incredibly stressed with the murder attempts, and now the devil being involved . . . Or should we call him Sam? I'm unsure what is more appropriate at this point. Sam doesn't have the same foreboding ring though, does it? Sam . . . Saaam . . . SAM . . ." Katarina sounded out the name in varying tones, attempting to make it ring with power, to no avail. "Maybe he has a last name. That'd make it—"

"Kat, why didn't you tell me the maids had stopped tending to you and that they were bullying Poppy?"

The redhead stilled, completely caught off guard by the question.

"Er . . . because it's fine! I like taking care of myself, you know that! And you've had enough on your plate with the coronation, and then your brother was missing . . ."

"It's my job to protect you though! The staff and their behavior are tasks I've already started to oversee, but I had no idea Rebecca had ordered them to—"

"She's your mother-in-law, Alina. You have to live with her until she's dead. I only have to put up with this for a year. It isn't a fight that's worth shouldering when you haven't even established yourself yet. Poppy's fine as long as she does what they ask, and it isn't like they attacked her or—"

"Kat, how they look at you is how they look at me. If they don't respect you enough to take care of you, then it's a reflection of what they estimate to be my own influence. Furthermore"—Alina turned around, her stare fierce—"Even if you thought there wasn't anything that could be done, why didn't you tell me?"

The redhead grimaced. "Well to be honest, I was getting a little tired of their snarky attitudes. At least when I'm ignored, it's more peaceful."

"That isn't the point! That's the kind of thing you are supposed to confide in your friend about!" Alina's bluster dwindled as her concern mixed with hurt.

"Okay . . . you know you're heartbreaking and adorable when you look at me like that. I'm weak to cute things. I mean, just look at Pina . . . She's spoiled rotten!" Kat nodded to her familiar, who was asleep peacefully in the window ledge. "How did you even find out about the maids, by the way?"

At her last question, Alina's expression grew irritated.

"My brother tore Rebecca Devark and me apart for not being a proper friend and for being wildly disrespectful to you. Apparently, he found out everything last night after you all returned."

"Eric did what?" Katarina's eyes flashed.

"He was right to inform us of this, but I was a lot more upset that I hadn't heard it from you, Kat. Wait . . . what are you . . ." Alina trailed off as the redhead's aura burst to life anew, flickering about her wildly, and her golden eyes glimmering.

"I can't believe I'm saying this, but Kat, don't be mad at my brother. Just focus on being prepared for the coronation tomorrow . . . I'm sorry to say this after everything, but I'm afraid I'll need you tomorrow more than ever." Alina's eyes drifted down to the ground, and her hands clasped in front of her middle.

Kat's aura dimmed, but there was something else that was peculiar about her friend's behavior that prompted her to shelve her anger toward Eric.

"Kat, I . . . I had wanted to wait a few weeks after the coronation to be safe before telling anyone but . . . I think I have to share this with you . . ." A light blush rose in Alina's cheeks as she finally met her friend's eyes. "I'm pregnant."

Kat didn't move.

Nor did her eyes budge from Alina's.

"Kat?" Alina slowly waved her hand in front of her friend's face.

Then, every reaction imaginable burst from the witch.

"Gods, Alina, congratulations that's incredible! Are you well? Are you vomiting a lot? I hear a lot of people have to vomit endlessly . . . How dare that lughead of a husband of yours do this to you! Doesn't he know how much you hate gross things? I ought to kill him . . . Where's my sword? You stay here while I deal with him." Kat started pacing around her room until she spotted her sheathed sword beside her wardrobe.

"Kat!" Alina grabbed her friend's hand, laughing. "I'm fine! Honestly, everything is fine. I feel a bit strange, but no problems so far. Also, please don't kill my husband; he's terrified enough for me."

"Good," Kat responded ominously. "Because if his giant foreheaded children are the death of you, I'll have no one to hold me back from killing him."

"His forehead isn't that big!"

"With his receding hairline, it will be."

"His hairline is not receding!"

"I'm pretty sure that it is along the sides, and damnit, Alina, then what will you do? I really don't think he can pull off being bald!"

The conversation continued to digress in a similarly ridiculous fashion for the better part of an hour. The entire while, both young women jested and teased like they hadn't in weeks, and that in turn made the larger threats that awaited them outside the castle walls seem a little easier to manage . . .

Though Kat was still furious with Eric Reyes, she figured she'd get the chance to stomp on his toes as much as she pleased and give him an earful at the coronation feast and ball the next day, and that notion significantly improved her mood.

CHAPTER 4

THE RISING REYES

Alina's hazel eyes were hard and unforgiving, her lips flat in displeasure. Katarina, on the other hand, was for once . . . unreadable.

"We are terribly sorry, Your Highness. It must have been—"

"Guards. Shorn their hair. They are exiled and shamed from the castle," Alina called out, her voice barely rising in volume.

The maids froze in shock.

Katarina's gaze followed them as a predator would its prey as they were escorted from the room, trembling.

"Do you think it was your mother-in-law?" Kat mused while striding forward to stare at the ruined ceremonial gown they had discovered the morning of Alina's coronation.

Someone had sent a rather clear message by writing the word *DIE* in black ink across the snowy white bodice.

"This is too inelegant for her. My money is on one of the noblemen opposed to the coronation."

Letting out a small sigh while shaking her head, a smile began to creep up Kat's face.

"Honestly? To me it seems they keep expecting you to crumple over the slightest of inconveniences."

Alina turned to Kat with a raised eyebrow. "I wouldn't exactly call the kidnapping of my brother, or even this 'slight.' Serving staff went into my chambers and willingly destroyed royal property. I know those two maids didn't do it, but if they'd been paying attention, it could have been prevented."

"Well, what better way to make an impression on your first day as queen?" Katarina's smile was perfectly devious, and Alina wasn't entirely certain what her friend was thinking while making such an expression.

"Kat . . . you normally are the first person to lose your temper over something like this. What's going on?" the princess asked slowly.

Katarina gave a languid stretch of her neck, her eyes innocently brushing along the ceiling.

"Well, I *am* your most senior handmaiden until you are crowned, and I mean . . . I have learned a thing or two in the past year . . ."

Alina faced her friend squarely, her brows lowering and her arms crossing over her chest. "Kat, I'm not exactly in a patient mood right now."

The redhead finally slid her golden eyes to her friend.

"Well, you see, before we left for Daxaria, my mother helped me think of all the worst possible scenarios and plan for them for your coronation. So I actually prepared another dress for you."

Alina's jaw dropped in astonishment.

"You . . . You did?"

"Yes. I did. And might I just say? I'm actually a little glad that they ruined this dress of yours, because if you are intent on not being a traditional Troivackian queen, it only seems fitting you don't wear a traditional Troivackian white dress."

Alina's momentary excitement turned to wariness. "What kind of dress did you prepare?"

Kat began to giggle in a most disconcerting fashion as she casually strode toward the door of Alina's chamber.

"Let's just say . . . it'll make a statement. Excuse me, I'll be right back."

Then without allowing Alina the chance to demand more answers, Katarina was gone.

Staring after her friend in the quiet of her chamber, Alina dropped her forehead to her hand.

"Gods . . . at least with Lady Annika Ashowan's influence, it shouldn't be anything too shocking . . . I hope."

Brendan regarded his mother's bowed head for a long while, his heart pounding against his chest, though his expression remained neutral.

His brother, Henry, stood with his arms crossed and face pale. The Troivackian prince was unable to bring himself to stare at either of his family members.

Eric stood to Brendan's right side, his gaze cold and unfeeling.

"For the insult you've given Lady Katarina Ashowan and for the blatant disregard of not only her safety but also of the good will with which she was entrusted to us, you are stripped of all duties and privileges permanently, and you will not be permitted to set foot in this court for a year." Brendan's voice was quiet but steely.

"I understand, Your Majesty," Rebecca responded without any hesitation.

"You will wait in your chambers until you are summoned for further questioning."

While Brendan's voice could have sounded like his usual growl to most people, those who truly knew him understood it was an emotional rasp.

Lady Rebecca Devark, former queen of Troivack, left the chamber, not once having met her son's eyes.

When the door had shut behind her, Eric stepped forward and bowed to the Troivackian king.

"I am satisfied with your ruling. I will send a letter to the Daxarian court with the details and let you know when I have received a response."

Prince Henry spoke up then. "Did you have to push for such an extreme disciplinary action? While our mother has been misguided with Lady Katarina, she has been instrumental in running the castle staff and even planning this coronation. To remove her, I'm afraid, will give the princess even more enemies."

Eric's deadly stare cut to the king's brother.

"The way I see it, everyone from the nobles to the lowest ranking servants will believe it is acceptable to treat not only Lady Katarina but also my sister however they please with no fear of repercussions. This has gone on long enough. Daxaria is not a weak kingdom, and Troivackian citizens should be aware that if they think they can behave disrespectfully, there will be consequences."

Henry opened his mouth to respond, but Brendan raised his hand and silenced him.

"Brother, please leave us. I need to have a private word with His Highness."

The Troivackian prince cleared his throat, displeased with not being able to say his piece, but he did as commanded.

Alone at last, Brendan folded his hands over his desk, his features hardened.

"I agree with my brother that this decision to remove my mother from the courts may not be a wise choice. Especially in light of all the changes that are about to take place. However, I confess that the former queen has made too grave an error in judgment, and I am displeased that Lady Katarina has been treated thusly without anyone's awareness."

Eric said nothing.

"This offense of the former queen's is far from the worst of what I would unfortunately expect to see in the near future. If I am banishing my mother and exposing a weakness in my position, then I expect you to be more involved in my court. Understood?" Brendan explained cryptically.

Slipping a hand into his pocket, Eric met his brother-in-law's gaze. "I will defer to your authority from here on out, but I will then ask that you allow Sir Gabriel Vohn to serve directly under me so I have an ally that I trust at my side while I start to . . . interact more with your vassals."

The Troivackian king gave a humorless smile. "I was surprised you didn't ask for him to be reassigned to you sooner."

"I know why you assigned him to guard duty, but I didn't have a need for him then. However, things have changed."

Brendan's stare sharpened. "You believe you know why I placed him as a guard when he is supposedly one of Daxaria's finest knights?"

Eric's expression barely changed. "You made him a familiar face to the Troivackian nobility. No one will think much of him now, as he has been in the background for the past month or so, guarding the banquet hall and your council room."

At first, it appeared the Daxarian prince had struck the king speechless, but when Brendan rounded the desk and stared down at his brother-in-law, there wasn't an aura of astonishment. No . . . it was suspicion.

"In less than two days, you not only learned the activities of my serving staff but also traced back their orders to my mother. I know from experience she is not careless. Now you are aware of the guard placements. How did you learn all this so quickly?"

Eric's only reaction to the question was to lift an eyebrow.

When no answer was forthcoming, Brendan let out a grunt.

"I will see you at the coronation, Your Majesty." Eric bowed and turned to leave without another word to spare for the king.

He had accomplished everything he had wanted to in that meeting.

First, he had ensured proper punishment had been dealt to Lady Rebecca Devark. Second, he had regained Sir Vohn under his control, and third, he had illustrated that he was paying close attention to the Troivackian court. The future Daxarian king knew that Brendan Devark, a shrewd and straightforward man, had learned that if he was going to make extensive demands and entrust Eric with more responsibility, everyone would need to be on their toes. He would not be anyone's puppet.

Stalking down the castle corridor, Eric glared at any servant that passed by him, making them flinch.

He typically would never behave so beastly toward those of lower status, but they had abused their positions, and they would pay for it.

As he continued making his way back to his chamber to prepare for his sister's coronation, the only reservation Eric couldn't fully ignore was whether he would be able to abstain from his favored vices . . .

Particularly when, on top of the new responsibilities he had taken upon himself, he was also sending a letter to his former friend, Finlay Ashowan, informing him that his daughter had indeed been mistreated on his watch, and worst of all, the devil himself was involved.

In other words . . . it was only a matter of time before the infamous house witch of Daxaria would be joining the Troivackian court, and who knew what kind of chaos would ensue then.

Katarina stood outside the closed throne room doors.

Within, hundreds of nobility stood awaiting the start of the coronation.

Somber traditional Troivackian music rang out from the front of the room, entertaining the guests as key figures took their positions.

Kat paced in front of the guards, her hands on her waist as she waited for Alina to arrive with her additional guards and handmaidens.

"Good day, Lady Katarina."

The redhead nearly jumped out of her skin when Rebecca Devark's voice sounded behind her.

"Gods almighty!" She breathed after forcing her flickering magic to dwindle back down after she realized who had startled her.

The former queen was dressed in all black as was her norm, her head wrap still twisted tight. The only difference in her appearance was the tired lines etched in her normally formidable expression.

"Ma'am, what can I do for you?" Kat managed while facing Rebecca and noting the guards had flinched at her initial outburst.

"A word here if you please." Rebecca gestured to the other side of the corridor, placing them beside the window that reached the ceiling and allowed the pale clouded day's light to pour in.

Eyeing the woman skeptically, the redhead obeyed and made her way over, though her eyes were already aglow.

"Lady Katarina, from here on out, Princess Alina's every breath will be endangered. Remember, exercise caution and do not act rashly. Believe it or not, my recent actions were to show you that there are consequences. All I wanted was to make you aware of how easy it would be to place you in a vulnerable situation." As she spoke, Rebecca straightened, the sincerity and conviction of her words bringing her no small amount of self-assurance.

Kat smiled, but there was something dark in her face that made the former queen become hesitant.

The redhead shifted closer, then leaned in, making Rebecca feel an unfamiliar flicker of fear . . .

"I think that is the lesson *you* should be taking here. If you hadn't betrayed your son by undermining his ruling and disrespecting someone he vowed to care for, not only would there be a united front to protect Alina, but you wouldn't be suffering the *consequences* in a *vulnerable situation*. I believe *I* am doing just fine. Though I do thank you for at least joining us at the end when we summoned the coven. It just would've been better if you'd realized I've been right for a while now."

The former queen glared at Katarina.

"You—"

Rebecca's words died in her throat when her gaze was drawn to the sudden appearance of Alina at the end of the hall with her remaining three handmaidens and six knights.

"That dress." The former queen gaped in horror.

"I think I made an excellent call on the color. It certainly makes an impression, doesn't it?" Kat asked delightedly.

"What did you do?" Rebecca struggled to breath as she turned her infuriated stare back to the redhead.

"Oh, well remember how you diminished Alina's and my own authority by using the maids in your schemes? Right, so you made an opening for a noble to ruin the traditional dress we had prepared. Well done, ma'am. Your sabotaging has again proved that we should be doing things our way."

"Even her lips are—"

"Mm-hmm." Kat smiled as Alina strode up beside Kat and her mother-in-law. The white fur mantle around her shoulders clasped with a gold chain appeared all the more luxurious against the scarlet red dress she wore, her lips painted to match.

"I believe it's time. Everyone's inside?" Alina asked, her eyes clear and calm.

Kat's grin widened as she stepped away from Rebecca. "They are, Your Highness." Kat curtsied, then moved to the back of the dress where Lady Sarah stood at the ready to fan out the train with her mouth pursed.

The Daxarian princess locked eyes with her mother-in-law one final time, but there wasn't an ounce of warmth in them, before she turned toward the great doors.

"Right. I'm ready." Alina straightened her shoulders, took a deep breath in, then nodded to the guards at the doors. "Open them."

CHAPTER 5

THE NEW TROIVACKIAN QUEEN

As soon as the doors to the throne room opened, the music halted and the faint murmurs of the awaiting nobility fell silent.

Katarina stood beside Lady Sarah Miller and behind Alina, her hands folded. Behind the redhead was Lady Wynonna Vesey and behind Lady Sarah, Lady Kezia.

They all proceeded into the room until the women noticed the red flower petals marking the start of the aisle. Their eyes remained fixed on the sliding train of Alina's dress and mantle. The handmaidens accompanying the princess were not permitted to look up and around themselves, and so Katarina had no idea if the former queen of Troivack was still watching from the corridor behind them, or if she had already left in an outrage.

Katarina didn't get a chance to think further on her exchange with Rebecca Devark either, as the music started once more, signaling the procession to continue up the aisle to the thrones where the Troivackian king and magistrate awaited.

The music that filled the still space was somber. The deep, droning tones of an instrument Katarina had only ever heard in Troivack echoed out, almost sounding like a funeral processional.

Inwardly, Kat was wondering who had chosen such depressing music . . .

Beneath their feet, the carpet was white with black trim running along the sides, making Alina's red dress easy to spot as the nobles around her shifted in surprise.

Katarina was struggling to stop her aura from flickering externally as her heart pounded in her chest, and she resisted with all her might the urge to stare at the faces watching them. Ever since she had faced the devil, her magic had been harder to control.

Brendan Devark stood atop the dais at the end of the aisle, his crown fixed atop his head. His clothes were entirely black, his beard cropped close to his face, and his presence as formidable as ever as he waited for his wife.

Alina reached the dais and ceremoniously climbed the twelve steps until Brendan was able to reach his hand out, helping her the rest of the way up.

Meanwhile, the handmaidens split apart at the bottom and filed down to the front rows of the audience.

The magistrate of Vessa strode across the dais from its far left side.

"Today, we have gathered to crown our long awaited queen of Troivack." His voice boomed out across the sea of heads, which cued the noblewomen present, who only then were allowed to raise their eyes to the scene.

Held in the magistrate's hands was a golden bowl containing frankincense oil.

Alina's eyes locked with Brendan's only for a moment before he released her hand and stepped back to his throne, sat, and nodded toward his wife. She then slowly knelt before the magistrate.

"Do you, Princess Alina Devark, swear to uphold Troivack's strength and discipline?" He turned to the young woman, his eyes hard.

The magistrate was a man in his early forties with a bald head and sharp light brown eyes that were barely resisting openly glaring at the princess and her scarlet dress; his air of disapproval wasn't hard to miss.

Katarina raised an eyebrow.

Brendan Devark took it one step further and emitted a low rumble that could only be heard by his wife and the magistrate at the top of the dais.

The magistrate immediately lowered his insolent gaze.

Alina barely suppressed a smile directed toward her husband. "I swear to uphold Troivack's strength and discipline."

"Do you swear to be a role model for your people, to support your king with dignity and loyalty?"

The magistrate made the wise decision to remain toneless.

"I do," she answered.

Dipping his thumb into the frankincense oil, the magistrate briefly touched his thumb to Alina's forehead as two noble stewards stepped forward with the crown and scepter.

"By the power vested in me by the king of Troivack and the Goddess herself, I declare you, Alina Devark the First, queen of Troivack."

Alina accepted the scepter that was a simple two-foot shaft wound and twisted with gold and iron.

The magistrate then lifted the golden crown with its points, intricate filigree, and two iron bands nestled in the gold band and placed it atop Alina's dirty blond hair that had been braided and pinned in a low bun at the back of her head. Kat felt a prickling at the back of her neck, and a strange tension rustled through the crowd.

She turned her chin slightly and stared down the row of nobles to the other side of the aisle. Her movement caught Kezia's eye, and she sent a quick frown at her fellow handmaiden.

Kezia's gaze shot up then to her brother-in-law in silent warning.

Brendan caught the look instantly and swiftly rose from his seat to walk over to his wife.

He offered his hand to her so she could stand, making the entire room burst out in whispers.

Never before had a king stood beside a recently crowned queen.

Normally, she would curtsy to the people as they would applaud her while her husband looked on from his throne, then he would rise and step in front of her. Once this was completed, only then could she stand and move to his side and they could proceed back down the aisle.

That is not what happened.

Instead, when Alina stood once more, she turned to face the people— while *in front* of her husband.

Then she nodded to Mage Sebastian, who stood along the perimeter of the room.

People were beginning to look to see who she had made the gesture to, when the stone bowls that had been placed to line the aisle suddenly began to reverberate with power, making a few people gasp and shift away.

Alina shot a subtle smile toward Kat, who grinned openly back.

"My people of Troivack." Alina's voice rang out across the room, resonating from the bowls and scaring the people into shrinking away from them in shock and awe. "I thank you for attending my coronation today and bringing with you the strength of your houses to swear your loyalty to me."

The people were gradually recovering from the terrifying effect of hearing Alina's voice project and echo so loudly around them. The volume seemed impossible coming from such a small woman . . .

"While I know I have much to learn, please know I have already beheld Troivack's power, and I have come to understand the potential of this kingdom during my time amongst your beautiful towns and cities."

The people eyed her warily, still displeased at being addressed with such grandeur by a mere woman.

"I only seek to make this great land greater, and to accomplish this, I will lead alongside His Majesty King Brendan Devark as shared souls belonging to Troivack with nothing but your well-being and pride in mind."

At the mention of her ruling jointly with their beloved king, several noblemen shared dark glances with each other.

Their identities were noted unbeknownst to them by certain knights that stood guard around the room . . .

"I will bring honor to you all, Troivack. Now, raise your voices to the Gods, for tonight we will celebrate!"

Despite her ringing conclusion, the room fell into a breath of uneasy silence.

It was then three archers amongst the crowd rose, their sights set on Alina.

"NO!" Katarina shouted, her aura busting out, its gold, orange, and reds making several people leap away from her. Her skirts were clutched in her hands, already prepared for running up the dais.

Several shrieks echoed around the room, and Brendan had his sword drawn in a flash, but there wasn't time for any further action to be taken, as the three assassins were suddenly hoisted into the air, their weapons falling to the ground below their feet. One of the crossbows even fell and knocked into the temple of a nobleman.

Mage Sebastian had moved forward, the crystal dangling from his ear a bright white light in the confusion as he held out his hand, murmuring the guttural magic language of mages.

Chaos erupted when the doors behind them closed, sealing the room off.

The three archers were then magically swept through the air and dropped into a heap before the steps where Alina and her husband stood at the top.

Brendan's arm had wrapped protectively around Alina's middle, his shoulder and back already shielding her from view of the rest of the room.

"It's alright," Alina whispered, despite her voice warbling ever so slightly. "This is our chance . . . to show them."

Brendan blinked down at his wife in shock. His blood was roaring in his ears for vengeance on behalf of the attempt on her and their unborn child's lives, but Alina, on the other hand . . . It almost was as though she had anticipated the attempt, but he could tell by her pale face that it was not the case.

Moving in front of Brendan again as people screamed and raised their voices, fearful of the attack as well as the taboo use of magic, Alina shouted.

"BE STILL!"

The loud ringing from the bowls activated and once again made the room gradually fall back into a quiet.

"Captain Orion." Alina turned her gaze to the military leader who stood in the first row of the audience, her hazel eyes flashing as she pointed to the three assassins who were still gathering their wits after being dropped from a great height. "Execute these men."

Everyone froze.

Captain Orion swallowed with great difficulty.

He was not accustomed to taking orders from anyone other than upper noblemen or the king himself, but the look in Alina's eyes and the attention directed at him forced him to act without further calculation.

Striding forward haltingly, the young man did as commanded, making several noblewomen shield their eyes; some were sobbing. When he struck down the first of the archers, Alina spoke, though Katarina noticed her friend was avoiding looking at the carnage as much as possible.

"I believe now is an excellent time to tell you, Troivack, that despite what you may have heard or previously thought, I *will* be your queen. If anyone believes that I am unsuitable or too *weak* as a Daxarian to earn my place here . . ." As she paused, she was a vision of drama with her crown, red dress, and position over the crowd . . . the ferocity in her face and ice in her eyes making several nobles stiffen.

The second assassin's head thudded to the floor, further staining the white aisle.

"Then I will continue to carve my place into your kingdom until you understand. Even if that means I sit atop the graves of those who have opposed me. Those of you who seek to plot more attempts and coups? I will see Troivackian justice is dealt without mercy. Now, Troivack . . . am . . . I . . . clear?"

The third and final assassin's head fell from his shoulders.

Katarina felt like she was going to be sick. She had no idea how Alina hadn't vomited or fainted.

Few people dared move, and no one could deny that beneath the room's surface appearance of grandeur and elegance, a bloodthirsty primal essence was breathed into the air by Alina's words.

Then, in the wake of the hush and awe . . . the first stomp rang out.

The lone nobleman from somewhere in the heart of the crowd brought the heel of his boot down hard against the marble floor yet again and continued to repeat the movement.

It was soon joined by another boot . . . and another . . . and another.

As the pounding of hundreds of feet echoed up as one large unanimous din, they began to chant.

"RA! RA! RA! RA!"

The booming approval of their new queen filled the throne room and overwhelmed Alina's senses, though she did not show it. Instead, she discreetly grasped her husband's roughened palm and squeezed his hand to help quell her trembling.

No one in attendance could have foreseen such a reception to Alina's coronation, but then again . . .

She had taken the crown in a true traditional Troivackian manner.

Amongst violence, and with strength and great bravery.

With this beginning, Queen Alina Devark began her reign, and she quickly, with great love, would be known amongst her people as the Blood Queen.

Her dress and lips only fueled the fire of her nickname, and the dress would forevermore be looked upon as the perfect garment for her ascension to the throne.

However, despite this great success, the king and his new queen, along with their closest friends and family, knew that it would be far from their hardest hurdle.

No, there was far, *far* more to come, but at the very least, they knew they had those that were loyal and willing to fight at their side in the trials and battles ahead.

CHAPTER 6

WORN WOUNDS

The throne room had been emptied for the palace servants and knights to clean up the blood and bodies, while also questioning the nobles present to see if anyone had noticed anything helpful during the assassination attempt.

Despite the echo of voices in the throne room gradually dimming as guests filed out into the corridor, the excitement of the day did not diminish.

The recently crowned queen of Troivack and the king had retired to the antechamber just behind the stairs that would save the couple from having to cross the blood-soaked aisle.

While most people at the end of the aisle had gone around the gory scene to exit the room, Katarina had instead skirted around everyone and followed the royal couple into the antechamber, despite more than one steward attempting to stop her.

Kat arrived in the gilded room, with its cream-colored walls, gold bordering, and its bright red cushions, and didn't bat an eye as she registered Alina half collapsed, her husband holding her upright.

"Blood . . . Beating . . . No . . . Please, no . . . Let them go . . . Please . . . It's my fault . . ."

Katarina half threw the steward closest to the door out, then leapt nimbly over the back of the nearest sofa, shoving Brendan's hands off his wife and placing herself in front of her friend, her golden aura burning and her eyes shimmering.

"Alina, love, remember that morbid new song you discovered? Where you go, I cannot follow . . . But you know that I'll try . . ." the redhead began to sing.

Alina Devark's tear-filled gaze that was lost to reality searched desperately but was not registering her friend before her.

Katarina gently grasped Alina's cheeks, then continued. "Give my life, woe is the night . . . in the dark among the shadows, where the light leaves my eyes . . ."

Alina's quiet voice at long last joined at the final line, but her mind was still lost to the present reality.

"Where . . . the light . . . leaves . . . my eyes . . ." Alina gripped Kat's arms tighter and tighter . . .

After several long breaths in the room filled with somber silence, Alina finally lifted her face, her eyes gradually clearing.

"Oh Gods . . . it happened again?"

Katarina smiled in relief down at her friend, the warmth in her expression comforting.

"Don't worry, you're here with your favorite person in the world, and the tree trunk you call a husband is over there."

Brendan was on the verge of growling, but when Alina's whispering laugh left her lips, he suddenly didn't feel the need.

"I'm tired," Alina managed, her voice weak.

"I know, love. Don't worry. You can nap. I'll make sure to create a fabulous scene as always." Kat grinned while she gently pulled Alina into her embrace.

"Lady Katarina." Brendan's voice for once was not a rough tumble of low tones, but instead was pleasantly gentle. "I can take her to rest. Thank you, for your help."

At first, the redhead didn't register having heard Brendan, as she clutched her friend to herself, her eyes closed tight.

In truth . . . perhaps she had needed just as much comfort as her friend after the assassination attempt.

Brendan's gentle touch on his wife's back had Alina clumsily releasing Kat before she then turned wearily to her husband and hugged him around the waist.

"Thank you again, Lady Katarina." Brendan gave a small bow.

Kat would've felt more annoyed or angrier at his interference were it not for his brown eyes that were so vulnerable and appreciative . . .

The king's gaze was reminding her that there was never a doubt that he loved Alina more than anyone.

Katarina swallowed. Hours earlier, she had felt thick as thieves with Alina, and yet once again, an overwhelming sense of loss and loneliness was overtaking her.

Pinching the fabric of her skirt to try and control the emotions bubbling up within her chest, she watched her friend retreat from the room without moving, and it wasn't until the poor footman she had chucked from the room nervously reentered that she snapped out of her trance.

Looking to the ceiling and taking a deep breath, Katarina left the antechamber and proceeded to quickly glide past the knights that were still in the process of cleaning up the bodies in the throne room.

What the redheaded noblewoman didn't see, however, was Eric Reyes casually resting in the shadows, his arms crossed. Frowning, he watched her disappear into the crowd, most likely to prepare for the banquet and dancing that was to begin shortly, however . . . Why had she run like that to the antechamber?

Furthermore, why hadn't she been kicked out immediately?

Eric knew she was most likely checking on his sister to make sure the new queen was alright after witnessing brutality she was not accustomed to, but there had been fear in Katarina's eyes too . . .

The Daxarian prince turned, slipped his hand into his pocket, and made his way out of the throne room.

Something told him there was a great deal more he needed to uncover.

Once he'd reached his own chamber, he ignored its usual state of disarray with the bed unmade, its sheets twisted and rumpled from multiple nights of sleeplessness and nightmares. Instead, Eric began to pace. Dirtied clothes were strewn over the floor, making for an interesting track for him to circle around. At one point, he shot a glance at the inconspicuous sack that leaned against the wardrobe. It was filled with empty wine and moonshine bottles that he would see to disposing of discreetly on his own.

However, ridding the evidence of his poor habits was not the most pressing matter . . .

He had just started becoming more aware of his surroundings in the Troivackian court, but there was still much to learn before he could become active in some of the dealings of the castle.

A knock interrupted Eric's intent thoughts, making him pause.

He treaded over to the door, and upon opening it a crack found himself staring at Lady Kezia.

Wordlessly, he stepped aside to allow her entry.

When the door was firmly shut once more behind her, she turned to the Daxarian prince urgently.

"Did you learn anything by observing the cleanup of the men?" She breathed quietly.

Eric's brows fell to a furrow. "Not much. Their clothes and crossbows were the best quality money can buy, but they carried no identification or other tokens. They were professional, and they intended to get caught. Most likely their families were paid handsomely for them to carry this out. I'm surprised my sister was able to handle the situation so well."

Lady Kezia smiled beautifully. "She is a lioness. I've suspected it for some time, but she played her hand very carefully upon arrival. She waited until receiving actual power before showing her true capabilities."

Eric let out a sigh and scratched the back of his neck. "Why did Kat run after her like that? It wasn't just out of concern, and to make matters even stranger, neither she nor my sister seemed entirely unaccustomed to the violence . . ."

"Well, I'm certain the events of last summer have something to do with it. This wouldn't be their first time seeing something of this nature."

Dropping his hand from his neck and straightening, Eric fixed Kezia with an alarmed stare. "What happened last summer?"

Drawing herself back in surprise, Kezia regarded the Daxarian prince with concern. "Surely you know about the kidnapping of your own sister?"

Eric's face drained of color and his stomach lurched sickeningly. "What?"

Kezia's hand flew to her mouth and her eyes rounded.

Eric's face hardened instantly as he took a step closer to Kezia, the air about him growing ominous.

Another knock on the door prevented the prince from asking another question.

"Your Highness, I've been instructed to tell you that the guests are now returning to the throne room for the banquet," the reverent tone of a steward called out from the corridor.

"Got it," Eric growled while his attention remained on Kezia.

The two remained locked in place, silence thick between them.

"Speak." The prince's eyes glinted dangerously.

"I honestly thought you knew . . ." Kezia trailed off while giving her head a small shake. "Last summer, Princess—oh, Her Majesty Alina and Lady Katarina were abducted. They were missing for around four days . . . I understand that both kings wanted to keep this matter quiet, but I assumed you would've been told."

Eric swallowed with difficulty, his nausea growing worse. "Tell me everything you know."

"I-I can't say much. I wasn't permitted to know all the details . . . I just know that they were taken due to some kind of misunderstanding, and that the only reason they were able to find Her Majesty before she was murdered or sold to Zinferan slave traders was because Lady Katarina managed to escape and find help. She then returned to save her."

A wealth of powerful emotions overtook the prince.

"What did they . . . what did the abductors do to my sister?"

Kezia shrank back. "As far as I know, nothing past what I've said. Lady Katarina protected her, though she herself was gravely wounded after . . . Aside from that, no permanent damage was done, though it is why both Her Majesty and Lady Katarina always wear bracelets or long sleeves to cover the scars around their wrists that were left from the ropes they were bound with."

Eric couldn't think clearly.

Couldn't manage a full breath.

He lunged for the castle door, making Lady Kezia give a small squeak of surprise as he reached around her and stalked from the room, slamming his chamber door behind himself.

Half blind with fury and pain, Eric made his way to his sister's chamber, and despite the guards making a move to block him from doing so, he proceeded to pound on the door. They decided it wasn't worth interfering when they took stock of the urgency in his features and slight tremor that ran down his hand.

When Brendan Devark opened the door, it took every ounce of self-control Eric possessed not to shove him aside.

"I need to talk to my sister. Alone."

The Troivackian king barely reacted outwardly, but he spent a breath observing his brother-in-law carefully. "I will permit you entry, but I am staying in the room."

That was enough permission for him. Eric shouldered passed Brendan into the chamber and found his sister half slumped in a plush armchair in front of the crackling fire, a pitcher of water with a goblet sitting beside her on the table and a basin in her lap.

When she turned her darkened hazel eyes to him, Eric could see the weariness on her pale face. Once he heard Brendan close the door behind him, the prince barely managed to keep his voice down as he rounded the chair to stand in front of his sister.

"Why did no one tell me what happened to you last summer?"

Alina's unfocused gaze sharpened; the question had taken her aback. "Ah . . ."

"How did you hear about this?" Brendan's quiet insistence went wholly ignored.

"What the bloody hell, Alina? What happened?!" Eric exploded, dropping to his knees before his sister, his face contorted in anguished guilt.

In that moment . . . he looked every bit the loving brother Alina remembered in her past. It was as though nothing had changed and he had simply been absent until that very moment, his gaze filled with love and sincere care . . .

It was too much.

She burst into tears, her hand flying to her mouth as she bent forward.

Eric gently grasped the basin in her lap and removed it, then pulled her into his arms.

Brendan was momentarily stunned. He had recognized the prince's heightened emotions when he'd first laid eyes on him, but he had been expecting more of his unrelenting anger. The king had not anticipated . . . this.

Quietly, Brendan turned and left. It was most definitely a private moment between the two siblings.

"Gods, Alina . . . I should have been there. I am so . . . *so* Godsdamn sorry." Eric's cracked whisper bore with it his own tears that he had only recently discovered he still possessed.

Alina could do nothing but cling to him like a child, her tears soaking the royal blue coat he had donned for her coronation.

For once, he didn't reek of moonshine or cigars.

He even smelled like his old self . . . sandalwood and a hint of bonfire smoke . . .

"I was trying to find you . . . Kat told me not to go . . . and they took us."

"Who? Who did this?" Eric's throat throbbed as he continued holding his baby sister.

"T-They were men after Reese Flint, and . . . and I had gone to see him because he seemed like the only other person who had seen you that could've known where you were."

When Alina pulled back, Eric's rough thumb gently brushed away her tears, his eyes searching her face.

"I never liked that bloody bard," he rasped, a flush of angry color rising in his cheeks.

Alina gave a quiet, watery laugh. "He is a good man, Eric. He gave me voice lessons for a year, and he protected his family the entire time we were held hostage. And I had Kat there protecting me."

At the mention of the Ashowan woman, Eric felt an even stronger force grip his heart painfully. "What did they do to Kat?"

Alina's eyes grew distant and shifted toward the fire. It was then Eric recognized why his sister had looked so out of sorts when he'd first entered . . .

A soldier's spell.

He carefully grasped her hand and drew her focus back to him.

"Please, Alina . . . What did they do? What happened?"

Fresh tears began to rush down Alina's face as she became even more distressed at the arrival of unwanted memories appearing in her mind. "They hit her. A lot. The whole time she kept goading them on, so they'd leave me alone. Then, when she came back to rescue me . . . she beat Roscoe to death with her bare hands, and she was stabbed while that was happening, and then she had used up too much of her magic. It was my fault. All my fault. It was all my fault, I couldn't help, I couldn't save her, I couldn't—" Alina's frantic words were pushing her closer to hysteria as she kept agitatedly pulling at the sleeve cuffs of her dress.

Eric seized her in another embrace, quieting her heartbreaking words, his own tears overflowing and a scream echoing up inside from the darkest recesses of his tired soul.

He had never hated himself more than in that moment, and he knew then that there was very little he wasn't willing to do to ensure the happiness of two particular people . . .

The first, his sister, whom he had abandoned.

The second, Katarina Ashowan, the woman he suddenly did not have the strength to deny any longer that he was horribly in love with.

CHAPTER 7

THE CUTTING EDGE

Y ou know"—Alina blew her nose in the handkerchief her husband had given her an hour earlier before continuing to address her brother— "Your hair really does look awful."

Eric, who sat on the ground with his knee propping up his left arm, raised an eyebrow toward his sister with a smile.

"Really? You're going to start in on my hair?"

"Yes. You not only appear barely fed, you look mangy. I always remember how the noblewomen loved your hair." Alina smiled deviously at her brother, the tip of her nose bright red from her tears moments before.

Eric rolled his eyes, but his smile didn't fade. "Would cutting off my ponytail make you feel better?"

"Absolutely."

Eric laughed but dropped his chin to his chest in defeat. "Ugh. Fine."

Alina's smile was radiant.

For the first time in four years, she finally felt like she had her brother back.

"You know, some women prefer men with long hair," Eric announced defensively.

"Not when it looks like a sad dog's tail."

"Now you sound like Kat . . . or Mom." Eric groaned while closing his eyes in exasperation. "Where did my sweet little baby sister, who thought I was the Green Man himself, go? Now you are a cynical, critical, tough sort, that—What did I say?"

Alina's good-humored smile had faded to sadness yet again. "You mentioned Mom . . . Am I truly like her?"

Eric's own expression turned morose. "More than you know, and I, unfortunately, am far too much like our father."

Alina dabbed her nose on the well-used handkerchief. "Hardly. Our father, if he isn't being the perfect leader, was doting on our mother. You're more . . . roguish."

"Is that a compliment or an insult?" Eric asked with an interested grin.

"Both. Why do you think you're like Father?"

"Hm. I let my emotions get the best of me. Mom only ever did that when she was pregnant. She had a lot of troubles with having children and— Gods, did I say something else wrong?" Eric grew increasingly concerned when fresh tears overtook Alina.

"N-No. Not really, but . . . did Mom really have as much trouble as people say with pregnancies? Many said she had multiple miscarriages and even stillborn babies . . ."

Eric's brows lowered, and his gaze saddened. "She did. She had at least four, perhaps five before me, and after, I couldn't tell you . . . but it was quite a few . . . You were her final miracle she used to say. Though she didn't like talking much about her experiences. Are you worried for when you and Brendan are ready for children?"

Alina shifted uncomfortably, her eyes no longer capable of meeting with Eric's. "Not . . . exactly . . ."

His stomach flipped, and his eyes widened with realization.

"Oh . . . stop staring at me like that. Yes!" the new queen of Troivack snapped, her cheeks deepening in color.

Eric was struck speechless.

Opening and closing his mouth, he eventually rubbed feeling back into the lower half of his face and was able to respond.

"Gods, congratulations, Lina! Are you . . . feeling alright?"

Giving her brother a small knowing smile, she leaned forward and clasped one of his hands. "Yes. I've been feeling perfectly fine. Aside from being nauseated after the beheadings today . . ."

"I could see that being a bit off-putting," Eric agreed with the faint note of sarcasm in his tone.

Alina responded with a sigh while releasing her brother's hand and slowly rising to stand. "Yes, it was. Though thankfully, no one else was hurt. Now, we don't have much time before the banquet. Should I cut your hair now?"

Eric stared up at his little sister for a beat before holding out his hand for her to haul him up to his feet. She wound up laughing as he made a show of having her drag him to his feet.

"I was truly hoping you'd forget all about the hair thing already . . ."

"Not a chance. Sit on the chest over there, and I'll grab Brendan's knife."

Casting one more look of exasperation toward his sister, who was already quickly walking to her husband's side of the bed where a sheathed dagger lay, Eric obediently seated himself down on the chest and waited.

"How is it you found out about last summer?" Alina asked while carefully unclasping the small black leather sheath. "I'm guessing Kat told you?"

Eric snorted. "Oh, right. Kat, the woman who would lie just to hide a mosquito bite."

Alina halted and stared quizzically at her brother. "I thought you said you two were friends?"

Turning to his sister, Eric stared at her momentarily perplexed before shaking his head with an exhale and a smile. "Oh, we are, but Katarina Ashowan is a far more private person than she leads people to believe."

Alina hesitated, her previously contented air fading to uncertainty. "What does that mean? Kat tells everyone anything that's on her mind. Are you being biased against her because of her father again? Or—"

"No, no. Alina, forget I said anything, alright? I didn't mean to insult her. I just find that she doesn't like to let on when she's hurt is all. You had to have noticed that after the whole ordeal with your mother-in-law, right?"

Alina tilted her head, her eyes becoming shuttered. "Is that the only reason why you are saying that?"

Sensing the conversation was taking a dangerous turn, Eric put every ounce of conviction he could muster when he said, "Lina, if you aren't going to cut my hair right now, I'm going to go get ready for your coronation ball."

Unable to hide her skepticism, Alina let out a small grumble before she stepped to Eric's side and lifted the blade under his ponytail. "I swear. Whatever happened between the two of you on the trip to Vessa has me feeling like you're hiding something."

"Did she tell you she bought a sword?" Eric supplied helpfully.

"A sword? Well, I guess she would be eager to start learning. I'm surprised Brendan waited so long to begin her lessons. I understand of course he wanted to give her time to settle into Troivack, but perhaps having her start by staying with Leader Faucher's family would have been a better way of going about that. I've heard his wife is a good woman."

"Hm," Eric responded noncommittally as he continued to avoid having to rat Kat out to his sister about the fact that she had, in fact, been stabbed a second time.

It was then that there was a small tug at the back of his head, a sigh of gladness, and then a draft that brushed the nape of Eric's neck. Resisting the urge to give an involuntary flinch, the prince was further distracted by the additional tugs and pulls he felt along his head.

"It wasn't enough to cut off the back?" he asked dryly.

"Well, then you'd just look even worse. I have to clean up while I'm at it to make you look presentable."

"Is that so? I swear, all women are the same; you give them an inch and they take a league."

Unimpressed, Alina leaned back to stare at her brother, the dagger wielded casually in her hand. "When men are as bloody stubborn as you, we take what we can get, got it?"

Eric raised both hands into the air. "I've also learned in my old age to never argue with a woman who has a knife and access to my throat."

Alina chuckled before Eric tenderly reached out and grasped the hand that did not have a weapon in it. "I missed you, Lina. Really, I did."

As the queen of Troivack stared at her brother's clear eyes that seemed brighter than before, she managed a small smile. "I'm honestly surprised you hadn't heard about the kidnapping. During the whole thing, Father and Finlay Ashowan were scouring for every mercenary individual and group. If you were anywhere near Rollom, I would've thought—"

"I was in Zinfera last summer. Or on a ship going there, anyway . . . I didn't return to Daxaria until spring of this year."

Alina blinked in surprise. "Why were you in Zinfera?"

Eric attempted to grin flippantly but didn't quite succeed. "A story for another day. Are you finished shaving me bald? I really do need to get back to change."

Alina swatted his shoulder then resumed her careful examination of his hair. "Sit still and don't distract me, and it'll be done in no time."

"Yes, Mom."

At this barb, Alina couldn't help but smile again as a corner of her heart that she had been previously forced to ignore began to fill with pure aching love and happiness. The corner where formerly her grief and anger had existed alone found itself something better to nourish in its confines.

Katarina had gotten through the dinner without making any kind of scene or unladylike comment. A fact she was rather proud of, even if it *was* because no one had attempted to talk to her. Whether it was due to the rumor that she had had a horrific and contagious flu recently, or if it was simply her growing reputation for being a difficult Daxarian woman, it was hard to say.

Though one thing Katarina did find odd was that she couldn't spot Eric anywhere around the long table. Additionally, the royal couple had sent a messenger to announce they would join everyone after the first course of dinner due to the security breach and investigation of the queen's near assassination.

When they eventually joined, Alina had donned a magnificently cool noble mask, showing no sign of her earlier bout of a soldier's spell.

In Daxaria, everything would have of course been canceled immediately in order to find the mastermind behind the attempt as quickly as possible. However, in Troivack, it was merely dinner and a show.

A fact that Katarina couldn't help but note was disturbing.

The banquet carried on in all its planned opulence, though Lady Rebecca Devark's absence cast a few nobles off balance.

When the final vestiges of the meal had been removed, and the guests were invited out to the terrace while the servants cleared the room for dancing, Katarina thought it was at long last the perfect time for her to drink to her heart's content. She could finally forget about annoying things like the devil, nasty nobles, or the horrible feeling of drifting further from her best friend . . .

But of course, there was something she had forgotten.

Suitors.

Noblemen young and old, who had all learned at the king's recent council meeting that Lady Katarina was no longer *just* the daughter of Daxaria's hero and a wealthy viscount, but now the daughter of a duke. A detail that, unfortunately, Katarina was unaware of earlier in the evening.

When she had seized the first goblet she could from a passing steward and turned to stare out at the clear Troivackian night sky, she couldn't help but smile as she recalled flying on a broom over the city of Vessa. The quiet, the beauty . . . The evening when she had gone stargazing with Eric in the library appeared suddenly in her mind.

"Excuse me, Lady Katarina, I am Lord Adam belonging to the Marquess house Cirillo. Would you do me the honor of being my dance partner for this evening?" The Troivackian noble who performed a quick bow to her looked to be in his mid-twenties, and had curling black hair that reached the base of his neck. He wore a silk charcoal gray coat that Kat noticed he had left unbuttoned near the top of his throat, making him look a bit rakish.

"I think I will be keeping myself company for this evening, Lord Adam, but thank you for your invitation." Katarina curtsied and kept her expression blank. There was no need to be churlish with someone who was only being polite and asking a reasonable question.

The Troivackian noble stared down at her with a small twitch of his eyebrows, obviously displeased with her response, but before he could open his mouth to say more, another man approached.

"Ah, still adjusting to the Troivackian dances, Lady Katarina?"

This time it was a man in his early forties who approached her. He smelled heavily of oils and had his black hair slicked back, leaving his curls to sit behind his scalp. He bowed to Kat, his thin mustache shining in the light of the nearby brazier. He wore a long dark red vest over a black tunic and pants and a large golden ring bearing a family crest on his pinky finger.

"I am Viscount Sanchez, I would be happy to instruct you while dancing to one of the slower numbers this evening, Lady Katarina." The viscount bowed magnanimously to Kat, his chin raised haughtily while Lord Adam frowned at him.

Kat fought with all her might not to cringe in disgust at his condescension.

"While I . . . *appreciate* . . . your offer, Viscount Sanchez, I am well-versed in Troivackian dances. I simply would prefer to quietly enjoy this evening in solitude," she informed him jarringly, only clenching her teeth once or twice.

There. Hard to ignore that direct response.

Or so Katarina thought.

"Come now, Lady Katarina, it is rather unbecoming for a guest to be seen excluding themselves on such an important occasion."

Rounding on the new interloper, Katarina's instincts prickled fiercely. Before her was a tall, lithe man with long white-and-black hair he kept bound behind his head and small oval gold-rimmed glasses perched on the end of his nose. His dark eyes were calculating and cold . . .

He reminded her a lot of Mage Sebastian in appearance.

Only Mage Sebastian didn't make her stomach roil at the sight of him. Annoy her? Absolutely, but he did not incite the same level of repulsion as this man . . .

"I am Duke Icarus. I don't believe we have had the pleasure of meeting before as I have only just arrived for the coronation this afternoon."

Katarina turned to stare at him directly.

So this is the man suspected of trying to kill Alina.

Katarina raised an eyebrow and straightened her shoulders. Her gaze turned cutting, and her features hardened to marble.

"I have heard of you, Your Grace. I am pleased to make your acquaintance."

She then did something she never had before, as she loathed to do it, but she held out her hand for him to bow and kiss.

For a brief moment, his lip twitched as though wishing to curl in disgust, but he seized her long fingers and performed the courtesy as seamlessly as his ranking dictated he should.

Wishing desperately she could wipe her hand off somewhere, Kat hid her true emotions before looking back to Lord Adam, the least unpleasant of the men before her.

"I suppose I would be dampening the mood to ignore all invitations. Very well, Lord Adam, will you be my partner for the first dance this evening?"

The son of the marquess smiled smugly. "I would be delighted to, my lady."

Kat gave the politest half smile she could muster. Though there was a vague demonic glint in her eye that only Duke Icarus noted when she held out her hand to Lord Adam and allowed herself to be guided off the terrace and back to the party.

As she stared at Lord Adam's profile, who was already waving to his friends in triumph, Katarina's excitement for the dance tripled.

Oh, just you wait, Lord Arsehat. I'm going to get my quiet night, and you will be my sacrificial lamb. I wonder where your pulsing vein will appear . . .

CHAPTER 8

A DARING DANCE

Eric approached the throne room that had been cleared of the banquet tables to make way for dancing and managed to enter without causing too much of a stir thanks to some sort of excitement happening near the center of the room.

As he raised a curious eyebrow and began to step toward the edge of the crowd, he was distracted by a hand clapping his shoulder.

"Eri—Your Highness! I haven't seen you properly since Norum!"

Turning toward the speaker, his body tensed by the sudden contact, Eric relaxed when he stared into the familiar brown eyes of his old friend Sir Vohn.

"Looks like someone finally found their way out of guard duty." The prince grinned at the knight and faced him more squarely.

"I did indeed, though I have no doubt that a certain Daxarian noble I know might've had something to do with it . . ." Sir Vohn removed his hand from Eric's shoulder and instead passed the goblet he was holding back into his other hand. "It's been a few years! Whatever happened to you after I left you on Quildon?"

The prince shrugged ambiguously. "You know me. I go where the fun is."

The Daxarian knight chuckled. "Sounds about right. Your sister was hell bent on learning about you for a while there . . . Might have told her about that little incident with the boat getting to the island of Quildon not knowing you hadn't told her . . ."

Eric closed his eyes with a wince and a pained breath. "You didn't tell her we were out of our minds drunk when we did that, did you?"

"Oh sure, I'd just casually mentioned we'd been kicked out of two taverns that night and semi-stole a boat. To your sister. The princess known for her sweet innocence."

Eric rolled his eyes and found his gaze landing on Alina, who was seated on her throne beside her husband, watching the dancing with pointed interest. "Not so innocent now it seems."

"Yes, well, the whole incident last summer was a rough turning point, I'll admit."

Eric's attention snapped back to his friend. "You knew about last summer as well? How is it no one told me?"

"Forgive me . . . but it wasn't the best topic to bring up on Her Highness—now Her Majesty's wedding day, and I thought you already knew about the . . . event." Sir Vohn bowed.

Eric shifted his feet uncomfortably, his guilt still fresh over discovering the details of the kidnapping. "We'll talk about it later. What seems to be the commotion on the dance floor?"

Sir Vohn straightened, his brown eyes cutting toward the backs of the nearby nobles.

"Ah, who else? Lady Katarina Ashowan is . . . well . . . being herself."

Frowning, his friend's response prompted the prince to carefully move forward while navigating around the sea of colorfully clothed nobles until he could finally see what new scene Kat had crafted. When he laid eyes on the five couples whirling around the floor, it wasn't hard to find the woman with her blazing red hair, her pale blue skirts fluttering with every turn of her hips, her golden eyes alight . . .

She looked like an otherworldly being. Effervescent. Charming, and— Eric's dazed thoughts halted.

He noted her partner's red cheeks and his barely suppressed scowl.

Tilting his head, it took the prince all of three breaths to realize what new havoc Katarina was wreaking.

She was making her partner look like an oaf, and the nobleman who was her dance partner clearly had no idea how she was doing it. From afar, Eric understood exactly how the redheaded troublemaker was accomplishing it.

Katarina was doubling both the number of her steps as well as her speed, making it appear as though she wouldn't remain on beat . . . But that was not the case. She had timed it perfectly. Instead of two slow turns, she was spinning rapidly four times, having doubled the speed exactly. However, that wasn't all she was doing. She then would step and wait twice as long for her next movement. Once again, she matched with the timing of the music, but her rhythms were throwing her partner off in the worst way, making her look like a fairy dancing with a lumbering dullard.

Eric covered his mouth and did his best not to laugh. The poor lad must've annoyed her.

As it happened, Katarina was in the process of whisking by the prince at that very moment, and as Eric dropped his hand from his mouth and folded his arms, he shot her a knowing smirk.

Katarina's exuberant expression froze as she passed, her golden eyes widening a fraction as she registered the prince.

She was so stunned, in fact, that she forgot to change her steps with her partner and instead danced normally for at least two bars of the music. Only, by this point, her partner was practically frothing at the mouth and was still clumsy as he grabbed her roughly by the waist and half shoved her along.

Eric's good-humored expression disappeared, and his hazel eyes fixed on the nobleman.

By the time the dance ended, Lord Adam was sneering while bowing to Kat.

When he straightened, however, his instincts bristled uncomfortably, prompting him to turn and find the crown prince of Daxaria staring at him as though he were considering slicing his throat right then and there.

The shadows that consumed the prince's eyes made Lord Adam's gut roil as he gingerly stepped back from Lady Katarina, barely resisting putting his hands in the air in surrender.

As he melted into the crowd, Kat peered around, wondering what had issued such a change in Lord Adam's demeanor. She was in the process of searching the crowd more carefully, when another young man stepped forward to speak with her.

Meanwhile, Eric slipped away from sight.

He needed to have a private word with the Troivackian noble who had deigned to push around Katarina Ashowan . . .

Katarina was struggling to resist rolling her eyes at her third dance partner of the night. As much as she had hoped her earlier act of rebellion with her first suitor, Lord Adam, would deter the other bachelors, it seemed the Troivackian men took it as a challenge to see who could manage her during the dances. Of course the fact that she was stunning didn't hurt, nor did the thought of a fat dowry should they manage to woo her.

However, each partner failed to match her changing tactics of humiliation.

For the second gentleman, she slowed her steps drastically but kept her spins quick for the first half, then when he started to get the hang of her strange deviation, she reversed the order. By the time the dance was over, he was red in the face and his throbbing vein revealed itself in the middle of his forehead.

Her third partner was an older Troivackian man in his late forties. He was large and strong, and so she had taken it upon herself to execute her steps perfectly, except when it came to the man's role to clap at the end of each spin, she joined him. It was a mark of dominance in the dance that had his expression morphing dangerously, but she met his gaze head on, her own golden stare sharp.

When he had bowed to her at the end while she curtsied, he opened his mouth to let loose his displeasure in hopes of educating her, only when he did so, something over her shoulder made him close his lips and pull back. He turned and walked away stiffly, leaving Kat to stare after him in confusion. She'd been looking forward to a good argument to further deter the sudden rush of suitors . . .

"I think if you try to get a drink right now, you'll have more partners waiting."

A flush swept through Katarina's body and her stomach leapt as she turned and found herself face-to-face with Eric.

Despite having seen him earlier that evening, his new appearance startled her to the point of speechlessness.

His wavy dirty blond hair had been cut and tidied and even swept to the side, revealing his intense hazel eyes. The dark navy coat he wore with ornate silver buttons matched his vest beneath, though the snowy white tunic that peeked through was neither buttoned nor tied at his throat—a hint of his lax nature. While his clothes were well-crafted and of fine quality, there was a subtlety to them that stayed true to Eric's nature. It was unlike the clothes he wore at his sister's wedding that Kat realized, especially in that moment, had been ill-suited to him.

He still didn't look like a polished aristocratic prince, but . . .

He looked more put together, and handsome. A small internal voice told Kat there was a different kind of danger in this new focus of his . . .

"So what if there are more suitors? I'm having a wonderful time adding a wide array of vein locations to my notes!" She placed her hands on her hips and hoped that the warmth she was feeling in her cheeks wasn't a blush.

"Let's see . . . Lord Adam had his by his right temple. Lord Sheldon had his in the center of his forehead . . . I didn't quite catch the last one."

"Both sides of his neck," Kat supplied while narrowing her eyes. "You seem like you know your courtiers."

Eric raised an eyebrow at her but didn't respond to her speculation.

"You cut your hair," Kat observed instead as the next wave of couples joined the dance floor, allowing her to fade back into the crowd with Eric.

"Correction: Alina cut my hair."

Kat grinned. "Is that your gift to her for her coronation?"

Eric let out a grunt while shaking his head, though he was obviously on the verge of smiling. "I swear you put her up to it."

It was Kat's turn to innocently avoid answering his accusation as she looked around them pointedly. It was then that she remembered that she was, in fact, angry with him.

"Why did you tell Alina about Rebecca Devark bothering me?" she demanded, a frown crashing her previously lighthearted expression and her arms crossing.

Eric blinked at her flatly. "Because she should have noticed and done something about it. Alina's supposed to protect you while you're here, Kat."

"She's got enough on her plate without worrying about me! You could have talked to me about—"

"You would've told me to hide it for you, Kat. It's not a bad thing to need help."

"Says the man who needs it the most," she snapped, her index finger tapping against her bare upper arm.

Eric let out a sigh of annoyance before noting that several courtiers around them were eyeing them interestedly.

"Dance with me, otherwise people are going to start trying to talk to us," he insisted, his voice dropping in volume.

"Pfft, what is it with everyone wanting to dance with me tonight? It's—" Kat didn't have a chance to finish her tirade before Eric reached out and grasped her hand and turned toward the dance floor. He paused a moment after doing so, giving her the chance to reject him if she truly abhorred the idea.

When her only objection was a small snarky side-glance, the prince proceeded to escort her. As the rest of the noble couples situated themselves while waiting for the next song to begin, Eric observed once again that a mischievous glint had entered her eyes.

"Now back to what you said about my needing help. There is a difference between you and me here in Troivack, and you know it," Eric continued quietly despite being out of earshot from the others.

"I'm not entirely helpless you know, and I don't exactly like the idea of needing a 'protector,'" Kat informed him seriously.

"That's funny, because according to Mr. Kraft, that's exactly what you referred to me as," Eric pointed out mildly.

Taken aback, Kat could tell that despite her best efforts, color had risen in her face. "That was different! I had to give him a good reason to get involved—"

The music began.

Eric shot her a wry raise of his eyebrow. "Don't stick your tongue out at me here. People are watching."

"I wasn't—"

"You were about to," Eric interjected before bowing to her.

Kat glared as she curtsied. Oh, how she wanted to torment him horribly for that, but she was a little distracted.

What had happened to him during his kidnapping? He seemed like an entirely different person since that morning . . .

He was becoming involved in Troivack's court, he cut his hair, and there was something else that had come alive in him that hadn't been there before.

It doesn't matter. He's being annoying. He should know better than to dance with me.

The first steps began with the couples meeting each other's palms and slowly circling one another, followed by another curtsy and bow.

They weren't steps that left a lot of room for creativity, so instead Kat bided her time.

Then came the part of the dance where the couples moved down a quarter of a circle together, the men gently touching their partner's waists from behind while guiding them with their other hands outstretched.

Then they would step away while the women spun toward them.

Kat smirked, excited to toy with Eric the same way she had her previous partners.

She intended to throw him off by changing her first and last spins. In turn, he would either try to adjust his step to be closer or farther away from her and look clumsy . . .

Kat executed her spins, her hand held out expecting to either bump into Eric or meet dead air, but his warm calloused palm met with hers exactly as the dance indicated they should.

When her eyes locked with Eric's, Kat found him smiling devilishly at her.

A fiery burn of competitiveness rose in her chest that wasn't entirely unpleasant . . . Her aura gently flickered to life. And due to his proximity to her, Eric found his surroundings growing hazy as a result.

The group of dancers traveled another quarter circle down with the men guiding their partners from behind.

Once again, the women were to spin to the men, and this time, Kat did so without adapting her speeds, only when it came time for the men to clap, she joined him on the first, but for the third clap . . . he held out his hand to her.

Catching her off guard, Katarina realized that slapping her hand down with his continued the rhythm, but it also took away her control of the dance.

She stared at him, her eyes glinting.

He let out the softest of laughs as he began to once again guide her back up the quarter circle.

"You think I'd dance with you without preparing beforehand?"

Kat grumbled, but only Eric could hear her, making the corners of his eyes crinkle in the way she had always liked best on him.

"Eric, I really don't like the idea of being dependent. I've been waiting my whole life to prove myself, and that's what I've wanted to do here in Troivack. I need to use this chance," she explained, her profile turning over her shoulder as they finished the quarter circle before her next set of spins.

Eric's teasing expression softened before he bowed to her, and she curtsied again. "Kat, we've been over this. It takes time to build your own power. If you get beaten down before you can even take that chance, then you lose your opportunity anyway."

Kat carried out her spins gracefully, her aura flickering magically about her, making her even more enchanting to watch. When Eric caught her hand again, her earnest gaze found his, her answer prepared.

"Then fight at my back, not in front of me."

Eric's eyes lingered on her face as they clapped twice in unison, and then as they had improvised before, palm to palm together on the third.

Right before she turned her back to him to be guided for the final stretch of the dance, he replied.

"Alright, Ashowan. Have it your way."

Katarina couldn't help it, she smiled, then he was yet again gliding with her up a quarter circle back to where they started.

With the music coming to its conclusion, Eric bowed and she curtsied. The room burst out in polite applause as the prince grasped her hand and, right before leaning over to kiss her knuckles, addressed her.

"You're going to do well in your footwork training with the sword. Your ability to add and alter intricate moves while staying on beat disproves my earlier theory about you being unable to keep to the tempo." He kissed her hand and, as a result, missed the burst of prideful glow from both Kat's aura and smile from his words.

When he straightened, she had regained a modicum of control over her features, though as he released her hand, she startled.

"Why do you have fresh cuts on your knuckles?"

Eric's expression grew shuttered. "Ah. Don't worry about it. Now if you'll excuse me, I see a wonderfully full decanter of moonshine."

Then without waiting another moment for Katarina to question him further, the prince disappeared into the crowd, where there were several pairs of noblewomen's eyes following him.

Kat blinked after Eric in confusion, but shortly thereafter decided he wasn't an entirely different person like she had at first thought after all.

As she turned to stare back at the crowd, stepping out of the strange trance she had been in while dancing with Eric, Katarina was subjected to a different type of attention. The disapproving gazes had turned calculative and even hungrier . . .

Her eyes darted up to Alina and Brendan, who sat perfectly still while watching her. Despite their intense observation of her, however, they didn't seem angry despite most likely having seen her tormenting the noblemen . . .

Kat decided a breath of fresh air was in order to settle her nerves, prompting her to stride purposefully toward the terrace. For reasons she couldn't quite place, she was feeling a little embarrassed, but as she moved, she plucked up a goblet from a passing servant's tray.

I've done my duties for the night . . . Time to drink.

CHAPTER 9

DOUBLE TAKE

Katarina downed the goblet of moonshine in a single toss and didn't falter for a moment as she placed the empty cup down on a nearby table and seized another full one from a passing footman.

She then let out a long breath while closing her eyes and allowed the cool fall breeze to cast her red hair aflutter. Her heartbeat was only just starting to slow down after her dance with Eric.

Why did it have to beat so hard anyway? With her magic, she could perform far harder physical tasks and not be even the slightest bit winded!

"That was quite the display, Lady Katarina."

Kat nearly vomited her moonshine. She opened her eyes and looked to see Duke Sebastian Icarus standing only a few feet away.

"Whatever do you mean, Your Grace?" Kat turned to face him, her expression icy.

"Humiliating your well-intentioned suitors in such a public manner, then allowing the prince of Daxaria to dance with you without problem," he pointed out, his tone light, but his gaze cutting.

"I'd prefer to think of it as His Highness merely being more *open-minded* to my interpretations of the dances than my first few partners," Kat countered evenly before taking a sip of moonshine, though her golden eyes never moved from the duke's face.

Duke Icarus raised a lone disapproving eyebrow. "It was an insult to our courtiers."

"I believe it is also an insult when a noblewoman declines an offer to dance but is bullied into accepting. Some could say it is a rather *conniving* and *underhanded* practice." Kat's index finger that held her goblet began to tap.

The duke moved forward while peering down his nose at her. "You seem to be misguided in your understanding of Troivack's tolerance for rebellious behavior from the weaker sex."

"Speaking of rebelliousness, isn't it horrible how there are rumors that some of Troivack's very own nobility are turning on their king?" Kat's feigned wide-eyed innocence infuriated the duke instantly.

"What are you insinuating, Lady Katarina? And before you answer, I will be kind enough to warn you that I am not a man to be trifled with lightly."

Kat's free hand flew to her mouth. "Your Grace, how could *I*, a mere, brainless, swoon-prone woman, *deign* to insult you?" She breathed before continuing. "I just thought it was an interesting topic everyone was aware of."

Duke Icarus's right cheek twitched as he leaned down. "You can fall out of Prince Eric's favor just as easily as falling into it. Then you may find yourself more mindful of your place."

Kat's smile spread slowly across her face as she tilted her head, and she leaned in closer to the duke, instantly disarming him.

"And you can perhaps reconsider eating so much garlic before breathing in someone's face."

The man jolted back, his entire face flushing red.

"Lady Katarina, Her Majesty Queen Alina has summoned you to aid her in the antechamber," a familiar voice interrupted Katarina and the duke.

When the two nobles turned, they found themselves staring at Mage Sebastian Vaulker, and it was then Kat realized that without a doubt, the two were father and son.

The duke hesitated at the sight of Sebastian, whereas the mage didn't seem to be able to look at his father.

Kat awkwardly moved away from Duke Icarus, though she did manage to give a semi respectable bob of her head in his direction before she reached the other Sebastian's side.

"Mind escorting me, Mage Sebastian? It'd be an honor to have such a knowledgeable and *admirable* magician give me a few minutes of his time," Katarina gushed while smiling sweetly up at the mage, who looked pale and uncomfortable.

Sebastian shot her a flat look, but he still offered her his arm and proceeded to escort her back into the ballroom.

"What was that about?" he demanded under his breath once they had returned to the bustling room that was growing more heated as the nobles drank and danced heartily.

"Your father's a nasty snake," Katarina replied breezily.

A shock ran through Sebastian's body that the noblewoman could feel in his arm under her hand.

"He told you he's my father?"

Kat felt her heart become uneasy as she stared at the mage's uncharacteristically vulnerable wide eyes. "No, but you two look far too much alike. Anyone who sees you side by side will know. I'm sorry."

Sebastian recoiled at hearing her apology, and it was clear he was about to snap at the redhead, but she spoke again before he could.

"It's not easy having a father that looks like you. My own da had to deal with looking like his own arse of a parent . . . He said that he would sometimes have nightmares of looking in a mirror and seeing his father staring back."

Sebastian's mouth clamped shut.

"The fact that your mother still chose to name you after the duke only makes it worse. No offense intended. Children aren't responsible for choosing their parents, but just so you know . . . and believe me, this isn't easy for me to say but . . . I like you significantly better than your father. You seem capable of decency."

The mage looked at Kat, his expression gentling a little before she cast him a sly sidelong glance.

"Don't worry, Sebbie, I doubt Alina is going to let him get his way for much longer."

Sebastian's flare of kind feelings toward Kat instantly dissipated.

Letting out a small huff, the mage rolled his eyes. "Gods, I can't wait for you to get out of this castle. I can't handle the stress."

Katarina was dangerously close to laughing when Lord Adam, her first dance partner of the night, stumbled in her path, doubled over, sporting a cut over his left eye that was turning a deep shade of purple. Though when he realized whom he stood before, he quickly rounded his shoulders and limped away.

"What happened to him?" the redhead asked bluntly.

Sebastian stared after the nobleman with a frown before his gaze drifted over the nobility to find Eric Reyes standing by a refreshment table. He was watching Lord Adam's retreat from Katarina and was about to return his attention to the three noblewomen who were fawning over him when he locked eyes with the mage.

The cold darkness that had passed through the prince's eyes when he'd watched Adam move away from Kat provided Sebastian with a strong hunch on what exactly had transpired.

"When you danced with Lord Adam, did he say or do something?" he asked, his voice quiet.

Katarina cast a questioning stare at the mage as they continued toward the antechamber. "Ah, he started getting a bit forceful by the end of the dance, but I still feel like I came out the winner of that exchange," she finished with a small laugh.

"More than you know," Sebastian muttered while filing the information away to address with Faucher later.

Katarina casually glanced toward the same beverage table Sebastian had been eyeing a moment before and recognized the back of Eric's head as three beautiful Troivackian noblewomen peered up at him from under their dark lashes. One in a midnight blue gown even reached out and touched his arm.

"He's a prince without a wife or even betrothed. He's going to be sought after," Sebastian pointed out with feigned casualness.

Kat's attention flew ahead of herself as though she hadn't realized she'd been staring.

"Well, those ladies are welcome to try to win his hand as much as they like."

Kat mentally cursed herself. She hadn't meant to sound so bratty.

Sebastian studied her for a long moment. "You know . . . it doesn't seem like a passive interest you two share. You keep orbiting each other."

Something her father had said months ago echoed in Katarina's mind then . . . It had been about how he couldn't avoid her mother back when they'd first met . . .

She gave her head a shake.

"Ah, Sebbie, look at you trying to be a matchmaker. Ever think about changing your profession? You could make a fortune."

The mage rolled his eyes. "I told you before to stop calling me that, and mark my words, Lady Katarina, the longer you play dumb, the madder you'll drive him."

"You speak as though Prince Eric is already smitten with me. He's not. Just because he likes to insult me—"

The pair had finally reached the antechamber door, but Sebastian had stopped and turned to face Katarina a few feet from the guards so that his next words wouldn't be overheard.

"You want to prove you are a capable woman? Stop pretending you're a fool who sees nothing. Everyone knows what is between you and His Highness. We have enough to concern ourselves with without this angst carrying on."

Caught off guard by his serious confrontation, Katarina wasn't able to respond to Sebastian's reprimand at first.

"I . . ." she began, then was forced to clear her throat. It wasn't like her to become shy, and so instead of stalking off, Sebastian waited patiently. "Eric—His Highness . . . Well . . . he can't be anyone's partner. And I . . . I've already hurt one person enough, so I don't want to attempt any kind of relationship. Ever. I don't think I'm cut out for it. So whether there is—or isn't—anything . . . let me be ignorant. As you said, there is enough going on . . . so . . . Please."

The mage was stunned.

How was it she always managed to catch him by surprise?

Katarina turned and continued on without Sebastian toward the ante-chamber. However, the mage glanced back at Eric, then toward her retreating back, and he couldn't help but develop a bad feeling in light of her response.

Apparently, while Katarina Ashowan was aware of *something* brewing between her and the prince, she had no idea of just how important she had become to him. To insist on remaining ignorant of such a thing . . . ? Sebastian looked back to Lord Adam, who was catching his breath against the throne room wall while a friend appeared to be asking him questions. Most likely about his battered state.

Sebastian shook his head, his hands curling into fists.

This might become a problem . . .

"Time for you to go, Kat," Alina informed her friend gravely before looking to Lady Kezia, who moved forward with a cloak and change of clothes in her hand.

Kat blinked in alarm. "Go . . . ? To Faucher's keep you mean . . . ?"

"Yes. You angered a lot of nobles tonight with your dancing prank, so now is a perfect time to say I've asked you to spend some time outside of court to ease you into Troivack's customs. This will give you a few months to train without suspicion. I can't say this is how we planned to sneak you away, but we're going to be turning tonight in our favor. Plus, if we do it swiftly, it will both appease them and also eliminate any attempts to attack you before you leave. We won't tell them exactly where you're going, just to be safe."

Staring at her best friend, then at Brendan, and finally at Kezia, Kat finally processed what was happening. "Alright, but before I go, in my defense, I had told them I didn't want to dance, and they said I was being rude for saying no."

Alina raised an eyebrow at Kat. "Did I sound like I was mad? It was bloody hilarious. You never dance at balls, so I knew they'd done something."

Kat's defensive expression shifted to a coy smile.

Brendan meanwhile looked concerned. "Who was it that was pressuring you?"

"Let's see . . . Lord Adam, eldest son of house Cirillo, Viscount Sanchez, and of course, our favorite duke in the world, His Grace Sebastian Icarus."

Brendan let out a low growl.

Alina rested her hand on his forearm while addressing her friend. "Don't worry, Kat. We'll deal with them."

The redhead shrugged. "Did I seem worried?"

Alina grinned back at Kat as an unspoken understanding passed between them.

"Besides," Kat continued, "Lord Adam looks as though he attempted to fight with a set of stairs and lost."

Alina's eyes flew to her husband's, a strange knowingness in both their gazes.

Kat frowned in confusion but was stopped from asking anything more when Lady Kezia cleared her throat and waddled forward.

"You should be off, Lady Katarina. We will send Lady Wynonna to provide you with missives and updates, but I'm afraid with my delivery date nearing, I won't be taking any unnecessary trips from the castle."

"Oh, you magnificent creature, I'm going to miss you horribly." Kat sighed before leaning forward and seizing Lady Kezia in an embrace.

The expectant mother smiled as she welcomed the hug and held on to the redhead for several long, happy moments before she carefully pulled herself away. "I am another moon away from the time the babe is due, but I will be sure to write to you."

The door leading out of the antechamber into the corridor away from the throne room opened, and in stepped Prince Henry, Leader Faucher, and Sir Cas.

"Lady Katarina, we will be escorting you to my keep. Mage Sebastian will meet us at the servants' exit soon," Faucher explained grimly.

Kat beamed. "I can't wait to meet your family, Faucher! We're going to have an absolutely *delightful* time living together."

Faucher let out a loud grunt, unable to hold her delighted gaze, then turned and swept out of the room with his cape swishing behind him.

Prince Henry shared a grin with Kat before he bowed and followed the military man.

"See you outside, my lady!" Sir Cas waved with his usual bright expression before he, too, bent forward respectfully and left.

Brendan rose to his feet. "I will leave you to say your goodbyes, but don't take long. Alina and I need to return to dance together before anyone thinks it's strange we're all gone."

The new Troivackian queen smiled and nodded at her husband as he leaned down and planted a quick kiss on the top of her head before he took his own leave.

Lady Kezia stepped back quietly, though she remained in the room.

"I'll miss you, Kat, but . . . you have to tell me all about your training, and you must become an absolutely amazing swordswoman so we can really show some of these arses what we can do." Alina stood and grasped Kat's hands, her eyes glistening with tears as she stared up at her friend.

"Don't worry, I've been waiting for this ever since I was a child. I'm going to give it everything I've got," the redhead assured confidently.

Alina smiled. "I know. Plus, you have to be relieved that you don't have to join me in the council meetings."

"Whaaat?! Of course I'll miss them! Sitting for hours . . . and hours . . . listening to endless conversations . . . endless complaints . . ." Kat's gaze grew haunted as her eyes drifted to the wall behind Alina.

"Oh, will you, now? I suppose I can always send you a compilation of my reports with Lady Wynonna for you to—" the queen of Troivack began smugly.

Kat yanked her friend closer to her, her golden eyes wide. "I'm burning my quills tonight and you can't stop me."

Letting out one final watery laugh, Alina threw her arms around her best friend.

The two hugged, and when they pulled apart, Alina's cheeks damp with her tears, set to helping the redhead untying the back of her ball gown. Kat then privately changed into a pair of men's britches, tunic, leather vest, boots, and lastly, a cloak.

Fully dressed, Kat marched toward the door but suddenly stopped and turned to face Kezia and Alina one final time. Unable to find the perfect words to leave with them, she settled on giving a wolfish smile. Then, she left and faced her new adventure with unbridled excitement and hope.

Though she did wonder if perhaps she should have left a note or message with Alina to communicate to Eric that she was leaving . . .

CHAPTER 10

THE FAUCHER FAMILY

Katarina awoke the morning after the coronation feeling . . .
Well . . .

Wonderful.

For whatever reason, the four hours she had slept had been deep, restful, and filled with dreams of little stress or consequence.

She stretched out, feeling perfectly comfortable in the bed, the sheets warm, and the small, weighted pull of the blanket to her right alerted her that Pina was curled up by her feet.

Kat had arrived in the dead of night, been shown to her room by a servant, and from there bathed and donned a fresh night shift before crawling into bed.

The room she had been given had dark wooden floors polished to a gleam, maroon curtains hung around a four-poster bed that reminded Katarina of Faucher's cape, though they also matched the upholstery of the chairs in front of the stone fireplace as well as the background of the detailed rug on the floor.

It was a much smaller room than her chambers at the castle, but . . . it felt cozy, and something about the space made Katarina feel at ease.

Perhaps there was the sense that it was a home and not a political battlefield. Though this raised several questions for the redhead as she sat upright and cracked her neck over her left shoulder, then her right.

For one, she would have guessed Faucher's wife and children to be models of traditional Troivackian decorum. However . . . there was a glow about the space . . .

The glow of a happy home.

Folding back her coverlet and sliding her legs over the edge of the bed, an easy smile came to Kat's lips as her toes reached down to the floor and found a small plush rug cushioning her feet.

Beside her bed were slippers never worn before, lined with lambswool and encased with soft leather . . .

"Faucher, are you secretly a sweetheart?" Kat murmured to herself as she slipped on her new footwear and locked eyes with her familiar momentarily.

Pina gave a slow, sleepy blink before a knock on Katarina's chamber door snapped her attention upward.

"My lady, do you need assistance dressing yourself?" a maid called out from the corridor.

Putting a hand to her chest and taking a calming breath, Katarina realized she had grown a little too accustomed to forgoing serving staff during her time at the castle . . .

"No, thank you!"

"Not a problem, my lady. I will wait outside to guide you to the banquet hall."

Nodding to herself, her fingertips pressing intermittently against her palms as excitement built in her chest, Kat turned toward the wardrobe to her left and set to finding what clothes she was expected to train in.

Upon opening the doors, her good mood dipped when she saw many of her dresses from the castle already hung and waiting.

She shifted through them with a small frown drawing her brows together, until at long last, she arrived at her trousers and men's tunic.

Odd that Faucher hasn't arranged for any other clothes . . . but maybe that comes later.

As she dressed, Katarina took stock of the room and further speculated just what it was that reminded her of her home back in Daxaria . . . and after careful deliberation, she came to the conclusion.

It was because it had a similar style, taste, and level of grandeur as her childhood home.

The realization brought a renewed sense of contentment, and with it, the same peace she had first awoken with.

After tugging on the leather cuffs around her wrists, Katarina strode over to the door, and she was once again surprised to see a maid standing there waiting for her.

The woman, perhaps in her late thirties, curtsied dutifully, her dark brown hair was braided and tucked underneath a white hair wrap. She wore a long sleeve sandy brown dress with a white apron tied around her waist that was modest but well-kept and tidy.

"Good morning, my lady. My name is Rosemary, I am one of the maids serving the Faucher household. I have been assigned to you to ensure you have a comfortable stay."

Kat smiled and craned her neck to the side in hopes she would see the woman's features a little more clearly but, despite this move, found that Rosemary was keeping her face turned downward.

"I'm happy to be in your care. Feel free to call me Lady Katarina, or Lady Kat if you feel like saving a bit of breath," Kat greeted happily, which prompted the maid to give a polite curtsy.

"I understand. Please follow me this way, my lady."

Kat watched curiously as Rosemary then gestured from her lowered position to her right down the corridor.

Closing her chamber door behind herself, the redhead's gaze darted to the arched windows that sat open all along the corridor, revealing a wide expanse of land that disappeared into the horizon of long brown grasses and weeds. Though there was a stretched number eight that had been tracked in the ground a short way from the courtyard. Katarina leaned closer to the window ledge, gingerly touching one of the gauzy curtains that had been swept to the side.

Peering around, she noted two other walls of the keep to her right and left that faced each other, making the structure form a U around the courtyard. Looking down, Kat then regarded the large courtyard that each of the three floors looked down upon. There were training dummies, benches along the borders, and barrels filled with weapons.

Kat barely resisted the urge to begin bouncing and instead settled for biting her lip before turning and moving down the corridor in the direction Rosemary was still gesturing toward. Though the woman had straightened from her curtsy, her head remained bowed.

Upon descending the keep's stairwell, its walls constructed of warm brown stone and its floors dark wood, Katarina eyed family portraits, intricate tapestries, and pottery along the way.

Once on the first floor, she was then guided to the left. At the end of that corridor, two tall peaked wooden doors with round iron handles stood propped open to reveal the banquet hall.

Faucher was seated at the head of the table, for once not wearing his cape or armor. Instead, he looked rather . . . normal. He was in the process of reading over some paperwork and wore a cream tunic that wasn't fully laced to his throat with its sleeves rolled to his elbows.

To his right sat a woman Katarina presumed to be Faucher's wife. Her black-and-white hair was piled atop her head, but she was the epitome of elegance.

Unlike the former queen Rebecca Devark, who had also been a model of class and grace, however, there was a kindness woven somewhere along her high cheekbones and small mouth, the dark bags under her eyes the only indication of her age in her face.

Then there was the young woman seated to Faucher's left. Her cheeks were round with youth, and her long frizzy hair was tied in a low, haphazard ponytail as she ate her breakfast with hunched shoulders.

"Morning!" Kat crowed.

The three nobles turned.

After a beat of silence, Faucher rose from his seat, already looking exasperated by her.

"Lady Katarina, this is my wife, Lady Nathalie Faucher, and my daughter, Dana."

Kat grinned and noted the subtle quirk of his wife's brows. Lady Nathalie was surprised by the friendly expression, but . . . there was a warm shine in her eyes that indicated she didn't mind Kat's smile in the least.

"It is wonderful to meet you, Lady Nathalie and Lady Dana. Thank you for welcoming me into your beautiful home." Instead of curtsying, Katarina bowed. She figured it'd look too silly if she attempted to act like a noblewoman while wearing trousers.

Unbeknownst to Kat, the bow made Dana look to her mother in astonishment, while Lady Nathalie in turn regarded her husband with a hint of amusement.

Faucher shook his head with a sigh.

"Lady Katarina, we've placed you beside Dana this morning."

Kat smiled at Faucher, then his daughter as she made her way over to the place he indicated and pulled out the ornately carved, high-back wooden chair that she then slipped into.

As she settled down, however, her boot nudged against something unexpected.

A loud whine followed by a yawn echoed up from somewhere unseen.

Startled, Kat shifted to the side to look under the table to see . . . three dogs.

The one she had just nudged was a large, slobbery mutt with red eyes that beheld her lazily. The dog behind him popped up and tilted his head to look at the newcomer curiously, his gray ears bent at the tips and his black eyes fixed on Kat.

Then a small dog that couldn't have been much bigger than most cats sat up behind the big dog's head and immediately bared its teeth.

"Cozo! Shh! She's a guest! We talked about this!" Dana whispered hastily while looking nervously to her father, who had his eyes closed as though he was preparing to reprimand her.

Kat almost laughed when she looked at Dana, who was already bowing her head in apology, though even with her face downturned, her freckles sprinkled across the bridge of her nose were still visible.

"S-Sorry, Lady Katarina, I should've warned you that—"

"Warned me that you have some wonderful beasties here? Pfft, pets are part of the family! What're their names?" the redhead asked jubilantly as a servant stepped forward and filled her goblet with water while another set down a plate of thick sausages, eggs, and tomato slices before her.

Dana peeked up nervously at Katarina, but when she met her golden eyes couldn't hide her shock.

"You've got eyes like a wolf!" she exclaimed.

"Dana!" Faucher growled, making her cringe, though Kat noticed she didn't seem fearful of her father, merely chastened.

"I take that as a compliment, Lady Dana! Yes, I do. I'm a mutated witch, though my abilities lay most strongly with fire, so my eyes have a unique color. Tell me, other than your little fighter dog, Cozo, what're the other two names?" Kat lay her napkin across her lap and stared interestedly at the young woman, who already looked fascinated by the Daxarian.

"O-Oh. Well, t-the large one is n-named Bruff, and the gray-bearded one is named Nickel. W-What kind of powers do you have?"

"Dana . . ." Lady Nathalie's soft voice called over the table while giving her head a small shake.

"No worries, Lady Nathalie, I get this question a lot." Kat began to load her fork with sausage and egg but kept her torso turned toward Dana. "I can see in the dark, eat a lot, am always warm, have a terrific constitution, and don't need much sleep. I'd say my eye color is the most interesting thing about my abilities." Katarina nodded to Dana once, then began to eat with great gusto while Faucher watched her pointedly.

He noticed she hadn't mentioned any of the strange happenings Sebastian had been reporting about her magic, once again making him think that perhaps the mage had been exaggerating . . .

"Lady Katarina, once you are finished with breakfast, we are going to the courtyard to meet the other young men training alongside you," he explained, drawing Kat's attention at long last away from his daughter.

He was already nervous about her influence over his youngest child . . .

"Sounds great! I'm very excited to start. Thank you for agreeing to teach me, Faucher." Kat's right cheek was filled with food as she spoke.

Faucher let out a breath mixed with a grunt of displeasure.

Lady Nathalie eyed her husband with interest, then Katarina.

"Lady Nathalie, you and my mother have such similar taste in decor; I must admit it's nice to be reminded of home." Kat turned to Faucher's wife, who placed her fork down and leaned back in her chair at the compliment. She nodded her chin in thanks.

"Is your mother Troivackian?" Dana couldn't help but ask, her wide doe eyes brightening with excitement.

"She grew up here until she married her first husband, yes."

"What family was she from?" Lady Nathalie asked gently.

"Oh, um, Earl Piereva's household." The hesitancy in Kat's voice made Faucher's dark gaze rest on her curiously.

"Ah, I remember your mother. She was very beautiful," Lady Nathalie recalled, though she had suddenly become very still.

"According to my da, she still is," Kat recounted fondly as she neared finishing her meal.

Lady Nathalie's attention fell to the table, her eyes lost in thought, which in turn made her husband stare at her in mild concern.

When she didn't appear to be any closer to snapping out of her silent musings, however, Faucher decided whatever had caught his wife off guard could be discussed later.

"Lady Katarina, if you are finished eating, we can—"

"Faucher, erm . . . is there a diet you put your students on or something . . . ?" Kat interrupted, looking a little sheepish as a servant stepped forward and removed her clean plate.

It took a moment for the military man to understand what she meant.

With a shake of his head, he waved forward a servant while still watching the redhead. "Lady Katarina usually eats three plates for breakfast."

Both Dana and Lady Nathalie's eyes shot upward to Faucher.

Kat blushed, but once the servant returned with the two loaded plates, she refocused her attention on finishing the food.

Meanwhile, Dana looked to her mother, her expression openly astonished and questioning. She had never seen someone interrupt her father and not be exposed to the full power of his glare, let alone have a woman behave so boldly . . .

Lady Nathalie's lips pursed as though fighting a smile.

While her husband hadn't been entirely forthcoming in his description of the Daxarian noblewoman who would be staying in her home, he had hinted that she was a little eccentric.

Catching Faucher's eyes, she raised an eyebrow and gave a small nod.

Apparently, his gift for understatement hadn't dwindled in his older years, but she wondered if even he knew the full implication of having proximity to a descendent of Earl Piereva's household in their midst.

Lady Nathalie openly studied Lady Katarina and noted the movement of her hands, the slope of her forehead, and found she could see faint traces of similarity to the former Annika Piereva . . .

So . . . the daughter of the Dragon is in my care. I wonder why I didn't receive a warning about this . . .

CHAPTER 11

KNOCKS AND KNIVES

The men stood in a line and openly gaped.

Kat met each of their gazes head on, her hands clasped behind her back, as she bobbed her head with a close-lipped smile aimed toward them. Faucher stood at her side, his expression flat.

Broghan Miller raised his hand tentatively. "Leader Faucher . . . is this . . . a jest?"

"It is not," the Troivackian military leader replied firmly.

The young man slowly lowered his hand, though it was not an easy feat as he continued to blink in open bewilderment at the redheaded woman.

"Can she not . . . train elsewhere?" Caleb Herra asked, his voice strained.

"No. She will be training here. With all of you. If she quits of her own volition, that is another matter, however, I will remind you that she is the daughter of the hero of Daxaria, and her father recently accepted the title of duke. Furthermore, she is here under my protection with the blessing of His Majesty King Brendan Devark. You will behave yourselves and keep this information private, or else you may find your necks relieved of your heads. Am I clear?" Faucher's voice rose, and his tone sharpened.

The men shifted their feet uncomfortably.

At last, Joshua Ball raised his hand, a blush already crossing his cheeks. "P-Pardon me, Lady Katarina, but . . . you aren't eighteen or nineteen years old, are you?"

"Oh, for the love of—" Faucher began to roar but stopped himself as the young man nearly leapt out of his skin.

"Erm . . . I'm twenty," Kat replied uncertainly.

The lad, who appeared younger than the others, let out a relieved sigh while closing his eyes and pressing his palm to his chest.

"Enough of this. Ashowan, fall in."

Kat looked around the courtyard. "Where? I don't see a hole anywhere..."

"The line." Faucher pointed at the row of his students. He could feel his anger boiling higher in his chest.

"Ah, right . . . Never had that order directed at me before." Kat made her way over to her fellow knights in training and decided to stand beside the young man who had been questioning her age, as he looked the most harmless.

The other men subtly shuffled farther away from her.

Faucher watched as Kat slowly clasped her hands behind her back and widened her stance.

"Shoulders back, Ashowan," he barked while starting to pace in front of the students.

Everyone including Kat drew their spines as straight as possible.

"Chests out, eyes forward. When I give you orders, you respond with one thing and one thing only: 'Yes, sir.' Understood?"

"Yes, sir!" they all chorused.

Kat's heart was hammering in her chest.

"Today we are running twenty laps, and then you will work through the stances I taught you, and may the Gods help you if I see you trying to practice something I did not tell you to." Faucher eyed Caleb Herra on this last point.

"Yes, sir!" Everyone's voices boomed back to their leader, continued stalking back and forth in front of them all.

"Ashowan!"

"Yes, sir?" Kat called back, the smallest lift appearing in the corner of her mouth.

"Because this is your first day, you will run thirty laps, and then I want you to wear the coat."

"Yes, sir." The redhead's response lacked its former vivaciousness.

"Is there a problem, Ashowan?" Faucher insisted as he bore down on Kat.

"I'm sure it's nothing, but what's 'the coat'?"

While Kat's golden eyes had remained fixed forward, the very startling sight of Faucher smiling snapped her attention to his scarred face.

Well, that can't be good . . .

Kat stood in the dirty padded coat and leather helmet with Faucher standing in front of her. He raised an eyebrow while the rest of the students practiced their attacks on nearby straw dummies.

"You will dodge my attacks. Watch my eyes, not my feet," Faucher ordered.

Taking a steadying breath through her nose, Kat readied herself, but it was during this inhalation that Faucher lunged forward with his sheathed sword and jabbed her ribs.

Doubling over, Kat coughed, then felt the sheathed sword rest against the side of her neck.

"Your opponent will not wait for you to be ready. Stand up straight."

"Way to go for the knife wound," Kat wheezed while pressing herself upright again.

"Assume your enemy knows your injuries. It is your responsibility to either protect your weaknesses or to pretend they don't exist and bear whatever pain that causes you." Faucher swung his sword and was about to jab at Kat yet again when she leapt back out of his way.

Without hesitating for a moment, Faucher proceeded to swipe his sword toward her middle. Despite her once again bouncing back, he next sent his blade toward her knees. He succeeded in hitting his target, knocking her down to a kneel.

"Don't let me force you in any given direction. Five more steps back, and you would've been pinned against that wall. Keep aware of your surroundings. Get back up." Faucher lay his blade against his shoulder and watched dispassionately as Katarina rose with a small wince.

He waited for her predictable irritation or an indignant outburst . . .

But none came. Instead, she frowned with concentration and locked eyes with him.

Then he began again.

The third time, he did in fact get her pinned back against the wall. The fourth time, she managed to dance away, but after a few minutes, Faucher stopped his advancement and stared at her sardonically.

"Right now, you keep putting more and more space between us. That is running away, not properly facing your opponent."

"What if I could fight you from here though?" Kat called out seriously.

Faucher huffed; he was unimpressed with her attempt at arguing with his teachings.

However, there was a sincerity to her question that stopped him from outright dismissing it.

"How would you do that when you are outside of arm's length? You aren't carrying a bow into battle."

"No, but knives are common, right?"

Faucher blinked and tilted his head over his shoulder. "Are you talking about throwing knives?"

"Yes."

The young men training off to the side of the courtyard all laughed.

Faucher shot them a withering stare, and they swiftly returned their attention to their tasks.

"Throwing knives is not a reliable method of fighting. Furthermore, in battle, men carry shields."

"Still, if I hit your sword arm with one, I'm still technically fighting you, aren't I?" Kat continued.

Faucher studied her without saying anything, mulling over her words.

"Alright, Ashowan. Come here. I want to see just how good you are with these alleged knives."

Kat burst into a smile and stripped off the bulky coat and helmet before jogging back to Faucher.

The military man noted she was already perspiring heavily, but she didn't seem to mind in the slightest.

Turning toward where the rest of his students trained, Faucher stalked over.

"Ball, step away from your dummy. Lady Katarina is going to show us her skill with a knife."

The young man limped away hastily.

"What happened to you?" Kat asked as he positioned himself a short distance away from her side.

"Ah, the first day I started training, Leader Faucher had me run laps to try and stop me being so superstitious about the numbers eight, nine, eighteen, and nineteen, but I ended up fracturing my ankle. It's almost healed up though!" Joshua Ball explained while the tips of his ears grew red.

Kat pressed her lips together to stop herself from laughing as she slowly looked over to Faucher with a knowing gleam in her eyes.

The storm cloud that darkened his features as he pointedly ignored her stare only made it that much harder not to cackle.

She could tell the lad was already driving him half mad.

When Faucher regarded her again, it wasn't hard to guess that he didn't appreciate his aggravations being the subject of her humor.

"What're you standing around for? Go get knives from the weapons shed," he growled.

Kat smirked at him, then reached behind herself, under the back of her shirt, and withdrew two knives.

The men all stiffened in surprise. Then without further ado, Kat threw both knives in the blink of an eye. Each dagger landed firmly in the arms of the dummy.

A pregnant pause followed.

"Do it again."

Kat's golden eyes slid to Faucher, and she smiled proudly.

Striding forward, she pulled free the knives, returned to her teacher's side, and then threw the blades into the arms with perfect precision yet again.

Faucher rounded on her. "Do you only know how to throw them?"

Without replying, Kat retrieved the two blades from the dummy and then faced the military man. "No. That isn't all I know how to do with these."

Faucher drew his sword free of its scabbard, making all the men training freeze in alarm.

"Show me what you can do, Ashowan."

"Thank you very much for escorting me yourself to the courtyard, Lady Nathalie." Sir Cas smiled at Faucher's wife as they walked through the keep.

"Of course, Sir Cas. I'm given to understand you are going to be helping my husband train his new students?"

"Yes, my lady."

Lady Nathalie bobbed her head in response as the pair reached the large arched open doorway that led out to the training grounds, where the sight before them made the knight and lady halt in their tracks.

Faucher was attacking Lady Katarina with an unsheathed sword, and she was combating him by dodging and attempting to stab him with two smaller knives in her hands.

While Faucher was clearly holding back his full strength and expertise, it didn't diminish the fact that Katarina was a worthy adversary . . .

"Oh my," Nathalie said breathily as she watched the redhead dip and dive.

"I didn't know she could do that!" Sir Cas announced—openly impressed—as he crossed his arms to watch.

Lady Nathalie looked on in awe, her gaze sharpening as she watched Kat continue to fight against her husband . . .

When Faucher finally noticed the arrival of his wife and Sir Cas, he stopped his attacks.

Katarina, however, was not aware of their presence and so she lunged forward yet again, only for Faucher to instinctively backhand the dagger from her grasp.

She blinked in surprise, then turned to follow his eyeline. When her gaze met with the Daxarian knight she had grown to befriend on their journey to Vessa, she broke out into a broad smile.

"Sir Cas! I didn't know you would be coming!" Kat straightened her shoulders.

"Ah, yes." Sir Cas shook his head, freeing himself from the trance of watching the duel. "His Majesty Brendan Devark ordered me to help Leader Faucher with your training."

Kat nodded happily before she held up one finger to prompt him to wait, as she then turned and retrieved her blade that Faucher had sent skittering across the courtyard stones.

When she returned to stand beside her teacher, the military man homed his attention on her without bothering to greet Sir Cas or his wife.

"Where did you learn to use knives? You fight like a Troivackian with them. If I hadn't been prepared for it, you would've been quite deadly."

"Ah, my m—"

"I'm sure her father, Lord Ashowan, brought in teachers for the sake of self-defense for her time here in Troivack," Lady Nathalie cut in smoothly before fixing her husband with a brief, unreadable expression.

Faucher was instantly taken aback. He was not used to his wife interrupting anyone.

Kat blinked in equal bewilderment, but given her limited personal relationship with the woman, she shrugged it off. "Yeah, close enough of an explanation. Though my brother is a little better than I am, and he is also pretty cutthroat with a sword . . . though don't ever tell him I said that," Kat insisted when she looked to Sir Cas, who laughed.

Faucher sighed while shaking his head. "The way you could dodge just now was far better than when I had you in the coat. Why?"

Kat fiddled with the knife in her hand awkwardly. "Well, because I didn't have a weapon, and I've never really learned hand-to-hand combat. Not to the extent that I'd be a proper match against you."

It was the second time that day that Faucher found himself confounded by the redhead.

He hadn't anticipated that Katarina possessed humility, or that she thought so highly of his own skills . . .

Sir Cas noticed the conflicting emotions crossing Faucher's face and winked at Kat, who remained unaware of what was happening.

"Regardless of whether you have a weapon, you need to be able to dodge.

Go get the coat. We'll try it again. If you can dodge my attacks until sundown, we will move on to the wooden sword training."

"Yes, sir!" Kat replied brightly as she jogged over to where she had discarded the coat and leather helmet.

Lady Nathalie silently curtsied and left the courtyard while Sir Cas made his way over to the other students to see what they were working on.

Meanwhile, Faucher stared after Katarina, his gaze calculative and his thoughts burrowing deeper . . .

If she had been permitted to practice every day . . . she would be a flawless master of those knives. I can tell at one time she was . . . Faucher hefted his sheathed sword in his hand. *She doesn't complain when she gets sweaty, and she takes her hits well without complaint. She was definitely taught by a brutal Troivackian . . .* He turned to stare over his shoulder where his wife was disappearing into their home.

Why was it the more he learned about Katarina Ashowan, the more questions he ended up having?

CHAPTER 12

BEGINNER BATTLES

Katarina sat on the wooden bench with her flagon of water, her elbows resting atop her knees. The light was fading from the sky, cooling the courtyard even more until her breaths could be seen in the light of the nearby braziers that had been lit.

Kat had finally been able to manage dodging Faucher's blows just in time for the other men to wrap up their own practices under the helpful tutelage of Sir Cas.

While screwing the cap back onto the flagon, she ruminated on how her first day seemed successful and began thinking about how lovely a bath would be, when the shuffling of boots on cobblestones alerted her to her fellow students gathering around her.

Lifting her golden gaze up, she noticed Caleb Herra stood at the center, a nervous-looking Joshua Ball on her left, and Broghan Miller on her right.

"Why are you learning the sword?" Caleb loomed over her, his arms crossed as his small dark eyes glared down at Kat.

"I like big sharp things," the redhead replied glibly.

Joshua Ball let out a small snort, but one cutting glance from Caleb had him schooling his face.

"You shouldn't be here," Caleb continued tersely. "You're going to bring shame to Leader Faucher, and he is the greatest teacher in all of Troivack."

Kat slowly lifted her shoulders up until she was sitting perfectly straight, then cocked her head over her shoulder, her attention never wavering from Caleb's face.

"Well, will *you* shame him because he teaches me?"

Caleb grunted.

Kat turned to look at Joshua Ball, who startled under her attention.

"Don't worry lads, I'm taking this seriously. I happen to like Faucher, so I don't plan on being too big of an annoyance. Now"—the redhead stood with a stretch and drew herself up to her full height, which in turn made the three young men around her do the same—"I reek like soured milk. I'm going to bathe, so are you going to get out of my way?"

The faint pulse of a vein on the left of Caleb's shaved head appeared.

"Another idiot Daxarian." Broghan Miller sighed while shaking his head.

Kat swung around to face him, smiling, though her eyes were wide with incredulousness.

"You just insulted the daughter of a duke and a witch! And *I'm* the idiot?! Pfft!" Kat laughed, then looked toward Joshua Ball. "Now if you'll excuse me, I'm leaving first."

The young man stepped to the side despite Caleb's scowl and Broghan's eyeroll.

She had taken all of three steps from the trio, but her fellow students decided they weren't quite through with her yet.

"You should tell that ridiculous knight, Sir Cas, to watch his back. We don't need direction from some lowly Daxarian knight who doesn't deserve to lick our boots."

Stopping in her tracks, Kat turned around, her golden eyes flashing dangerously.

They could antagonize her all they wanted, but . . .

She wasn't about to let them threaten Sir Hugo Cas.

"The men haven't come in for dinner? What about Lady Katarina?" Faucher asked the maid, Rosemary, with a frown. He had been pacing in his office and verbally reviewing the results of the day's training for Sir Cas to log before dinner when the personal maid he had assigned to the lady had sought him out.

Shaking her head, the young woman didn't raise her face. "We prepared a bath for her, but she has not come in yet."

Faucher shot Sir Cas a knowing look as the young man stared back from the desk where he was making notes.

The two were flying out of the office in an explosion of movement.

When they rounded the corridor that led toward the courtyard, they could hear the furious grunts and shouts echoing down, instantly prompting the two men to break into sprints.

When they reached the courtyard, the sight before them brought a roar bellowing from Faucher.

Caleb Herra wielded a real sword drawn from its scabbard, and Katarina had one of her knives in hand, while Broghan Miller clutched his bleeding upper arm that appeared pinned to one of the straw dummies by Katarina's other blade.

Joshua Ball was standing to the side, looking around nervously, and so he was the first to jump and turn at the sound of Faucher's furious shout.

Kat continued glaring at Caleb, but he was already standing at attention with his shaved head bowed to his teacher.

"WHAT DO YOU THINK YOU ARE DOING?!" Faucher's voice boomed as he bore down on his two students.

The redhead's jaw was clamped shut as she too gradually fixed her posture before her teacher.

Faucher stared between Caleb and Kat. Neither of them spoke.

Meanwhile, Sir Cas was already working on freeing Broghan from the training dummy.

"One of you better speak or you will both be punished accordingly," Faucher informed them while glaring menacingly at the two.

When no answer was forthcoming, Faucher rounded on Joshua Ball, whose face drained of color.

"You. Explain."

"W-Well . . . Caleb w-was talking with Lady Katarina a-and—"

"Was he threatening her?" Faucher demanded.

"N-No, but he . . . took exception to her . . . and m-might have said something about how Sir C-Cas shouldn't be teaching us . . . Lady Katarina attacked first . . ."

Sir Cas strolled over to the scene with Broghan at his side (who was still grasping his bloodied upper arm) and raised an eyebrow at hearing the last of Joshua Ball's recanting.

The Daxarian knight turned toward Faucher, looking remarkably relaxed despite the insult he had apparently received behind his back.

The Troivackian military leader, however, was not as calm.

Pivoting back to face Katarina and Caleb, he eyed the pair angrily.

"Lady Katarina, you will run the track in the field until your legs give out under you. If you try to enter this keep without your knees knocking together, I will send you back out here to run until your feet bleed through your boots." He then stepped closer to Caleb, his eyes boring into his student's blank expression.

"You, Herra, will duel with Sir Cas every day in front of your fellow comrades. You will learn to respect your betters, or you will be dismissed."

Caleb's jaw flexed, but he did not speak.

Faucher's gaze flit to Kat, a dangerous shine in his eyes in the dying light of the day. "Did I not say to run?"

The redhead turned from him and marched off with her head held high toward the long figure eight track without bothering to look directly at him or Caleb.

When she was out of earshot, Faucher seized Caleb by the front of his tunic and half threw him toward Broghan and Joshua.

"Did I not warn you?" he seethed at the young men.

Neither Caleb nor Broghan displayed any emotion. Joshua Ball, however, gulped.

When the trio said nothing, Faucher looked to Sir Cas, who had his arms folded but still looked completely at ease as he gave a small shrug.

Letting out a grunt mixed with an exhale, Faucher's toes turned toward the keep's entrance.

"None of you will be given dinner or breakfast. I will see you all here before the sunrise. Understood?"

"Yes, sir," the men responded in unison.

Faucher stared at them for another long moment, already sensing that the issue was not, in fact, over.

However, he had anticipated that such problems would arise . . . He only hoped that his strategies and Lady Katarina would succeed in placating their displeasures, though he already had his doubts that they would.

At last, the military leader retreated to his keep to inform the serving staff of his orders pertaining to everyone's meals, Sir Cas following close behind.

Oddly, the young knight, who was annoyingly prone to smiling, didn't seem all that bothered by the fact that he was being disrespected and looked down upon.

Faucher had heard that Sir Cas was one of the most gifted swordsmen in all of Daxaria, and he had supplied multiple brilliant points to teach to the students . . . but he still was only . . . twenty-five? His youthful face made it all that much more difficult to discern.

I'll be able to study his style tomorrow when he faces Herra. Hopefully he is as talented as his reputation has led us all to believe.

With his thoughts turning to the more comfortable topic of men and their abilities, Faucher proceeded to completely forget the redheaded noblewoman running laps behind his keep . . .

A mistake he wouldn't ever make again.

*   *   *

Eric sat in his chamber, reviewing the list of names Sir Vohn had supplied him.

His assistant, Thomas Julian, busied himself with putting his chamber to rights, and the elite knight contented himself with sipping his goblet of moonshine by the fire.

"You're certain these are all the nobles that have businesses reliant on Duke Icarus's investments?" the prince asked after a moment while leaning back into his chair with wrinkles appearing between his brows.

"That just includes the nobles in Vessa and Biern. I haven't even begun to investigate Norum or Rozek."

Eric closed his eyes with a groan.

"The only noble family that was keeping him in check until recent years was the Piereva house. However, that was more out of competition than any sort of honor," Sir Vohn explained while reaching for the decanter and topping up his drink again.

"With a backing like this, why doesn't *he* want to be king?" Eric asked while tossing the list onto the side table with no small amount of aggravation.

"He honestly respects the Devark family. Though he takes exception to your sister. He is also one of the nobles who was instrumental in exterminating magic from the kingdom. The amount of cold-blooded murders on his grounds was unparalleled."

Eric gazed into the fire in silence.

He knew that Duke Sebastian Icarus would be a formidable opponent, but he hadn't known he would be so well connected throughout the entirety of Troivack. It was difficult to find any weakness in the duke's web. It made Eric tempted to talk to Finlay Ashowan about how he could bring the man to ruin . . .

"He doesn't have an heir. Or one that he's named anyway . . . He has only daughters. You've met his illegitimate son, though I'm given to understand that the two aren't in contact."

"Mage Sebastian? Yes, I might ask *him* if he knows anything that would be of help, but I don't know that he's trustworthy yet." Eric leaned forward until his hands lightly clasped together. After another moment of careful thought, he rose to his feet.

"Alright, Gabe, I want you to find out which of these business associates and expenditures he began investing in after my sister's engagement was announced. Mr. Julian?"

The young lad nearly dropped the pair of trousers he was in the process of putting away. "Y-Yes, Your Highness?"

"I want you to find out anything you can from his servants. Find out how he treats them, if he does anything illegal, if he has a vice. Anything that could be exploited," Eric ordered while striding over to the desk that, until the past few days, had been untouched by the prince.

The assistant bowed and scurried from the room at once, though Eric opened his mouth to tell him that it didn't have to be that instant.

Shaking his head with a sigh, the prince instead started scrawling down notes that Sir Vohn couldn't see from his seat by the fire.

"So you want to take down a duke from another kingdom?" the knight questioned in a more serious tone. He hadn't wanted to ask such a direct and incriminating question in the presence of Mr. Julian.

"Yes, and to also find out who are the other powerful figures he is working with . . ." Eric trailed off. He had yet to relay to Sir Vohn his encounter with the actual devil.

"Hm. That's pretty ambitious of you all of a sudden. It isn't even *your* kingdom."

Eric's hazel eyes briefly rose to meet his friend's stare, who froze when he saw the darkness that appeared in the prince's features.

"He tried to have my sister killed and he is intent on hurting Katarina Ashowan. I'm not leaving Troivack until he is dealt with."

Sir Vohn found himself speechless.

For as long as he had known Eric, he had come to see him as an easygoing noble. Someone who enjoyed fine drink and fun. Perhaps a little bit devious, and of course he carried out his duties well, but he had never gone out of his way to hurt someone . . . not in the way he wanted to with Duke Icarus . . . No. He'd always been the precious prince of the kingdom.

I suppose no one has tried to kill his sister before . . . and after learning about her being kidnapped last summer, he must be feeling guilty.

Sir Vohn rose with a long yawn and turned toward the door. "Well . . . we'll do our best. Though the way you're talking, it's a good thing Lady Katarina was exiled for a while. It'll be hard for Duke Icarus to—"

Eric was on his feet in the span of a breath, his chair scraping across the stones as his sharpened gaze fixed on Sir Vohn.

"Kat is exiled?"

Yet again, Sir Vohn found himself being cast off balance by the prince's uncharacteristic reaction.

"Er . . . yes . . . last night she was sent to be cared for by Faucher's wife to help her adjust to the Troivackian court. Most likely extra etiquette lessons and the like . . ."

For whatever reason, Sir Vohn had the distinct impression that it would be wise to remain very, *very* still.

At first, Eric's face seemed to relax, until it hardened to marble. "I'll go visit Faucher in the morning. I'll make sure she is settled in, and he has the appropriate number of guards. Has she brought her maid, Poppy, with her?"

Sir Vohn carefully looked to the prince again, and he instinctively began to stand at attention. "I don't believe her maid was able to go with her last night. I'll see about arranging for you to go for a ride early in the morning. You probably don't want more rumors going around . . . right?"

Eric didn't respond immediately. His expression remained ambiguous and his eyes unblinking for a lengthy moment.

"Of course. I'm just making sure she is being treated properly after the incident with the former queen. It's bad enough we have to write to her father about it."

Sir Vohn let out a long breath as his face broke into a smile. "Right! Her father! I thought it was strange you were so concerned, but I guess you and Lord Ashowan patched things up at last?"

The prince didn't offer any confirmation on the knight's supposition, but as he seated himself back down at his desk and returned his attention to his paperwork, replied with, "I'll see you in the morning."

Sir Vohn blinked, and his smile drifted from his face.

When had his friend changed so much?

With a final lingering glance, Sir Vohn took his leave for the evening, though he couldn't help but grow curious to see how Eric would interact with Lady Katarina the next day . . .

Perhaps then he would have his answer once and for all regarding whether there was any truth to the rumors or not.

CHAPTER 13

MORNING MAYHEM

M aster Faucher! Master Faucher, pardon me, but there is a visitor!"
The strained whisper of a steward along with the relentless sharp
knocking on his chamber door were what awoke Faucher the morning following his first day of teaching Lady Katarina Ashowan.

Faucher let out a long grunt, blearily opened his eyes, and slowly brought
himself up to a sitting position while wincing at the aches in his right knee
and back.

"Nattie, can you go see what that's about?" he murmured while pinching
the bridge of his nose.

It took a few more moments of quiet before Faucher registered that his
wife was not responding to him as usual.

With his eyes finally adjusted to the shadows of the room, Faucher
turned, reached out, and found Nathalie's side of the bed cold.

Frowning, he wondered where she had gone so early in the day, when
the frantic knocking resumed.

"Sir! The prince of Daxaria is downstairs in the entrance!" The steward's
voice had become painfully desperate to the point of almost sounding like
begging.

Hauling himself out of his bed and stalking across his chamber, Faucher
threw open the door and glowered down at the servant.

"S-Sir, His Highness is awaiting you," the steward repeated, though he
visibly gulped at his master's obvious disgruntlement.

Without speaking so much as emitting a series of animalistic growls, Faucher closed the door and proceeded to dress himself in a hurry before leaving the chamber and making his way down to his home's entrance.

By the time Faucher descended the stairs and found the prince with a Daxarian knight and a young maid he recognized as the one Lady Katarina had traveled with, he could hear the faint thunder of barking from the other end of the keep. His daughter's many dogs had awoken as well apparently . . .

Eric raised an eyebrow at the sound but returned his attention to Faucher, who had finally touched down on the black-and-white marble floor.

"Morning, Faucher, pardon the intrusion so early in the day. We wanted to avoid anyone seeing me leave."

The military leader openly glared at Eric, unaware that crumbs of sleep were caked into the bags under his eyes.

"I'm here to return Lady Katarina's maid. If I might make my greetings to her, I will be out of your hair in no time." The prince gave a slight incline of his head as was appropriate, and that was when Faucher noticed it . . .

Eric was tidily dressed in a clean white tunic and navy blue leather vest that was fastened with fine silver hooks. He wore pressed tan trousers and black riding boots, his hair had been cleaned and tidied, and his eyes were no longer bloodshot.

He looked as a prince should.

Save for the hardness and haunted look in his eyes . . .

"What happened to you?" Faucher demanded without bothering with the customary formalities.

Eric gave a humorless smile. "I've been a bit busy as of late. Now, knowing Kat, she's already awake and prowling around somewhere."

Faucher studied the prince for another lengthy moment before letting out a huff and shaking his head. He then turned toward the corridor that would take them to the banquet hall.

"I doubt she'd be awake. She already started a fight with my other students. She had to run laps after a full day of training, so you might as well leave her maid here and be off, Your Highness."

"Faucher, what do you mean Kat started a fight?"

The ice in Eric's voice made the Troivackian hesitate before facing him again, a sharp glint entering his dark eyes.

"She attacked a student. I punished the participating parties accordingly," the military leader announced firmly. His tone left no room for argument.

The prince stepped closer, his features neutral, but the air around him ominous.

"I'm going to see Kat before I leave. After that incident at the castle, I'm not going to be entirely trusting of anyone, Faucher."

Faucher squared his body and was opening his mouth to argue with him further when Rosemary, the maid who was assigned to Lady Katarina, appeared.

The woman looked exhausted and pale, and her eyes . . . The brief moment Faucher glimpsed them before she curtsied, he saw fear.

His stomach clenched.

"Master Faucher, Lady Nathalie has asked that you come to the courtyard."

The military leader didn't wait long enough to thank her for the message, and he instead tromped past Rosemary toward the corridor that would take him to the training space, already sensing that something pertaining to the infuriating redheaded noble had run amok.

Eric didn't need an invitation to follow along, but he did wave to Sir Vohn to stay behind.

When the two men reached the exit to the courtyard, they found Lady Nathalie standing with her arms crossed, her attention fixed ahead.

"Nattie, what is the meaning of—"

"Gregory, look." His wife nodded toward the distance, her stare not wavering for a moment.

Faucher followed his wife's gaze and felt his eyes go wide.

He stepped down into the courtyard as though in a trance.

"Faucher . . ." Eric's alarmed tone as he stepped beside the military leader failed to snap him out of his stupor.

"By the Gods . . . what . . ."

"Godsdamnit." Eric broke into a run.

Faucher remained rooted to the spot.

"Apparently, the glowing began a little before midnight, according to Rosemary," Lady Nathalie informed her husband quietly at his back.

"Has she been . . ."

"Running ever since you ordered her to? Yes. Rosemary was sent to keep an eye on her after you left the men. She hasn't stopped to take a break or drink any water the entire night." Nathalie's voice was quiet, but there was mix of concern and amazement in her face.

"How long have you been out here?" Faucher asked sternly.

At last, Nathalie looked to her husband. "Rosemary came to get me when Lady Katarina started glowing. We tried to ask her if everything was alright, but she insisted that she had to run until she couldn't anymore."

"Why didn't you come get me?"

Nathalie tilted her head thoughtfully over her left shoulder. "Curiosity, I suppose."

Faucher let out a breath of displeasure as he turned back in time to see the prince reach Katarina, and he watched as the two spoke and gestured back to where he stood.

The military leader cursed softly under his breath.

He should have known better than to doubt Sebastian's warning.

"I can keep going though! He said to run until I couldn't!"

"Kat, you know he had no idea you could run all night—Hell, even *I* didn't know you could." Eric held out his arm to stop Katarina from running yet another lap, and he stared at her flatly. Once he had been able to receive a response from her and noticed her eyes weren't consumed with magic, his initial panic had calmed considerably.

Kat sighed, then stuck her tongue out at him. "Spoilsport."

Eric rolled his eyes as he gestured back toward the keep.

Kat casually strolled beside him as she proceeded to crack her neck side to side." Gods . . . if only I could always do this . . . I feel twenty times more relaxed . . ."

Eric shot her an incredulous glance before snorting. "You're mad."

Kat smirked. "I appreciate the compliment. So what're you doing here? Did you miss me already?"

Eric shook his head while looking to the sky with a smile. Kat's golden gaze lingered on his profile. His eyes were crinkling again . . . He really did clean up nicely . . .

"I heard you got into a fight with some of the other students," the prince said instead.

Kat squinted and pointedly avoided looking in Eric's direction. "Hm . . . fighting? That doesn't sound like me . . ."

"It sounds exactly like you."

"Your Highness! Just what do you think of me?"

"That you're a troublemaking hellion, who should never be left to her own devices." The prince snorted.

"I'll have you know I only acted out when they tried to threaten Sir Cas!" Katarina fired back with a small note of indignation.

Eric laughed heartily then. "Faucher's students threatened Sir Cas? Gods . . . that must've been funny."

Kat turned to face Eric more as they walked. Something was peculiar about his tone . . .

Sensing her gaze, the prince decided to explain his reaction. "Do you know the youngest age an elite knight in Daxaria can be?"

"Twenty-seven?"

Eric grinned. "Exactly. Sir Cas was granted special permission to join when he was twenty-three. He's twenty-five now."

Kat balked. "What?! I know he mentioned he was a bit gifted with the sword but—"

"Yes. He doesn't like people knowing or talking about it. I haven't gotten to see him fight yet, but I've heard it's incredible."

"Well, he's supposed to spar with Caleb Herra today. Do you want to stay and watch? It's supposed to be Herra's punishment, and I must say I'm especially excited now," the redhead invited casually while also slowing down as her boots crossed onto the cobblestones of the training courtyard.

Eric sighed while struggling to supress a smile once he glimpsed Kat's barely hidden eager expression. "I'm not supposed to be out for long, but . . . I might have to make an exception."

Kat beamed.

After a beat or two of happy silence, Kat stared at Eric in the final moments before they reached Faucher—who did not look all that pleased to see the two of them taking their time reaching him.

"You know, you should've given up on moonshine a lot sooner; you're a lot more fun now." Kat couldn't help but begin to skip as her hands clasped behind her back.

"I'm not giving it up. I'm just moderating it somewhat." The prince's good-humored expression faded tenuously then.

Kat felt herself bite the inside of her cheek. "Well . . . you seem a lot better now is all."

Eric didn't bother responding to her observation as the pair at last arrived before Faucher, who already had his arms folded over his chest as he noted Kat's flickering aura.

"You. Go bathe and go to bed. You will be back on these grounds by lunch."

"But I wanted to see Sir Cas and Caleb Herra spar!" Kat burst out, earning herself an unimpressed scowl from Faucher.

"You will see it tomorrow. Go."

Shoulders slumping forward, Katarina trudged toward the keep where Rosemary and Lady Nathalie stood waiting for her.

"Oh, Kat?" Eric called out.

The redhead peered back over her shoulder, still glum.

"I brought you your maid. You really do need to stop forgetting to tell people where you're going."

Kat didn't say anything, but she did break out into another bright smile before she turned and darted into the keep, obviously excited to bring a familiar face to her side.

When she had disappeared inside and Faucher and the prince were once again alone, the two eyed each other.

"Will Your Highness be visiting often?"

"I might," Eric answered ambiguously while slipping his right hand into his pocket. "In fact, I might stay longer today. I, too, am curious to see Sir Cas spar. He tends to train on his own at odd hours, so I have yet to see him in action."

"Mm." Faucher's black brows knit together.

"Besides, I think there are a few things you should really be aware of when it comes to Kat if you are going to train her," Eric added more seriously. "We had intended for Mr. Kraft to come be a part of her lesson planning, but he is going to be occupied for a few weeks at most."

"I received the notes from Mage Sebastian and Mr. Kraft regarding her abilities. I have things in hand."

Eric looked over his shoulder at the track that Katarina had been tearing around all night, then back at Faucher.

"It was an oversight on my part to assume she would inform me of abilities, like being capable of running all night."

Scuffing his boot against the stone courtyard, Eric nodded quietly while looking around in a deceptively casual manner.

"I know you were forced to teach her, Faucher. I also know she's eager to show the world what she can do, and that can make her reckless. My advice to you, whether you want it or not, is that you should push her harder than you've ever pushed anyone before."

"His Majesty already gave me his blessing to push her. I—"

"No, Faucher, you're not hearing me. If you think there is a method of training or a standard of learning that is impossible for a normal person? Expect it of her. She *isn't* entirely human. I, too, had to learn to stop expecting her to act like one. After all, how many people do you know that have faced the devil and not only survived, but nearly beaten him?"

At this, Faucher stilled. "You've certainly had a radical transformation in your ways of thinking, Your Highness."

"Kat hurts herself when she tries to force an opportunity to prove herself. So let's just give her the right opportunity. Isn't that what His Majesty was aiming for when he ordered her to be trained?"

Faucher didn't respond.

Mostly because he knew he shouldn't reveal to the prince that the purpose of the king ordering him to teach Lady Katarina was to prove that he was the superior teacher, who could turn even a woman into a competent beginner swordswoman. All so that he might further his own career.

Though, despite Brendan Devark having claimed that to be the reason . . . Faucher *was* starting to wonder if there was perhaps an even bigger plan surrounding Lady Katarina that the king had kept to himself.

CHAPTER 14

UNEXPECTED UNDERDOG

When Kat was at last permitted to rejoin her fellow students in the courtyard after the luncheon hour, she found herself still lamenting having missed Sir Cas's duel with Caleb Herra. Not to mention she hadn't been able to bid a proper goodbye to Eric . . .

With a sigh, the redhead swung her arms as she strolled toward the courtyard with Rosemary following behind her. Poor Poppy had been awoken terribly early to join her mistress at Faucher's keep, and so Kat had instructed that she was to have the rest of the day off to rest and recoup.

Rolling her shoulders, Kat mused how she would need to make Poppy wash her clothes first thing the next morning, as she only had three pairs of trousers and tunics, and given that she was sweating through them each day, could not wear them more than once unless she wanted to repulse anyone who happened to stand downwind from her.

Once Kat faced the pale daylight at the courtyard exit, she noted Caleb, Joshua, and Broghan hard at work with their wooden swords, facing their dummies while Faucher and Sir Cas stood side by side and observed.

Taking the two steps down to join them, she straightened her spine and lifted her chin.

She had avoided Faucher's attacks the previous day, so she was bound to be able to hold a wooden sword for the day's lessons like he had promised.

Pacing forward, Kat stopped a short way from Sir Cas and Faucher, then widened her stance and clasped her hands behind her back.

"Katarina Ashowan reporting for lessons, sir."

Both Sir Cas and Faucher looked to the redhead, but the two men bore very different expressions.

Sir Cas was smiling as warmly as ever.

Faucher only gave her a glimpse before he returned his attention to the new recruits.

"Faucher?" Sir Cas prodded gently, his smile barely dimming.

"Grab a wooden sword from the barrel. Your dummy is on the right."

Kat grinned and nearly ran to the aforementioned barrel. She pulled out the wooden sword and then looked in the direction Faucher had nodded for her dummy. Her smile faltered.

Her dummy was far from the rest of the other students, alone in a corner of the courtyard . . .

Hesitating, Kat gripped the handle of her practice sword even more firmly.

She was used to people segregating her.

She'd show them.

So she stood in front of the dummy and waited.

Her magic burned under her skin, begging to be released despite running all night and not receiving an adequate amount of food or sleep . . . Her determination and excitement had drawn it forward regardless.

"Lady Katarina, Sir Cas will teach you the basic stances. You will practice them, and before the dining hour, I will have you spar with Herra. Understood?" Faucher shouted over to the redhead without moving a step.

"Yes, sir!" Kat called back without shifting her stare from the dummy.

Sir Cas made his way over to the redhead and began instructing her without a single glance back, his breezy attitude earning him several looks of disapproval from the young men.

Faucher kept his attention fixed on the other students, feigning disinterest in Kat.

He needed to ensure she'd be accepted by the others if they were to have any success.

The spar would be the first test to see if that was possible . . .

"Herra!"

"Yes, sir!"

"Step forward."

The young man did as commanded, separating himself from his peers and meeting Faucher in the center of the courtyard.

"You will now spar with Lady Katarina."

Caleb frowned deeply, though he didn't verbally express his displeasure.

"You will not use any attacks that aren't the ones I've shown you in the past week. This is meant to be a training session."

"Yes, sir."

Faucher's stern gaze lingered on Caleb before he made his way over to where Kat was working with Sir Cas. Her golden eyes were intently fixed on her dummy as she moved through each stance fluidly.

The longer he watched her, the more impressed Faucher became. He found himself nodding along to each repeated stance that she worked through masterfully.

He looked at Sir Cas, and the young knight nodded knowingly.

"Lady Katarina, come here," Faucher called out after ensuring every one of her moves was flawless.

The redhead stopped and straightened. While sweat shone along her hairline, she seemed otherwise unfazed by the long day of training, regardless of her lack of sleep or nourishment.

Kat gave a single nod of affirmation to Sir Cas, then another brief bob of her chin toward Faucher as she hefted her wooden sword and strode toward Caleb Herra, whose disdain could be sensed from across the courtyard.

Once the pair stood toe-to-toe, Kat raised a single eyebrow.

"If you insist on being here, I won't go easy on you," Caleb informed her with a whisper. "Even if your crown prince is watching."

Despite intending to remain neutral in her countenance, the news that Eric was somewhere nearby observing her spar caught Kat completely off guard. "Eric's here? Where? I thought he left already."

The redhead began looking around and at first didn't see where the prince was allegedly watching from until she looked up toward the second-floor balcony. There, Eric stood with a bored expression, and a knight that looked familiar was at his side.

Kat was beginning to grin up at him, but that was when Caleb swung his wooden sword and landed a firm blow in her gut.

"Point to Caleb," Faucher's voice boomed. "Ashowan, keep your attention on your opponent."

Kat wheezed and slowly straightened, though it felt as though one or two of her ribs were bruised.

"If you were just going to get married and be queen, why bother learning the sword? Are you trying to humiliate Troivack?" Caleb growled while flipping the wooden sword in his hand.

With narrowed eyes, Kat reset her stance and struck her first defensive pose.

Caleb attacked again, but this time she was ready. She blocked his blows, though the strength he put behind them made the wood of her sword rattle painfully in her palm.

Gritting her teeth, Kat continued deflecting his attacks, but she was getting forced backward and she knew it.

"Ashowan, stop letting him lead you like a dog!" Faucher shouted from the side.

At last, Kat stepped back far enough that she didn't need to avoid Caleb's attack, which gave her time for an extra breath to shift sideways and advance to his left.

With a grunt, Caleb tried to put her back on his favored side, but she kept sidling around him, making him follow her in a circle.

After another moment, he stumbled.

"Keep your eyes fixed on one point, Herra. She's dancing with you," Sir Cas called out, his voice uncharacteristically stern.

From behind Caleb, guffaws from Broghan and Joshua reached his ears, making his lip start to curl.

Kat remained focused on him, but despite this, she couldn't have prepared for the wide arc he drew as he brought his weapon down over her head.

"HERRA! I SAID USE ONLY WHAT I TAUGHT YOU THIS WEEK!" Faucher roared as soon as he saw his student draw his weapon back, but the anger in Caleb was too ravenous.

Kat managed at the last minute to get her sword above her head and stop him from cracking her skull, but she could hear the wooden sword splinter under the full force of his blow.

Caleb bore down on her, his face inches from her own, his ire heavy in his gaze.

Kat felt her magic ignite.

Her aura burst from her body, and her eyes brightened to a shine, making Caleb rear back.

"Godsdamn witches," he spat while readjusting the grip on his sword.

He came at her again, but his moves weren't what he was supposed to be using . . . No, they were brutal.

He struck the handle of her sword, bruising her fingers and making her leap away with a small yelp.

"HERRA! YOU WILL DESIST THIS INSTANT!" Faucher was stomping forward, but the hotheaded youth didn't listen.

Caleb swung his weapon toward her knees. Luckily, Kat stopped the attack with her own sword, but the weapon snapped completely, the wooden blade dangling by a splinter, making it useless.

Smirking triumphantly, Caleb pulled back his arm again to strike at her, but the redhead had had enough.

She felt all rational thoughts snap free.

"Fuck this."

"HERRA, YOU ARE GOING TO BE IN A WORLD OF TROUBLE IF YOU DO NOT—"

Kat lobbed the broken sword at Caleb, who attempted to deflect it with his own weapon, but with the dangling blade whipping about, he wasn't able to cast it off cleanly. With his weapon and movements occupied, Kat darted forward, and with her aura burning even brighter and wider, her eyes flashing like a divine being of wrath, she crashed her fist into the corner of Caleb's jaw.

A wave rocked the young man's body once, and then . . . he crumpled in a heap on the ground.

The courtyard was quiet as Katarina stared down emotionlessly at her opponent.

"If you fight like a dirty bastard, I'm going to beat you like a dirty bastard," she informed Caleb's unconscious face passionately.

The redhead lifted her face to see Broghan and Joshua gaping at her, fear and uncertainty in their eyes as they beheld her magical aura.

Kat turned to Faucher, who had frozen in place at the scene, looking completely stunned.

Sir Cas was staring in open wonder . . .

Then, Kat turned her face up to see Eric.

He was smiling.

He nodded to her.

She nodded back.

Shifting her body to square herself in front of Faucher, she stood at attention.

Despite this, no one was able to move or speak for several moments . . . not until the glow around her finally dimmed.

The first to move was Sir Cas, who strolled over to where Caleb lay unmoving. Kneeling, he set to checking the young man's pulse, then head, before gently slapping his face to revive him.

Kat didn't look anywhere else but at Faucher, who held her gaze steadily.

"Herra's fine. Just knocked out cold," Sir Cas announced to everyone before standing again.

"Lady Katarina . . ." Faucher began at last.

"Yes, sir?" Kat asked while lifting her chin.

"Because you acted in self-defense, you will not be punished for this. Caleb Herra"—the military leader turned his furious gaze to the young man, who was opening his eyes and staring around him dazedly—"for dis-obeying my orders, you are banned from lessons for the next week."

Caleb didn't look as though he was in a state to understand what was being said.

Fortunately for him, both Broghan and Joshua stepped forward to help him stand.

"Take him to his chamber, and then the two of you go eat your dinners." Faucher returned his attention to Kat. "You are dismissed."

Kat bowed her head, then proceeded toward the keep without bothering to look back at her fellow students.

Though she did sneak a glance toward the balcony and found that Eric and his knight were no longer watching.

With a sigh, Kat shook her head.

She didn't relish the feeling of winning the spar. Though before Caleb had begun to use underhanded tricks, she had been enjoying it thoroughly . . .

No, it was the hatred he bore for her that made her uncomfortable.

Stopping in her tracks in the keep's corridor, Kat felt her composure slip as the unpleasant feeling of being unwelcome and unwanted began to twinge in her heart.

Start doing things the Ashowan way . . . Eric's voice echoed in her head.

Closing her eyes, a smile slowly climbed up Kat's face, and a comforting warmth rose to life in her stomach.

He was right.

She would handle her pesky comrades in a way that would make her father proud; she just needed to wait for the opportunity to turn things around.

Eric sat in Faucher's study, his legs stretched over the low table in front of the well-worn sofa. His hands were lightly clasped atop his belly. Sir Vohn waited for him outside in the corridor.

When Faucher entered and locked eyes with the prince, he grimaced as he turned and closed the door behind himself.

"Do you have something to say, Your Highness?" the military man asked with a rumble as he trudged over to his desk and plunked himself down.

Eric turned a mystifying smile on Faucher. "I didn't think I did."

Letting out an annoyed yet exasperated breath, Faucher regarded the prince directly.

"You have a problem with the way things are here with Lady Katarina? Then say something. I fought against it happening, and I warned His Maj-esty that the students would most likely take exception—"

"Faucher, why do you think I have a problem?" Eric's voice was too calm, his expression and posture too casual . . .

"Because you're acting like a politician who's about to come at my back with a knife."

Eric blinked. "Has that actually happened to you?"

"Yes," Faucher answered bluntly.

"Well, you can rest easy. I don't plan on stabbing you in the back in your own keep." Again, Eric smiled charmingly, and again, Faucher felt a wave of uneasiness overtake him.

"Why are you here?" The Troivackian tried a new angle while moving as little as possible.

"I figured we could chat before dinner. Your wife was gracious enough to extend an invitation to Sir Vohn and me despite us imposing upon you for the full day."

Faucher grunted. "You seem rather active these days, Your Highness."

Eric tilted his head over his shoulder. "Oh, believe me, Faucher, there is nothing more I'd like to do than crawl into a hole somewhere with my weight in moonshine. I'm just trying to make it so that I can do so in peace."

While Faucher stiffened, he said nothing.

In fact, neither of the pair said anything else for a while, until at last, Eric rose to his feet with a brief glance around the cramped study overflowing with bookshelves and a single stag's head over the hearth. An oddly small office for a man of such import . . .

"Relax, Faucher. I had no problems with what I saw today. You're training her well and fairly. You aren't abusing your power or showing favoritism. You're as skilled a teacher as I was told you'd be. Besides, I made a promise to Lady Katarina recently that I'd fight at her back rather than her front, so if there were to be a . . . *conflict*, you'd be dealing with her first and foremost."

"Are you trying to threaten me?" Faucher asked darkly.

Eric slowly placed his hand in his pocket. "No, Faucher. I'm saying I like how you're doing things. Just keep doing what you have been and remember that if the tides turn when the other Troivackian nobles find out about her being here with their sons, I will be on Katarina Ashowan's side. If a fight starts between her and *anyone*, I'll be there to finish it."

Faucher regarded the prince and noted his steely expression and sharp eyes.

Whatever the devil had done to Eric, it had had a rather drastic effect.

A bell clanged from somewhere in the keep, drawing both of the men's attention.

"Sounds like dinner is ready." Eric turned toward the study door and moved forward.

Faucher pushed himself off of his own seat as the prince exited into the corridor, and he couldn't help but ponder for the hundredth time what his life would've been like if he had retired, when he suddenly remembered which bell he had just heard.

"Wait! Your Highness! Stay in here!" Faucher burst out while rushing for the door.

Eric turned with a puzzled expression toward a scattering commotion and a series of bangs that could be heard thundering down the corridor.

"Oh, sh—" Eric lunged back for the office but unfortunately wasn't quick enough, as a stampede of twenty-five dogs swept him down the corridor in a blur of fur and lolling tongues.

CHAPTER 15

DEAR DAUGHTERS

K at speared the tender piece of beef on her plate with pursed lips. She kept her gaze fixed on her meal, her red hair falling in curtains around her face.

She couldn't look.

If she did . . .

She was done for.

"Lady Katarina, could you . . . ahem . . . perhaps pass the gravy?" Sir Vohn asked delicately.

With trembling fingers, Kat carefully slid the porcelain gravy boat down to the knight while turning her head away from him with her eyes closed.

"I-I'm sorry again, Your Highness . . ." Dana squeaked from Katarina's right side.

Katarina let out a garbled choke as she felt the grip on her composure rapidly deteriorating.

"It isn't your fault, Lady Dana. Do not worry. Though . . . I am curious . . . How did you come to acquire . . . that number of dogs?" Eric's voice was polite and kind.

Katarina then made the mistake of assuming his appearance had changed since she'd first glimpsed him in the aftermath of the dog tsunami, and she peeked through her hair to her left.

She instantly burst out in hysterics.

Eric's recently cut blond hair was frizzing high above his head, and his formerly white tunic had several muddy dog prints of all sizes patterned across.

Sir Vohn, on his other side, was in a similar state, though the knight also sported a single eyebrow with its hairs raised straight up. Either the result of an errant lick or simply from the brushing past of a canine, it wasn't clear.

It didn't matter.

Katarina was uncontrollable as she laughed, her palm slapping the table repeatedly while doubled over.

Poor Dana blushed a bright red, Faucher was looking at the ceiling in exasperation, and his wife was wiping her mouth with her napkin for a suspiciously long time.

Meanwhile, Broghan Miller and Joshua Ball were staring pointedly at the wall behind the prince, their eyes watering in their efforts to not succumb to peals of laughter alongside Katarina Ashowan.

Eric casually turned to face Dana and pretended that there wasn't a red-headed witch who was slowly slipping out of her chair as she let out wheezing gasps between guffaws.

"I-I got my first pup when I was a little girl, and then I . . . I get them as presents, a-and find them in the marketplaces. Sometimes they are in the field behind the keep . . ." the young woman managed, though her blush was starting to look painful. "T-They are all really well trained, s-so I—"

Katarina let out a squawk and completely fell off her chair, her laughter suddenly rejuvenated.

"T-There are dogs under the table. . . . and they're staring at them! L-Like they know!" she managed to explain, though she squawked immediately afterward.

The smallest of laughs then broke free of Lady Nathalie, making her husband's gaze snap to her, but she couldn't help it. She lowered her forehead to her hand and surrendered to laughter. Broghan Miller and Joshua Ball weren't far behind.

Faucher looked to Eric, who, while no one else was looking, reached up and flicked one of his wavy strands of hair that was standing nearly upright. It bounced.

Clearing his throat, Faucher stood abruptly, then stalked from the banquet hall as quickly as possible.

Eric grinned, then resumed paying attention to Dana, who looked caught between a grimace and a smile. "I'm serious, Lady Dana. You have nothing to apologize for. If anything, it's impressive that you have so many dogs trained so well and living peacefully together."

Katarina was in the process of climbing back up into her chair while wiping tears from her cheeks and taking deep breaths.

"H-He's right, you know! I had no idea twenty-five dogs lived here! Normally they'd be tearing around making all kinds of noise and mess," Kat agreed while facing the younger girl.

Unbeknownst to Kat, Eric was looking at her with an adoring warmth in his eyes, something only Lady Dana could see, as everyone else was still recovering from their outbursts of laughter.

"Er, I-I think it's all in how you train them. I also think that . . . that if trained properly, they could make assets to the military! I mean, it just makes sense. They use dogs for hunting. Why not to help in battle or in emergencies?" Dana's shy countenance was quickly being replaced with pure excitement as she looked to Kat and even once toward the prince.

"That's an interesting idea, Lady Dana," Eric commented sincerely. "Do you have any specific ideas on how they could be of use?"

By this time, Faucher was reentering the banquet hall, his cheeks suspiciously pink . . . as though he had fled simply to laugh . . .

"Yes! I think dogs would be the best scouts! They can smell and hear things we can't, so if we could train them to give us hints from what they see or hear . . .''

"Communication would be a problem. Do you think you'd be able to work a way around that?" Eric asked interestedly while also ignoring both Lady Nathalie's sudden wariness and Faucher's discomfort.

Dana sat straighter than anyone had ever seen her before. "Yes. I can find a way. I know I can."

"Very well. Train them, and if you think you've succeeded, I want you to send me a letter at the castle."

"Your Highness—" Faucher interrupted loudly.

Eric looked at Faucher, his expression turning stony. "Your daughter has a good idea, Faucher. We've used dogs to find game and even missing people. Why not see if they can be of even further assistance?"

"Because they are just dogs. All the enemy would have to do would be to plant a pork leg in the ground and they'd be leading an army in the wrong direction," Faucher explained with his fingers curling into fists.

"You're wrong!"

The outburst had come from Dana, and this succeeded in stunning everyone back into silence.

The young woman stood from her seat, color once again returning to her cheeks, her own hands clasped into fists . . . She looked a great deal like her father.

"I can train dogs to ignore temptations better than some foot soldiers in a brothel!"

"Dana!" Lady Nathalie's breathy chastisement was mixed with shock.

The young woman flinched at the sound of her mother's stern voice, then dared to lock eyes with her father.

The hardness she found reduced her to tears in an instant, and then she was fleeing from the room.

As she half ran through the banquet hall doors, she happened to push past Sir Cas who watched her fly by in her distressed state in great alarm.

Eric and Katarina looked at Faucher and Lady Nathalie and noted that they looked every bit the part of worried parents.

Dana's mother was staring at her husband imploringly, and Faucher . . . He looked as though he himself was the one who had been hurt instead of his daughter.

Katarina had seen that look on her own father's face countless times. Seeing it on a man as rigid and stoic as Faucher made her feel all the gentler toward him.

For all the Troivackian military leader's faults, he loved his family dearly even if he didn't always show it.

"Go talk to her." Kat's quiet voice made Faucher's black stare snap to her, but when he regarded the redhead's empathetic expression, he hesitated. "Sometimes it's hard to tell if Troivackians love even their own children. It helps to hear it."

"This is not your business, Lady Katarina. You've done enough." Faucher's warning growl made Kat go quiet, but she held her ground. While her teacher's gaze was fierce, she did see a flicker of uncertainty in it . . .

She shrugged and turned back to her meal. The tension in the room remained high, but it wasn't quite as stifling as it had been when Dana had first stormed out.

Sir Cas, meanwhile, was warily seating himself beside Joshua and looking at Eric and Sir Vohn with a frown.

"I know I took a bit longer than I had intended writing to my family, but . . . what happened, Your Highness?"

Katarina's lips pursed.

"I swear to—You still find it that funny?" Eric finally addressed the redhead. While his tone was incredulous, he smiled as he spoke.

Kat began to giggle, but it was nowhere near the same voracious laughter as before.

After managing to consume a single spoonful of the soup in front of her, she grinned at the bewildered blond knight across from her. "Sorry, Sir Cas, His Highness is feeling a little bit *dogged* after his visit today."

Joshua, who had been taking a drink from his goblet, choked.

Sir Cas's gaze dropped to the paw prints dotting Eric's shirt, then at his wild hair.

"You didn't know about the feeding bell?" Sir Cas asked with a good-humored smile of his own.

Sir Vohn eyed his fellow knight wryly. "Thanks for the warning."

"Now, now . . . we've all had a *ruff* day. I think we can just enjoy the rest of our meal," Kat interjected breathily.

"Godsdamnit, you are your father's daughter," Eric muttered under his breath while taking a drink from his own goblet.

Kat shot him a sidelong glance that he met with a small, cheeky grin of his own.

He really does seem to be making that expression a lot lately . . . Kat found herself thinking dazedly, unaware that she herself was starting to blush. Happily, she refocused her attention onto her dinner. She couldn't remember the last time she'd been in such a good mood.

Lady Nathalie watched the pair interact with pointed interest, then glanced around the table to see everyone else's reactions. Sir Vohn was watching the scene while looking perplexed, Sir Cas appeared as nonplussed as usual, Joshua and Broghan looked concerned . . . and her husband?

He wasn't touching his food, his eyes lost in thought.

Nathalie smiled lovingly, knowing that Faucher wouldn't notice.

She knew he was thinking about their daughter and worrying endlessly about her. It was one of the many wonderful things about him she couldn't help but adore. Casting one final glance toward Katarina Ashowan, Nathalie felt her smile briefly widen before once again regaining control of her facial expression.

Just as she predicted . . . things were getting interesting.

Faucher stood outside his daughter's chamber door, lantern in hand.

He wore his robe, his tunic, and pants but stood barefoot . . .

It was in the middle of the night after all.

As quietly as a thief, he stole into his daughter's room and gently closed the door behind himself.

He sensed one of the multiple dogs that were permitted to stay in Dana's chamber raise its head at his arrival, but a hastily tossed piece of dried beef had the beast granting him a peaceful entry.

Faucher padded across the floor without making a sound until, at last, he came to Dana's bedside.

Gazing down at his daughter's face, he could tell she had cried herself to sleep . . .

His heart ached.

Slowly, Faucher placed the lantern on her bedside and knelt.

Reaching out a hand, he gently stroked her frizzy hair away from her face and couldn't help but smile tenderly at her freckles.

He remembered Katarina's words . . . about how Troivackians didn't always show their love, but . . . how could Dana not know? How could she not know she had him wrapped around her smallest finger? She always had. From the day she'd been born, he would've given anything and everything to her. His love for his daughter had humbled him countless times, and he'd let it continue to do so as long as he could ensure she was happy and taken care of.

Dana shifted in her sleep, her face scrunching, and Faucher hesitated his gentle strokes to allow her to settle back down. She had always been a heavy sleeper.

"Dana," he whispered quietly. "I'm sorry I upset you today. I never mean to make you cry."

Faucher's hand drifted to her limp one, then plucking it up, he brought his daughter's hand to his forehead. "I love you, Dana. If you want more dogs, I'll get you a hundred . . . but don't go near the military. Please. I don't think I could take it."

A tremor entered Faucher's hand as he imagined his sweet daughter facing down the brutes he shouted at and trained to be as deadly as possible . . .

"Please . . ." Faucher closed his eyes and kissed his daughter's fingertips before gingerly releasing them and rising. He grasped the lantern once more, then swept out of the chamber.

A lump was rising in his throat as he walked purposefully back to his chamber, and his head was starting to ache with emotion.

How could Katarina's father send her here to learn swordsmanship? Unless he isn't the family man he makes everyone think he is. Faucher mused bitterly while recalling the way Brendan Devark had threatened marrying Dana off for the sake of training Lady Katarina.

He had cited that the Daxarian noblewoman was needed for change.

A new concern appeared in Faucher's chest, giving him a feeling of . . . unpleasantness.

While he had known Lady Katarina to be important in terms of finding the literal devil and possibly helping prove that he was more fit to be the captain of Troivack's military . . . the king had alluded to even *more* plans riding on her success.

By his next breath, Faucher had become more than a little incensed on behalf of his student.

Just what is being planned exactly? Does her father truly know how much pressure the king has placed on her?

Frowning, Faucher wondered if perhaps he should send a letter of his own to Finlay Ashowan and —

He stopped and shook his head, blinking himself back to sound thoughts.

Gods . . . Treason. I was considering treason just now, for the sake of Lady Katarina.

Sighing, the military man deftly calmed his whirling emotions back down; they would do him no favors. So instead, he decided to go to bed, and in the morning, he would once again work on training the wild redheaded witch. Though after her sparring match with Caleb, he was going to be adding several revisions to her lesson plan.

CHAPTER 16

GRAND GUESTS

K at's breaths came out in puffs of steamed air as she practiced her defenses on the dummy repeatedly, her mind lost in thought as she moved through the motions gracefully.

She hadn't looked at her fellow trainees once since they had entered the courtyard, and she had managed this by starting her training earlier than any of them.

In fact, starting the week after Eric's visit, she was in the training grounds even before Sir Cas or Faucher had finished their breakfasts.

The sky above was clouded, and there was a bite in the air that hinted at snow.

It was the perfect weather for a fire witch prone to overheating.

"I think you made an impression on Herra." Sir Cas's friendly voice behind Kat pulled her free from her intent focus.

The redhead hesitated her practice, her wooden sword held near her ear as her gaze cut to the brutish young man with his shaved head.

Caleb Herra was staring at her as though in a trance, his eyes starry.

"Pfft," Kat scoffed, then turned back to the dummy. "I was warned this might happen."

Sir Cas glanced at Caleb Herra, then the redhead. "Warned about what exactly . . . ?"

The tip of Kat's sword caught on the loose burlap of the dummy, making her fumble her sword. Sighing in agitation, she turned to the Daxarian knight.

"Hannah, my father's old friend, she warned me that if I stand up or even become violent toward some men, they, for whatever reason, develop an interest."

Sir Cas barely suppressed a smile. "I'm not sure it's that kind of interest, Lady Katarina. I think it has more to do with admiration."

Kat spared another glance toward Caleb, who blinked dazedly and then turned back to Broghan Miller, who was talking to him.

"Well, if he doesn't want to kill me anymore, I'm happy about that. Though I wouldn't trust him courting a meek woman, if you get my meaning."

Sir Cas's levity faded. "I do. Though perhaps you can start to show him the error of his ways. I heard your father reformed a few knights in his time, one of them being the current captain of the Daxarian military."

Kat sighed then turned back to her dummy. "I don't have the patience or position to discipline Troivackian men."

"Not yet." Sir Cas grinned.

Caught off guard by the unexpected words of encouragement, Kat smiled back at the knight. "I appreciate your faith in me, but something about the wooden sword isn't lending me a lot of confidence."

Kat returned her efforts to her dummy with a deep inhale and resumed working through her stances under Sir Cas's observation, when Faucher strode into the courtyard from his keep.

"Herra! Time for your spar with Sir Cas!"

Kat chucked her wooden sword to the ground and bolted onto the bench where she half slid, half leapt.

Joshua Ball, who had been in the process of pulling on his wristbands, jumped at the sudden movement and shifted away from her.

Broghan rolled his eyes and sat on the other side of Joshua.

Caleb Herra, for once, looked reluctant and uncertain, making Kat even more curious given that she hadn't been able to witness the fight the day Eric had visited.

Sir Cas meandered forward, his expression as pleasant as ever as he pulled his sword from his scabbard.

Caleb licked his lips and stepped his left foot back.

Raising his free hand, the Daxarian knight waited, his own breaths coming out in plumes, his blond hair almost silvery in the pale daylight.

While Kat had been eager to watch for the sake of vengeance against Caleb, what she had failed to anticipate . . . was the rumored swordsmanship mastery that Sir Cas possessed.

There was a moment of stillness, and then Herra rushed toward the Daxarian knight.

Two taps of his sword, and Sir Cas sent Herra's weapon clattering to the ground.

Sir Cas looked unfazed.

"I didn't even see how he did that . . ." Joshua whispered to Broghan.

"Again," Faucher called out. "Herra, you did well attacking his nondominant side, but your grip on your sword and your footwork were sloppy."

The two men faced each other again, though the second time, Caleb stepped a little too close to Sir Cas and he promptly found himself knocked onto his arse.

Again, Sir Cas waited while looking completely carefree.

Kat was mesmerized. Watching the Daxarian knight's fine movements and easy reactions . . . It was like he defended himself as easily as he breathed.

After the fourth time of Sir Cas besting Herra, Kat slowly raised her hand.

"What is it, Ashowan?" Faucher called out from where he stood at the other end of the bench.

"Can you and Sir Cas spar? It'd be interesting to see two masters go head-to-head."

Broghan and Joshua looked to Faucher hopefully. Herra, meanwhile, was wincing as he limped back over to the bench.

"That would not be beneficial to you all at this stage of your lessons— Herra, did I say you were finished? Try again. Stop using your brute strength to win."

The young man had only just begun to lower himself down onto the bench, when he was forced to stop himself with a grimace, then push himself back to standing with labored movements.

Kat didn't mask her disappointment before she then stared at Sir Cas with her newly discovered admiration.

The fifth time Caleb dueled with Sir Cas, it was more a lesson in how much avoidance one could put against their opponent before Faucher lost his patience.

The sixth, Herra was clumsy and flinched when Sir Cas's second hand joined the hilt of his sword.

"Gods, Sir Cas is around the same age as Caleb . . . How did he get so skilled?" Joshua mused aloud to his fellow students.

Kat couldn't answer; she was too enthralled to properly register the question.

At last, Faucher sent them all to their individual training dummies, save for Katarina.

"Today I will teach you three attacks. This will be your new starting stance. Ready? Good."

The military leader walked her through the moves, and in no time at all, she was executing them expertly in the air.

Nodding to himself, Faucher was about to dismiss her to practice against her dummy, when the Daxarian prince's words echoed in his ears.

"Push her . . . harder than you've ever pushed anyone before . . ."

Warily, Faucher turned back to Kat. "Ashowan, I want you to take those three moves I just showed you and attack Sir Cas."

The Daxarian knight turned around swiftly at hearing this new order, and as he stepped closer to Faucher, he bore an uncharacteristic frown.

"I thought we were only showing her three to five attacks?"

Kat blinked in surprise. "You spar with Herra though . . . ?"

"Herra has years of lessons under his belt. He's recovering his skill and his memory after the injury to his head," Sir Cas replied, though his eyes remained fixed on Faucher.

Kat looked over at Caleb Herra, who had resumed training against his dummy, though he was slower than usual after his sparring earlier that morning.

"Lady Katarina bested Caleb yesterday. So let's see how she fares," Faucher announced firmly, his dark eyes locking with Sir Cas's.

The knight looked like he was about to continue arguing, when Kat moved forward. "It'll be alright, Sir Cas. Though do I get to spar with a real sword?"

Faucher shot her a wry sidelong glance. "No. Sir Cas, go retrieve a wooden sword."

The Daxarian knight gave the Troivackian another dubious look before turning and making his way toward the nearest weapons barrel and plucking out his own training sword.

Faucher and Sir Cas passed each other as the knight approached Kat and the Troivackian elder removed himself from the sparring area.

Admittedly, Kat felt her pride sting at seeing Sir Cas's reluctance. He wouldn't have shown such hesitation if it had been one of the other young men intending to fight him . . .

Gripping her sword tightly, Kat resolved to do her absolute best. She needed to show Sir Cas she was strong enough to cross blades with, even if she didn't have the experience as the others did.

When Sir Cas struck his beginning position again, Kat wasted no time in lunging forward with the first attack Faucher had shown her.

Sir Cas defended it easily. "The tip of your sword drooped when you were aiming for my side. Keep it raised or you might get the blade caught in armor."

Kat nodded and attacked using the first form again.

Sir Cas gave a small smile. "Perfect."

Kat didn't acknowledge the compliment. Instead, she struck again using the second maneuver she had been shown.

This time, Sir Cas still blocked her easily, but a stiffness entered his features. "You're too eager for the attack. It makes you impulsive. Remember to stay cool-headed at all times, or it could cost you your life. There is no emotion in a fight."

Kat's brows furrowed, but she nodded. Closing her eyes, she took a steadying breath. She tried to calm the fluttering pulse in her throat and settle her earlier disgruntlement . . .

She heard Sir Cas's boot scrape against the stones, and her eyes snapped open. She defended his sudden attack while backing up with a small stumbling step.

"Always be ready for an attack. *Always*." Sir Cas's blue eyes never wavered from her face, his training sword still clasped in hand. "You responded much faster than I thought you would. Well done."

"Yeah. Great. Was just trying to work on that first thing you told me about not being emotional with attacks," she said breathily with a subtle note of annoyance.

Sir Cas made his way back to his position opposite her again. "You won't get to take a moment during a fight. Remember, Faucher told you this on your very first day. You need to calm yourself in whatever way possible, while staying alert."

Katarina attacked again using the third method Faucher had taught her. "Easier said than done."

Sir Cas blocked her weapon, and her poor footwork had her stumbling as a result.

"Emotions go to the back of your mind the moment you pick up a sword or someone attacks. You practice this every day until it is second nature."

Katarina didn't say anything as she reset herself and struck again while minding her footwork, but she still fumbled.

"You're stepping into the attack with your front foot; start with your back. This attack sequence relies on the strength and speed of the second strike, not the first, so you need to set yourself up in the first part."

Sir Cas and Katarina continued sparring for most of the morning in a similar fashion, but by the time the luncheon hour arrived, the knight was nodding encouragingly. "It seems like you've mastered them. I'm going to try attacking you at random here on out. See how you fare."

Kat raised an eyebrow but then grinned. "Sounds fun. Maybe just don't creep into my chamber or anything. I might throw things."

Sir Cas blushed brightly. "Lady Katarina, you really shouldn't jest like that . . ."

A shout from Faucher drew everyone's attention. "Alright, everyone, I will see you in the banquet hall. Afterward, Herra, Ball, and Miller, I will be showing you—"

"GRANPA! GRANPA!"

A loud shriek interrupted Faucher's final words as a little girl in a dark red dress bolted down the steps to the courtyard and straight over to the military leader.

Faltering in surprise, Faucher's legs were then seized in a bear hug by the little girl, who couldn't have been older than four or five years old.

"GRAPPA!" Another young voice drew Katarina's eyes over to the steps, where a large Troivackian man with long, straight black hair that was tied back stood with another little girl, only around three years of age, clutching his pant leg, her thumb placed in her mouth despite hopping up and down at the sight of Faucher. The large man also happened to be holding a cherubic baby boy.

For a brief, bright moment, Katarina thought Faucher was about to smile, but instead he cleared his throat, then bent down and scooped up the little girl.

"Isabel, you know you aren't supposed to come out to the courtyard when Grandpa's teaching, yes?" Despite attempting to sound stern, the little girl, with her long brown hair already tousled, still smiled while gingerly fiddling with Faucher's tunic ties.

"But . . . But she's here . . ." Isabel mumbled while pointing at Katarina before dropping her head to Faucher's shoulder while still peeking at the redhead.

Kat smiled at the little girl named Isabel, but the child turned her face shyly into the crook of Faucher's neck in response.

Glancing at his students to his right, the military leader managed to regain his scowl. "I dismissed you. Why are you all still here?"

The three male students jumped into action and immediately filed through the courtyard exit, passing by the Troivackian man, whose gaze was fixed on one person . . .

Kat.

Shooting a somewhat apprehensive glance in his direction, the redhead made her way up the steps after her peers, and she, too, passed the man Kat assumed to be Faucher's son, and she entered the keep.

Faucher meandered over to his eldest son with Isabel still in his arms while Sir Cas remained behind and tended to the training dummies that needed more hay added to their burlap.

"Father."

Faucher nodded. "Dante. What brings you here?"

"Mother sent me a letter mentioning the crown prince of Daxaria being here for dinner." Dante raised a thick eyebrow as he stared at his father, his hand idly patting the head of the daughter, who still clung to his pant leg.

"And?" Faucher asked tersely.

Dante's eyes briefly widened before he blinked in disbelief. "Sounded like something important was going on, so I thought I'd come find out what it was about. What is a woman doing training here?"

"Private business."

"Granpa! Can I play with Auntie Dana's dogs?" The little girl in Faucher's arms asked pleadingly.

"It's lunchtime. Go find your grandmother, and perhaps afterward Aunt Dana can take you and some of the dogs out to play."

"'Kay!"

Faucher kissed his granddaughter's cheek, then set her down on the ground.

When Isabel had scampered off into the keep, Dante shifted his infant son to his other arm.

"What's going on? I haven't heard from you since you returned from escorting the Daxarians."

Faucher said nothing for a moment and instead proceeded to pick up his second granddaughter, who didn't give any objection.

"Is Mabel here?"

"She's with Mother." Dante's expression hardened as his father turned from him and instead of answering the original question gave his undivided attention to the little girl in his arms.

"Carmen looks more and more like your wife," Faucher observed idly.

Dante's eyes narrowed. "What is happening here in Vessa that has you going to the extent of making small talk?"

Faucher began to bounce his granddaughter in his arms, making the little girl giggle. Though once he did finally meet his son's unimpressed stare, he acquiesced with a grunt and finished climbing the stairs to his keep.

"Come, let us have some lunch and . . . try not to talk to the redhead."

CHAPTER 17

AN UNCOMFORTABLE
UNCOVERING

Katarina was making silly faces at Faucher's granddaughters that had them giggling mercilessly. Joshua, Broghan, and Caleb were questioning Sir Cas about his former and present swordsmanship teachers Captain Antonio and Captain Taylor. Lady Nathalie and Mabel Faucher (wife to Dante Faucher) sat talking politely, while Dana held her nephew in her lap and avoided looking at her father, who was talking with his eldest son.

All in all, it was a boisterous luncheon.

As the meal progressed, Lady Nathalie turned her attention from her daughter-in-law to the redhead. "Lady Katarina, Mabel is wondering if you are enjoying your time here in Troivack."

Katarina looked up from the children to her hostess, then the younger noblewoman, who kept her eyes averted and fixed on the table.

"It's been an adventure. From assassination attempts to the coronation—where there was actually another assassination attempt—I can't say I'll leave without any stories!"

"Oh my!" Lady Nathalie interrupted, her eyes wide and fearful as they moved to Faucher. "Your parents must be terribly worried!"

"Ah . . . well . . . they would be . . . if they knew." Katarina grinned, then was forced to look at the ceiling as Dante Faucher rested his muscled forearms on the dining table and homed his attention on her while his father grimaced.

"You haven't relayed to your parents about the dangers you've gone through? Lady Katarina, who is your escort here?"

"Ah well . . . technically His Majesty Brendan Devark, but we all had to split up after arriving, so . . . Faucher, I suppose?"

Dante cast a dark look toward his father.

"Lady Katarina, you are not to disclose private details pertaining to His Majesty." Faucher's voice was sharp.

"What about this swordsmanship training?" Dante carried on regardless of his father's aggravation.

"Oh, *that*, everyone is on board with! Well, almost everyone . . . Herra! You still hate me?"

Katarina turned to her fellow pupil, who balked under the sudden question.

"Wh-What? I-I . . . No. It's . . . not . . . Y-You're . . ."

"Right, well that's an improvement!" Kat cheered happily while pointing at Caleb with her fork and smiling at Dante, who did not share in her exuberance.

When she noticed that Dante was not looking all that impressed, Kat acquiesced to committing to a slightly more serious tone. With a sigh, she leaned back in her chair and fixed Faucher's son with a good-natured expression. "I'm going to have to start coming up with fun responses to all these questions that keep being repeated. I'm a witch, too, by the way. Mutated. Not just a pure fire witch. Don't ask about my magic powers—How about I have you guess? That could be fun."

Dante's face drained of color before he turned to his father.

"A witch?"

Faucher recoiled.

"Er, sorry, thought my eyes made it obvious . . . ?" Kat looked to her teacher awkwardly.

The silence in the room was just as deafening as the noise before.

"Should we go play with the dogs now?" Katarina turned to the little girls, who broke out into excited smiles.

"No!"

Kat jumped and turned to see Dante's wife staring fearfully at her. It was the first time the woman had looked directly at the redhead.

Though it wasn't for long, as Mabel was already on her feet and rounding the table, one arm seizing her infant son from Dana, and her remaining free hand herding away her daughters.

"P-Pardon me, Lady Nathalie, we will be taking our leave." Dante's wife hunched her shoulders toward Katarina as she tried to keep both her daughters hidden.

Kat watched in astonishment as the children were ushered out of the room, though their objections and cries carried on in a steady stream.

Dante's fury remained directed at his father. "You know she's terrified of witches."

Allowing his hand to fall to the table, Faucher looked at his son irritably. "Didn't I tell you not to talk to the redhead?"

Dante shook his head and stood. "I knew His Majesty's time in Daxaria had changed him some, but to think things would become so eccentric *here* as a result . . . I'm going to tell Conrad and Piers about this."

"Who're they?" Kat interrupted loudly in the hope of trying to engage with Faucher's son on a safer topic.

"My brothers. Do you realize your presence here puts my father and his family in jeopardy?" Dante asked accusatorily.

"Alright, I understand I am a little bit prone to getting in trouble, but I'm not *deadly* unless I'm really hungry, then that's a whole other—"

"She's the daughter of a duke, Dante. Mind yourself," Faucher interrupted while staring at his son somberly. A startling amount of fight appeared to have left the normally hardened military leader.

"A duke?! The only witch amongst Daxarian nobility is Viscount Ashowan. The house witch."

"He accepted a dukedom recently," Faucher explained calmly.

Dante's neck snapped back toward Katarina, who smiled and gave him an encouraging thumbs-up as the younger man put the pieces together.

"You're an Ashowan."

"Actually, your father dubbed me *the* Ashowan when we first met, and I am quite fond of the title."

Dante looked like he was about to start in on his father with renewed vigor, when surprisingly, his younger sister Dana interjected.

"She's nice, Dante . . . My . . . my dogs like her, and they . . . they are great judges of character, as you know."

Dante's expression softened when he looked to his little sister, who had to be a decade his junior.

"That's not the problem, Dana. If word gets around that a witch is here? There's a chance people could try to set the keep on fire or attack us."

"You would think we were defenseless ducks listening to you," Faucher grumbled beside his son, who tensed.

"What about my girls, father? What about Dana? Or Mother, when they are out in the markets? I know this isn't entirely within your control, but you should have told us so that we could be better prepared."

"You were better off not knowing. It was safer that way. Now you must mind that your wife doesn't run to her parents and tell them everything. Nathalie, why in the world did you send them a letter when—" Faucher had started to turn to his wife, but upon remembering that all his students were still present, along with his daughter and Sir Cas, stopped himself.

"Everyone but my son and wife, get out."

None of the dismissed parties needed any further encouragement, and with Dana's three dogs on their heels, they all took their leave, allowing the three older Faucher family members to continue their argument alone.

Once everyone stood outside the banquet hall doors, Kat pivoted to face Dana, who was petting one of her dog's head lovingly, though there was worry in her eyes.

"Things will be fine. This happens almost every time I meet someone new here in Troivack." Katarina clasped a hand on the young woman's shoulder.

"Doesn't it bother you? I can't imagine having so many people mad at me for no reason . . ." Dana managed to say as Caleb, Joshua, Broghan, and Sir Cas made their way back to the courtyard.

The redhead reached down and began scratching Cozo's ears. "Sometimes it does. I didn't like that your sister-in-law was so afraid of me, but . . . my friends here in Troivack have helped a lot."

"You mean the new queen? Or the crown prince of Daxaria?" Dana asked ambiguously, though she was watching Kat carefully.

At first the redhead stared blankly at the dogs by her feet before she gave her head a small shake.

"Both, I suppose. How is training the dogs to alert soldiers about enemy rebels going?"

Dana sighed, her posture relaxing. "It's tricky, but . . . I'll get there. I know I will. By the way is . . . Sir Cas . . . by any chance . . . um . . ." The young woman trailed off, her ears already turning red.

Kat smiled knowingly. "He isn't married or betrothed. Though he is twenty-five, so you two have a bit of an age gap."

"Well, you and the prince are twenty and twenty-nine, so—"

"I beg your pardon?" Kat interrupted with a burst of surprised laughter.

Dana shifted uncomfortably. "S-Sorry, I know there isn't an official engagement yet, but I'm sure soon—"

"No, no! It isn't like that! Prince Eric and I are just friends. I promise. Just like you and Sir Cas. Though, we have an even bigger age gap." Kat chortled, while starting to shuffle away from Dana.

"S-Sorry, if it was supposed to be a secret. I won't tell anyone," Dana squeaked.

"Why do you . . ." Katarina trailed off and cleared her throat while at the same time glancing around the corridor to ensure no one was within earshot. "Listen, I'm going to get back to training, but you need to stop thinking strange thoughts. Go train your dogs."

Despite her jesting tone in her final farewell note, Kat's posture and steps had grown awkward as she took her leave without sparing another glance back.

Dana gnawed on her lower lip for a moment before looking down at her dogs that sat contentedly panting at her side.

"Well . . . at least Sir Cas is single . . . Not that I can even talk to him . . ." She sighed. "Maybe I'll just go play with Boots . . ."

As Dana continued down the corridor, her three dogs in tow, she once again recalled how Prince Eric of Daxaria had looked at Katarina Ashowan the night he had come to dinner.

I wonder if she really doesn't know . . . I've only seen that look on my brothers' faces when they met their wives. She smiled. *I'd bet my best dog treats that he'll be back to see her in no time.*

"What is she doing?"

"She's probably trying to watch us train."

Broghan and Caleb chortled as they stared just past the courtyard to where Dana and a large dog none of them had seen before played a game of fetch.

The two had halted their training to watch her, when Sir Cas stepped in front of them, blocking Faucher's daughter from view.

"I don't recall telling you to take a break."

With quick apologetic bobs of their heads toward the knight, the two younger men resumed their efforts between the dummies, though off in the distance by her own dummy, Katarina had noticed their arrogant smirks and was gripping her wooden sword handle even more tightly.

"Ashowan, focus. I'm going to teach you three more attacks and two more defenses, then you will be sparring with Sir Cas until dinner. Tomorrow, we are going to attend to your footwork training." Faucher drew the redhead's attention back to him, though his own dark eyes briefly went to his other two students. It was painfully obvious in that moment that if Herra and Miller weren't more careful about leering at his daughter, the likelihood of them being shoved into a deep hole and buried alive was quite high.

"What happened to Caleb Herra, Faucher? Sir Cas mentioned this morning he had years of training . . . He has that scar on his head and face, and given his age, he probably could be a knight already," Katarina wondered aloud interestedly.

Faucher's attention homed in on the redhead's idle expression. After a moment of silent consideration, the military leader turned back toward the dummy as though intending to ignore her query.

"Caleb was an exceptional swordsman. So much so in fact that his older brother, Sir Seth Herra, had him attacked and left for dead a week before his knight's test."

Kat faltered. "What?! Why isn't that arsehat in jail?!"

Faucher shot her a sardonic look laced with wordless chastisement over her cursing.

"Let me guess. A dark alley? Couldn't see who it was?" Kat straightened, her golden eyes becoming furious.

"More or less. Troivackians aren't proud about being successfully betrayed. So while Caleb Herra knows with great certainty that his older brother tried to have him killed, he will never admit it. Instead, he must start over again. Though it isn't coming back to him as easily as we had all hoped when the physician announced he'd live, though with memory loss . . ."

Kat stared at Caleb, a pang of compassion and sympathy welling up in her chest.

"Are there stories like that with Joshua Ball and Broghan Miller as well?"

Faucher fought off a smile at her reaction.

Despite their animosity toward her, the fact that Lady Katarina was angered on their behalf was a hint of maturity Faucher often doubted she possessed.

"Lord Ball doesn't want his half brother anywhere near a sword or the courts. He is determined to protect his position and instead sees to . . . other means of keeping Joshua in check. Suffice it to say, Lord Ball has no idea that Joshua is here. He is a bastard after all."

Kat winced. It wasn't difficult to guess that Joshua had been kept under his brother's thumb and suffered humiliation and wrath when she recalled her own first meeting with his elder brother during her first dinner at the Troivackian castle . . .

"Broghan Miller is the youngest son of Lord Milo Miller. His older sister, Lady Sarah, is one of Her Majesty's handmaidens, and his eldest brother, Sir Cleophus Miller, is one of our best knights. You may recall that was the one in charge of guarding your familiar."

Her expression falling flat, Katarina was indeed able to remember with great clarity the battle-hardened giant, who became as soft as sponge cake when it came to her kitten, Piña Colada.

"Ah."

"He has a lot of pressure on him to live up to everyone's expectations. His brother is infamous as a knight, and his sister a pillar in society . . . Broghan falls through the cracks, though he at least has his entire family supporting his endeavor to become a knight," Faucher expounded, his own eyes roving over his ragtag group of students.

"And then there's me . . . a spoiled Daxarian witch, who recently became a duke's daughter," Kat supplied glibly while once again facing Faucher with her wooden sword over her shoulder.

Faucher regarded her quietly for a moment, and it was in his lack of agreement about her self-deprecation that Kat realized Faucher was going to give her own personal summary straight to her face.

"You are a Daxarian witch, who has been scorned, stabbed, and has faced adversity from the moment you stepped foot on Troivackian soil. Not to mention being the first woman to be publicly and professionally trained with a sword in two kingdoms. The expectations are highest of all for you. The fact that you are a witch means—" Faucher faltered.

He finally understood.

In his mind, he saw the plan that the king and queen had crafted . . .

"You have been tasked by our king to be the figurehead of change for an entire kingdom."

The redhead blinked. "What's this about a figurehead of change for a kingdom . . . ?! I didn't sign up for that! I just like sharp things! And maybe I'd show a few nobles that women can learn sword fighting and that witches are useful, but—"

"You want to change the outlooks of the most powerful men in an entire kingdom, and you're telling me you didn't realize the implications that this, in turn, would change our entire land?" Faucher asked in genuine concern.

He wasn't about to admit he was ashamedly behind in realizing it himself.

Katarina opened and closed her mouth several times. "I-It's Alina who is going to change the kingdom! I'm just . . . I'm just an example she wishes to use."

"An example that would make Her Majesty's efforts futile if you were to fail."

Kat stared wide-eyed at Faucher, who held her gaze. It was integral that she understand the stakes on her performance and success. If he were being honest, he was hoping he'd scared Kat so succinctly that perhaps when her father arrived to help them all deal with the devil, he would whisk his willing daughter away back to Daxaria.

"Godsdamnit . . . when you put it like that, I need to be training earlier and later! Don't worry, Faucher, I won't make you stay up with me; I know you need your beauty sleep. Though maybe ask the kitchen if I could have a snack before breakfast."

Katarina's earnest plotting to improve her swordsmanship and subsequent prattling made Faucher's spark of hope die instantly.

With a sigh, the military leader left the witch to go check on the others, but as he turned from his most troublesome pupil, he looked up and found himself staring at none other than the crown prince of Daxaria, Eric Reyes, standing at the top of the steps to his keep.

Faucher's brow crashed down as he opened his mouth to ask the future king just what the hell he thought he was doing there again, when Eric leaned around him and called to Kat.

"Oyy! Ashowan! You forgot your sword at the castle. Did you honestly give *any* thought to packing?"

CHAPTER 18

A ROYAL RATTLING

Katarina caught the sword Eric threw to her by its scabbard and grinned. "Gods, Your Highness, at this rate, I'm inclined to think you can't live without me."

Eric scoffed. "The maids were talking about throwing out that junk you call a sword. I have to keep you happy, or else when your father comes, there'll be hell to pay."

Kat stuck her tongue out cheekily and—interestingly enough—Eric did the same.

"Your Highness, is there another *important* reason you have come to my keep today?" Faucher ground out, his agitation shining brightly in his eyes while his upper lip twitched.

The prince turned to Faucher, and the shift in both his expression and air was chilling. "Aside from bringing the sword? Yes. I heard your son paid a visit yesterday."

Faucher's breakfast burbled uneasily in his gut. "Who told you that?"

Eric shrugged ambiguously. "How are you going to ensure he and his wife don't reveal what you're doing with Kat here?"

"My family is my business, Your Highness." Faucher's vision began to turn into a tunnel, and at the end was his target . . . the target that was starting to no longer be an annoyance, but a threat.

"Gods, Eric, you sound creepy as hell." Katarina's voice snapped the rising tension between the two with her glib tone.

The prince turned to look at her, his hard expression gentling once more. "It isn't that difficult to figure out. Your neighbors down the road mentioned seeing your son's carriage, Faucher."

"Why were you talking to my neighbors?"

"Lady Darchamp flagged down my carriage today and asked why there was so much traffic going by," Eric supplied while folding his arms over his chest.

"So you really did just come here to bring Lady Katarina the sword."

Silence settled over the trio.

Eric blinked, stunned momentarily by the verbal trap, then slowly smiled, while Katarina turned to look at him with a mix of expectancy and uneasiness.

Faucher's presence had grown formidable, and the sharpness in his gaze indicated his mind was transitioning to a different function than that of the patient but irritable teacher.

"My third reason for coming here was to let you know what's going to be happening at the council meeting in His Majesty's court." Eric's right hand slipped into his pocket, and he didn't dare look at Katarina. He knew the military leader in front of him was considering violence to start his morning off.

Faucher let out a small, grumbling huff, then turned back to Katarina. "You. Keep practicing what I taught you until Sir Cas can spar with you."

"You're already sparring with another person?" Eric asked interestedly.

The redhead beamed.

"Your Highness, you can't keep interrupting her training." Faucher looked like he was about to seize Eric by the front of his tunic and drag him away.

Holding up his hands to ward off the Troivackian man, Eric shot him one final steely look before once again addressing Kat.

"You need to get that sword fixed. In a fortnight, I can take you to a blacksmith in Vessa."

"She'll have better swords available to her sooner—"

"That sword is a piece by Theodore Phendor, I'll have you know!" Kat cut Faucher off indignantly, her arms folding over her chest.

"You were swindled. How many times do I need to tell you that?" her teacher insisted briskly.

"Either way," Eric began pointedly, already sensing the pair were about to go head-to-head. "Knowing Kat, she's going to want to try using it when she's allowed to. Faucher, we need to convene in your office. And you, I will see in a fortnight. Unless you get grounded." Eric had started moving away from the redhead, but at his final farewell gave her an upward nod over his shoulder before continuing back toward the keep.

"I'm not a child!" Kat barked irritably before rounding back to her training dummy and muttering curses under her breath.

Faucher watched Eric from the corner of his eye as they walked, and he noted the right corner of the prince's mouth that was tugged upward.

The two men made it inside the keep, where the biting winds were reduced and fires lit in the hearths subdued the cold, and they continued through the halls in silence. The occasional maid or steward passed and bowed or curtsied, but nothing needed to be said until at last they'd reached Faucher's office and the door was closed behind them.

"You shouldn't be seen in Vessa together."

Eric ignored the abrupt declaration from the Troivackian and made his way over to the couches, where he plopped himself down. "I'll take care of things there, Faucher. Sit. We have bigger concerns here on out."

Not liking being dismissed by a man he had only two months prior been half dragging in a drunken stupor across the kingdom, Faucher proceeded to stalk behind his desk and sit heavily.

"Alina's sitting in on the council meeting today."

Faucher was back on his feet in an instant. "What?"

"His Majesty is having her attend the meeting, and we've received word from Duke Ashowan that he will be setting sail shortly. With the Alcide Sea being especially unpredictable this time of year, it could take him close to two months to get here. Maybe even longer if they run into a lot of trouble or if there are any surprise issues he must deal with before his departure."

"Gods. I thought His Majesty was going to wait to bring the queen into the meetings . . . at least until Lady Katarina was closer to being ready . . ."

"Ready for what?"

Faucher wasn't fooled by the airy tone Eric had used to ask the question. He sensed the newly born beast that bellowed and reared whenever there was a matter involving Katarina Ashowan.

"That information is under the discretion of His Majesty."

For a long, dangerous moment, Eric didn't show any emotion or move a muscle.

Then he shrugged and cast his sights around the office. "If you say so."

"How is it you were able to leave the castle and come here undetected?" Faucher changed the subject hastily.

"Faked being drunk last night and stumbled out with a couple knights for some cards. They'll all assume I'm sleeping the drink off in the inn Sir Vohn is currently guarding." Eric stood and strolled over to a large framed painting depicting Faucher's family tree.

"What will His Majesty do if the nobles revolt the instant Her Majesty sets foot in the council room?"

Eric took his time answering as he squinted at the names scrawled along the branches of the tree.

Faucher's hands curled into fists that rested atop his desk.

"Neither Brendan nor Alina told me anything about their plans, but they have asked me to tell you that you are expected to go to the castle by the dining hour to help placate some of the nobles," Eric finally explained.

Faucher's mood blackened as he took a deep breath in.

Why had Brendan Devark kept so many secrets from him . . . ?

"Oh, and Mr. Kraft, the Coven of Aguas leader, will begin attending Kat's training twice a week around the time I return to have the sword repaired."

At his wit's end, Faucher pushed off from the desk and drew himself up to his full height as he regarded Eric.

"I believe I have the training in hand. I do not—"

"Have you ever seen Kat's eyes filled with nothing but golden light before?" Eric asked suddenly.

"No. I haven't."

"You'll want Mr. Kraft here if it does happen . . . And Faucher?" Eric turned and faced the Troivackian squarely, his expression momentarily anxious. "Do your best to stay calm when you see it."

Faucher took a deep breath in and at first said nothing . . .

"Your Highness, I'm going to speak bluntly, as my patience ran out the moment you set foot in my keep for the second time within a fortnight."

Eric tilted his head over his right shoulder, nonplussed.

"Your love for Katarina Ashowan is becoming a new fixation for you to replace your addictions with. You are behaving erratically with her being at your center, and it will not end well. Not for you, and consequently, your kingdom."

Faucher waited for the anger or the denial . . . He waited for the flippant response . . .

"You're mad with your king, not with my awful life choices. Talk with him."

Eric then turned and strode toward the office door, though as he reached for the handle, he hesitated. "There isn't another tidal wave of dogs coming, is there?"

Faucher was almost too infuriated to reply. His left hand ached for a dagger or sword . . .

"No, Your Highness. It is not even the luncheon hour yet."

Eric grinned and waved to the military leader. "Thanks . . . Oh. One more thing . . ."

"What?"

"If you knew someone with unimaginable, unlimited potential, wouldn't you also try to clear the way as much as possible for them? To see how far they could go?"

The question caught Faucher off guard, and so he said nothing.

Fortunately, the prince wasn't waiting for a response, and so he left the office with a coy smile tossed over his shoulder.

With the door closed and the stillness of the room resting over him, Faucher collapsed into his chair and dropped his forehead to his hand.

He almost wished the prince was still nothing more than a drunk . . .

The members of the entire council stared in ominous silence.

All the men present, young and elderly, sat in the massive cold room, in their high-back chairs, their bodies pointed down the long table toward their king . . .

And Alina.

She sat beside Brendan on his right, wearing a bright red dress, and her lips painted the same color. She wore her crown, as did he. Alina looked similar to how she did the day of her coronation, a detail that was not lost on the noblemen.

The cloudy colorless daylight did little to offer brightness in the hall, even though its windows rose high into the shadowed ceiling.

"I will begin this meeting with an announcement," Brendan called, his voice booming over them with an edge that made some flinch. "Her Majesty Queen Alina Devark will be sitting in and speaking during all meetings henceforth."

"Your Majesty cannot be serious," an older Troivackian noble declared from his seat near the couple.

"This is preposterous. She has poisoned your mind and should return to the solar with her handmaidens," another older nobleman huffed while thumping a fist on the table.

"This is an insult to the kingdom of Troivack, and I will not stand for it!" A younger noble farther down the table declared while even going so far as to rise from his seat and stare around righteously while those around him nodded in agreement.

Brendan's obsidian eyes lingered on each speaker, though his gaze was devoid of emotion, which succeeded in sending a chill down each of their spines (not that they would ever admit to it). He then turned his head slowly toward Alina.

"What is your response to this, my queen?"

The men glared daggers at the only woman in the room, each of them readying to object all at once.

Alina raised her fingertips just under her lips and tilted her head. Her dirty blond hair and elegant face were a striking visual interruption from the grim, whiskered men surrounding her.

"Hm, this *is* troublesome. You see, my lords . . . I agree with all of you. I *shouldn't* be here."

Her response made everyone falter in surprise.

"Well . . . there you see it, Your Majesty! Even your queen has spoken!"

"Then you agree she has valuable insight that should be adhered to?" Brendan asked bluntly, his attention flitting to the same nobleman that had first objected.

"You think us children? I see your ploy, Your Majesty! You are making the queen argue in our favor so we will be forced to agree with her!" Another nobleman accused angrily.

"What if I *do* disagree with His Majesty though? Am I a disobedient wife? Is it treason?" Alina wondered, her eyes rounded in an imitation of innocence.

No one had an answer in the face of such a baffling question.

Until Duke Sebastian Icarus calmly leaned forward. "You agree you should not be here, and the king believes it is important to listen to you. So we are. We thank you for respecting our customs. I'm certain His Majesty struggles to part with you in the mornings, so he has made a small oversight."

"Are you saying I am incapable of separating my base urges with my ability to rule, Duke Icarus?" Brendan's voice increased in volume, making most of his vassals wince.

"I merely tried to offer a compliment to Her Majesty, that she has clearly satisfied our king. It is a praiseworthy endeavor." Duke Icarus bowed his head to the couple.

While Alina remained cool and composed on the outside, she was imagining her husband pinning the duke to the ground while she slapped him repeatedly.

Brendan's daydream involved a significantly greater amount of blood.

"How about this . . . ? If by the end of this meeting, ten of you vote to exclude Her Majesty from future meetings, she will be excused for at least a year," Brendan countered regally.

"Why not rule this out entirely?" One of the lords asked acidly.

"Because it is my order. If you wish to defy me, step closer. The blood will blend in perfectly with my wife's dress."

The room once again fell into a hush.

Brendan raised an eyebrow and stared down the table at the most powerful nobles in his kingdom. "Shall we begin?"

CHAPTER 19

DAXARIAN DALLIANCES

Kat barely let out a sound as she deflected Sir Cas's blows, then retaliated with her own practiced attacks. He was almost smiling the entire time.

"I must . . . admit . . . Lady . . . Kat . . . arina . . ." Sir Cas struggled to parry. She was speeding up the steps . . .

He didn't say anything until he was forced to knock her practice sword out of her hand and swipe his own to her throat.

"I may be a genius with the sword, but you are something else entirely," Sir Cas said, grinning and panting. Kat smiled back for a breath before swatting his sword hand away and attempting to strike him in the face.

"Of course I am. I'm a witch." Sir Cas dodged her fist and was putting several feet of distance between them while Kat's eyes were aglow in delight.

Sir Cas rolled his neck with a laugh. "It's been a fortnight since we've started sparring, and you've not only caught up to the others, but you're starting to get the edge on them. It's impressive."

Just behind the Daxarian knight, Broghan Miller had turned and openly glared at Katarina. She shot him a hard look back but didn't let her attention linger any longer than that.

Noting the exchange, Sir Cas let out a sigh. "Miller's still holding out, is he?"

"Yeah. Herra is strange with me now, but at least he isn't calling me names under his breath. Ball is just a crate of fluff, so no issues there. That leaves only Miller set on hating me until he dies."

"Maybe you should try introducing your familiar to him?" Sir Cas suggested with a teasing glint in his eyes.

Kat chortled. "Pina refuses to leave the chamber. Probably because of the dogs . . . But even if she did, I'm not sure I want her charming the younger Miller."

Sir Cas nodded in understanding. They hadn't forgotten the jarring sight of the terrifying Cleophus Miller fawning over the kitten.

The sound of the luncheon bell clanged then, making everyone perk up.

While most of the men wore their winter clothes while training, their breath coming out in steaming plumes, Katarina remained unbothered in her tunic and leather vest with trousers.

However, that didn't mean she didn't enjoy a hot meal after her days of rigorous training.

As the students stowed their weapons, Kat lagged as usual in order to avoid having to come in close contact with any of her peers.

"I've noticed I don't see your aura as often as I did while we were traveling and even during our time at the castle," Sir Cas announced interestedly.

Kat, who was pointedly looking at the ground and lifting her toes experimentally while the young men filed past her on her right, didn't respond until they were once again out of earshot.

"Yeah, I get to move all the time, so I'm a lot calmer generally. Though you probably have already heard Faucher grumbling about the cost of feeding me."

"You really don't feel tired?"

Kat shook her head while moving forward and placing her training sword in the barrel. "Not at all. If anything, I can think a hundred times more clearly. It's like . . . I'm finally doing what I've been meant to do."

Sir Cas noticed that while she claimed the benefits of her new lifestyle, there was a small frown etched on her face . . .

"Do you know why I didn't want to spar with you?"

Kat's widened gaze flew to the Daxarian knight. He was aware how reticent he had seemed at first?

Sir Cas smiled sheepishly. "It's because . . . I love swordplay. I think about it constantly, and if not swordsmanship, my family. But when I become focused during a spar? All I can think about is winning."

"You were worried about hurting me." Katarina's realization finally dawned on her.

Sir Cas nodded, his eyes filled with knowingness as he tilted his head and stared at her in perfect understanding. "You're worried what it means that this life suits you so well, aren't you?"

Katarina's heart fluttered.

He had cut through to the truth a little too well.

Sir Cas deposited his wooden sword in the barrel and turned toward the keep's entrance.

"Well, I can honestly say that I've enjoyed teaching with Faucher these past few weeks, and I haven't had to kill anyone. Then the times when I *have* had to fight during my time as a knight, I'm glad I was able to protect others. No job or lifestyle comes without a price, and being a knight is a hard job. We face horrific scenarios so others don't have to. It's one of the many reasons why knights are revered for their strength."

Kat nodded along. "I'm just . . . I guess I worry that after a while I won't care about hurting people, and that is especially terrifying."

Sir Cas's lips tightened reluctantly. "You won't always care the same way, it's true. It's another price of the job. To be efficient and effective, you can't mourn every life you take or person you maim. You'll lose your mind if you do. While it is important to keep sight of your morals and principles, sadly you must accept the burden of possibly destroying another person's world."

Kat could feel her resolve to learn the sword waver. Her hands started to tremble as dread began to fill her heart.

"I have a hard enough time knowing I killed someone that deserved it."

Sir Cas reached out and gently grasped Kat's elbow, stopping her right before the keep's steps.

"I remember the first man I killed. It's worse when it's personal. You're a good person, Kat. If you ever are worried that you're becoming something that scares you, feel free to talk to me. It's what being brothers-in-arms do for each other."

Gratitude overwhelmed Kat as she stared into Sir Cas's kind blue eyes to the point where she felt warmth behind her own gaze.

Unable to resist, she hugged the knight.

"Thank you."

Sir Cas was taken aback, but after a moment, he smiled and gently returned her embrace. "Anytime."

The loud clearing of a throat interrupted the two.

Pulling free of each other, Katarina and Sir Cas looked up to see Prince Eric and Sir Vohn at his side, regarding the scene with wry expressions.

"Getting along well, I see." Eric raised an eyebrow at Kat, who blushed while sticking her tongue out at him.

"Gods, Sir Cas, if you keep treating women like they're your sisters, you most definitely are going to die alone," Sir Vohn jested with a smirk.

The blond Daxarian knight laughed. "Well, you keep treating them like

mistresses, and that hasn't gotten you much aside from the occasional burning—" Sir Cas caught himself at the last moment and glanced at Katarina
apologetically.

The redhead blinked at him, bewildered, before turning back to Sir
Vohn. "Do you often have sexual diseases?"

Sir Cas burst out laughing while Eric let out a long-suffering sigh.

Sir Vohn's jaw dropped along with his brow as he looked back and forth
between Sir Cas and the prince. "I'm getting lanced by my juniors, Your
Highness. I think we should have them run laps."

"Ask Faucher how that went for him last time, and you'd think otherwise," Eric replied while casually descending the steps.

Katarina rolled her eyes toward the sky while Sir Vohn cast a curious
glance in her direction and Sir Cas let out another *ha* before trying to
stifle it.

"Are you ready to go?" Eric asked Kat, his hazel eyes softening.

"Go? Go where?"

Eric looked back at Sir Vohn, who was still grinning. "You'd think I was
a footman for all she thinks of her crown prince."

Kat frowned in bewilderment until her memory returned at last. "Right!
The sword! I thought you were coming in the evening?"

"Change of plans. My sister is sending you a handmaiden with updates
from the court tonight, so I came earlier."

"Aren't we supposed to go under the cover of darkness?" the redhead
asked with a small hunching of her shoulders to add a theatrical tone.

"Since when are you opposed to sneaking around?" Eric queried with a
chuckle.

Kat rounded on him, her hands rising to her hips. "I don't sneak around!"

"You used to sneak out quite regularly from what Alina has told me."

"She lies! I would never—"

"Stop insulting the queen. Let's go. And anyone ever tell you that you
look exactly like your father when you stand like that?" Eric turned and
began climbing up the steps accompanied by Sir Cas and Sir Vohn.

Kat spluttered. "Of course they have! Oyy! I should bathe before we
head out!"

"Your stench will help people avoid us. Come on, I can't be gone for
long today," Eric called over his shoulder as he continued into the keep.

Kat was left on her own, self-consciously moving her hands from her hips
to her sides, and her mouth opening and closing as she struggled to think of
a comeback.

When none was forthcoming, she dropped her head back with a loud groan, then followed behind the men. However, she couldn't help the cheek-aching smile that split across her face as she then jogged to catch up with Eric, who, unbeknownst to her, had the exact same expression at that moment.

"Is this really necessary?"

"Yes."

"I look stupid."

"Yes, you do."

Kat punched Eric's shoulder and scowled.

He had forced her to shove her hair under a tight leather cap with earflaps and then wear a cloak to hide the length of her ponytail. Eric wore a hat of his own, but his was a wide-brimmed farmer hat and didn't look nearly as ridiculous.

"It sounds like you and Alina are meeting more often," Kat noted idly as she and Eric strolled down Vessa's bustling city streets, where merchants and neighbors shouted and cajoled with one another.

It was another overcast, dark day, and the icy wind was especially piercing. Faucher had been saying only that morning it was an unusually cold winter for Troivack, causing many people to worry about heating their homes in the coming months.

"We have. Especially since she started attending council meetings. We go over some of the proposals together—and we make sure the other nobles hear about us meeting. She was barely allowed to remain in the meetings, and it was entirely thanks to the plan she and His Majesty mapped out. With my sister and I conferring together, the nobles are inclined to think it's my wisdom they are listening to. Meanwhile, Brendan Devark fights against every policy and suggestion from the council, and Alina fights in favor of it. He then caves, but only to her."

Kat grinned. "Definitely sounds like an Alina plot."

Eric nodded as he gently pressed Katarina to his other side away from the road as a cart with sacks stacked high trundled past them.

"Yes, but the nobles aren't stupid. They know what His Majesty is doing and aren't pleased with it. Alina needs to win more of their favor . . . though she's hiding her nature from them, which is what makes them uncertain just how angry to be with her. They wonder if His Majesty or I am just using her. Disturbingly enough, that makes them less angry . . ."

"Oh, Alina will find a way to take the lead. I have no doubt."

"She already has, but she isn't forthcoming with her plans." Eric didn't sound pleased with the fact, and Kat decided not to prod any unpleasant feelings so early in their excursion.

"What have you been doing if you aren't attending these meetings?"

At first, the prince didn't respond as they continued to navigate their way through the crowds, but he finally stopped and gestured with his thumb down a dark alley, where halfway down a blacksmith's sign hung gathering dirt and cobwebs.

Only once they had turned down the alley did he answer.

"I've been training and familiarizing myself with more of the nobility."

Katarina briefly wondered if any of the aforementioned nobility were of the female gender but decided she didn't want to ask in case the answer made her feel strange . . .

"Are you sure about this blacksmith? He doesn't seem very popular," she observed as they neared.

Sirs Vohn and Cas casually placed themselves at the end of the alleyway the prince and noblewoman wandered down, stopping any idle foot traffic from passing down the inconspicuous path.

"I heard he's one of the best, though he isn't one to care much about appearances. He lives for his work."

Upon reaching the wooden door with its sturdy wrought iron handle, Kat looked to its square windows and noticed a white film over them thanks to age and dust, which prevented her from seeing any of the wares.

If she hadn't been told otherwise, she would've presumed the shop abandoned.

Rapping his fist against the wood, Eric waited.

When no one came to answer the door after several more moments, he knocked again, this time for longer.

The door swung open during the barrage of pounding to reveal a man who appeared as broad as he was tall, who wore darkened goggles encased in steel strapped over his eyes. His bushy beard reaching his chest had more than a few patches that seemed to have been singed off, and his leather apron looked as though it had been pulled from a garbage.

"What do you want?" he boomed irritably.

Kat blinked in surprise, while Eric simply raised an eyebrow. "We have a sword that needs to be fixed up. Supposedly one of Theodore Phendor's early works."

"Mm." the blacksmith let out a rumble deep from his chest that felt as though it could rattle the glass of his shop.

"We know it could be a fake, but my companion here is still willing to pay good money to see it restored."

The blacksmith let out another grunt, then turned and walked back into his dark shop, leaving the door open behind himself.

Looking at each other, Eric and Katarina grinned. Without a word, they both resisted laughing.

It looked like they were in for another interesting encounter, and so the prince entered the shop followed closely by the redhead to find out once and for all if the sword she had found was in fact one of the infamous weapons crafted by the master forger Theodore Phendor.

CHAPTER 20

A WINTER CHILL

Clutter and debris appeared to make up the entire blacksmith shop save for the space of the anvil, the hearths, and the ovens.

How the blacksmith managed to work without light baffled Eric, though it didn't occur to Kat, who navigated the stacks of broken hammers, axes, cauldrons, and random pieces of furniture with ease thanks to her ability to see in the dark. At one point, the Daxarian prince tripped over a rusting spear that lay in the way, making Katarina reach out instinctively and seize the back of his tunic.

"I've never thought of myself as fussy about cleanliness, but this place is a disaster . . ." Eric murmured to her under his breath while steadying himself.

"You can leave if you're going to complain," the blacksmith barked from his anvil.

Eric blinked in surprise; the man shouldn't have been able to hear him from that distance.

"Are you going to keep wasting my time, or are you going to show me the tin sword?" the blacksmith bellowed while seizing a large pair of black leather gloves.

Eric opened his mouth to make an equally smart-ass remark, but Katarina stepped past him, unclipping the sword from her belt with its scabbard and presented it to the man.

The blacksmith seized the weapon with a huff.

He peered at the sheath's leatherwork and metal tip with a disapproving shake of his head. Then he gripped the fine chain link handle and pulled the blade free. He dropped the scabbard on the dirtied floor and stared at the weapon. His goggles hid his eyes, but his round, heat-scorched cheeks and thick lips stilled.

Katarina was about to ask him what he thought, when he flipped the blade in his hand.

Then he did it again.

And again.

And again.

He frowned. He slapped the flat of the blade down on his hairy, scarred forearm and turned toward his hearth.

He didn't move a muscle, but his nasally grunting breaths quickened . . .

Rounding back to Eric and Katarina, he thrust the hilt toward her.

"Hold it," he ordered, his gravelly tone restraining some other larger emotion.

Katarina cautiously reached out and took the sword from his beefy, calloused hand.

She stood with its tip pointed toward the sky, feeling perfectly foolish.

The blacksmith scowled. "Say you'll sell it to me."

"Hold on here; we just asked—" Eric began, but the blacksmith waved off the rest of his words.

"Just say it. I won't buy it."

The prince blinked and settled back down hesitantly.

Kat briefly looked at Eric in open bewilderment, and he gave a small tilt of his head as if to say, *Might as well* in response.

"Erm . . ." She turned back to the blacksmith awkwardly. "I'll sell you this sword for the right price."

"Great." The blacksmith reached to grab the weapon from Kat only for a ringing pulse to flutter from the sword, filling the cluttered room as though they were encased in stone or marble designed for the best of acoustics.

It sounded exactly as it had when Katarina first found the sword back in the market, only this time as the echo faded, she could hear whispers . . . and they sounded angry . . .

The blacksmith's hand dropped to his side as he let out a shuddering breath. "That. That is a true Theodore Phendor sword in the hands of its master."

Kat looked at the sword in her hand, stunned, but an excited, triumphant smile slowly climbed up her face.

"Really?" she asked while barely resisting the urge to shout and jump up and down like a child.

Eric was staring at the blacksmith with a calculative eye. The prince wanted to make sure the Troivackian wasn't trying to swindle Kat in order to charge her more for the sword repairs . . .

"Theodore Phendor created pieces for retail sale, but you know that his most famous skill was crafting remarkable weapons for knights and nobles," the blacksmith spoke, startling the two Daxarians by revealing to them that when it came to his craft, he was fully capable of becoming chatty. "It was said that Theodore Phendor managed to bind a weapon of his creation to its owner's soul, but once the owner died, it would search for a new master. Even if its original owner was killed in battle. He made all his clients promise on their lives that they would not be buried with their weapons. Some still tried . . . but one way or another, the weapon always found a way out of the grave and into the hands of its next master."

"How is it no one caught onto the fact that he was a witch?" Eric mused with a small chortle and shake of his head.

"Deficient witches weren't as common then as they are now," the blacksmith explained seriously.

A peculiar reaction for a Troivackian . . . Most wouldn't talk about witches or magic so casually.

Katarina didn't notice this, however, as she continued staring at the sword in her hand. "So, will you fix the handle for me? I'd like to be able to fight with it, but currently it's more fit to be a decorative piece."

The blacksmith turned and inclined himself to Katarina. "It would be . . . one of the biggest honors of my life if you would allow me."

The burly man sounded as though he were willing to beg.

Kat grinned. "Well, you seem to know what you are doing, so . . . here. When will you have it ready—Oh, and what's your name?"

The blacksmith reached out and carefully took the sword Katarina offered to him as though it were a newborn babe. "I will work as diligently as possible, but I will take my time to ensure there is no one who could say they'd have done better by this weapon. I will aim to have it done in a fortnight, but if it takes a month, I ask for your understanding."

Kat nodded with a smile. "That works for me. Let me know your fee at the time of completion, and you still haven't told me your name."

The blacksmith puffed his chest out and raised his chin. "My name is Dimitri Phendor."

Both Eric and Katarina's jaws dropped.

"I am the great-grandson of the witch who crafted this sword."

Katarina and Eric walked down the Troivackian street side by side without a word.

Both were still recovering from the multiple shocks of the afternoon.

"You . . . you have a sword by Theodore Phendor . . ." Eric spluttered haltingly.

"Yeah."

"And we just stumbled upon his great-grandson, who is capable of fixing it for you."

"Yeah."

The prince turned to look at Kat, who was staring ahead in a daze.

"It really does seem like you were fated to come to Troivack."

Kat swallowed. "Do you think . . . I mean . . . is it possible I'm supposed to kill the devil?"

Eric frowned. "He said he was worried your fates would become tied . . . Perhaps that's what he didn't want."

"Do you think the devil will avoid me then?" Katarina asked hopefully while turning to look at Eric's profile as they started to descend a sloping street that wound around an old carpenter's shop.

"I don't know. It didn't sound like he became involved with us because he wanted to. He said someone hired him to kill Alina, and we are all confident it was Duke Icarus. And let me tell you, Sebastian Icarus is a hard nobleman to deal with just on his own; he has ties to almost every integral business in this kingdom."

"What if he died? What happens then?" Katarina mused casually.

"He has a brother, who is more than ready to take over. After the brother, cousins . . . So on and so forth. Plus, if the family starts to halt businesses because of being targeted, it could expedite the civil war."

Kat felt her stomach roil. "It all seems so tangled."

"It is. His Majesty has a real mess on his hands. Hopefully Alina can make some headway in helping him."

The pair stopped when they came to the back of the unmarked carriage they were supposed to ride in back to Faucher's keep.

Sir Cas and Sir Vohn were trailing behind them but were out of earshot.

"What if I've put Alina in greater danger because the devil is linked to me now?" Kat couldn't bring herself to look at Eric.

However the prince stared directly at her anxious expression with the right corner of his mouth turned upward. He then reached out and tugged on the earflap of her hat. "Don't give yourself troubles that don't exist yet."

Kat's eyes rose and locked with Eric's, making every inch of his face soften.

Warmth flooded her being as she saw the crinkle in the corner of his eyes she loved so much, and she could feel a deep peace grow in her heart as she basked in the comfort of his presence.

She didn't want to look away.

She just wanted to be looking at Eric in a quiet side street in the cold for as long as possible . . .

For the rest of her life . . . Kat, for some reason, wanted to remember how he looked at her that day.

Then something white drifted down and landed in Eric's wavy blond hair.

Snow.

It was snowing!

Both Eric and Kat looked to the sky as the dark clouds above them released fluffy flakes on the bleak earth below.

"Gods, this isn't normal at all in Troivack." Eric breathed while looking back at Kat and seeing her brilliant smile still directed at the sky.

When she realized he was watching her and not the wintry wonder above, the redhead lifted an eyebrow and tilted her head. "Is the hat still that funny?"

Eric laughed, then reached out and, after looking over her shoulder to confirm the only two in the quiet alley other than themselves were their two knight escorts, plucked the hat off her head, revealing her mussed fiery hair. Kat grew rigid from the move, her heart pounding in her ears . . .

"Not sure that's much better," Eric teased while studying her with a smirk.

Kat's momentary trance was broken as she snatched the cap from Eric and slapped his shoulder with it. "At this rate, I should just shave my head."

"Oh Gods. As if I'm not going to hear enough from your father about the trouble you've gotten into." Eric turned toward the carriage, his expression hidden from Kat.

"Are you and my da going to make up?" she asked without thinking.

Kat hadn't been prepared for Eric to suddenly stop moving after he reached for the carriage handle.

With his back to her, he didn't say anything, and instead, after three plumes had appeared and disappeared from under his hat, he opened the carriage door and stepped back to let Kat into the vehicle first. His face was unreadable and distant. Caught off guard by the shift in his mood, Kat got the distinct impression he did not want her to ask any more on the topic . . .

So she entered the carriage without commenting on the abrupt change in Eric's countenance, even though she desperately wanted to.

* * *

The journey back to Faucher's keep was spent in silence until at last, they turned down the long desolate dirt road where no other building stood. Only trees and weeds for as far as the eye could see . . .

"If it is just because of the drugs or drinking, why wouldn't you be able to make up with my da?" Katarina couldn't help it. The question was itching her throat too terribly.

Eric's marbled features didn't change, and when his gaze moved to her, the shadows that Katarina had almost forgotten about reappeared.

"I'm nowhere near the man Fin expects me to be, not to mention I have other issues with him."

"Such as?" Kat prodded as she fought with all her might not to fidget.

The prince took in a short breath and let it out in an aggravated grunt before moving his attention back to the passing scenery out the carriage window.

"It's private, Kat, but your father isn't entirely in the right in everything that went wrong between us."

The redhead was about to pester him even further, but Eric shot her a warning look that had her dejectedly slumping back against the leather carriage seat for the rest of the trip to Faucher's keep.

When the horses finally pulled to a halt, Eric managed to gentle his former hardness when he addressed Kat again.

"I'll be bringing Mr. Kraft here soon to start helping you train. I'll see you then."

Kat nodded and waved but didn't say anything.

She understood that Eric and her father had once had a close relationship, and she didn't deserve knowing all the details of their feud, but the prince's cold handling of her questions had made her previous high spirits turn sour.

After stepping down from the carriage and closing the door behind herself, Katarina moved toward the keep's entrance only to be startled when Sir Vohn jogged past her and opened the tall heavy front door for her.

"Are you in a hurry of some kind?" Kat asked with a chuckle once she had overcome the surprise from the burst of movement.

Sir Vohn grinned at her, unaware of what had transpired in the carriage between her and the prince. "Sorry, Lady Katarina. His Highness has a courting date back at the castle he must get ready for. Today's errand just ran a bit long."

Kat felt as though she'd been punched in the gut. "O-Oh."

"Didn't mean to rush you! Take care, my lady, and please pass along our apologies to Leader Faucher for not saying our goodbyes!" The Daxarian knight darted back to the driver's seat of the carriage and leapt up, while Sir Cas, who had been following behind him, stared at Kat wide-eyed.

The carriage wheels made the gravel crackle as it once again set itself into motion, leaving Kat standing in the empty doorway awash with horrible, sickening feelings.

"Lady Katarina, I'm so sorry. He shouldn't have told you like that—I don't think Sir Vohn is aware of—" Sir Cas rushed forward, his face pale.

"Aware of what? Oh . . . I suppose he shouldn't have told me something that could be confidential, right? Jeez, I wonder if we've missed dinner . . ." Katarina disappeared into the keep, but despite her breezy words, she refused to look at the knight, and her voice sounded a mite too choked.

Sir Cas turned to stare at the back of the swaying carriage with a cringe. Did Sir Vohn really not know?

The Daxarian knight sighed. *Well, I guess it's better she finds out here than later at the castle surrounded by nobles . . . Still. I hope the prince and Lady Katarina can have a meaningful discussion before things go too far.*

CHAPTER 21

FAUCHER FOLDS

F aucher stalked down the center of the castle corridor, his pace steady and his glower ominous enough to cause any servants or nobility that happened to be in the same vicinity to shrink back. Ever since Prince Eric had summoned him the previous day, the military leader had been doing his due diligence in calming down multiple council members in the castle with regards to the queen joining in the meetings.

Without locking eyes with anyone he passed in the corridor, Faucher instead focused on calming his mind for the conversation ahead.

When he reached his destination, he pounded the solid surface of the door. At first there wasn't a response . . .

Then Faucher heard shuffling and whispered voices.

At last, the door swung open to reveal the queen of Troivack.

"Ah, Leader Faucher! Good day! I apologize, His Majesty wasn't expecting you." Alina blinked up at the military leader, stunned. She wore a long sleeve black dress with a plum-colored shawl loosely wrapped around her shoulders.

"Your Majesty." Faucher bowed. "I need to speak with the king. Now."

Alina's eyes widened with worry before she glanced back to her husband, who looked equally concerned.

"I will leave you two then. Good health to you, Leader Faucher," she replied hesitantly. He could tell she wanted to ask to stay, but he was sincerely grateful that she did not push the matter.

Faucher waited as the queen curtsied to her husband, then strode out of the office with her head held high.

Upon entering, the Troivackian leader closed the door behind himself and marched over to the king's desk, where he sat and bowed.

"What's happened?" Brendan asked, his index finger gently tapping the desk.

"How much are you intending to use Lady Katarina for?"

Brendan straightened and carefully folded his hands over his desk. "I already told you; she is going to show that you are the superior teacher, and she is going to confirm to everyone that Alina is aligned with capable people of her sex."

Faucher's eyes bore into his former pupil. "So I was right . . . You are intending to use Lady Katarina to improve the stigma against witches."

"That would naturally occur, yes."

"My lone student is responsible for changing our entire kingdom on the front lines of both gender and witch inequality as well as job assignment, but if she fails, she is buried with her efforts while you and Her Majesty remain safe?" Faucher accused, his tone rising.

Brendan stood from his seat, the set of his jaw growing firm. "Faucher, there is risk to everyone. Not just Lady Katarina."

"Lady Katarina isn't beholden to this kingdom like we are. You are asking a lot of a foreign woman."

"She is a close friend of Alina's," Brendan answered ambiguously.

"What does she get in return?" Faucher countered, his eyes glinting dangerously.

Brendan raised an eyebrow. "She gets to prove herself and learn the sword as she has always wished."

"She proves herself to your people and then goes home. Is that it?"

The Troivackian king studied his friend in silence, but Faucher wasn't having any of it.

"You are betting too much on her. Yes, she is capable. Yes, she has talent. But Lady Katarina's life is in far greater jeopardy than she knows."

"Given that there have been multiple attempts on her life, I'd say she is perfectly aware."

"And her parents? Are they in complete agreement with these plans?" Faucher was glowering, and his presence swelled in the cluttered office.

Brendan carefully rounded his desk, his eyes never leaving his vassal. "Faucher, you had no problem with this before."

"That is because I didn't anticipate you bringing Her Majesty into the council room with you so soon. If you had waited until after Lady Katarina had swayed some of the men or I had obtained a higher position where I could help you, I wouldn't be as concerned."

The king folded his arms over his thick chest. "I wanted to see what

Duke Icarus would do. He only just got here, and there's a chance that if we agitate him enough he will try to go visit the devil, which would help us keep track of him."

"Or you aimed fifteen new daggers at your wife's throat," Faucher added frostily.

"Alina is doing well. She is placating the men and most of their wives," Brendan responded tersely. "What else is bothering you?"

"Are you keeping an eye on the Daxarian prince as of late?"

The Troivackian king tilted his head to the left. "He drinks heavily and has been spending his time surrounded by women of all stations when he isn't training."

Faucher couldn't hide his incensed reaction. "He's been doing what?"

Brendan's mouth quirked upward in a humorless smile, but he said nothing.

"Are you aware he has been spying on my house?" When the king didn't react, Faucher snorted bitterly. "So you are."

Brendan shrugged.

Faucher shook his head and turned away from his king. "I am too old for these games you are attempting to play amid the chaos."

"I'm glad you have warmed to Lady Katarina." Brendan reached for the goblet of water on his desk and took a drink.

Faucher peered back somberly, and the look in his eyes made the Troivackian king set his cup back down.

"I'd like to wash my hands of this, Brendan."

"Faucher, I'll tell Prince Eric to stop—"

"No. You are playing with war, and you hid the spark for it to ignite in my house. Take Lady Katarina back to the castle and have her train here with Sir Cas."

Brendan pushed himself away from his desk. "Have you forgotten what I mentioned I might do when we first had this talk, Faucher?"

The military leader's fortitude left so swiftly that it alarmed Brendan.

Faucher suddenly looked old and tired . . .

"Are you referring to your threat to marry off my daughter to Lady Katarina's brother? Fine. Arrange it. Perhaps it's better she is far from Troivack with this recklessness carrying on in the court."

The military leader made his way back to the exit, his steps heavier than they had been when he'd first entered the office.

"Greg, I'm not trying to punish you; I am just trying to create a better kingdom."

Faucher hesitated as he reached for the handle of the office door, and for a moment, it seemed as though he was going to leave without another word.

However, when he turned back to face the king, Brendan almost wished he had.

"I've always been at your back. I've always taught you that the direct approach, with integrity and strategic thinking, could build the future you wanted for Troivack. What you are doing now with plots and gambling everything you have built with your sweat and honor, I can't support." Faucher paused, his eyes drifting to the floor briefly before taking in and letting out a long breath.

"I've always been able to hold my head high around my family, and while I've not always been able to share the details of our work together, I could always confidently say the decisions we came to were wise and worthy of pride. All that has happened and all that we are doing . . . If it were to fail in the worst way possible, your *and* my entire family could be slaughtered. And Lady Katarina . . . If she remains here when the literal devil himself is after her because of the loyalty she holds for your wife? She will be buried right alongside us all. Daughter of a house witch or not."

Brendan didn't say anything, nor did he display any emotion to the words of one of his most trusted teachers and friends, who had been like a father to him growing up . . .

"I'm disappointed, Brendan. I cannot condone these plans and stand by you."

The Troivackian king tensed. Deep in his black eyes, his pain shone through.

"I never knew you could talk so much." Brendan's voice came out a growl, but Faucher knew he had hurt him.

With a bow, the military leader left the king's office and, shortly thereafter, the castle. Despite having had a meeting arranged to help Captain Orion with his own training, all Faucher wished to do was go home to his wife and not have to speak to anyone for days.

The second Faucher set foot on the stairs leading to the front doors of his keep, he knew something was wrong.

For one, he could hear people talking inside, and for another, he was noticing his stable hands were in a hurry to hitch multiple horses.

He threw open the door, his cloak billowing in the wintry wind, and he was greeted with his servants dashing up and down the entrance hall.

"You! What is the meaning of this?" Faucher shouted and pointed at one of his stewards, who was in the process of running to the left while carrying two long scrolls.

The man screeched to a halt and opened his mouth to respond, when Faucher's wife, Lady Nathalie, came rushing over.

"Thank the Gods you're here. Was Lady Katarina training this morning before you left for the castle?" she asked breathily while laying a hand on Faucher's forearm, her light brown eyes gazing up at him intently.

Faucher frowned while casting his mind back to earlier that day before the sun had risen and a thin blanket of snow had coated the courtyard stones. "Yes. I gave her another two attack combinations to work on before I left and that was all."

"Alright, that means at most she should be only a short ride away. Marco, please send Dante into Vessa to search, Piers to the south, and Conrad to the northwest. There could be farmers that spotted something. Gregory, I doubt they would have gone to the west, but—"

"Nathalie, are you telling me Lady Katarina is missing?" Faucher felt decades of his military expertise hum to life.

"Yes. When Sir Cas and the other men went out after breakfast, she was nowhere to be found. Her wooden sword was gone, and she hasn't been found anywhere in the keep."

"What of the snow?" Faucher asked while thinking about the half inch of snowflakes that lay across the land.

"The snow had been cleared by the stewards by the time we realized she was missing. They didn't say they noticed anything—at least they don't think they did. You know how it is with training; she would have been walking all over that area."

"Was anything other than the sword missing?" Faucher turned to the steward named Marco, then back to his wife.

"No. She was wearing her normal clothes and boots, and nothing from her chamber was gone."

Faucher reached up and rubbed his beard carefully. "No servants heard or saw anything?"

Nathalie shook her head.

"What are Sir Cas and my students doing now?" Faucher began to stride toward the right of his keep toward his office.

"Misters Herra, Ball, and Miller are in their chambers, and Sir Cas is checking down the road with Lady Darchamp. I called our sons here once it grew close to midday and there still was no sign of her; they only just arrived."

Faucher frowned, then continued heading in the direction of his office, while his wife remained in the entrance hall to speak to more of their staff. When the military leader opened the door to his study, he found his three sons standing and waiting for him.

Dante had his arms folded and his legs braced apart. His long, straight hair was fully tied back, his sword on his hip and his winter cloak over his shoulders. Conrad was in the process of rubbing his short curly hair, his eyes cast to the floor as he stood across from his brother, his crossbow on his back and his beard neatly trimmed as usual. Piers had his hands gripped into fists at his sides, clean-shaven cheeks and his mop of curly black hair swept over his left ear, revealing the two silver hoops hanging from his right earlobe.

"Father, did you already speak with Mother about the situation?" Dante asked as soon as all three of Faucher's children looked up upon their father's entrance.

"I have. She wants to send you out in all directions to look for Lady Katarina, but before we do any of that, Dante, I need to ask . . ." Faucher stalked over toward his eldest son, his stare unwavering. "Did you or Mabel tell *anyone* that Lady Katarina is here?"

Dante's face hardened. "No. We both agreed that it's too large a risk for our family to tell anyone other than my brothers."

Faucher rounded on his other two sons. "Conrad, Piers, did either of you say anything to anyone?"

Conrad shook his head rapidly. "I haven't even told Ruth."

Piers looked at his father with his usual prideful air. "Nicole is away with her parents until the spring. There isn't any way I could have told her."

"Did you two fight again, Piers?" Dante voiced disapprovingly.

Piers's lip curled. "No. Her sister is having a baby, and she's gone to help. Not all wives are nervous of their own shadows, brother."

Dante drew his sword and aimed it at Piers's throat. "Insult my wife again, and I will—"

Faucher stepped forward and cuffed Piers on the back of the head, then gave a single look to Dante that had him reluctantly sheathing his sword.

After making sure none of his sons were about to enter into a ridiculously juvenile fight, Faucher addressed them. "If what you all say is true, then Lady Katarina should be close by."

"What do you mean, Father?" Conrad queried, confused.

Faucher let out a long-suffering sigh and walked toward his study door.

"Come. I have a guess about what might have happened."

CHAPTER 22

ROCKY REVEALS

K at's temple throbbed painfully.

Her wrist was stinging, and her right knee felt bruised . . .

When her eyes fluttered open, she was forced to close them again with a grimace, as the light made it feel as though a dagger was being driven through her skull.

"Godsdamnit . . ." She groaned while reaching her hand up and shifting on the cold ground.

Her thumb was met with sticky blood that was already drying on the side of her head.

Pushing herself up into a sitting position, Kat tried again to open her eyes, and while it still hurt, she at least could begin to take stock of her surroundings.

She was lying on hard-packed ground with gravel and other large slabs of rocks, and . . . she was in a small gorge. Stone walls rose around her, and a few inches from her boot was a frozen stream. She then noticed her wooden sword laying a few feet away on the ground . . .

Kat's memory surged back to life.

She had been training, and she'd gone out even earlier than normal after learning about Eric's courting date . . . Faucher had come and given her new offensive moves that she was already mastering shortly after he'd left, when Broghan Miller had come out.

"Ashowan, let's talk."

Kat looked at him, her expression hardening for a moment before closing her eyes and letting out a sigh. She had to start dealing with those *types of people like an Ashowan.*

"What's up, Miller?"

"Let's go for a run. I want to see if you can keep up." He lifted his chin arrogantly at her, his hands stowed in his pockets.

Kat scoffed. "No, thanks. I generally don't go out alone with someone who has made it magnificently obvious that they hate me."

The young man lifted an eyebrow, his jaw working side to side while the redhead resumed her attacks on the dummy.

"You're doing better than I thought you would. For a woman, I mean," he called out.

Kat grinned but didn't bother stopping her training. "What do you mean 'for a woman'? I'm a witch, Miller, and I'm pretty sure I've already surpassed you in our lessons. Faucher's talking about me fighting with a real sword next week. Aren't you another month from that?"

Broghan's eyes narrowed. "I don't know about that, but if you're so damn confident, run with me."

Katarina stopped attacking the dummy and faced him. "You're being suspicious as hell."

"If you think you're stronger than me, then it shouldn't matter what I do. That's true strength here in Troivack, or were you never taught that in Daxaria?"

Kat considered her peer for a moment, her golden eyes sharp on his face.

She should've held on to her common sense for longer . . . but she was still struggling to put Eric out of her mind . . .

"Tell you what, Miller. If we go on this run together, then you have to do something for me."

Broghan's lip curled. "What's that?"

"You have to buy me a bottle of moonshine and share a cup with me, and you're not allowed to insult me during the entire time we drink."

"Only if you impress me," he countered haughtily.

Smiling, Kat slipped her wooden sword into her belt.

"You're going to run with that?" Broghan scoffed.

"I'm going to need a handicap to try and make it less boring," Kat responded cheekily while stretching each of her arms across her body in turn.

Her fellow student was about to make another snide remark, when she took off at a sprint, leaving Broghan behind in a whoosh of cold air.

He clenched his hands into fists and took off after her.

If she wanted to be a knight so badly, then she could handle a little hazing . . .

* * *

Kat stared at the rock wall before her with fury burning in her chest.

They'd run for an hour . . . Kat hadn't even had her aura begin to show, and honestly, she had found it rather refreshing. But then, sweating, panting, and pale, Broghan Miller had lunged at her with his right shoulder and shoved her into the gorge, his eyes burning as he watched her fall. Only, for some reason, he'd also looked surprised . . .

"He could've killed me." Kat stared up and guessed the fall had been around ten or eleven feet. "If I wasn't a witch . . ." She trailed off.

Gazing down at her hand that had grown calloused and bloodied from her days of training with Faucher, Kat then regarded her discarded practice sword.

"Did he even check to see if I was alive?" She looked up and down the chasm but didn't find a way to climb up.

Kat bent down and plucked up her sword, her aura bursting to life for the first time in weeks as a potent urge to tear Broghan Miller apart limb from limb coursed through her.

"Fine. You wanted to see Troivackian strength? Have it your way."

Katarina launched the wooden sword at the stone wall across from her and embedded it nearly to its hilt, which cracked from the pressure of being suddenly encased in rock.

With a flying leap that was in no way within the realm of humanly possible, Katarina landed on the sword hilt and sprang up to the ledge, her aura burning hot and broadening with every breath she took.

Faucher rolled up his tunic sleeves as he descended the steps into his courtyard, where his three male students and Sir Cas stood with their hands clasped behind their backs.

Meanwhile Piers, Conrad, and Dante waited to the right, watching with various looks of confusion and uncertainty as pale sunlight broke through the clouds to illuminate the wisps of snow that lazily drifted down from the sky.

Without bothering to acknowledge any of the men that stood before him, Faucher finished tucking his sleeves above his elbows.

"This morning, Lady Katarina Ashowan went missing," he began evenly.

Caleb Herra glanced at his two peers standing at his sides. "Yeah, we heard."

Faucher's fist caught Herra unawares in his gut, its iron strength forcing out all air and thoughts from his head and bringing him to his knees.

Both Joshua Ball and Broghan Miller stiffened.

Sir Cas, unsmiling, stared ahead, nonplussed.

"My staff have been instructed to be on alert for any intruders or strange happenings since Lady Katarina joined my keep. None of them heard or saw anything out of the norm this morning. This means that if someone they were *used* to hearing and seeing had been around the lady, they wouldn't have thought anything of it." Faucher's tone was distant. It was a far cry from his normal roars and bellows, and it made the man's calm even eerier.

"S-She was out with the prince yesterday. Perhaps they went off together this morning," Joshua began while the heel of his left boot slid half an inch backward.

Faucher's back hand flew out, crashing into Joshua's cheek and knocking the student flat on his arse.

"I'm aware of your feelings about the lady's presence, but I gave you all my warning the day she arrived," Faucher continued while he paced to stand before Sir Cas, who hadn't moved despite the casual violence being doled out.

"Did she sneak out?" Faucher asked, his brows lowered.

"If she did, I did not help her do so," Sir Cas answered without emotion.

Faucher nodded, then turned and paced back toward the last of his pupils.

"Miller, you've had the biggest issue with her as of late. What did you do with her?"

Sir Cas's head gradually swiveled to stare at the young man, his blue eyes paler in color than anyone had ever seen.

"I haven't done anything. Just woke up, ate breakfast, and she was gone when we all came out here." Broghan's voice was as confident as always, but he smelled of old sweat despite not having trained for even an hour before they were sent back to their chambers.

Faucher seized him by the front of his tunic and drew him up to meet his nose. "Boy, if you've done something foolish, no one can save you. Not your brother, not your father, and I most certainly will not throw my own family before the beasts that will come for you."

Broghan didn't say anything, but his complexion shifted toward a sickly gray as he beheld genuine pity and sincerity in his teacher's eyes.

"I didn't do anything to her. I'm sure she just flounced off and will come skipping back here any minute—"

"FAUCHER!"

The roar that tore through the courtyard made everyone *but* Faucher tense.

Instead, he shook his head in resignation and bid Broghan a quiet farewell. "I warned you."

Still gripping his student's tunic, Faucher turned his head and looked up to the second-floor balcony to see Eric Reyes standing there with Mr. Kraft, the leader of the Coven of Aguas and the air witch who had helped rescue the prince from the devil.

They came the instant they'd heard Katarina was missing, and Nathalie had tried to buy her husband time by sending the prince to the second floor.

He must have been tipped off by Lady Darchamp when my boys came, Faucher thought grimly as he released his student and faced Eric, who looked as though he were ready to slit every one of their throats himself.

"It was risky to fly here in daylight, Your Highness," Faucher called up.

"We didn't fly. We merely . . . expedited the carriage ride a mite," Mr. Kraft explained with a prim clearing of his throat.

Eric leaned his palms on the balcony ledge, then studied the young man Faucher had just released.

Broghan Miller subconsciously flinched under the prince's eyes that bore into him, filling him with mortal dread.

"Oh Gods, there she is." Mr. Kraft let out a disapproving sigh, snapping everyone's attention to him.

Then, seeing the direction he was staring, all turned to witness the bright flaming streak making its way to them.

It was moving fast.

Too fast.

"Faucher . . ." Eric's voice was loud, but there was a crescendo of concern in it that made everyone else become even more uneasy.

"Godsdamn." Faucher's youngest son, Piers, breathed in awe as he watched the blazing woman draw closer to them, her feet a blur against the ground and her face gradually coming into view . . .

"FAUCHER, GET EVERYONE THE HELL OUT OF HERE!" Eric bellowed.

Everyone jumped, but no one understood the prince's panic, nor did they move quickly enough before Katarina stepped back onto the courtyard stones . . . her aura whirling around herself and her eyes consumed in golden light.

"FAUCHER!" Eric shouted again, spittle flying from his mouth.

Katarina was still moving unnaturally fast, and so when she blurred and appeared in front of Broghan Miller, his knees went weak as he stared into the face of her magical fury . . .

Kat's hand snapped out and seized him by the throat, then hoisted him toward the sky. As everyone began to spring to action, she slammed him down onto the stones as though in slow motion.

It would've been fatal. She would've bashed his head open easily, but Conrad had fired his crossbow and graze the inside of her elbow, and so she dropped Broghan the final three inches to the ground.

Faucher was upon her next, attempting to wrap her in a hold that would render her immobile, but she turned and knocked him with her elbow and sent him flying.

Caleb and Joshua scrambled away from her on the ground, tears rising in their eyes.

Sir Cas moved forward, his hand on the hilt of his sword. "Lady Katarina—"

A burst of wind magic struck Kat . . .

Or, it had meant to.

Her aura flared up and consumed the blast.

Katarina's head snapped sideways, her unseeing eyes turning up toward the origin of the attack.

The air witch was quickly being thrust behind Mr. Kraft, but it was too late.

Kat took three long strides, and despite another arrow being launched at her, she missed being hit as she threw herself into the wind, crossing an incredible distance, and managed to seize the stone of the keep.

She scrambled up the wall like a demonic animal, vaulted the window ledge, her aura nearly wide enough to completely fill the corridor.

Eric stood in front of her.

"Kat," he called out softly, both his hands in the air revealing he held no weapon.

The burning witch regarded him the same way she had the night she'd rescued him from the devil.

Her head tilted interestedly, staring at him. She moved closer to Eric, but she wasn't moving aggressively . . . No, she looked more curious than anything.

"Kraft, tell whoever has a bow and arrow not to shoot," Eric murmured without turning to address the man. "And for your own sake, don't make any sudden moves."

The leader of the coven looked too petrified to make any such attempt, but Lady Nathalie, who had retreated into the shadows of the corridor, gingerly shuffled forward while sticking to the wall of the keep.

For a terrifying moment, Katarina's power-filled gaze shifted to the woman.

Nathalie froze.

No one breathed, but Eric stepped closer to the redhead. "Kat, mind looking at me?"

The redhead's magical sight returned to him.

"Thank you. Now, could you return to your usual self? You're a bit hard to look at when you're brighter than a bonfire."

Behind the prince, Mr. Kraft let out a guttural noise of disbelief.

Kat once again moved closer to Eric, her head angling over her other shoulder as she did so.

It was uncanny how similar she was behaving to the night of the prince's rescue . . . It was then that Eric belatedly remembered how last time she had been consumed with magic, she hadn't snapped out of it until they'd . . . they'd . . .

"Oh, shit." Eric's eyes widened as he fought against tearing his gaze away from her and instead toward the many onlookers. He sidled farther away from the balcony edge. If she kissed him like last time, that would lead to even more problems than they already had . . .

A loud clang rang out.

Behind her mother, at the other end of the corridor, stood Dana. She trembled as she held the large brass bell in her hand. She stared at Kat despite looking as though she were about to faint, and when the witch began to turn away from Eric toward her, she hiccupped.

Thundering paws echoed down the hall, nails scraping the floorboards in great haste, and Eric had only a moment to turn and shoot Dana an appreciative smile over his shoulder before he grabbed Kat and, for the second time in a matter of weeks, was overtaken by a throng of dogs.

CHAPTER 23

SAVED AND SENTENCED

K atarina had fallen limply into Eric's arms under the barrage of dogs. He clutched her, stopping her from being dragged down the hall with the beasties, and secretly relishing the moment.

He hated himself for this.

He hated that having her nestled in the crook between his neck and shoulder made him feel more at peace and calm than he had felt in years. He hated that he was noticing a unique amber scent from her hair mixed with the smell of winter . . . because he loved it.

When the last of the mutts had galloped by, everyone looked to the red-headed woman, who no longer glowed, and in fact, remained half collapsed despite there no longer being any reason to be.

Eric locked eyes with Mr. Kraft, then Lady Nathalie, gave them each a small nod, and proceeded to pick Katarina up into his arms with a grunt.

"Mm?" the redhead moaned softly as the prince began walking down the corridor, giving a small flit of his eyes toward Lady Nathalie in silent question of where her chamber was.

The woman proved herself to have the composure and presence of mind of a battle-hardened soldier as she gave a small curtsy and silently led Eric down the corridor without a flicker of fear or hesitancy.

"You might need to sleep for a bit," Eric murmured at the top of Kat's head as they moved back into the warmer confines of the keep and away from the open balconies.

"Noissfine. Gottatrain. GottabeatupMiller," she slurred while giving a weak effort to break free of Eric's hold.

The prince stiffened but resisted asking anything about her ramblings as he struggled with her weight. She had gained a good amount of muscle due to her training, and it was making it significantly more difficult for him to continue carrying her. As a direct result, the prince resolved to start following the Troivackian strength training methods for himself the very next morning . . .

Once they reached Kat's chamber, Eric strode in and laid her down on her bed, startling her familiar, Pina, from her napping spot by the footboard. He set to brushing back her mussed fiery hair away from her face, but when Kat flinched, he froze.

Blood.

She had a cut by her hairline surrounded by bruising.

She'd hit her head, and Eric could tell from years of work as a mercenary that a normal human would've been bedridden for days from such an injury . . .

He then began checking over the rest of her body and noticed her palm and wrist were scraped and bleeding. He wanted to check under her tunic sleeve for any other injuries aside from where Conrad had grazed her with an arrow moments before but could tell with their present company of Lady Nathalie and her daughter, he wouldn't be permitted to go quite so far. Instead, he settled for removing her leather wrist cuff, but he ended up taking a sharp inhale.

Eric had forgotten what Alina had said.

The reason Kat and Alina had always worn bracelets or, in Kat's case, a leather wrist cuff, was to hide the scars.

Encircling both of Katarina's wrists was worn, puckered pale skin from having had her hands tied together for days . . . She had bled and blistered with them . . . and protected his sister.

His thumb gently brushed the tops of the scars as he worked on swallowing with great difficulty.

"Eric, what are . . . Wait, what happened? I just remember reaching the courtyard . . ." Katarina's eyes fluttered partially open. She stared dazedly at Eric's pained expression but didn't understand why he was making such a face.

"Kat, what happened?" he asked softly.

The redhead winced, making the cut near her hairline reopen as a result and causing her head to subsequently pound once more.

"Fell."

"Your Highness, I'm sure the lady needs to r—" Lady Nathalie began to glide toward the bed, but one deadly glance from Eric had her freezing in place.

He turned back to Kat. "You attacked one of your peers. Tell the truth, Kat."

She tried to take back her hand that was still in Eric's grasp, but he rested his other palm against her cheek, and she was thoroughly trapped.

"I just went for a run. And fell. Don't worry so—"

"Godsdamnit, Kat, save yourself for once. They can kick you out of Troivack for this." Eric's voice was hoarse, and his eyes were filled with such intensity that Katarina couldn't look away. "What did he do?"

For some reason, the truth was the only thing able to leave her lips. "He pushed me. Down a small gorge. My . . . My wooden sword is still down there. In the rock wall. It was an hour run from here."

Pina, hearing her witch's confession, hopped over Kat's hip and lightly pawed over to her face, where she worriedly pressed her pink freckled nose into her mistress's cheek with a loud rumbling purr.

Momentarily caught off guard by the kitten, Eric felt his heart ease a little when Kat smiled at her familiar's tender nuzzling.

The prince removed his palm from Kat's cheek, gently scratching Pina's cheek before he forced himself to lock eyes with the redhead. He was worried it would be too obvious to her how much he loved her right then.

Luckily, she was far too worn out from the use of her magic and injuries to see much, as her vision blurred, and she drifted off into a deep sleep before either could say another word.

Unfortunately for Eric, to everyone else in the chamber, it was plenty obvious.

Giving a small bow to her wrist, the prince touched his forehead to the scar she'd received while kidnapped with his sister before giving her hand one final gentle squeeze and slowly rising back up to standing.

Lady Nathalie, Dana, and Poppy, who had come running to the chamber when she'd heard the ruckus, waited behind Eric.

He didn't turn away from Katarina's bedside despite the heavy silence in the room, and no one dared to try and address him again.

Then he spun around and stalked out of the chamber. Mr. Kraft and the air witch, who had been standing just outside jumped as he stormed by and tentatively began to follow in his wake.

Eric's bloodthirst was palpable in the sharpness of his eyes and lowered brow, ensuring that everyone gave him a wide berth as he walked.

He made his way across the second-floor balcony to the stairs, then out to the courtyard in record time, where Leader Faucher was inspecting Broghan's damaged head. The young man was visibly struggling to stay awake while clutching a towel someone must have handed him to put pressure on the wound.

Eric had almost reached Faucher and Broghan when Dante moved in front of him.

"Your Highness, we are going to summon Captain Orion to arrest Lady Katarina in light of—"

Dante was not a small man, nor was he unskilled, but when Eric drew his sword hilt with a sharp jerk and crushed the inside of Dante's hip, he doubled over like a rag doll. The prince then seized his broad shoulder, and with his right leg braced outside Dante's, sent him tumbling over it to the ground before anyone could blink.

"Dante!" Faucher shouted, reaching for his son but not having a chance to check on him before Eric was crouched beside him and now in front of Broghan Miller.

"Lady Katarina says you pushed her down a gorge," Eric informed the younger man with a low, threatening growl.

Broghan's eyes momentarily widened, and he shifted uncomfortably before his expression turned defiant. "That witch is a liar. What proof does she have?"

"She says her wooden sword is still in the gorge, and that it is an hour's run from here. I also happen to know that Piers Faucher over there is one of the best hunters in all of Vessa. So if we take a ride out across that field, what are the odds we will find your boot prints?" Eric leaned forward, his lip curling.

Broghan went rigid.

Faucher gave his head a weary, knowing shake. "We've summoned your brother, Miller. Are you going to bring this to the king's court, or are you going to confess here?"

The young man began to tremble. If the matter was taken to the king's court, his death was certain with a guilty verdict.

"I . . . I hadn't meant . . . There was an entire river there months ago . . . I didn't know it had dried up . . ."

Eric's left hand shot out and seized Broghan by his bruised throat while his right hand drew out the dagger from inside his boot at the same time.

However, Faucher was prepared for this reaction, and his arm snapped out across the prince's chest.

"We assign his punishment to the letter of the law. His brother must be in attendance at the very least."

Eric's terrifying stare didn't move from Broghan's face as the young man choked for air beneath his hand.

For a moment, Faucher worried the Daxarian prince wouldn't listen to him.

Everyone knew he didn't want to.

Dana, who stood beside Lady Nathalie at the entrance to the courtyard, was trembling as she clutched her mother's arm and shrank away from the murderous air emanating from the prince.

A small mewl in the deathly quiet abruptly drew everyone's attention down to the adorable Piña Colada, who was padding down nervously onto the courtyard stones toward the scene. She halted at the bottom of the steps and gradually crouched, her stare fixed on the prince.

Locking eyes with the familiar, Eric let out a huff while also releasing Broghan, who was gasping and coughing desperately the instant he could draw breath.

The prince stood at the same time Dante Faucher brought himself to his feet. Eric folded his arms and stared down at the young man, his features hardening once more.

"Very well. We can wait right here."

Broghan Miller cowered before him.

Faucher's hand curled into a fist as he, too, rose. "I'll send Piers out to ensure there is evidence. He should be back around the same time as Sir Miller arrives."

Eric said nothing.

Facing his youngest son, who looked uncharacteristically serious in light of the brutality he had just witnessed, Faucher nodded to Piers, who nodded back and made his way to the edge of the courtyard and began walking.

Faucher let out a breath and turned away from his student, who still lay on the ground.

There was nothing he could do to save him. He only hoped the young man's brother could perhaps make a fair bargain for his life . . . though Faucher wasn't particularly hopeful.

"What is the meaning of this?"

Everyone but Eric turned to the booming voice of Sir Cleophus Miller, who strode into the courtyard. He looked even larger with the bear fur cloak around his massive shoulders, his shaved head pale in the dwindling winter light.

"Sir Miller, we have a matter pertaining to your brother that we are trying to settle outside of the king's court," Faucher explained diplomatically after the two exchanged curt nods of acknowledgement.

Cleophus let out a grunt.

"Your brother . . . assaulted—"

"Attempted manslaughter," Eric interrupted, his attention at last moving from Broghan, who hadn't seen the prince blink once in the time they had waited for his brother.

Cleophus looked down on the ground where his brother lay with a bloody towel pressed to his head.

"He pushed Lady Katarina down a gorge. Were she not capable of using magic, she could have been killed. My son, Piers, as you know is a skilled hunter. He has found numerous tracks proving your brother's presence at the time, and we have Lady Katarina's testimony as well," Faucher continued calmly.

"Brother, I swear! I thought the river was still high enough! Sh-She's told everyone she is never cold; all I meant was to push her into a river. J-Just a little bit of hazing, I never meant to—"

"Why didn't you tell anyone she was lying in the bottom of a gorge and in need of help then?" Sir Cas's steely voice caught everyone off guard.

It was strange enough that the kindly knight wasn't smiling, but hearing his chilling tone was even more ominous.

"I-I-I figured she'd . . . she'd be fine! And she is! She nearly killed me when she came back, and she almost hurt a lot more people herself—" Broghan defended desperately.

Cleophus's chin suddenly jerked down as Pina proceeded to rub herself affectionately against his thick ankles, alerting him silently to her presence. Her tail swished against his muscular calf as she peered up into the toughened knight's face and let out two sweet mews.

His attention completely absorbed, the knight crouched and lovingly scratched the kitten's cheek. She pressed her soft forehead into his palm, then craned her neck upward, her whiskers fluttering in the chilly wind.

"Princess, it's cold out here; why are you—" Cleophus murmured, while utterly ignorant of the baffled onlookers. The knight wasn't able to finish his thought as Pina nibbled on the tip of his nose and brushed her cheek against his after, her tiny paw pressing herself closer to him by using his beefy forearm.

Then she abruptly stopped and stared directly at Broghan, who blinked back at the familiar. She pushed off Cleophus's arm while still looking at his younger brother. She squinted as though she was glaring. The familiar then turned and trotted her way back into the keep, darting past Lady Nathalie, who remained in the doorway—Dana had retired to her chamber by then.

Not a word had been said, and yet it seemed as though the kitten had given her greatest fan a scathing reprimand.

Cleophus straightened gradually, looking utterly crestfallen. His shoulders hunched and his mouth twisted as though he were a little boy who'd just been abandoned by a friend.

The spell was broken when Cleophus's beady eyes snapped to his brother.

The giant stalked over to Broghan, and with a snarl that turned into a rumbling roar, he seized him by the back of the neck and dragged him from the courtyard while the young man yelped in protest.

Even Eric had no idea how to react. He looked to Faucher. "I might be a little rusty on understanding Troivackian punishments, but what does that mean?"

Faucher didn't reply. He merely let out a breath and faced his sons, who were looking at one another in equal confusion.

"Come, let us all have some supper. I think we will learn what becomes of the youngest Miller tomorrow. Will you be dining with us, Your Highness?"

Eric glanced at Sir Cas, who inclined himself in response.

"No. I better get back. I already missed a meeting this afternoon. Send a missive to my sister when Lady Katarina wakes up. Mr. Kraft will stay with her for the next week to help her with her magic." The prince started to make his way toward the keep with Faucher at his side—the Troivackian more than a little relieved that the Daxarian royal was leaving without having killed anyone.

"I will be sure to keep Her Majesty apprised of the lady's condition. Though I imagine Lady Katarina will be seeing the queen shortly. I informed the king this morning I am no longer going to be instructing her."

Eric rounded on Faucher, his head tilted over his left shoulder, his stare hard.

"I don't think so. Now more than ever, you owe her. You failed to protect Lady Katarina, Faucher. She stays with you whether you like it or not."

Shaking his head, the Troivackian responded firmly, "She is too large of a threat to my family."

"You don't abandon your students, Faucher. Especially when they've done nothing wrong. She was attacked and she shouldn't pay the price for it," Eric countered, showcasing that he was capable of making reasonable conversation pertaining to Katarina Ashowan at times.

Faucher felt his teeth set themselves on edge. "I'm doing this for her own good."

Eric laughed dryly. "You just said it was for *your* family. I don't think so, Faucher. Like it or not, you're in this now, and the only way you're getting out of it, is by seeing it through."

Without waiting to hear the military leader make any further arguments, the prince continued on into the keep. He didn't glance back, instead stowing his right hand in his pocket as he walked purposefully ahead.

Faucher looked to his sons, who had hung back. He could tell by their expressions that they had heard the entire exchange . . . and none of them had liked what they'd learned.

CHAPTER 24

EXTRA EDUCATION

My lady, are you sure you're alright?" Poppy wrung her hands.

"It's fine. I have to face everyone sooner or later." Kat sighed while fastening her leather wrist cuff. Despite her tumultuous day before, her injuries weren't fatal, and the noblewoman knew being bed bound would drive her mad in no time. So she prepared to return to her regular schedule immediately.

"L-Leader Faucher's sons are a little frightening . . . and they don't seem happy that you're here."

"Nonsense. They're thrilled!" Katarina looked at her maid, who was a heartbreaking portrait of desperate and terrified for her. "It'll be fine, Poppy. Once I figure out the Ashowan way we'll be thick as thieves in no time."

Poppy tilted her head curiously. "You keep saying that lately, my lady, but I'm not sure I understand."

Kat began tying back her long hair. "I'm not perfectly clear on it either. I keep thinking about what my da would do in my boots . . . but I can't do a lot of what he does. He starts magically cooking, or makes terrible puns, and whoever he's trying to win over usually becomes too busy watching him do things that they forget he's annoying."

The maid gingerly fiddled with her skirts. "You were plenty loved in Daxaria, my lady."

Kat shot Poppy an appreciative smile. "Well enough I suppose, but I'm an infamous hellion."

"To be honest, my lady, that is what makes you so interesting to be around. Your stories and how no one can guess what you'll think of next are unrivaled."

Kat turned to the young woman and paused as she took in her words.

"Thanks, Poppy. Gods, have I told you how much I missed you?"

The maid blushed. "Only seventeen times."

"Make it eighteen. I'm as happy as Faucher when I don't talk to him all morning." Kat pulled Poppy into a hug before leaning back and clasping her upper arms.

"My lady, I-I think Leader Faucher cares for you a great deal. To me . . . he simply seems stressed."

Kat absorbed this insight in thoughtful silence but couldn't bring herself to agree, so instead of responding, she settled for giving Poppy's arms an extra squeeze before turning to her chamber door and taking a steadying breath.

"Time to face the dragons."

Striding purposefully from her chamber, she made her way down to the banquet hall, though by the time she made it there, her nerves were thoroughly frayed from multiple servants having nearly bolted at the sight of her as she passed.

When she entered the banquet hall, she found Faucher, Lady Nathalie, Conrad, Piers, Dante, and Dana all seated and avoiding eye contact with each other, then Mr. Kraft and the air witch she had met when she'd rescued Eric—Celeste, who gave her a respectful nod in greeting. Of course there was also Joshua and Caleb, but the two of them were intent on picking through their breakfasts as quietly as possible.

Kat felt disappointment flicker to life in her chest when she realized Eric hadn't stayed . . . She was then reminded that he was most likely busy galivanting around with other noblewomen.

"Good morning, Lady Katarina!"

Startling her, Sir Cas's voice rang out behind the redhead, making her aura flare and her hand fly to her chest.

When she realized who it was, she let out a small groan and allowed her shoulders to slump forward.

"Morning, Sir Cas."

When Kat faced the room again, she was greeted by the sight of all the men save for Mr. Kraft and her fellow students on their feet with a weapon in hand.

For a moment, Kat winced and recoiled, but after dropping her gaze to the breakfast table, she cleared her throat and proceeded into the banquet hall while pretending not to be bothered.

"Morning, everyone. No need for the dramatic greeting."

Kat made a point of sitting at the end of the long table, several seats away from anyone.

Sir Cas, however, was having none of it and immediately sat on her right-hand side.

"Lady Katarina, did you rest well?" he asked with a warm smile.

"I . . . did. Yes. Thank you." Kat bobbed her head to the steward, who half threw her plate of breakfast at her before he fearfully retreated.

A beat of silence followed as Kat slowly plucked up her silverware.

"I'm sorry my dogs trampled you!" Dana's voice was unnaturally loud and succeeded in making her brothers, who had only just begun to sit back down, jump.

Kat looked to the youngest Faucher family member. At first, Dana looked like she was going to avert her eyes, but she pursed her lips and forced herself to hold the redhead's gaze with a nervous but firm nod.

"Oh, don't worry about that. Who could be mad at dogs that are so well trained?" Kat winked in both thanks and good humor, making Dana break out in a tentative, relieved smile.

"Lady Katarina, do you mind if I explain to everyone present why they shouldn't be afraid of you?" Mr. Kraft queried with a bow.

Kat blinked in confusion, then looked at Faucher. He seemed to be equally perplexed.

"I haven't said anything about it, as I have not had your consent to share the details of your magic," Mr. Kraft elaborated, while reaching for his napkin and wiping his mouth.

Lowering her chin in confirmation, Kat watched the man warily. He was treating her completely differently than before . . .

"Lady Katarina is not a threat to you if you do not bear her any ill will. It is one of the reasons His Highness was not afraid to approach her when she was in the throes of her . . . outburst," the coven leader began. "Her magic feeds off the aura or intentions of others. Witch or not. If you mean her no harm, her magic will not seek to consume. It only wishes to dominate what is directed against her."

Katarina was pointedly avoiding looking at everyone, but Mr. Kraft's explanation made her go still.

Eric was confident about approaching her when her magic controlled her . . .

The first time she had faced him in her magically enhanced state, she had kissed him.

Was that because—

"So she only attacked Broghan Miller because of how he felt about her?" Piers scoffed while twirling his fork.

"More or less. I imagine her magic had been feeding off his resentment for quite some time, and then it mixed poorly with her being in a life-threatening situation," Mr. Kraft continued calmly.

"Mind if I ask why you lot are all so angry with me?" Katarina blurted a little too loudly as she at last looked at the rest of the people present. "Troivackians are supposed to revere strength. Broghan Miller shoved me down a gorge and didn't give a shit if I died. If I'd simply beat him to death, no one would've cared and respected me for it. So . . . what the hell?"

Dante looked to his brothers with a raised eyebrow; Faucher let out his usual grunt.

Lady Nathalie leaned forward. "It was your inhuman strength. No one could overcome it. You even struck Gregory, and so my sons feel concerned at your presence. Especially how little we all know of witches here in Troivack."

"Well, I'm here to be an ally, not an enemy. Why are you all trying to change that?" Kat stared at the Faucher family men accusatorily.

No one could think of a response.

"Look, I *know* how terrifying my abilities are. That's why I've hidden them. I'm here with Faucher because, at the very least, I want to learn to control them. I want to protect people, not hurt them."

"It isn't just your magic though, is it?" Piers added while setting down his cutlery. "You are also the prince of Daxaria's intended, and you are under our family's protection. If we slip up or your magic hurts an innocent *once*, we will pay for it."

"Whoa-whoa-whoa, I'm not engaged to Eric." Kat balked, holding up her hands defensively.

Piers looked to Faucher. "She's powerful and stupid, Father. We can't let her stay here."

"But I'm not!" Kat interrupted fiercely, leaning forward to stare at Faucher's youngest son.

Everyone except Sir Cas rolled their eyes.

"Didn't you say she was beyond gifted with the sword?" Dante asked his father while pointedly ignoring Kat's exclamation.

"She is remarkable. See for yourself during our training," Faucher replied grimly while tearing into the chunk of bread that made up his breakfast.

Piers snorted, Dante continued eating as though nothing had transpired, and Conrad looked uneasy.

Katarina regarded Faucher desperately, but he didn't meet her stare.

Her teacher merely continued eating and, as a result, made her feel all the worse and even more out of place.

Kat stared glumly at her breakfast.

Sir Cas glanced at the Faucher family members angrily before he turned back to Kat. "You know . . . I'd not seen your familiar come out of your chamber before yesterday. She is as cute as ever."

Kat barely managed to lift a corner of her mouth. "Yeah. Adorable."

"What if you ask her to watch you train today?" Sir Cas asked while trying to add an extra level of cheer to his voice.

Kat gave a halfhearted chuckle. "She might. Though I think she's scared of the dogs."

"I can have the dogs stay in the south wing of the estate today!" Dana interjected eagerly.

Her brothers looked up in alarm. None of them had heard her speak so clearly or loudly before . . . and it had already happened twice in one sitting.

"What do you say, my lady? Should we have Piña Colada join us?" Sir Cas emanated warmth as he waited for the redhead's response.

At last, Katarina looked up and found her sorrowful mood lighten when she noted Sir Cas's and Dana's encouraging expressions. "Alright. I'll ask her."

Sir Cas's eyes twinkled happily at her response, and he returned his attention to his breakfast but not before smiling appreciatively at Dana, who blushed scarlet as a result.

The Faucher men straightened and glared daggers at Sir Cas, but the Daxarian knight had tucked into his breakfast and was quite oblivious to the multiple men he was causing a disturbance amongst.

Kat grunted as she showcased her attacks and defenses against her dummy.

Her irritation was unbridled as all three of Faucher's sons stood to the side and watched her train along with Sir Cas, Mr. Kraft, and Faucher himself.

When she had completed demonstrating the full extent of her knowledge, she turned to face them, snow continuing to fall gently around her, her golden eyes bright in the daylight.

Dante raised an eyebrow and looked to his father. Conrad was frowning but nodding silently to himself, while Piers continued to openly stare at Katarina with a calculative expression.

"You say she hasn't had any other training and has only received instruction while she's been here?" Dante questioned his father seriously.

"Aside from daggers and archery, that is correct."

"Daggers and archery?" Dante repeated in alarm. "Gods, the Daxarians really are a different breed."

"She's good," Piers interrupted without taking his gaze from Kat, who lifted her chin at the compliment.

"Better than good," Conrad added as he, too, turned to Dante.

"When her right foot is at the back, it becomes locked, which could make it problematic if her opponent tries to back her up," Dante continued conversationally.

"Agreed. She needs to spar more with Sir Cas, but I don't want Ball or Herra falling behind either," Faucher explained while looking over his shoulder to where his other two pupils were pretending not to watch Katarina's display.

"Well, if the well-being of our family rests on her being trained properly and quickly, then I suppose I can spare some time," Piers announced with a resigned shake of his head.

"Might as well. My ships aren't due to return for another three months," Conrad agreed while nodding to his younger brother.

Faucher looked to his two sons, his arms falling to his sides. "I didn't ask you to get involved."

"We are involved whether we like it or not," Dante pointed out coldly, his gaze moving once more to Kat's stubborn face. "I'll come a few days a week as well. The sooner we finish training Lady Katarina, the sooner she is out of our hair."

Conrad leaned forward to address the Daxarian knight then. "By the way . . . Sir Cas, when you are fighting her, are you swinging with your full strength?"

The knight bowed. "Not quite."

"If I might make a suggestion?" Mr. Kraft spoke up. "Lady Katarina's ability should allow her to overpower any of us, as we saw yesterday, but perhaps train her so that it is her last resort. Or, we can try having her use her abilities in small doses."

Kat blinked. Use her power in small doses? Was that possible? She had only ever been able to use any of it when she was desperate or beyond her human limits . . .

She started to open her mouth to speak, when something brushed past her ankle.

Glancing down, Kat found Pina peering up at her.

Breaking into a smile, the redhead bent down, stroking her familiar's cheek briefly before the growing kitten leapt nimbly up onto her shoulders.

Rising back up, she couldn't help but feel more emboldened by Pina's presence as her purrs rumbled around her neck.

The men had collectively stopped conversing and stared as Kat raised her arm to Pina so that she could rest her front paws on her forearm.

"I don't think any of you got a formal introduction. This here is Piña Colada. Pina for short without the fun accent. She's my familiar. Pina, say hello!" Kat couldn't stop grinning at the stricken looks she was receiving from the men.

The kitten closed her eyes slowly, the corners of her mouth appearing as though to be curling upward in a smile.

"Your familiar is . . . quite charming." Mr. Kraft cleared his throat.

"Of course she is." Kat turned and nuzzled the kitten's cheek and relished in the purrs that grew louder.

Sir Cas stepped over until he was within reach and tentatively offered his hand for Pina to sniff.

"Good to see you, Pina. Remember me?" The kitten's eyes opened as she leaned her face into Sir Cas's palm. "I'll take that as a yes."

The familiar carefully reached a paw out and rested it on Sir Cas's shoulder. The knight stilled himself as she crossed over to rest on his shoulders.

Kat laughed. "So you want to watch me work from his superior height, hm?"

The kitten nuzzled Sir Cas's cheek in response.

"Ashowan, come here. I'll show you why you need to work on your right foot," Faucher called out.

Kat bopped the tip of her finger against the freckle on Pina's nose and turned back to her teacher, already feeling leagues better than she had that morning.

After she had left the men and returned to the middle of the courtyard to spar with Faucher, Sir Cas walked back to Faucher's sons, who remained standing in line.

"Anyone want to pet the familiar?" he offered as the kitten peered up through the falling snow at the towering Troivackians.

Dante's eyes narrowed. "I don't like cats."

Conrad inched away. "I'm not sure about touching anything magically tied to a witch."

Piers snorted and didn't bother answering.

Mr. Kraft was the only one to reach out and allow Pina to smell his own hand. As she did so, she looked up at him, her pupils growing wide and making her even more adorable . . .

"Well, aren't you sweet," Mr. Kraft murmured as he continued petting the familiar, unaware that he was starting to smile . . .

Sir Cas grinned, then peered over his shoulder to where Kat was training.

Don't worry, Lady Katarina. Things are starting to change. Bit by bit . . . Just hold on a little longer.

CHAPTER 25

DEVIL AND DEMONS

Leo kicked over the wooden chair and glared. His breaths came out in plumes as his men moved in chests and firewood behind him. His ire was heavy in his chest as he glared at the humble surroundings.

"Was that really necessary?"

Swinging around, Leo stared at Sam, who stood reading their most recent missive from Duke Icarus, still wearing his heavy wool coat.

"I never wanted to come back here."

"Come now. It isn't all bad. I'm surprised the roof is in somewhat decent condition after all these years." Sam accepted a goblet from one of the mercenaries behind them. "Have some moonshine. It'll numb the chill until we start a fire."

"What the hell are those creatures doing all over Troivack? I thought you said they were superior beings that roamed the Forest of the Afterlife. Why are the Gods sending them here? Why now?"

Sam sighed. "I'm sure *that* meddlesome woman had something to do with it, and until I see them for myself, I can't know the reason they are here. They haven't attacked anyone as far as I'm aware."

"Then why are we hiding?" Leo snapped.

"With Duke Icarus now in court and the Daxarian prince making a successful escape, we need things to settle down again. I'll see if we can orchestrate another poisoning of Alina Devark, but the Troivackian king is being incredibly vigilant about his new bride . . . Makes me speculate that there may already be a future prince or princess planted in her belly."

Leo ran his hand through his hair. "Well, that's good. It might kill her."

"Mm," Sam answered ambiguously. "Tell me, have we figured out where they are hiding Lady Katarina? Did she leave with the former queen, Rebecca Devark?"

"No. The witch is with Leader Gregory Faucher, though we haven't been able to get any other information from anyone in the keep. It seems he's well prepared as always."

"What of the prince?" At last, Sam looked to Leo.

The mercenary flinched but tried to hide the fact by pretending to watch the men carrying in the rest of their things.

"Apparently, he is more or less doing the same things he always has, only now he seems to be courting every single woman in the entire castle."

Sam's lips curled upward coldly. "I see he's running from his feelings. No surprise there. It won't be long before he destroys himself completely."

"Master, what are we going to do about the house witch when he comes?" Leo asked suddenly.

Sam let out a long breath and at last turned to face his subordinate. "He won't have any magical abilities while here, and furthermore, odds are he is intent on removing his daughter from Troivack. Though, we'll see if he gets here before things go awry."

"Oh? Are we going to try and take Lady Katarina?" Leo straightened, his dark eyes eager.

"Not at all. It's bad enough I have ties of fate with her now . . . No, we will leave her be. She's in the middle of a storm, and it's only a matter of time before things come to a head. Right now, all we need to do is wait until she leaves, then we can go back to what we've always done."

"I thought you wanted to 'take care of' Lady Katarina because she might be able to kill you?" Leo's brows furrowed.

Sam closed his eyes and stretched his neck, as though weary from having had to converse for so long. "I've already figured out how her power works. I'm in no danger."

"What if . . . What if *that* woman is behind everything?"

The devil glanced at the men behind Leo, who were carrying trunks up to the second story. "It's possible . . . or all this is an incredible coincidence. Something I'm more likely to believe than *that* woman having a hand in all this. It doesn't benefit her." Ambling farther into the room, Sam placed the missive down on the table and seated himself. "No. All I'm hoping to do is keep an eye on Lady Katarina until she departs. I think she has served her purpose in my life as it pertains to a warning, so once she leaves Troivack, all will be as it should be again."

"What's the warning exactly? If you've already figured out how her magic works, then it isn't very effective," Leo mused while being forced to pick up the chair he had knocked over in order to sit across from his master.

"The Gods are warning me that they will create beings that can make my forced penance here on earth far more painful. They're going to keep giving witches abilities to possibly hinder my efforts, or they will send me someplace even worse."

Leo glanced over his shoulder briefly before dropping his voice. "A worse place? Like the Grove of Sorrows?"

Sam shrugged. "To me, the Grove of Sorrows holds little threat. I'm at peace with my decisions. My hand in murders and kidnappings—I've always given a less severe option, have I not? I have given countless people other choices to meet their objectives. *They're* the ones who will have to face the demons they've turned themselves into."

The devil began to remove his coat, his attention moving to the rafters. "It's remarkable your parents were able to keep this place so well tended even in their older years."

Leo's hands curled on the table.

"It wasn't all bad growing up here, Leo. Your mother and father were two truly decent humans. Don't let your experience with the villagers cloud that," Sam chastised while folding his arms.

Leo resisted growling. Ever since they had been chased from Vessa, he struggled to stay in control of his emotions. Sam knew it was a result of his wounded pride after facing a witch who was significantly more powerful than himself.

Pride once damaged often makes way for even worse demons. For now, it appears as anger and envy . . . We shall see if it turns to greed or not.

Sam's bored expression didn't shift despite the nature of his thoughts as he waited for Leochra Zephin, the boy who had been raised with him in that lifetime as a brother, to regain control of his emotions.

"What did Duke Icarus say?" Leo finally asked after cracking his neck.

"He says Her Majesty continues to support the nobles, and she is beginning to sway more of them. She is proving far more capable than he had anticipated. She hasn't mentioned bringing in the Coven of Aguas or making his bastard son a court mage yet. A wise move."

"Sending Lady Katarina away was an especially good idea," Leo added, his stormy mood calming.

"Mm-hmm. Though I'd feel more at ease knowing what she is doing at Gregory Faucher's keep. Double our efforts in trying to find out what is happening there, bribe a servant to quit if you must, or try poisoning a family member and offering a cure in exchange for the job. Send . . . what's his name . . ." Sam trailed off while pinching the bridge of his nose.

"What's wrong?" Leo stilled in his seat.

Sam didn't respond for a moment as he took in a deep breath of air. "Those blasted ties . . . They're really proving to be a nuisance. Lady Katarina's threads are pulled tight around me. This will be harder to ignore than I'd hoped."

"Do they make you want to kill her?" Leo queried interestedly.

Sam waved his hand dismissively. "Of course not. They make me want to be around her. The threads want me to stay close to her. I have to second-guess every instinct and choice I have for the foreseeable future."

Leo frowned in concern. "I can see about killing her—"

"Don't. Not unless you want to bring calamity to our doorstep. Even I can't fathom how to handle what would undoubtedly break over us," Sam warned, his gaze cutting to his subordinate ominously. "I'm serious, Leo. Stay clear of her. If she goes back to Daxaria, it should fix itself."

"Wouldn't attacking her give more reasons to send her back?" the mercenary mused hopefully.

Sam lifted his chin, and the chilly winter air around them turned even icier. Leo recoiled as he felt the familiar nightmarish fear fill him.

"I said no. That is the end of discussion. We will advise Duke Icarus on how to dethrone Her Majesty, but that is it. Am I clear?"

Leo's hands drifted to his lap as he attempted to hide their trembling. "Yes, master."

Sam continued staring at his subordinate, the room gradually filling with more and more shadows, until Leo broke out into a cold sweat.

"Good."

All at once, the ethereal chill and demonic shadows disappeared.

"Duke Icarus hasn't even begun to execute the idea I proposed at our last meeting. Give it time." Sam stood from his chair, his narrowed eyes watching Leo's pale face and hunched shivering shoulders dispassionately. "I'm going to retire for the evening. Have the men send up my dinner when it's finished. I'll be dining alone."

Then Sam drained his goblet and turned to the set of stairs that would lead to the second story of the small house where he had spent his one hundred and forty second boyhood.

He needed to try and gain control of the uncomfortable urges he was feeling to return to Vessa and survey Lady Katarina himself, and he didn't want Leo to see just how powerful the pull was.

Sam slipped his hands into his pockets as he mounted the stairs.

Why on earth did the Gods send a witch like Lady Katarina now of all times? It feels like I'm missing something . . .

". . . And after discussing the matter of the cold winter, they are trying to figure out what to do if it carries on for too long. It might lead to a firewood shortage, so whether we start recruiting men to go into the woods to start stockpiling wood to store now is being decided at the next meeting. Oh, and Lady Kezia had her child!" Lady Wynonna finished while topping up her goblet for the third time.

Katarina had her cheek smooshed against her palm until hearing the last bit of news from the Troivackian court, making her sit up with renewed vigor.

"Kezia had the baby?! Why in the world did you not lead with that! Is it a boy or a girl?!" the redhead demanded excitedly.

"Well, there were a great deal of notes Her Majesty wanted me to relay to you. Of course, once you study these, make sure you burn them as usual so that—" the widow started to ramble.

"Winnie! The baby! Tell me about how Kezia's doing!" Kat demanded while clasping the woman's arms to draw her attention back.

"Right. It's a boy! They named him Elio. Both he and Kezia are perfectly healthy and happy."

Kat beamed. "Gods, that's wonderful! How long ago was this?"

Lady Wynonna's unsteady gaze drifted across the room thoughtfully. "Less than a fortnight back?"

The redhead sighed. "Well . . . I'm sorry I missed it. Did Her Majesty attend to Kezia herself during the labor?"

"No, she was in a long council meeting at the time, and to be honest"— Wynonna leaned in closer and dropped her voice—"she's started getting morning sickness, so it was better that she avoided making herself ill."

Katarina winced as she thought of her poor friend having to pretend she wasn't going through her first pregnancy woes. Though she was glad the queen had decided to confide in her handmaidens about her condition.

"Well, I believe that is about everything I—Oh. I nearly forgot. I handed a sword His Highness Prince Eric Reyes sent with me to your maid when I first arrived." Lady Wynonna rose unsteadily and hesitated while trying to regain her balance.

"Oh, I . . . I thought I was going to retrieve the sword with the prince." Kat balked while blinking rapidly. A sharp pain in her chest made her want to hunch over her middle.

"Ah, he's been busy courting every available female under the castle roof. He even asked *me* for a cup of moonshine in Vessa . . ." Lady Wynonna shook her head with a smile. "Though I doubt he was being serious."

Katarina was finding it oddly hard to breathe just then.

"Well, I must be off. As always, it's been wonderful getting to see you." Lady Wynonna gave Katarina a wobbly curtsy, then turned her black shrouded figure to the chamber door and took her leave.

Swallowing with great difficulty, Katarina was reminded why she had been so reckless in the first place the day she had gone for a run with Broghan Miller. If she were to be honest with herself, she'd prefer getting shoved down a gorge twenty more times than have to hear how Eric was making his way through every eligible woman in the Troivackian court . . .

Biting down hard on her lip, Kat turned to where Pina lay napping.

"Come along. Might as well see what this sword looks like, hm?"

The familiar opened her eyes slowly, and, after giving a long yawn, she rose with a stretch.

Plucking up the kitten, Katarina was startled when Pina did something she hadn't ever done before—she licked her cheek.

Puzzled, it wasn't until the redhead realized that it was because she was crying that her familiar had done such a thing . . .

"Godsdamnit. No," she seethed, wiping her cheeks hastily while Pina leapt up onto her shoulder. "I am not going to let something as ridiculous as *that* make me upset."

Stomping out of her chamber, Katarina tried forcing her thoughts back to the happier news of Kezia, the most stunning creature to ever walk the earth, having her baby. However, this didn't last long before she began to pass by the entrance hall on her way back to the courtyard. She was compelled to stop, as there stood Broghan Miller, head hanging, while his brother—and a man she presumed to be his father—waited behind him.

"Ah, Lady Katarina, just in time. Now that you've finished with Lady Wynonna, we were hoping to talk about the punishment pertaining to Mr. Broghan Miller," Lady Nathalie called out to Kat from the entryway, Faucher at her side with his hands on his hips and glaring at Broghan.

Lady Nathalie's warm voice was soothing, as though she were trying to lessen the tension between everyone.

Meanwhile, Kat's heart hadn't fully slowed yet from hearing news about Eric, and when she stared at the young man before her who could've killed her . . . She hoped she could find a voice of reason somewhere in her being.

CHAPTER 26

THE PERFECT PUNISHMENT

Katarina sat in the solar with Lady Nathalie on her right and Faucher on her left.

Across from them, Broghan Miller sat with his face turned to his lap, and behind him, his father and brother stood.

Lord Milo Miller reminded Katarina of Prince Henry oddly enough. The man had smile lines around his eyes and mouth, though a pair of small round gold spectacles gave him more of a bookish appearance.

He was significantly shorter than his eldest son, Cleophus Miller, who stood beside his father with his thick arms crossed and his dark eyes narrowed.

"Lady Katarina, it has been decided that, in light of my son's recent offenses toward you, he be punished severely. He has come to offer you his apology," Lord Miller began seriously, his hands loosely clasped in front of him.

Katarina waited, her jaw flexing.

"He will never be permitted to take the knight's exam here in Troivack, and furthermore . . ." Milo Miller paused as he stared at the back of his son's downturned head.

There was a rare show of pure emotion on the elder noble's face that Katarina was not used to seeing on a Troivackian.

"His life is yours to take," the lord finished, his voice rasping.

Kat stiffened while Faucher grunted in approval at her side.

"But . . ." Lord Milo Miller continued. "I . . . beg of you. Please . . . Please don't kill my boy. He has behaved abysmally, and I cannot excuse it or offer proper recompense, but I—"

"Could all of you except Broghan Miller please leave the room?" Kat interrupted, her anger rattling around the deep recesses of her chest.

Everyone save for Broghan looked at her in stunned silence, but after Lady Nathalie and Faucher shared a brief look, they rose.

Lord Miller reached forward and clasped his son's shoulders, tears welling up in his eyes before he released him, and with halting steps made his way to the solar door with his eldest son trailing behind.

Kat gently tapped Lady Nathalie's forearm just as she was about to step away from the sofa, making her lean down, when the redhead beckoned her closer. After hearing Kat's whispered request, she raised an eyebrow but gave a small nod.

Faucher frowned at the odd exchange, but when his wife took her leave and addressed a servant waiting just outside the door, he joined the others in their departure.

The quiet emptiness of the solar settled heavily over the two nobles.

Kat continued observing Broghan as she eased back into her seat, folded her arms, and crossed her legs.

The young man trembled as he pushed himself off the sofa and onto his knees before her.

He then lowered himself even farther until he was on all fours.

"L-Lady Katarina Ashowan," he began, his breaths coming out unevenly. "For . . . For attacking you, I offer my deepest apology. I'm sorry for nearly killing you."

Kat lifted an eyebrow, then leaned forward so that her elbows rested on her knees.

"Why didn't you get help when I was knocked unconscious?"

"Your . . . Your magic was glowing when you fell, so . . . so I thought you'd be fine."

"That's not why." Even though Kat's voice was soft, it still carried every bit of acidity that would've come if she'd shouted.

Broghan Miller stilled on the floor, and there was a small *plipping* sound that alerted Kat to the fact that he was crying.

"I left you there because . . . because I'm a coward. I had only intended to haze you by shoving you in the river, and I only realized after pushing you that the river had disappeared. I didn't want to . . . to risk losing everything and be the one to shame my family."

"You already had lost it all when you saw what you'd done. Surely you—"

"I was terrified. Too terrified to . . . to think. It was bad enough when you kept besting all of us during training. I'm the one everyone expects the least of in my family . . . Cleophus isn't even my father's real son. He's my cousin we adopted when his parents died . . . but he's going to inherit the lord title."

"So that excuses Godsdamn murder?" Kat asked coldly.

Broghan broke down in a sob. "No. No, it doesn't. You just always seemed so . . . unstoppable."

Kat continued gazing down at the young man. She wanted to kick him in his ribs. She wanted to tell him he could rot in jail for all she cared . . .

This isn't the Ashowan way.

A light went on in Kat's mind, and all at once . . . everything suddenly became perfectly clear.

As though confirming this realization, a knock on the solar door had her rising and crossing over to find Lady Nathalie standing and holding the items she had requested.

Broghan Miller didn't know what was happening, but he heard clattering and the sound of something being poured.

"Drink."

He looked up blankly, his cheeks still damp from his tears, and noticed the goblet being offered that smelled distinctly of moonshine.

"I told you we would have a drink after that run."

Broghan stared up at her uncertainly.

She still was fearsome, her golden eyes bright and her features hardened, but he was not in a position to refuse, and so he took the drink from her.

Kat proceeded to cross her legs again and settle back into the couch. "I said drink."

The young man finished the moonshine in a single gulp and winced.

Katarina reached to the side of the sofa where the bottle sat on a small end table, plucked it up, and proceeded to fill his cup again.

"Sit over there." She nodded at the seat he had previously abandoned in order to grovel.

Hesitantly, Broghan made his way back onto the couch across from her, his posture awkward and his expression stricken.

Kat closed her eyes as she took a long drink from her own goblet, savoring it before she lowered the cup and once again looked to her peer.

"I'm not going to kill you. Or order to have you killed."

Broghan gasped and dropped his face to his free hand, succumbing to fresh tears.

"Oh Gods . . . thank you . . . thank you for your mercy. I swear I—"

"I'm not finished," Katarina interrupted airily.

He stopped his litany of gratitude, his eyes lifting to the redhead, who was starting to smile wolfishly . . .

"You're going to swear your life to serve me as my personal guard."

Broghan's face drained of color. "W-What?"

"You're going to serve me until the day one of us dies, and if I die first, you serve my next of kin. Your children will continue to serve my family until I release you. You're going to leave your family here in Troivack and come with me back to Daxaria to carry this on."

He couldn't say anything in response.

Katarina took the opportunity to finish her moonshine, then made a point of smacking her lips loudly.

She reached for the bottle and filled her cup again before looking back at the young man, her daunting smile still bright.

"So, Miller, still want to thank me?"

"It's been too long. Why hasn't either of them come out?" Faucher grumbled while he continued to stare at the closed solar door.

"I'm sure Lady Katarina is fine," Lady Nathalie soothed while glancing at Broghan Miller's brother and father.

"What did she want with a bottle of moonshine?" the military leader speculated next.

Unsure of the answer herself, Nathalie didn't bother trying to respond to him before she stepped over to the two Millers.

"I understand that this is a difficult time to wait, but perhaps we should—"

A shriek interrupted her, sending Faucher barreling into the solar in the blink of an eye with the others close behind.

The sight that greeted them, however, had the small group freezing in their tracks.

Lady Katarina was sprawled on the couch, laughing hysterically while Broghan Miller, completely disheveled, was swaying in his seat, a goblet loosely clasped in his hand as he stared at the redhead in open dread.

"Nooo! You can't be serious!" he slurred. "They . . . You mean . . . women just come up and . . . and can talk to you? All the time? Firsss' you say there's an earl named Dick Fuks . . . an' now—"

"What is the meaning of this?" Faucher bellowed, making his two students stare up at him blearily.

"Aah, Faucher! We're just getting to know each other better!" Katarina crowed, her magical aura flickering.

Faucher glanced at the empty moonshine bottle. "Are you drunk?"

"*He* is. It'd take a lot more than a shared bottle of moonshine to get *me* drunk," Kat informed him cheerily while pointing at Broghan.

"My lady, what is the punishment you've decided for my son?" Lord Milo Miller blurted before he could stop himself.

Faucher cast him a disapproving glare that made the man flinch, but Katarina sat up, then stood to face him, drawing her teacher's attention back to her.

"I've decided that your son is going to be my personal guard and serve me for the rest of his life. We can do a proper ceremony another day."

Faucher blinked in astonishment, though there wasn't any other indication of how he was feeling.

Sir Cleophus and Lord Miller, however, were an entirely different story. The two wore their reactions openly. Lord Miller was openly relieved and already beginning to weep, while Sir Cleophus almost seemed . . . envious . . .

"Lady Katarina, are you sure that is a wise idea?" Lady Nathalie asked seriously while moving forward with her eyes cast down.

Kat sighed and met Faucher's stare head on while responding to his wife. "I don't like the idea of killing people, and this way he makes up for hurting me for the rest of his life."

For a moment Katarina wondered if Faucher was fighting the urge to smile. The corners of his lips *were* twitching . . . Then again it was possible that he was resisting shouting at her in front of everyone. She decided to continue explaining the reasoning for her decision regardless of his reaction.

"This also means Broghan can be knighted in Daxaria and still train with us here at the keep. I mean, there's no point having a guard who can't even beat my father's friend Hannah . . ."

"Who is Hannah?" Broghan wondered while trying valiantly to uncross his eyes.

"Ah, my father's former kitchen aide, who is going to become the next head of housekeeping in the castle of Austice. She's infamous for nearly killing a man with a frying pan and possibly breaking the bones of a few other people," Kat recalled as her hands found their way to her hips.

"She sounds . . . wild." A small frown suddenly creased Broghan's face.

"Ah." Kat casually took a large step around the couch.

Faucher was about to ask her what she was doing, when Broghan Miller proceeded to vomit all over the solar floor.

"Unfortunate, but we've all been there." Katarina nodded sagely to herself while everyone else looked away.

Lady Nathalie turned swiftly toward the corridor. "I'm going to . . . to summon the maids."

Katarina tilted her head over her shoulder as she stared down at her new personal guard.

"Fish? For breakfast? I knew you were a bit strange, but—"

Sir Cleophus just about sprinted from the room. The mass of muscles that made up the knight had turned a threatening shade of green.

Even Faucher looked a little peaked.

Lord Miller was the only one to move toward the young man, who still swayed in his seat.

"Come, son. We'll take you home."

"Lord Miller, didn't you hear me?" Kat sidled around the sick on the floor to Broghan's other side. "He's going to stay here and become a better swordsman. Or, I swear to the Gods, I will add insult to injury and make him my *second* personal guard, and Pina will be the first."

The drunken man wasn't able to say anything as he struggled to stay in the land of the conscious, but that didn't faze the redhead. Instead, she looped her arm around his waist and tugged his arm around her neck.

"Come along. I'll dump you in your bed and laugh at you in the court-yard during training tomorrow morning."

At first Kat struggled to haul him onto his feet, and Lord Miller was about to offer his assistance again but was stopped when Katarina's aura flared back to life, allowing her to accomplish the task easily.

Once the two had staggered from the room, Lord Miller faced Faucher.

The military man had been uncharacteristically calm and quiet during the entire ordeal . . .

"Leader Faucher, I . . . I cannot thank you enough for the generosity you've shown my family." The lord bowed.

Faucher eyed him, his true thoughts unknown.

After another beat of silence, he clapped a hand on Lord Miller's shoulder and exited the solar without a second look back, leaving the nobleman to trail after him.

The reason for Faucher's stoic response was that he wasn't about to admit how he was more than a little impressed and proud of his student. Despite her justifiable anger and hurt over what Broghan Miller had done, she had chosen a wise and fitting punishment—one that showed the type of exemplary honor he had seen in her before.

Incredibly, Faucher was so surprised with the turn of events that he couldn't even find it in himself to be upset about the consumption of his moonshine or the vomit on his floor.

Though he had no doubt that it wouldn't be long before Lady Katarina had some snarky comment or antic that would dissolve his renewed regard for her, but . . . perhaps for a week or two, she might continue to stay on his good side.

CHAPTER 27

A BROTHERLY BARRAGE

Watch your back foot!"
"Move to the left!"
"You're going to lose a hand doing it like that!"
"Meeew!"

Katarina Ashowan's decision to have Broghan Miller continue studying with them at Faucher's keep had completely transformed the courtyard within a week.

Gone were the days of Kat training alone in her own corner of the space, as were the awkward tensions amongst them all.

Instead, her dummy was placed beside her fellow students, and she no longer only sparred with Faucher or Sir Cas but with everyone. Including Faucher's sons.

Even Pina had begun to join everyone at the training ring once Dana had succeeded in fencing the dogs in the south wing of the keep.

The familiar was, at present, perched on Dante's broad shoulders. She had been taking a languid nap until her witch had begun fighting against both Piers and Conrad.

Faucher paced around the sparring trio as Katarina continued fending off both Piers's and Conrad's attacks, then he stopped and stood beside his eldest son and Mr. Kraft. The coven leader's main job was to observe the appearances of her aura to discern precisely what it was attempting to consume when she was not warding off magical attacks.

"It's not normal," Dante murmured to his father as he watched the young woman continue to successfully keep his two younger brothers at bay.

"Hm?" Faucher responded, though his eyes never left his student.

"She knew nothing about swordsmanship, and in three months, she is good enough to fight against two opponents? *Trained* opponents?" the eldest of the Faucher children remarked seriously while reaching up to scratch Pina's cheek and earning a rumbling purr.

"You know she isn't human; it's been said many times," Mr. Kraft interjected, though he, too, refused to look anywhere else but at Katarina.

"Still."

No one said anything else for a stretch of time until, at last, Katarina dodged Conrad's attack and fell directly onto the sheathed point of Piers's dagger as his sword arm wrapped around her throat.

"Gotcha, witch," he uttered with a smug smile.

Conrad rolled his eyes at his brother's gloating while Katarina gave him a playful jab of her elbow into his ribs. "Only took you getting your big brother's help to finish me off, Baby Faucher."

Piers released her, allowing the redhead to use the back of her wrist to wipe the sweat rolling down her right temple.

"Ashowan! What did you do wrong?" Faucher hollered, drawing everyone's attention to him.

His sons were panting hard in the cold morning, but Lady Katarina . . . was fine. Aside, of course, from the steam that rose from the top of her head.

Kat shifted the wooden sword in her grip. "I let them overwhelm me."

"Do you know how you let them do that?" Faucher asked while taking Conrad's wooden sword.

Katarina frowned but didn't have time to think more on her answer before Faucher attacked her with a quick backhanded swipe of the sword toward her middle, making her jump back and clumsily block the assault. She continued defending herself from each of his stabs and slices that relentlessly flowed until Faucher's grip suddenly changed and he pulled the sword upward, the wooden blade of the weapon resting against her neck.

"You are training. Not winning. You need to end a fight as quickly and efficiently as possible. Stop thinking you need to practice showing off what you know. Start thinking about how you can use what you know to beat your opponent."

"She wasn't *trying* to win?!" Piers burst out behind them, his water flagon halting its journey to his mouth.

"She was trying to win fairly, but there are no fair fights in reality," Faucher replied, though his dark gaze didn't leave Kat's. When he spoke again, his voice lowered so that only she could hear. "You don't want to scare people away from you again, but this is the next necessary step. I held off having you fight with a real sword after everything that has happened, but it's time."

Katarina swallowed.

She looked at Broghan Miller, Caleb Herra, and Joshua Ball who were working on their own dummies.

They had only just started getting along . . . What if she lost control and they avoided her again?

Reading her thoughts easily, Faucher clasped her shoulder. "After lunch, get your sword, and we will begin sparring with real blades."

Kat hesitantly nodded. "Yes, sir."

"Good." Faucher turned back to face everyone in the courtyard, then frowned. "Is Sir Cas still not back yet?"

"No, Mother and Dana needed his help walking the dogs again," Conrad responded with a disapproving twist of his mouth.

He looked at Piers, who shared a similar expression.

Faucher took a deep, calming breath. "I'm sure everything is fine. Now, all of you head in."

The group gratefully made their way toward the weapons barrel save for Mr. Kraft and Dante.

"I can take Ms. Colada up to her chamber if you'd like to head to the banquet hall now," the Coven of Aguas leader offered while looking up at Faucher's eldest son.

Pina leaned her cheek against Dante's, and the man inadvertently smiled before giving her a peck on her whiskers. "She's fine where she is."

"I thought you didn't like cats, brother," Piers pointed out as he strutted by with his wooden sword casually resting against his shoulder.

"This one is different from other cats," Dante defended with narrowed eyes.

"Well of course, she's a princess." Kat stopped in front of Dante and gave her familiar even more scritches that made the kitten close her eyes and grin. "I just wish I could understand her like my father understands his own familiar."

"My sister understands her dogs perfectly well without having to converse with them. I wouldn't worry about it, Lady Katarina," Conrad remarked gently as he, too, stowed his practice sword in the weapons barrel.

"I know, but . . . who wouldn't want to hear what a sweet girl like this has to say?" Kat let her hand fall away from Pina's face and noted that Dante was smiling again.

She decided not to comment on it and instead relished in the knowledge that everyone in the past week had been notably happier. In fact, there had been more smiling than she'd seen anywhere in all of Troivack. Though she would've loved to take the credit, she had to admonish that it was most likely all due to Pina's regular outings.

With a sigh, Kat turned toward the keep and went along with the others. She wished she were half as charming as her familiar was, but . . . at the very least, the people who fell under Pina's infallible cuteness tended to treat her better as a result.

Hm . . . I wonder if that's why Pina has that ability in the first place . . . Maybe her role in my life is to help get me out of trouble.

The banquet hall was as noisy as ever as everyone talked amongst themselves. Katarina was listening with her fellow pupils to Joshua Ball attempt to tell a lewd joke despite stammering in her presence; Mr. Kraft was speaking with Piers; Dante with Conrad and his father; and last but far from least, Sir Cas, Lady Nathalie, and Dana conversed on the other end of the table.

Sir Cas was saying something to Dana that had her blushing and smiling, while Lady Nathalie nodded along in her usual dignified manner.

"What're you three talking about so closely?" Piers's loud question drew everyone's attention to both him and the trio he had addressed.

"Oh, we're just discussing Lady Dana's training with the dogs. She can make them do incredible things. A few of them can jump higher than I ever knew dogs were capable!" Sir Cas marveled, making the pink in Dana's cheeks turn crimson.

Piers glowered along with his brothers. "They're dogs. They aren't that impressive. As long as a mutt is loyal, that is all that matters."

"His Highness Prince Eric Reyes says if I can train them to track armies, he might be interested in my dogs!" Dana defended, her previously pleased expression notably dimmed.

Her three brothers turned to their father, who grimaced.

"You're going to let her get involved in the military?" Dante demanded.

"And with Daxaria?!" Piers added incredulously.

"We have not finished discussing it, Dana." Faucher didn't dare look at his daughter.

"You should see the dogs yourself, Faucher. I know I couldn't have imagined—"

Sir Cas began speaking, but the murderous stare Faucher gave him had the Daxarian knight falling silent.

Meanwhile, Dana's shoulders slumped forward dejectedly. "Excuse me, I . . . I'm finished."

Everyone fell silent as they watched the young woman hurriedly make her exit, and once her soft footsteps had faded away, they all looked at Faucher.

He didn't address any of them, however, and instead resumed eating his lunch.

"So . . . Sir Cas . . ." Piers started slowly, changing the subject. "Tell us about yourself. Our father says you're a gifted swordsman. One who has made Daxarian history by becoming the youngest elite knight in the kingdom."

Sir Cas bobbed his head. "That is true."

"Are you the son of a noble?" Dante queried next, his expression far less hostile than Piers's, but his tone was icier.

"Afraid not," the Daxarian knight answered shortly.

"Are you the son of a merchant?" Conrad steepled his hands over his lunch.

"Not that either," Sir Cas responded while gradually straightening in his seat. It was beginning to dawn on the knight that he was the subject of scrutiny amongst all the Faucher men present . . .

"Are you expecting us to guess?" Faucher's voice was gruff as he stabbed his pork chop with a notable amount of brutality.

"It's just not a pleasant story. I'm surprised anyone is interested. I thought Troivackians preferred to keep to themselves after all." Despite Sir Cas's innocent expression, Kat could see there was a defensiveness that was rising in his eyes.

"We like knowing who's in our house, eating at our table." Dante had stilled, and his dark eyes became fixed on the Daxarian.

"Well, I . . . I have five younger sisters. The two eldest are recently married, and—"

"What does your father do?" Conrad cut him off.

At that question, there was a dramatic shift in the knight, and it was the first time Katarina had seen Sir Cas look somewhat fearsome.

"I don't believe that is information that needs to be shared." His voice was even, but all pretense of friendliness had melted away from his eyes.

"It is if you're going to court our sister," Piers snapped angrily.

Sir Cas reared back in surprise, then looked at Faucher and then to Lady Nathalie.

"When was it decided I was going to court Lady Dana?" The shock of Piers's confrontation had brought back a more familiar light into Sir Cas's features.

"So you *don't* want to court our sister?" Conrad jumped in with a raised eyebrow.

"What's wrong with courting our sister? She's too good for you!" Piers threw his fork down with a clatter.

Sir Cas stared perplexedly at the three brothers.

He turned to Faucher, hoping for a voice of reason in the absurdity. Only Faucher stared right back at him and said, "Well?"

"I . . . cannot tell . . . if you *want* me to court Lady Dana . . . or if you *don't* want me to court Lady Dana . . ." Sir Cas began helplessly.

"What are *you* trying to do with her?!" Piers insisted, leaning closer, his chin jutting forward superiorly.

"I was just being friendly with—"

"Then you're leading our sister on? It's clear as day she is enamored with you, yet you keep indulging her." Dante seethed.

Sir Cas looked to Lady Nathalie, hoping for an ally, but the woman seemed strangely at peace with the situation unfolding.

"I . . . really . . . don't know . . . what I can say . . . that will allow me to leave this conversation." He inched away from the table as though faced with four hungry bears.

"In this situation, it's better to be honest. Or do you want to be like that coward Daxarian prince with Lady Katarina?" Piers growled while rising from his seat.

"Hey! Why was that—" Kat cried from the opposite side of the table, but Sir Cas raised his hands in surrender, cutting her off.

"Lady Dana is a lovely person. A smart, kind young woman, but she *is* young. I didn't want to avoid talking with her just because of how she seemed around me, because I thought it might be more hurtful if I did."

His answer succeeded in quieting the room for all of three breaths.

"Are you saying you want to parade around with other women until my sister is more mature for you?" Dante sprang to his feet followed by Conrad and Piers.

"Oh . . . dear . . . Gods," Sir Cas dropped his head to his hands.

"You should've just told them what your father does when you had the chance," Kat whispered down the table, only halfheartedly meaning for everyone to hear.

The knight shot her a weary, appreciative smile. "Alright, alright. I'll tell you a bit about my past, and perhaps then you'll all—Conrad, I didn't even see you bring the crossbow in here," Sir Cas observed flatly, while eyeing the small weapon that had appeared in the man's hands.

"Never hurts to have around," Conrad countered evenly.

"Unless you're the one getting shot at, that is," Sir Cas muttered, then looked up at Faucher. "My father is an infamous criminal in Daxaria. He is known as The Beast. He was hired to protect shady merchants and cargo. He loved my mum and all of us like crazy, but illegal work was all he'd ever known growing up in poverty. When he was arrested, I was only fourteen, and the former Captain Antonio and present Captain Taylor took me in and trained me. It's an even longer story of how that came to be, but . . . here we are. I earn a respectable living and support my family. My father might be released in another five years. So . . . I hope that answers your questions. I am lower than a commoner in origin."

No one moved or said a word.

Whatever story everyone had been expecting to hear from the endlessly upbeat knight, it hadn't been that.

"Now do you all see why it's absurd to think anything should or would happen between myself and Lady Dana?" he asked patiently, though he appeared to have aged five years in the span of a single meal.

The Faucher men half collapsed back into their seats, their former vigor seemingly stifled.

"Goodness, good looks and a tragic background where you overcame the odds with your own skill . . . I imagine you are *very* popular with women," Lady Nathalie noted casually.

The room exploded with fresh waves of accusations and questions, and Kat couldn't help but stare at the matriarch of the family with her jaw dropped.

She had thought Lady Nathalie to be the gentle sort . . . and even stranger still, she had thought that she *liked* Sir Cas. Shaking her head as Conrad wielded his crossbow and Sir Cas held up his pork chop as a shield, Katarina made a mental note to never underestimate or anger Lady Nathalie in the future.

CHAPTER 28

CUTTING IT CLOSE

Faucher had just finished begrudgingly ordering his sons not to attack Sir Cas in a misguided effort to keep him away from Dana. The Troivackian military man's mood was still bleak, however, as the unpleasant thought of his beloved daughter being married off and taken from him wedged a foothold in his mind.

As a result, he wasn't as aware of his surroundings as he normally was, and so he didn't hear the ruckus that was coming from outside until he was standing at the steps down to the courtyard.

What he saw had him setting off into a sprint.

"ASHOWAN! WHAT IN THE WORLD IS—"

"Easy! Herra, stop lunging! It's making it worse!" Kat called out while narrowly missing the swinging blade herself.

When Faucher had finally reached his students, they were all blissfully ignorant of his arrival, until he grabbed the back of Katarina's leather vest and hauled her backward so she could stare up into her teacher's livid gaze.

Her face drained of color, and then a tense smile gradually drew her lips taut. "Oh, hello, Faucher! Mind giving us a hand?"

"What the hell did you do?" the Troivackian demanded, his grip on the back of her vest tightening.

"Ah well . . . you see . . . Herra was saying he doubted that Lady Dana's dogs could be useful in the military, and I took exception on her behalf!" Kat announced defensively, her eyes flitting toward the sword that was waving around frantically.

Faucher didn't speak, only began to growl.

"Besides, how did you know it was me?" the redhead asked while blinking up innocently.

"I don't need to dignify that with an answer. You will get that sword off the dog's head by yourself." Faucher half threw Kat back toward his daughter's dog that had the handle of a short sword tied securely atop its head. He could tell the scabbard had been on the weapon initially but had been flung off during the mutt's excitement.

To make matters worse, the poor beastie was the excitable, friendly type that kept thinking everyone attempting to take off the weapon was either trying to play or wanted him to jump up on them for a good pet.

"Herra! Ball! Miller! Back to your dummies!" Faucher barked as the three students were unsuccessful at trying to grapple the dog.

Grateful, the young men started to retreat until Kat shot an accusatory glare at Broghan.

His head hung in defeat. "Sir, as Lady Katarina's new personal guard, I think I should—"

Broghan was cut off when Faucher dismissively waved his hand over his shoulder, signaling that he didn't care what his pupil chose to do. He was still earning himself back into Faucher's good graces after all . . .

The two began to sidle back up to the dog.

"Easy . . . easy . . ." Kat held up her hands toward the beast but eyed its wagging tail and tapping front paws warily.

Broghan was visibly sweating at her side.

"Still think dogs aren't useful in the military?" Kat couldn't help but ask with a grin as the two inched closer to the canine.

"This is only difficult because we can't kill Leader Faucher's pet," Broghan argued without allowing his sights to stray anywhere but the armed canine.

"Well . . . it'd make a hell of a—Shit!" Kat leapt to the side as the dog bounded straight for her, the sword aimed toward her abdomen. Sadly, the dog chased her new direction and nearly succeeded in stabbing her, but Broghan Miller took the opportunity presented and leapt onto the dog's back, wrapping his arms around its chest.

"Untie the sword! This beast is wriggling like a fish!" he ground out while Kat kept trying to inch her way to the dog's side only to have him whip his head back and forth delightedly to watch her.

"Can't get to him when his attention is on me! If you could—"

"What's going on here?" Dana's clear voice interrupted their exchange, her navy blue skirts hiked up in her hands as she bolted over to where Katarina and Broghan were manhandling one of her beloved dogs.

Thanks to hearing his master's voice, the dog squirmed away from

Broghan's hold, once again making Kat dance out of the way as the canine continued to bark and chase her.

"Why is there a sword on his head?!" Dana demanded breathlessly.

Neither Kat nor Broghan could answer, as they both were in the middle of trying not to get sliced by said dog, who was becoming even more excitable.

Dana clenched her hands into fists as she drew herself straight.

"PORK CHOP, SIT!"

The roar that exploded from the youngest Faucher resulted in both Katarina and Broghan sitting down where they stood along with the dog, whose name turned out to be Pork Chop.

From the opposite corner of the courtyard, the other men froze at the bellow that had come from the young woman.

She had sounded (incredibly enough) . . . like her father.

Stomping over to her dog, Dana set to untying the sword from his head as he sat obediently, his wide head lifted calmly as his master did her work.

Once the weapon was freed, she threw it down on the cobblestones and rounded on Broghan with a blazing fire in her eyes.

"Why did you do something like this to one of my dogs? He could've been hurt! You-You—"

"Dana, it was me. I'm sorry," Katarina interrupted while rising back up to her feet. "It was thoughtless . . . I hadn't meant for it to get so out of hand. I was just—"

Dana's attention snapped to the redhead, the ferocity in her face made Katarina halt her movements.

"Don't you *ever* touch my dogs, or so help me, I-I will sic them on your familiar!" Dana's chest heaved as she barely resisted going off on a tirade.

Kat held the young woman's gaze as she proceeded to bring herself up to her feet, her expression stony.

Dana was beginning to open her mouth to let loose another litany of curses, but Katarina stopped her by bowing.

"I'm sincerely sorry, Lady Dana. I had only meant to show the other students how brilliant your dogs are. I hadn't meant for things to become dangerous."

Swallowing with difficulty, Dana couldn't help but feel bitterness rise in her chest. Everyone was always thinking so little of her . . . treating her like a child . . . Well, if they thought she'd simply sit idly by while they put her dogs in danger, they were wrong!

"Lady Katarina, unless you are an absolute idiot, you just don't—"

"Oyy, what's that over there?" Piers unknowingly interrupted the start of his sister's chastisement.

Everyone looked up to where Piers was pointing toward the horizon.

There was something massive in the distance . . . and it was ambling its way closer.

"Gods." Mr. Kraft breathed, his eyes growing round as he stepped forward.

"What is it?" Faucher gawked at the hulking form that was larger than any animal or beast he had ever seen.

"That's . . . That's a stone golem. We've been studying them at the castle. This is the first time one has been seen so far south." Mr. Kraft looked toward Katarina Ashowan nervously.

"I thought all reports had indicated they were harmless." Faucher's voice dropped, preventing any of his sons or students from overhearing the question.

"That's true. No one has been harmed . . . even when a unit of soldiers from Norum attempted to capture one . . ."

Faucher regarded Mr. Kraft's apprehensive face, and after a moment, it dawned on him why the man was reacting as he was.

"You think Lady Katarina has something to do with this."

The Coven of Aguas leader's gaze flitted back to the Troivackian military leader, and he gave a slow nod.

Faucher took a deep inhale and turned to seize the short sword Katarina Ashowan's maid had brought down for her training that afternoon, which had been leaning against one of the benches.

It was the blade crafted by Theodore Phendor, the one that the redhead had become unexpectedly reticent about using.

Sword in hand, Faucher stalked over to where Kat stood watching the stone golem as it neared.

He thrust the scabbard in front of her face.

Blinking in surprise, the redhead looked at Faucher in confusion.

"Take it. We're on alert now. Dana, go back inside," he ordered while barely sparing his daughter a glance.

"Father, what is that?" the young woman asked, her former anger forgotten as she, too, couldn't move her attention from the strange creature.

"It's a stone golem. An ancient beast. Get back inside to your mother until either one of your brothers or I come to get you."

Dana pursed her lips, worry creasing a line between her eyebrows, before she turned to her newly disarmed dog, Pork Chop, and gave a short whistle that had him trotting after her eagerly.

She had made it perhaps halfway across the courtyard, when a blur from above dropped down and landed in front of her with a fluttering of a black cloak that rippled out like a splattering raindrop.

When the figure straightened before Dana, he revealed his long, pale purple hair and matching eyes with three pupils present in each eye. Even his height of seven feet was extraordinary, and it sufficiently caught everyone off guard.

The ethereal being stared at Dana, who stumbled back a step, making her dog growl protectively at her side.

"Hm, *you* aren't the burning witch . . ." The creature's pupils spun around in his eyes once, then he lifted his chin and smiled at Katarina Ashowan. "There you are."

Stretching out his arm, the otherworldly being started to press Dana to the side only to have Pork Chop lunge at his ankles.

The figure once again blurred.

No one could tell exactly if he had simply moved faster than they could see, or if he had disappeared altogether, but either way, he appeared again by Katarina, Faucher, and Broghan . . . with Dana clutched by her throat and held to his front with a knife's blade digging into her skin. Pork Chop was back in the center of the courtyard, looking around confusedly.

"Witch, you will be coming with me for—ARGH!"

Pork Chop hadn't been prepared to give up on saving his master just yet, and as a result had launched himself with great speed and agility, his teeth bared . . .

And sunk an impressive bite into the ethereal man's right buttock.

It was exactly the opening Faucher needed as he seized the intruder's wrist and thumb, and with a loud snap, wrenched his grip away from Dana's throat while Faucher's other hand gripped her shoulder and pulled her free.

The being's pain-stricken face flew back up toward Faucher, who was already pressing his daughter behind him, his own sword drawn. The intruder's pupils spun again, and suddenly Pork Chop . . . was gone.

Disappeared into thin air.

The ethereal man straightened.

"PORK CHOP!" Dana hollered from behind her father.

Faucher's grip on his sword handle tightened.

"Witch, you will come with me, or I will be forced to allow my friend to level this keep."

Kat still hadn't drawn her sword and instead found herself struggling with an inner debate of whether to release her magic full throttle . . .

"What even are you?" Broghan asked from the back of the group.

The being's eyes didn't bother shifting from Kat's. "I am an imp. Now, witch. I will not repeat myself, so—"

Faucher swung his sword, making the creature flit from view and reappear again, only this time, he had Katarina's arm clutched in his uninjured hand.

"Come, it won't be long."

"You're right about that much." Kat raged up at the imp, her aura flickering to life as she attempted to yank herself free from his grasp.

While the imp was pulled forward slightly, he didn't release her. Instead, he raised a bored eyebrow.

What was going on?

Katarina could feel her magic struggle against something . . . It felt like an invisible force was gradually winding its way around her aura . . . like it was snuffing it out . . .

"LADY KATARINA! HE'S BINDING YOU!" Mr. Kraft's shout made Kat look up in alarm.

"Binding me?" she asked in confusion.

The imp regarded the Coven of Aguas leader with a brief, impressed tilt of his head before he once again blurred away.

Katarina's world spun.

It was a whirl of colors and noises she couldn't fully make out, and she felt uncomfortably damp, but she could see her aura flickering around her. She felt her panic rising as she desperately allowed more and more of her power to leak out in hopes that she could break free from the dizzying wind she felt trapped in, but nothing seemed to work.

The spinning stopped just as abruptly as it had begun, but even though she was no longer in a flurry of magical movement, her vision still whirled, and she staggered when the imp released her arm.

"Ah, Lady Katarina, pleasure to finally meet you."

Kat gripped her head, and blinking warily, was able to see . . .

A man.

A normal-looking man.

With light brown hair that stuck up at odd angles, pale skin, and dark eyes . . .

If it weren't for his eyes, Kat would've assumed he was Daxarian.

What made this new person look out of the ordinary though, was his peculiar clothing. A forest green vest with gold buttons running up the far right side, buttoned over a snowy white tunic, all covered by a long, tailored green coat that matched his vest and cream-colored trousers. The most interesting thing of all, however, was that he had gold earrings pierced all the way up his left ear and a loose chain dangling from his right.

"My name is Ansar. I'm afraid we do not have much time, but if you could please stay still while I complete putting this on your wrists, that would be most appreciated."

Kat stumbled back when the man held up a long strip of grubby-looking material. It was dark green. Or was it gray?

"I've already cast the first of the spells on you; all that's left is to add the knot and—" Ansar had moved a step forward, but Kat had already taken the liberty of putting some distance between them.

"What the hell are you doing?" she said breathily while eyeing the imp, whose black pupils were whirling again.

"Binding you. This will be better for you in the long run. This way that pesky devil won't have any ties to you, and you can live on as a normal human. You've served your purpose in sending a message from the Gods." Ansar's tone was businesslike as he continued moving forward.

"Do you really think I'm just going to let you do that?!" Kat demanded, her hand gripping the hilt of her sword. She was so focused on the two strangers who had just abducted her that she didn't register that the handle was hot to the touch.

"Do you really want the devil, the first evil, the murderer of the first witch, to remain tied to you? Your loved ones are becoming ensnared, and he will destroy them as he sees fit," Ansar explained calmly as though they were discussing a fine meal they were about to enjoy.

"My da and his familiar can take care of him! I'm a witch, and you can't—"

"The familiar, Kraken the Emperor, is coming?" the imp interrupted, his pupils spinning even faster.

Kat stared at him sardonically. "Really? Kraken? That's who scares you? Not my father, who met the Gods?"

The imp didn't reply but shared an unreadable look with the man named Ansar.

"We have to stop *him* from arriving. We must go tell her—" The imp wasn't able to say more, as Ansar's gaze hardened.

He turned to Katarina, cloth in hand. "If you do not submit peacefully, then we will force you to surrender."

With another flurry, the imp was behind Kat. He wrapped his uninjured arm around her and gripped her to him, pinning her down.

Kat snarled as she tried to ignite her magic — and failed.

Ansar moved toward her briskly.

Kat's sword handle began to gently hum in her hand, and something in her *knew* it was her only way out of the mess. Neither the imp nor Ansar seemed to be aware of this happening, but as Kat realigned her grip on her weapon, she smiled.

"Fine! You're somehow stopping me from using magic, but you know what? Witch or not, I'm one annoying-ass woman with a sharp weapon!"

"You don't need to struggle, so —" Ansar's words were cut off as Kat fought against the imp's grip with every ounce of her remaining strength to draw her sword out, and amazingly . . . the moment the polished blade started to break free of the scabbard . . . it became easier to pull.

Sparks cracked in the air as Kat slid out her sword while loosing a frustrated roar as she battled the imp's strength. Her aura burst forward in an explosion, sending both the imp and Ansar flying backward.

The sword was free, and it was ringing in her hand right where it belonged.

Katarina looked at Ansar's shocked expression and flipped the sword in her hand, her vision slowly filling with golden light.

"Now, what was that about binding my magic?"

CHAPTER 29

A RELUCTANT RETURN

Sir Cas ducked under the golem's swinging arm, his sword stowed away in its scabbard—there was no use for it.

The magical figure was made completely of stone, with only two glowing orange eyes high above that were barely discernible under the moss and vines that draped over its body.

"CONRAD! FIRE AGAIN! I'M RUNNING TO YOU!" Faucher hollered while moving with impressive speed for a man his age.

His middle son reloaded his crossbow in record time and once again shot for the creature's eyes that followed Faucher as he approached, and yet again, the arrow fell to the ground as a thick ropey vine swung in front of its eyes, deterring the arrow's trajectory.

The golem had taken two steps into the courtyard, smashing the stones beneath its feet under its great weight, its head reaching above the keep's roof.

"Godsdamnit," Faucher huffed while the creature neared.

"It doesn't have any other weakness?!" Dante was half dragging Mr. Kraft over to his father, the witch's eyes were aglow as he searched the creature's magical prowess

"I-It's a creature of the earth—we'd need an air witch of some kind to subdue it, or an earth witch to bury it. Unfortunately, Celeste is back at the castle," the coven leader explained while watching and wincing as the golem flung back an arm and sent a corner of Faucher's keep crumbling down.

Sir Cas shouted up at the creature and managed to redirect its attention away from the keep.

"So we have no choice but to run?" Faucher asked while his eyes roved over the creature's being in hopes of finding another point of vulnerability.

"It's certainly looking that way."

"Then there is no point to any of this right now." The military leader's expression didn't change, but the grip on his sword handle tightened.

Piers jogged over to his father and brothers. Sir Cas was on his own to divert the golem's attention, though none of the Faucher family appeared bothered by the fact.

"What should we do about Lady Katarina?" Dante watched passively as Sir Cas barely leapt over the hand of the golem that attempted to grab him and somersaulted away.

Faucher took in a deep breath. "She has a sword. Between that and her magic, my guess is they'll have their hands full and she'll come running back here within the hour."

The group gave a unanimous silent nod amongst themselves.

"That imp was attempting to bind her abilities though!" Mr. Kraft burst out anxiously as another wall of Faucher's home was bashed down.

"Piers, did you make sure everyone evacuated the keep?"

"Yes, Father."

"Good. Mr. Kraft, what do you mean he was binding her abilities?" Faucher turned to address the witch once more.

"He had a thread . . . It wouldn't be visible to the rest of you, but he was already beginning to bind her powers. If the imp succeeded and was using some of the same cloth that bound the first witch before her death . . . Lady Katarina would no longer possess any of her magic." Mr. Kraft paused as he eyed Sir Cas darting between the golem's legs, drawing its focus back away from the keep. "Should you not be helping him?"

The men all looked to the blond knight for a moment. Sweat was pouring from his brow as he ran to and fro, his blue eyes steely as he played cat and mouse with the golem.

"If he dies, Dana might get weepy," Piers drawled.

"But maybe she'd mourn him forever, and we'd never have to worry about her getting married or courting ever again," Conrad mused ominously.

Mr. Kraft shot the younger man a fearful glance, then looked to Faucher desperately.

The leader of the Faucher family rolled his eyes, his reluctance painfully clear.

"Fine, fine. May as well see if we can save some of the keep."

The men were stepping forward to rejoin Sir Cas's attempts to subdue the golem, when suddenly, the beast turned and started stalking away . . . abandoning its former path of destruction.

Everyone stilled as they watched, mesmerized, as ripples in the air fluttered down its back, shifting about the golem until . . . it disappeared entirely. Neither the golem nor imp anywhere to be seen.

"What in the—"

"*Hell* is happening?!" Piers finished Conrad's exclamation.

Even Mr. Kraft stared in confusion.

Their baffled awe was interrupted, however, by a familiar bright light surging toward them.

"Ah, there she is," Faucher observed while Sir Cas made his way back to the group. "Mr. Kraft, is her magic consuming her awareness?"

The coven leader squinted and raised his hand up to shield his eyes from the dim sunlight that had brightened the sky. "Close, but not quite . . ." He blinked and dropped his hand from his face. "Faucher, did you say that her sword was a true piece of Theodore Phendor's?"

"I did."

Mr. Kraft said nothing else as Lady Katarina reached the destroyed courtyard. As she slowed to a walk, looking every bit the wrathful demon she had been rumored to be, her aura gradually reduced until she stood in front of the men without a hint of a glow; her eyes were the last to fade back to normal.

"Hi, everyone," she greeted casually. They gave various grunts and nods in acknowledgement while also attempting to peer around her in the direction the golem had departed.

Mr. Kraft stared incredulously at her then at the Faucher men. "Why are all of you responding so damn calmly?!"

"We're not calm," Piers replied breezily. "I'm about to soil these pants. Godsdamnit, Father. What. Is. Going. ON?!" He rounded on his father, his formerly blasé façade having dissipated.

Faucher let out a guttural sigh while closing his eyes and shaking his head.

He didn't respond to his son but instead addressed Lady Katarina.

"Are you hurt?"

Kat pondered the question for a moment. "No. Just tired."

"You looked like you were having problems with your magic," Faucher observed evenly.

She shrugged. "I had a sword, didn't I?"

A twitch that hinted at a smile teased the corners of the military leader's lips.

"This attack happened because of you. Why?" Piers interjected, brandishing a finger at the redhead, his brows lowered.

Kat looked to Faucher, who gave a small shake of his head.

"We are not permitted to discuss these matters," Faucher admonished, though he sounded utterly exhausted when he did so.

By that time, Sir Cas had joined the group, and while he was no longer panting, he was still coated in sweat and dust from the keep's destroyed walls.

"Thanks for the support out there," he interrupted dryly.

"You had it in hand well enough. We had to convene to figure out if there was another way to attack it." Conrad gave an innocent shrug. Apparently, his conscience felt perfectly clean.

Sir Cas scowled at him before he regarded Kat. "What happened after the imp took you?"

Kat glanced at Faucher, then smiled apologetically to the Daxarian knight. "Sorry, Sir Cas. I don't think I'm supposed to talk about that either. Faucher, do we have to go see the king now?"

Her teacher sheathed his sword and rounded toward the entrance of his partially demolished keep. "We do. Ashowan, follow me."

As he stalked up the steps, Katarina hesitantly followed but was forced to stop in her tracks as Faucher paused at the top and turned back around to face his angry sons.

"All of you. Dress for court and go find the rest of my students, your mother, and Dana. I think we're all going to be spending quite a bit of time at the castle, starting today."

Katarina stood outside the doors to the throne room, her heart racing. Her gloved hands were already sweaty, and she was fighting the urge to pace.

Caleb Herra, Joshua Ball, and Broghan Miller weren't in much better condition.

The four of them wore uniforms that marked them as Faucher's students—it was proof that Faucher was one of the highest ranked military men and, therefore, entitled to bestow a symbol of esteem to his protégés.

The uniform was a pale blue vest over a white tunic—each was fitted with a chest plate—brown trousers, and boots. Over their right shoulders were royal blue capes pinned over their left shoulders with silver brooches that bore detailed designs unique to Faucher's family. In addition to the uniforms, they, unlike other squires in training, were permitted to carry real swords into the castle once they had been dubbed skilled enough to do so.

Of the four students, only Katarina Ashowan carried a sword at her side.

She was to follow Faucher and his sons into the throne room, leading her peers in front of the nobilities. This marked her as the top of her class.

"H-How did it come to this? It's eight days until the full moon! Why now of all times . . . ?!" Joshua Ball moaned while scratching his head incessantly.

"Turns out, the golem attack was a bit more noticeable than we'd hoped," Broghan noted while leaning against the marble corridor walls.

"That nosy neighbor of Faucher's summoned the knights almost instantly," Caleb added with a disparaging grimace.

"I heard your prince was looking for you again when the knights came to investigate the grounds." Broghan shot a small smirk at Katarina, whose eyes narrowed in response. "But you were off changing."

"Of course he came to check on me. He would have to be the one to tell my da if I was crushed to death by a magic rock-man," she snapped back irritably.

Both Broghan and Caleb rolled their eyes knowingly.

"Stop that, or I'll make the entire Faucher family think that the two of *you* are interested in Dana as well." Kat bore down on the young men, who merely guffawed at her threat.

The redhead growled.

"Ashowan! At attention! Herra, Ball, and Miller, side by side behind her." Faucher's voice boomed from down the hall, making his students nearly leap out of their skins.

The military leader was clad in his official polished armor and maroon cape. His three sons were in a similar state of dress, save for the cape, and all wore matching strained expressions as they trailed behind their father.

Once Faucher reached his students, he stood before them with his shoulders straight and his chin lifted.

"I know none of us were prepared for this happening now, but here it is. Mr. Ball, you have good reason to be concerned, as your brother has had no idea you've been training with me all this time, but you will remain under my protection in this castle while we are here, and I will hide you elsewhere if need be. Mr. Herra, remember to play your cards close to your chest and avoid your own brother best you can. Mr. Miller . . . bear your punishment bestowed from Lady Katarina with dignity should it come to light. You're alive, and you should remember to be grateful for that."

The three young men stood with bowed heads. Faucher's blunt tone barely inflected at all.

"Lady Katarina"—Faucher's hard gaze softened for a fraction of a moment—"while I'd hoped we'd have more time before throwing you into this den of wolves, we'll turn it into an opportunity. At the very least, you have learned enough, if not more than I'd hoped you would, before we were forced to return to the castle. You no longer are the fidgeting, undisciplined, directionless, troublemaker you once were. You are a swordsman. You have honor, purpose, and training. You will conduct yourself with the dignity and respect you are owed while keeping in mind that you are a dangerous individual, and that comes with responsibility."

Katarina felt her cheeks burn.

She never in her life would've thought Faucher capable of breathing a kind word to her.

Even if he was saying these things to stop all of them from upchucking their lunches . . .

She could tell he meant every word.

"Are we going to pretend she *didn't* tie a sword to a dog's head this afternoon then?" Piers interrupted from behind his father.

Faucher gave him an acid glare over his shoulder, but the youngest Faucher son smiled back, nonplussed.

The military leader turned to face his students again, though this time, the shadow of uncertainty in his face made them simultaneously grow nervous again but also more attentive to his next words.

"You have been brave during our time together. You have worked hard day and night and have overcome not only physical shortcomings but also character faults that are not easy to admit, let alone improve upon. Keep your heads high no matter what is said, no matter how they look at you. You will show you are proud to be my students, and if anyone tries to say otherwise . . ."

Faucher trailed off, and his lips curled upward frighteningly.

"You make them regret it." Dante's cold voice pierced through his father's students, and at the same time, helped harden their hearts against their individual gut-clenching fears.

Faucher nodded, locking eyes with each of his students briefly before turning around, stepping past his sons, and facing the throne room doors.

Only when he stood alone at the head of the entourage with nothing but the iron doors in front of him did the military leader reveal the true depth of his apprehensiveness. He was terrified of what was happening in his homeland . . . around his family . . . Magical beasts? The devil? His daughter being interested in a man?

It was all horrifying.

But . . .

Dante pounded on the doors, and with a loud, echoing creak, they began to open.

I've survived this long, and at least I know Katarina Ashowan is almost ready for what comes next . . .

CHAPTER 30

NETTLING NERVES

The throne room was completely silent despite there being at least two hundred nobles and guards present.

Everyone was wrapped in their warmest furs and thickest wool; the large room was especially cold in the winter evening.

Alina and Brendan sat on their thrones, both looking as regal as ever. Alina's hair that was turning more brown than blond in the darker months was braided over her right shoulder. She wore a black fur cape that kept her warm, along with a long sleeve dark plum colored dress. Her husband, as per the norm, was clad from head to toe in black.

As Faucher marched into the throne room, his head held high and his expression fierce, he looked at no one.

At first everyone merely watched the familiar sight as one of the highest ranked and most respected military men in Troivack made his way across the marble floor. Then came his three sons, shoulder to shoulder as they, too, walked in. That was a little out of the ordinary, but when they saw who came next, well . . . a flurry of whispers and exclamations whirled into existence.

Katarina Ashowan strode forward alone, her chest plate and sword gleaming in the cool light of the room along with her golden eyes. Her hair was in a high ponytail as she followed the Faucher men down the aisle of the throne room without looking at anyone.

Already astonished to see her not only dressed as a man, and armed, what really drove the nobility into a fervor was the fact that she was leading the other students . . . and it suited her.

There wasn't the restless energy around her that there had been when she'd been at court, or the smiling mischievousness that had put many of them off her company. Instead, there was a serious focus in her eyes and militaristic purpose in her walk that made them struggle to disparage her presence entirely.

When they reached the throne, Faucher stomped his final step, signaling those behind him to do the same.

Then, in perfect unison, they all lowered themselves down to one knee before the king and queen.

"Your Majesties, I, Leader Gregory Faucher of the first rank, greet you."

"Leader Faucher, I was told there was a magical beast sighting at your keep this morning." Brendan's low voice rang out.

"Yes, Your Majesty."

A panicked flutter ran through the room.

"Was anyone harmed?" The king's volume increased, calming the brief interruption.

"Fortunately, no, Your Majesty."

"Did you kill the beast?"

Many people present held their breaths, terrified of the answer.

"The beast disappeared before we could, sire," Faucher replied after a moment. He knew to dread the reaction to such an inconclusive result.

Sure enough, no one could contain their fearful exclamations and desperate discussions.

Brendan held up his hand, and miraculously, the room once again settled down.

"This is alarming news, but I'm sure during this unexpected fight, you have learned about the beast so that we might better prepare for its return. Am I right, Leader Faucher?"

"We *have* learned a great deal about the beast. I will be happy to give you my observations and notes in my formal report, Your Majesty."

The king nodded. "Excellent. We will be discussing this in detail at the council meeting tomorrow morning. For now, you all must be tired. I understand damage was sustained at your keep, Leader Faucher. Therefore, your family and students are welcome to remain here in the castle until the necessary repairs are completed."

"Thank you for your generosity, sire."

"You are dismissed, Leader Faucher. Thank you for coming so swiftly."

"Of course, Your Majesty."

With another deep bow of his head, the military leader rose to his feet, and after a sharp turn, his sons and students parted to create an aisle for him to walk back toward the doors of the throne room. After his echoing steps passed them, they followed Faucher in the order in which they had first arrived.

None of them had spared a glance at any of the nobility, who continued to watch in awe and interest as Faucher, his sons, and his students left with their footfalls in perfect unison.

The quiet that followed their departure was not destined to last.

As soon as the doors closed behind the last of Faucher's students, the nobility exploded once more in anxious talks, questions, and not least of all . . . outrage over the presence of Katarina Ashowan as a student of one of their highest ranking military men in the entire kingdom of Troivack.

Katarina sat with her arms crossed in the servants' dining hall which was empty save for her peers. It was just past the dinner hour, and their chambers had not yet been prepared.

The four of them had tried to remain as inconspicuous as possible, all aware that Katarina revealing herself as she did would most likely result in irate nobles. Or in the case of Caleb and Joshua, irate brothers who also happened to be nobles.

The air was heavy, and the only light came from the flickering torches on the walls.

Katarina's index finger was tapping restlessly against her left fist, her glowing eyes lost in thought as she stared blankly at the wall before her while seated on one of the benches.

Caleb, Joshua, and Broghan glanced at each other somberly.

They had all settled easily into their fears.

"Good Gods, you'd think someone died." The loud voice belonging to Piers Faucher called out to them all from the entrance to the hall, making the students turn with a small startle.

The youngest of Faucher's sons strolled in with his usual swagger, though in his arms were three bottles of moonshine. Behind him came Conrad and Dante carrying similar cargo, though Dante also clasped goblets.

"We're holding an early funeral," Broghan replied grimly.

"Oh? Whose?" Piers asked while setting down the bottles on the rough wooden table Katarina was seated at with her back turned.

"Ours," Joshua responded while dragging his feet over to a bench.

"Ah . . . to be young and dramatic." Piers tsked while uncorking one of the bottles and pouring its contents into the goblets his eldest brother had set down.

"If it's youth that gets to be dramatic, what's your excuse?" Dante asked his brother dryly.

Piers waved off the jibe, then slipped his free hand into his pocket as he continued filling the cups.

"We weren't being dramatic. We really might die," Broghan interjected while stepping over the bench to seat himself down on Katarina's left-hand side.

"My brother didn't know I was training," Joshua confessed weakly while sitting on Katarina's right side. His eyes went wide as he imagined the untold horrors that awaited him after his older sibling sought him out.

"Neither did mine. He's already tried to kill me once," Herra added gruffly as he, too, sat on the bench, farther down.

It was the first the young man had ever admitted knowledge of the attempted fratricide . . .

"The other knights may try to kill me just for becoming sworn to Lady Katarina, and my brother still hasn't forgiven me for making her cat hate him. He's trying to manage his rage by staying busy . . . I've never seen him train so hard in all my life," Broghan recounted with a note of awe in his voice.

"I don't think I need to say why people might feel violent toward me," Kat supplied while turning to face the three Faucher sons, who now sat across from the students.

"Well, you're the least likely to die given your status as a foreign noble, if that's any help," Dante informed her bluntly.

"Yeah. It's not," she replied flatly while meeting his gaze. "If I've peeved off too many people, things will be horrible for Alina—I mean, the queen. Even if I can disappear back home, I don't want to leave her in a bad position."

"Regardless of when you revealed what you were doing, it would've been bad," Piers pointed out while handing out the goblets to everyone present.

"I disagree, brother. With the magical creature being revealed first, people will blame her somehow. It's the perfect way to test Her Majesty and put her in her place given Lady Katarina's close relationship with her," Dante argued unabashedly. He didn't seem to care if he contributed to the sinking mood of those around him.

Conrad noticed, however, and so cleared his throat as he raised his goblet.

"One day, one battle at a time. It's what our mother used to tell us when things got rough," he explained. As usual for the middle Faucher son, he didn't fully raise his eyes, his timid nature as present as ever.

"That's right," Piers chimed in while shooting his eldest brother an exasperated glare that Dante didn't bother acknowledging as he, too, leaned forward to grasp his goblet. "You all walked into that throne room proudly and represented our father well. Cheers!"

Everyone gradually picked up their goblets and toasted, albeit laboriously.

Katarina drained the entire drink in a single go and set the cup down with a long exhale.

"At last. I don't have to beg for moonshine," she admonished halfheartedly.

"Well, you've earned it." Piers nodded encouragingly. "Honestly, you're a hell of a swordsman . . . woman? Swordswoman? Anyway, you're the best student I've ever seen my father work with. No offense to the rest of you."

"None taken," Herra grunted while taking another gulp from his own cup. "I knew after our first spar she was in another realm entirely."

"Is that why you kept referring to her as a goddess?" Joshua asked, his cheeks already pink from the moonshine.

Herra sat up straight, his expression livelier than anyone had ever seen it as he stared in mortification at his fellow student.

A beat of silence rested over the group.

That is . . . until a slow smile spread across Piers's face.

"A 'goddess,' Herra? My, my. I didn't know there was such a crush between you."

"Leave him be," Dante warned his brother without bothering to look at Herra, whose entire bald head was blushing scarlet.

Katarina was momentarily taken aback, and as a result dropped her gaze to her cup where she dug her thumbnail into its side.

"It isn't like that," Herra managed, though his voice rasped. "I just . . . She's . . . impressive. That's all." He cleared his throat awkwardly and downed the rest of his moonshine.

Conrad was kind enough to fill up both Herra's and Katarina's cups again.

"You know, Piers, you remind me of my father's friend Lord Harris. He never knows when to shut his mouth either."

Everyone smiled at Kat's insult save for Piers, who regarded the redhead coyly and folded his arms over his chest.

"Well, someone has to air the dirty laundry. Speaking of, you didn't happen to notice the prince at the meeting today, did you?"

Katarina scowled at Piers.

"Let it rest for today, hm?" Dante ordered his brother while shooting him an unimpressed sidelong glare.

"Now where's the fun in that? Lady Katarina, is it that you have a sweetheart back home that you're saving yourself for?" Piers asked with glittering eyes.

"You know, from what I've heard about your own marriage, I'd think you should be giving *that* more thought than my love life," Kat bit back while once again finishing her cup of moonshine with ease and earning brief looks of impressed approval by everyone present.

Piers raised an eyebrow in her direction. "I don't need to give it much thought. Nicole and I are passionate. We fight and we love intensely. She's never dull, and that's exactly how I like it."

"Gods, you and Lord Harris could be brothers. Last time he and his wife fought, it was at our keep . . . The cows only just started recovering from the stress last spring," Kat recalled as the echoes of those terrifying days sounded off in her mind.

"What . . . cows? What did they do to the cows?" Joshua Ball queried nervously while glancing at everyone around the table to see if anyone else was confused. He was heartened to see he was in good company.

"It's best left unsaid to be honest." Kat sighed. "I mean . . . it did give my mother the excuse she was looking for to redecorate when they had to repair the fire damage."

"Alright, now you're full of it. You're just exaggerating the event to make us curious, aren't you?" Piers scoffed.

"I'm not! One day if you ever visit Daxaria, I'll make sure you hear from the multiple eyewitnesses," Kat assured him with half a laugh.

Piers blinked at her confident attitude before letting out a slow breath of air.

"Well, if it *does* turn out to be true, I'm going to be competitive and pick an even bigger fight than this Lord Harris person with Nicole. You say they traumatized cattle? We could petrify the chickens, the horses, set fire to an entire wing of the keep—"

"Their children were present, so the fight was a bit more reined in for them . . . Though I might have to implore you, if you are going to compete with their infamy, do it in someone else's home. Perhaps in the castle with Prince Eric. I don't think he'll care as much if a tower or two gets destroyed," Kat interjected while the others around the table began to laugh.

"Oh, I don't know. I might have a thing or two to say about destroying my castle."

Everyone jumped to their feet and turned to see Eric Reyes himself, his arms crossed and his shoulder pressed to the doorframe of the banquet hall.

"Coins on the table." After a beat of stunned silence, Herra's blunt voice drew everyone's attention back to him as he stared at the three Faucher sons.

Conrad reluctantly passed him an entire bottle of moonshine and a single silver coin.

Eric, meanwhile, was making his way over to the group.

"Do I want to know?" Kat whispered to everyone with a keen sense of foreboding.

"They bet His Highness would try and find you during dinner. We bet he'd wait so that he could do it in secret," Broghan supplied as he plucked up his own supposed trophy bottle of moonshine and coin while gazing at it lovingly.

"Tomorrow . . . I'm going to beat *all of you* into the courtyard stones," she hissed under her breath.

"Now, now." Piers looked over at the redhead just as Eric reached them. "All is fair in love and war."

CHAPTER 31

STORY TIME

Do . . . do you really not have anyone you're keen on?" Joshua Ball hiccupped as he and Kat sat apart from the others who were drinking and carousing amongst themselves.

After Eric had joined them, Sirs Vohn and Cas had come, and next thing they knew, they were having a small party in the middle of the night in the servants' banquet hall.

Unsurprisingly, Joshua Ball proved to be the one with the weakest alcohol tolerance amongst them, and so Katarina decided she'd keep him company . . . especially as it aided her in avoiding Eric.

Ever since she had learned about his courting dates and that he had gone to retrieve her sword from the blacksmith without her—anytime she thought of him really—she developed horrible nausea that made her feel like everything was wrong in the world.

She chose not to think about why that was.

Kat looked at Joshua with a half smile before ruffling his hair. "I'm free as a bird. No possible husbands for me."

The young man twisted his mouth as his glassy eyes moved over to where Eric was talking with Conrad.

"Honestly, you lot need to let that go. He's been busy courting everyone he can speak to here in the castle." Kat tried to sound good-naturedly, but there was a faint croak in her voice that betrayed her.

"You both love each other, and no one knows why you aren't with each other," Joshua mused aloud unabashedly.

Kat flinched as she downed her eleventh cup of moonshine.

"Ah . . . that was probably inappropriate." Joshua swayed in his seat. "So . . . are the stories about you all true?"

Grateful for the change in topic, Kat reached for the nearest bottle and refilled her cup. "Which stories are you thinking of?"

"Well . . . there's the one about you setting goats and a pig loose in the king's castle."

"Okay, it was not multiple goats. It was one goat. And . . . three piglets, and maybe one or two chickens."

"W-Why?"

"I was trying to prove to Alina that they could make suitable pets. She was worried about dogs or cats because of their fur. Then she didn't want a nice songbird because she worried it would defecate all over her chamber, so I was showing her alternatives. I was trying to point out that the chickens wouldn't be able to fly high enough that she'd have to worry about them showering her chamber with poop, but . . . I . . . erm . . . didn't know they actually *could* fly quite a bit higher than I realized . . ."

Kat busied herself with taking a drink from her goblet.

Joshua Ball howled with laughter.

"What about the story of the runaway ale barrels?" Sir Vohn joined the discussion interestedly while swinging his legs over the bench across from Kat and seating himself.

"Ah, that one was only partially my fault," she said while she swirled the contents of her cup with one hand, her other resting in the crook of her elbow. "You see, my da was visiting some of the businesses he invests in, and one of them was getting an ale delivery while I waited outside. I didn't know the delivery man had already untied the barrels and had begun unloading them when I offered his horse an apple from my lunch."

Sir Vohn smiled but with confusion, unsure of how the two correlated.

"Well, the horse lurched forward, and this particular establishment was on a hill . . ."

Sir Vohn let out a laugh of disbelief. "How many ale barrels did you send rolling down the streets of Austice?"

Kat stuck her tongue in her cheek as she feigned recalling the details. "Two . . . maybe three . . ."

Sir Vohn chortled again. "Thank the Gods no one was hurt."

"That is the one area I do seem to be quite lucky in. Whatever trouble I find myself in, I don't actually end up hurting people . . . unless they deserve it."

"Is it true you punched a noblewoman in the face and gave her a black eye?" Sir Cas joined the discussion, looking relatively inebriated himself.

Kat drank again, her eyes moving to the ceiling as she delayed her answer.

"She was defending her brother and family honor at the time if I remember correctly what her father told me." Eric stepped closer and eyed the two knights seated across from Kat.

The redhead met the prince's eyes only briefly before needing to look away. She was getting that horrible feeling again . . .

"The woman was actually a noble's daughter our age, who was picking on Tam. She wasn't aware that I was around, because she *knew* I wouldn't put up with it, but Tam is different. He'll pretend to ignore whatever anyone says." Kat scowled briefly at the memory. "She was spouting all sorts of nasty things . . . so I punched her . . . and maybe her older sister as well, when she tried to intervene."

Kat shrugged.

"What about the story about Harold?" Sir Vohn insisted next.

By then, the rest of the party had gathered around the redhead to listen to the infamous tales be confirmed or elaborated on with great interest.

"Ah, Harold . . . A very torrid relationship at first."

Everyone save for the Daxarian men stiffened in surprise.

"Well, it was my sixteenth birthday, and I'd had a terrible time at a tea party my mother insisted upon. The young women were awful, and Tam got to do as he pleased, which was horribly unfair. So I convinced Likon, the boy my parents adopted when I was young, to help sneak me away to perhaps go for a walk in Austice, and to maybe even try a glass of moonshine for the first time . . ."

No one dared interrupt as they all waited with captivated smiles.

"Well, I happened upon a brothel my parents owned stakes in, recognized one of the women from when I was younger, and she kindly helped me to their moonshine. They had a regular customer there with his cart and Harold, and he thought it'd be funny to see me a little inebriated. So he kept pressing drinks on me."

The Faucher brothers glanced at one another, their moods shifting to anger.

"He was trying to take advantage of you," Dante interrupted angrily.

Kat grinned. "Yes, and I knew that, but I also realized I wasn't feeling the effects of alcohol thanks to my magic—not that he had any idea who I was."

"You really need to work on developing a sense of danger," Piers commented dryly.

Kat rolled her eyes. "I was perfectly safe. Anyway, I drank his purse dry, and when he accused me of cheating, he got a might pushy, so I ran and took Harold with me. We had a rousing good time stopping at pubs all over

Austice, though I did wear him out and gave him ale, which I've learned since was a bad idea."

The Troivackian men had their jaws dropped.

"Well, poor Harold grew quite frightened of me as a result, and I, of course, felt terrible, but we mended our relationship. And now he even lets me ride him again!" Kat summarized while drinking again from her cup.

"Y-You . . . ride . . . Harold?" Joshua asked while glancing in shock around at the other men. "Your parents aren't worried about . . . about your reputation?"

"Yes, I ride him. He's not the strongest or best-looking, but he's a fine ass! Sure, I get disparaging comments from time to time, but I don't ride him regularly. I'd say twice a year just to make sure we're still doing well. I had to take responsibility for him after that day after all."

No one spoke.

"S-So you *do* have a lover," Conrad managed faintly.

Dante looked as though he might faint. "My Gods. I knew things were different in Daxaria, but—"

Eric roared with laughter.

As did Sir Vohn. And even Sir Cas grinned while Kat stared at the mortified Troivackians, perplexed.

"A lover? Listen, I may be a little adventurous, but Harold's far too hairy and the wrong breed altogether!"

"She took a commoner to bed and treats it as her plaything . . . And here I was thinking she was naïve." Piers breathed in awe. Despite the youngest of the Faucher men usually being the most unflappable, even *he* looked pale and shocked.

"A commoner to bed?! Piers! You take your jests too far!" Kat spluttered at the gall of his accusation.

Eric had tears rolling down his face as he clasped Sir Vohn's shoulder and tried to get ahold of himself.

"M-My lady, perhaps you are . . . a tad . . . inebriated. You don't realize you never said *what* Harold is." Sir Vohn wheezed.

Kat blinked then looked up at the Troivackians.

"Oh Gods." She opened and closed her mouth awkwardly, her cheeks burning as she finally understood what was happening. "I thought everyone had heard the story! Harold isn't a person! He's a donkey!"

The Troivackian men stared dumbfounded at her for a moment. Unable to speak.

Until at last Piers half launched himself across the table, pinched Katarina's cheeks, and shouted, "Good *Gods*, woman! Speak clearly next time! I was about to go write a lengthy letter to your father!"

"Pieeers! Ouch! Shttoop!" Kat called out through her squished cheeks.

Both Sir Cas and Sir Vohn pulled the drunken Faucher son away from the redhead, and thankfully, he did not resist.

"The ass she rides twice a year . . . I . . . I'm at an absolute loss as to how you didn't realize how that sounded." Sir Vohn was barely keeping himself together as he fought off the urge to continue laughing.

Even Eric was still letting out the occasional chortle.

"Like I said! Everyone has heard of the story in Daxaria . . ." Kat mumbled, though she was smiling as she took another drink.

"It's a very good thing that it isn't well-known here, Lady Katarina, otherwise everyone would be hiding their daughters and wives from you."

Kat looked at Dante, whose arms were crossed as he shook his head.

"Oh, don't worry, my bet is that after today, that's exactly what they're going to be doing," she added, her momentary spell of lifted spirits dimming.

None of the men had the ambition to lie and say otherwise; they knew she was completely accurate in that assessment.

"Speaking of your good standing, Lady Katarina, it is getting late. Perhaps you should go see about your chamber being ready." Sir Cas gave the noblewoman a half smile. "Tomorrow is going to be a long day."

Kat grimaced, then drained her cup and stood. "Right you are. I imagine I'll be facing a room full of angry noblemen, who are eager for me to be shipped back to where I came from."

"Don't worry, ye can always bash their heads on the courtyard stones till they change their minds," Herra blurted while his beady eyes fluttered. "Worked on Broghs an' me perfectly well.'

Kat perked up brightly. "You make a very compelling argument, Herra!"

Faucher's sons let out a collective groan as Eric rounded the bench and gently prodded her right shoulder.

She turned from him and walked the other way, not sparing a glance in his direction.

An exchange that was not lost on the rest of the men as Kat waved over her shoulder.

"Night, lads. Until the battles of tomorrow!"

There was a disjointed return of the farewell, but really the men that remained were watching Eric's confused expression as Kat exited the servants' banquet hall without having addressed the prince in any capacity.

Eric continued staring after her, a small frown drawing a line between his brows.

He then dropped his gaze to those present and noticed that a good many of them avoided meeting his eyes.

The prince slowly folded his arms over his chest.

"Someone here know something I don't?"

"Does she have to run into your arms anytime you show your face?" Piers asked indignantly while he lowered himself into a seat at the table with his brothers.

"No, but she is avoiding me completely," Eric continued, studying everyone closely.

None of the Faucher men replied. Piers scratched his lengthening chin whiskers, and Conrad gave a subtle shrug while keeping his eyes fixed on the table. Dante remained as immovable as always . . .

Eric adjusted his sights to Sirs Vohn and Cas and found that the blond knight was sitting with his hands lightly clasped around the base of his goblet, unwilling to acknowledge the question.

"Sir Cas . . ." the prince started, but the Daxarian knight didn't give him a chance to finish.

"Sir Vohn told her you've been courting all kinds of women in the castle and you went and got the sword without taking her with you, and she's really offended about all of it, and you should just start courting her officially at this point before ugly rumors start. Truly, Your Highness, this entire façade is tiresome, and while I don't like butting in on people's private business, this drama feels ridiculous when it's between—"

Sir Cas peered up, and when he realized everyone was staring at him, he didn't finish his rant and instead blushed.

"Right . . . I have trouble . . . hiding my thoughts . . . when drunk . . ."

No one said anything.

Instead, the group looked up at Eric and waited to see what he would say to what they all had been thinking for a good long while.

CHAPTER 32

A CRITICAL COUNCIL

E ric stared at the array of inebriated men, his arms folded, his gaze unimpressed.

No one spoke.

But they all stared at him (save for Joshua Ball, who had fallen asleep on the table) and waited to hear his answer.

When the Daxarian prince still hadn't said anything for an inordinate amount of time, Piers finally had enough.

"Good Gods, truly? Dante, you said you never thought someone as immature as me should get married; what do you think about this whole thing now?"

"I stand by what I said back then," the eldest Faucher son retorted without missing a beat, though his eyes remained fixed on Eric. "However, His Highness might be in fine company with you."

Piers had been opening his mouth angrily, but at the second half of his brother's words, the fight left him as he slumped dejectedly in his seat.

"Sir Vohn, why did you tell Lady Katarina I was going on courting dates?"

Eric's eerily calm voice summoned everyone's attention back to the matter at hand.

The Daxarian knight shifted uncomfortably in his seat but drew himself up straight.

"It was widely known. I mentioned it casually. I didn't know there was anything between you and Lady Katarina that warranted discretion."

Despite Sir Vohn's eyes appearing glassy and his cheeks tinged with pink, his answer sounded stone-cold sober.

"Then you are a blind man." Conrad shook his head and took another drink from his cup.

Eric's gaze narrowed. "That isn't why. You were testing her. Or me. Or both."

The knight wasn't hurried in making a reply as he gulped the last of his moonshine and stood.

"You've assured everyone, regardless of who asks, you have no intentions with Lady Katarina, and that all rumors about the two of you are false, Your Highness. If there is nothing as you insist, it shouldn't matter what I said. It would've seemed deceitful if I had willfully omitted saying anything. If I am wrong, Your Highness, I apologize." Sir Vohn bowed to the prince while clasping his hands behind his back and widening his stance.

Eric stared at his friend for another breath of time, his features hardening.

Then he wordlessly dropped his arms and strode out of the servants' banquet hall without another look back.

Sir Cas let out a long sigh while running a sloppy hand through his hair and dropping his forehead down.

Sir Vohn cuffed him on the back of his head.

"Good Gods, you know if someone presses him, he'll only get more stubborn and push back."

Sir Cas lifted his head again, his eyes half closed already. "Anyone know why he's avoiding being with her?"

Despite addressing the entire group, really the question had been directed toward Sir Vohn, who eyed the men around him warily before half collapsing back onto the bench.

"The epidemic a few years ago in Daxaria. The one that killed the queen? He hasn't been the same since then. He never thought or talked about getting married even before, but then again, he never seemed overly interested in women either. He had a couple *close* lady friends that he courted casually, but nothing warranting a serious discussion." The knight shrugged. "It could be he avoids Lady Katarina because of the fight he had with her father, but I honestly think His Highness is simply dead set against any relationship."

"Well, he is more than interested in a woman now. If he doesn't properly face it, he'll most likely do something foolish," Dante stated while sipping from his own cup.

"Or Lady Katarina will do something . . . I mean . . . being realistic . . . she's the far more likely of the two of them," Broghan Miller slurred in his seat.

Everyone around the table paused at that insight, then after properly processing it, all nodded in agreement.

They *had* just listened to some wild tales involving the redhead.

"Either way, this will end badly at the rate it's going." Piers yawned.

"Nothing to be done about it now. Let us retire for the night." Conrad stood from his seat, though he stumbled and revealed to everyone that he was in fact quite inebriated despite having sounded perfectly fine.

"A *great* idea. We all have a long day tomorrow." While Sir Cas was the one to say the words, his head remained resting atop his arms, his eyes closed, and he didn't seem all that motivated to move . . .

Dante looked down at him, then over to his brothers, who both wore devious smiles.

Sir Vohn, seeing this, eyed them warily as he bent down and threw his fellow knight's arm over his shoulders.

"Mind explaining what those looks are about?"

Both Piers and Conrad were unsuccessful in hiding their disappointed glances.

"Oh, no reason. Good evening, Sir Vohn." Dante turned without looking at the knight and made his way out of the banquet hall with Conrad and Piers reluctantly following.

Sir Vohn watched them leave, then looked at Broghan.

The younger man was rubbing his face with one hand while using the other to push himself up off the bench.

"Their sister is fond of Sir Cas. They've taken exception to him as a result."

Looking at the mostly unconscious blond knight, who was almost a complete deadweight, Sir Vohn grinned. "Been charming some Troivackian women, golden boy?"

"Golden boy?" Sir Herra asked as he stood with a grunt before casually bending down and throwing Joshua Ball over his shoulder.

"Ah. It's what the knights at home nicknamed him. He's rumored to become the next captain of Daxaria's military; he's wildly talented and brilliant. Women love him, but he never pays them any mind . . . Plus the hair. He's our golden boy. Innocent as a new lamb." Sir Vohn playfully tugged Sir Cas's arm that was around his neck, making the *golden boy* let out a sleepy grumble.

Both Broghan and Herra looked at Sir Cas—the knight who, at their first meeting, they had looked down upon and scorned—with shock and admiration.

The two younger Troivackian men then looked at each other and gave their heads a shake.

"Hard to believe he's already being considered for captain," Broghan lamented, leading the group to the banquet hall's exit with Herra and Ball not far behind. "Though to be honest, I don't think the Faucher family would care even if he were a king. No one will ever be good enough for Lady Dana."

Sir Vohn laughed, and once the last of the Troivackians had left, he regarded Sir Cas's sleeping face once more.

"Looks like you're finally getting yourself into a bit of mischief."

Sir Cas let out another mumble, but it was incoherent, so Sir Vohn resumed his work of half dragging him off to bed. Each member of the departed group was set on hopefully sleeping off the last vestiges of their impromptu night of drinking and revelry. The dawn was fast approaching with new threats and trials awaiting them all, and sporting a hangover for such exciting times was hardly ideal.

"Your Majesty, how could you permit such a thing to occur *here*?!" Lord Ball roared from his seat, his palms braced against the council table, his eyes flashing dangerously.

Brendan stared at the man in silence, but Lord Harriod Ball was not going to submit before his king today.

Alina's direct gaze on the lord also went ignored, but that wasn't new.

"This was a unique arrangement between the king of Daxaria and me. Lady Katarina is a witch and wished to learn discipline that could challenge her. An honorable ambition," Brendan announced while surveying the rest of the nobility present. "Are you telling me that the threat of magical beasts in our land is not the most prevalent matter on your minds?"

At least half the noblemen present shifted uncomfortably.

"Those beasts are most likely only appearing *because* of that witch! Just like when that Aidan Helmer devil led us to an abysmal defeat, he came with a dragon," Lord Ball continued while meeting everyone's eyes and making several men lean forward hungrily.

"These sightings began long before Lady Katarina arrived here in Troivack, and furthermore, what purpose would she have for doing so?" Alina asked imperially.

Most of the men ignored her, save for Lord Miller, who met her gaze with a neutral expression.

"What other explanation is there?"

Everyone waited expectantly for the answer.

"Perhaps it is because you angered the Gods by attacking the witches, who they had sent into the world in order to act as mediums between nature and humans." Alina's unblinking stare cut to Lord Ball, who barely resisted the urge to sneer.

"What proof is there?" another lord from farther down the table called out indignantly.

"There have been no sightings of magical beasts in Daxaria, Zinfera, or even Lobahl. Only in Troivack, and Troivack is the only kingdom that has turned its back on those chosen by the Gods," Alina pointed out while sitting tall in her chair beside her husband, who listened to the discussion without saying much.

At first, no one could think of another argument to the one their queen had presented, but Lord Ball was in a fine mood for a fight.

"Why now, then? This could be an attack you yourself arranged, Your Majesty, against Troi—"

"Finish that groundless accusation of treason toward your queen, and you will hang before sunset, Lord Ball." Brendan's warning sent shivers down many men's spines. Even Lord Ball knew well enough to back away from the dangerous ground he was stepping on.

"We have sent scouts to try and learn more from these creatures. We have gathered historical texts from both our remaining coven members as well as Daxaria's coven to try and learn more, but at this time still do not know enough." Captain Orion jumped into the conversation, looking in a rather foul state himself. The presence of Faucher and his controversial student had him feeling as though there was something suspicious afoot . . .

"Mage Sebastian Vaulker, you've been awfully quiet this entire time." Lord Ball looked at the young man, who sat inconspicuously on the opposite end of the table.

Despite having everyone's attention jump to him, however, Sebastian didn't react flustered or concerned.

"I am listening to the council like many of us here. As previously stated, I've already offered what little knowledge and resources I have at my disposal given that our own academy was destroyed years ago along with any records that could have been helpful."

The table once again fell quiet.

"If . . . If it is as Her Majesty suggests and these beasts are here because the Gods are angered, how would we go about rectifying the situation?" Lord Miller asked while looking to the king.

"I was considering bringing in the Coven of Aguas to further discuss the matter," Brendan responded calmly.

"Bring more witches in?! What if that summons even more beasts to our doorstep!" Lord Ball's palm slammed against the table.

"If you cannot refrain from theatrics and are unable to be a part of reasonable discussions, you should leave, Lord Ball." Brendan's tone had risen, and the nobleman's cheek was twitching as though trying to stop himself from glaring at his own king.

Brendan held his gaze and waited.

At last, Lord Ball seemed to settle down enough that he seated himself once more and waited, though no one believed that he was finished airing his complaints.

"Those in favor of seeking counsel from the Coven of Aguas, please raise your hands."

A little over half the room tentatively pressed their hands into the air.

"The council has voted. Now, on to our next topic—"

"Are we going to discuss the mockery of Lady Katarina Ashowan being trained as a knight?" Lord Ball couldn't help but murmur loud enough for everyone to hear.

Alina raised an eyebrow in the lord's direction.

"We are, but in this case, we are going to invite Lady Katarina to join the discussion with her teacher to best address all questions, including her account of the magical beasts," Brendan continued evenly.

"Why would we need to have the lady present, sire?" Duke Icarus, who had been abnormally docile that morning, interrupted.

At this, Alina leaned forward so that she could better stare at the lord, a cold smile on her face.

"Excellent question, Your Grace. The reason we are having her here is to not only have her answer questions about her abilities, which only she can answer, but also to gauge how her training is proceeding. What do you think of this, Duke Icarus?"

The nobleman stiffened, but unlike Lord Ball, he was far more adept at hiding his true nature and thoughts.

"I suppose we may as well see what could have prompted this . . . odd turn of events."

The men around the table began to whisper and discuss—more than half of them sounded angry.

Alina cast a sidelong glance at her husband, and the two shared an almost imperceptible twitching of lips, the urge to grin a little too tempting than was perhaps good for them in that moment. What could they say? They were both more than a little curious at what Katarina's time spent with Faucher had yielded, and both were betting that: it wasn't going to go as anyone expected.

CHAPTER 33

DEMANDING DAYS

S ay it back to me."

"Do I really have to? I swear, I'm not going to—"

Faucher's flat stare told Katarina that whatever denial she was about to make, his demand would still be the same.

Dropping her head back with a moan mixed with a sigh, she then flopped her chin back to her chest.

"I will not speak unless spoken to."

"And?"

"Even if someone's being an arsehat."

"Ashowan . . ."

"Even if someone is being an idiot."

Faucher growled.

"Fine. Even if . . . someone says *something* . . . that could be . . . interpreted unfavorably."

The military leader's eyes narrowed. "And?"

Kat scowled while placing her hands on her hips. "Don't smirk at anyone."

"*And?*"

The redhead frowned. "That was everything!"

Faucher carefully folded his arms over his chest, his armor clanking slightly as he did so. "No seeking vengeance on anyone after you leave the council room. Like putting cat shit in their shoes, or continually stealing their drinks, or cutting holes in the backsides of their trousers."

Katarina's eyes widened and snapped to the window to her right, her tongue poking the right side of her cheek.

"That's right. I know all about your small acts of defiance after someone's irritated you." Faucher nodded sternly at his student, the warning in his voice impossible to miss.

"Did you also hear about the pigpen?"

Faucher's arms dropped with his expression as he stepped closer. "What did you do to the pigpen?"

Kat held up her hands defensively. "Nothing! Not here in Troivack anyway. I just, erm . . . wondered if you'd heard anything from Daxaria is all . . ."

Faucher stared at Katarina in silence for several moments before addressing his three sons, who stood off to the side.

"All of you watch her every move in this castle from today onward."

Katarina's jaw dropped as she stared irritably at Faucher.

"Wait . . . *she's* the one who cut holes in my pants?" Piers looked at his father, the realization dawning on him.

"She was the one stealing my cup every time I put it down?" Conrad added in equal awe.

Faucher let out a long agitated breath, then looked at Dante.

He was staring at the redhead, looking quite concerned. "Did you do something to me?"

Kat shifted awkwardly on her feet while casually glancing around to ensure no one was passing by within earshot as they waited outside the council room doors.

"Alright, look . . . you all must admit you didn't really charm me when we first met . . ." she addressed Piers and Conrad, who both looked a mite annoyed. "And, Dante, I . . . Well, I didn't have to do anything to you."

"What does that mean?" Dante burst out with uncharacteristic panic.

Kat hesitated while glancing sheepishly at Faucher. "You see—"

"Leader Faucher, Lady Katarina, His Majesty and the council are ready for you now."

Mr. Levin, the king's assistant, had poked his head out the council room doors and called over to the group.

Faucher fixed Katarina with one final warning stare before looking back to his sons. "We will hopefully be out before the dining hour. See about arranging for Lady Katarina to eat in her chamber privately. Things might become hostile."

"Yes, Father." Conrad nodded.

"I still would like to know what she meant when—" Dante didn't finish what he was saying before a movement on the other end of the corridor caught his attention.

Following his eyeline, both Katarina and Faucher looked and found Eric and Mr. Julian walking toward them.

Katarina's face turned stony, and she straightened her shoulders before looking back toward the council room doors.

"Glad to see I'm not too late. Are we going in now?" Eric asked Faucher, though his eyes lingered on Katarina, who hadn't acknowledged him at all.

"We are entering now, yes."

Kat's head snapped back around to stare up at Faucher. "He's joining us in the meeting?"

Faucher studied her agitated expression, caught off guard by the emotion he saw in her eyes.

"Yes. He is the highest authority and representative here from Daxaria, and he had his father's assistant send him copies of the agreements between His Majesties King Norman Reyes and King Brendan Devark regarding your swordsmanship lessons," Faucher explained while watching Kat's cheeks turn a bright shade of pink.

"Faucher, can I have a private word with Lady Katarina before we go to the council room?" Eric requested suddenly, his hazel eyes fixed on the redhead, who was once again staring at the doors.

"That isn't necessary," Kat spoke before her teacher could answer the prince. "Everyone is waiting for us."

Before Eric or Faucher could comment or argue further, Katarina braced her feet apart, clasped her hands behind her back and lifted her chin.

"Leader Faucher, sir, I am ready when you are."

Between her militaristic tone and stance, everyone, including Mr. Levin, who was watching the scene, hesitated.

To anyone who wasn't Faucher and his sons, no one had ever seen Katarina behave . . . so . . . disciplined.

Moving in front of his student and noting her cold emotionless face and her flawless posture, a flicker of pride appeared in Faucher's eyes. Though he cast a final look of uncertainty toward the prince, who appeared troubled while staring at Katarina and then at Piers and Conrad, who were grinning behind her. Even Dante's expression had softened.

They may have been a little proud of her as well.

"I believe we are ready to enter, Your Highness. Whatever needs to be discussed can be done after the meeting." The military leader bowed to Eric.

While he didn't look pleased, the Daxarian prince turned to his young assistant, who handed him the paperwork that had been mentioned, and they crossed the corridor to the council room doors that Mr. Levin had opened for them.

Following Eric came Faucher and then Katarina. Mr. Julian bowed to them all as they passed, then was the final person to enter the council room before the doors shut behind him.

In the council room, a table filled with approximately thirty noblemen sat waiting. Alina was positioned at the end of the long table with Brendan, both facing the doors. The couple surveyed the entrance of the newcomers with their usual chilly dignity.

"Your Highness, Leader Faucher, and Lady Katarina, thank you for joining us," Brendan greeted.

All three of them bowed, including Katarina, who was wearing her uniform, which once again sparked murmurs of disapproval.

"We have summoned you here today not only to receive a more detailed recounting of the fight with the ancient beasts but also to go over the arrangement with regards to Lady Katarina's sword training."

Faucher barely resisted looking over his shoulder at the redhead.

Even though she hadn't even mumbled a word, he could hear her thoughts clear as day.

Oh sure. A woman learning swordsmanship is the same level of concern as magical beasts capable of flattening a keep. Faucher resisted growling. Instead, he explained to everyone the details of the attack, including how difficult it was to find a weakness in the stone golem, the appearance of a magical imp with three sets of pupils and purple hair, and last but not least . . . the man who tried to bind Kat's magic. Though any mention of the devil was tactfully omitted.

"Why would these attackers want to bind Lady Katarina's abilities?" Brendan asked Faucher from the opposite end of the table.

"While I can't say for certain, Your Majesty, it could be that they see Lady Katarina as a threat."

The council room members were unable to contain their reactions as they all burst out talking at the same time.

Lord Ball slapped his hand on the table, rising to his feet. "What *great* power does Lady Katarina possess that could be dangerous?"

Brendan eyed his vassal darkly.

Faucher noted this and so did not give an immediate response . . .

He glanced at Kat over his shoulder.

The military leader appeared to be debating something as he regarded her poised expression and gaze that had fixed itself ahead. She didn't fidget and hadn't made any comments thus far . . .

"I believe that is a question for Lady Katarina to answer."

Faucher heard himself say the words and instantly felt uneasiness in his gut, but it was too late to take it back. So he locked eyes with his student and tried to communicate as clearly as possible . . .

He was putting faith in her, but she had better come through.

However, Kat didn't move. Or speak.

The nobles around the table gradually fell quiet again as they waited.

Faucher almost gave a rueful chuckle when he realized *why* she hadn't spoken yet.

"Ashowan, you will answer the council's questions to the best of your abilities," Faucher called out for everyone to hear.

"Yes, sir," Kat replied loudly, her voice ringing as she obeyed, making just about everyone present ten times more uncomfortable.

One hand on the hilt of her sword and the other pressed over her heart, Kat bowed to Lord Ball, who grew more furious as a result.

"To answer your question, Lord Ball, it has been discovered during my training with Leader Faucher that I am stronger, faster, and more resilient than most humans thanks to my abilities. These factors of my magic could be why these mysterious new creatures see me as a potential threat."

It was a partial lie.

One she had been coached on, as no one save for a handful of people knew about her encounter with the actual devil.

"Why would you train here in Troivack and not in Daxaria?" Another nobleman sneered from his seat.

Katarina bowed her head to the man. "Of course because Leader Faucher is the best teacher of our two great kingdoms."

A full lie.

She had to be tested by her mother and Daxaria's king before they could decide she was worthy of taking on the responsibility, and she just happened to be in Troivack when she was finally allowed to learn.

The council room wasn't quite able to argue or scorn that response, however, so they were hasty in picking a new one.

"What do you know of these magical creatures?" Lord Miller interjected.

Once again, Katarina displayed the perfect conduct of a knight in training and bowed her head to the nobleman before responding.

"I know very little. Only that the being with the three pupils in each eye had abilities outside the elemental realm we are all familiar with."

"Daxaria has a growing population of mutated witches. What made this being's abilities so remarkable?" Brendan himself asked the question.

"The being disappeared into another realm altogether and had abilities no one has ever reported before. His appearance was also far more unique than a typical witch's variance. Having three pupils per eye and being over seven feet tall is not the norm."

For some reason, the repeated mention of the mutated pupils had Eric frowning.

"How is it you escaped this being after he had abducted you?" the queen queried next, making the room fall ill at ease yet again.

Kat looked at her friend, and for once . . . it was Alina's turn to become perturbed by the changes in her friend. There was no mirth in Kat's face. No hidden jest shining behind her eyes . . .

It was as though she was becoming a different person, even though she had only been gone a few months at most.

"As I stated before, Your Majesty, my abilities paired with Leader Faucher's training have made me a respectable adversary."

"My student is modest. If she were given another three months' training, I believe she could pass the knight's tests," Faucher added on seriously.

This certainly set the room off.

Some men laughed, others shouted, and some . . . well, there were a select few who studied Lady Katarina with her ethereal eyes uncertain of their opinions . . .

"I'm hearing boasts of Leader Faucher being the finest teacher and a fresh student being worthy of taking on the knight's test in an insultingly short amount of time," Lord Ball interjected, the outrage in his voice rousing several men to join him in standing.

Brendan raised his hand, and while the room did not fall silent all at once, it didn't take long.

"The claim you make is a bold one, Leader Faucher."

"Yes, sire."

"Would you be willing to prove its merit?"

The faintest of rumbles began in the back of Faucher's throat that only Kat could hear.

"I would, Your Majesty."

"Then why don't we select one of Captain Orion's own students to fight Lady Katarina? We shall match his best student that began training around the same time she did. Someone who should be ready for the knight's exam in three months?" Brendan leaned back in his throne and looked around the table.

Many noblemen voiced their approval of the proposition.

Once again, their king had come up with a fair and just way of handling the situation.

"Pardon me, Your Majesty." Duke Icarus inclined forward in his seat, peering through the small round spectacles perched near the end of his pale nose. "Lady Katarina should also spar with a seasoned knight to see if she is truly as capable as she says."

Brendan looked to Faucher. "Of course we will not expect Lady Katarina to win against one of our own well-trained knights, but a measure of how close she is to reaching the level you describe would be illuminating to everyone here."

Faucher and Katarina bowed.

"Of course, Your Majesty," the military leader agreed evenly.

The men around the table were feeling significantly more relaxed and assured that in no time things would be set right. They all knew Lady Katarina to be a mutated witch. However having successfully wiped out far more powerful witches than herself in their kingdom, they found little reason to hang on to their agitation, knowing that she was no match for true Troivackian strength.

"Lady Katarina, what do you have to say on this matter?" Brendan regarded Katarina, feeling more than a little pleased with how well his and Alina's plan was going.

By dinnertime that evening, however, he would be cursing the momentary lapse in caution.

"Yes, Your Majesty. As this is a test being given to me, a foreign noble, simply as a means of placating those here who have no business weighing in on my affairs or the decisions reached by not only yourself, but the king of Daxaria, I have my own terms."

Eric bit the inside of his cheek to stop himself from smiling.

He had been disheartened and almost worried when she had been too pliable with the whole meeting . . . and was rather enjoying how uncomfortable her accurate analysis was making the council.

"First and foremost, I want the wives and daughters of the men present to witness the duels."

The noblemen didn't get a chance to splutter their disapproval of her first demand before the redhead plundered on.

"Second, should I win my duels, I would like my exile to be lifted."

Ensuring her adversaries had absolutely no chance to recover, Katarina unabashedly continued.

"Last, but not least, I would like to summon Sir Seth Herra of Troivack's elite knights to offer me his apology in front of you all, as he insulted my honor and integrity on the journey here to Troivack. There are several eye-witnesses to this particular event. Leader Faucher, His Highness Prince Eric Reyes, and Mage Sebastian Vaulker are able to validate this."

Faucher turned and stared at Kat, his eyes wide, as, in the deafening silence of the room, a nobleman rose to his feet.

Unbeknownst to the redhead, it was none other than Sir Herra's father.

Katarina didn't bother looking at anyone else; she kept her eyes locked with Brendan's.

Eric was trying his hardest not to laugh. And Faucher?

Faucher was regretting allowing her to talk in the first place.

CHAPTER 34

APOLOGY AGONY

No one dared move as Katarina faced the king, her gaze unwavering. Lord Aaron Herra openly gaped at her, and Faucher stood beside her, debating whether she would make it out of the council room alive.

Both Brendan and Alina momentarily forgot to breathe.

"What was this alleged transgression?" the king managed to ask, though it was taking more effort than he'd like to admit to stop his voice from rasping.

"Sir Seth Herra accused me of lying and slandering Your Majesty when I informed him of the decision to allow me to learn swordsmanship. He questioned my integrity and honor, saying he did not believe me and demanded I apologize in front of our traveling company. A knight *below* my rank, attempting to punish and humiliate me, owes me a public apology at the very least."

The shock that filled the room was unfathomable.

"And while I have stated this as a condition of terms, that is out of my benevolence. As it really isn't a question of who was or wasn't right," Katarina's sharp voice rang out.

Faucher barely resisted the urge to clamp his hand over her mouth, but even if he had stopped her from shaming the entire room of powerful Troivackian noblemen, the triumphant predatorial glint in her eyes would've been enough to agitate them succinctly.

Eric had a half grin on his face, though he directed his eyes to the floor discreetly.

Lord Aaron Herra revealed his pulsing vein amidst his purple expression to be in the center of his forehead. The man was too incensed to even find the words to speak.

Though the way Kat's golden eyes moved to him, it almost looked as though she dared him to fight with her. It would give her a chance to further

wipe the floor with his honor using one of the well-known pillars of Troivack's court. Strength from power.

"Your Highness Prince Eric Reyes, as the highest ranking witness that
Lady Katarina cited, are the events she is recounting accurate?" Brendan
looked to his brother-in-law, his eyebrow twitching when he noticed the
gleam of pride in the prince's eyes.

"Yes, Your Majesty. That was what happened. Though it should also be
mentioned that Lady Katarina was also told that if she was lying, she would
be forced to apologize in court. Her request of a private apology during this
council meeting instead of a public one is more than fair."

Brendan looked as though he momentarily considered dropping his face
to his hands as his eyes fluttered, though he masked this urge to the best of
his ability.

"Very well. It was Sir Herra's error to insult a guest of rank, and so instead
of adding it to your terms, Lady Katarina, I believe this should be carried out
today regardless. Guards, please summon Sir Seth Herra."

Lord Herra half collapsed into his chair, his complexion had dramati-
cally shifted from an alarming plum color to that of a blanket of white snow.

"Lord Aaron Herra, do you perhaps have something you wish to say to
Lady Katarina?" Alina's icy voice drew all eyes to her.

It wasn't hard to deduce the queen was furious.

The nobleman let out a long breath that was imperceptible beyond the
two men seated at his sides. He looked on the verge of fainting.

However, he was saved from having to respond by Duke Icarus.

"Your Majesty, it sounds to me as though Sir Herra's son was merely
trying to protect the crown's prestige. No one could have predicted that her
claim at the time was true, as before yesterday, we all would've thought it
outlandish." The duke addressed the king, ignoring Alina entirely.

Brendan didn't react to the slight toward his wife, but he did note it.

"To insult and call into question a noblewoman's integrity and honor
is far from the appropriate method of handling the situation, particularly
a guest, Duke Icarus." Alina's tone rose, and it succeeded in drawing the
nobleman's eyes to her, though they narrowed almost imperceptibly upon
looking to his queen.

"You may be unaware of this, Your Majesty, but the respect and pride for
our king here in Troivack lives deep in all our hearts. We defend our leader
from any and all possible insult and questioning."

"Determining what I have and have not ordered without my consultation *is* an insult, Duke Icarus." Brendan's interruption sent a wave of fear through the noblemen.

"That's exactly what I said at the time," Katarina muttered under her breath so that only Faucher might hear.

Her teacher cast her a sidelong glance of disapproval.

Duke Icarus remained irritatingly calm, however, despite the royal couple's displeasure. "Far-fetched claims are reasonable to question, Your Majesty, particularly when I'm given to understand this Daxarian noblewoman has a history of deception."

"I beg your pardon?" Katarina burst out before anyone else could beat her to it.

Her aura flickered to life and her eyes flashed, making many of the nobles in the room draw back and share disapproving glances.

"You will mind your next words, Duke Icarus!"

It was the loudest Katarina had ever heard Alina speak before. Kat tensed and observed her friend's rapidly rising and falling chest. She normally was soft spoken because of her breathing troubles . . .

Duke Icarus did not so much as bat an eye as he regarded the queen for a lone moment before looking to Brendan.

"Is it not true that Lady Katarina was a part of a ploy that led Your Majesty to deceive the Daxarian king last summer? A secret outing with our future queen at the time that could have placed her at risk?"

The room broke out in whispers.

Meanwhile, both Kat and Alina's eyes widened.

How had he found out about their camping escapade the summer before? If he had learned about that small incident, then that meant he was also most likely aware of their kidnapping . . .

It was a subtle threat he was making to oust *both* the queen and Katarina and bring into question their honor.

Brendan's gaze blackened.

"The outing was a misunderstanding bred out of a lone serving staff's oversight. You dare to slander your queen and Lady Katarina Ashowan?"

Everyone froze.

The sense that things were about to escalate to outright violence was keenly felt by all present.

"Furthermore, the incident that took place more than a year ago was confidential in nature. You will explain yourself now or surrender your life to me for your insult and overstepping your bounds."

Duke Icarus bowed his head unbothered. "I merely heard about the incident as it resulted in the announcement of your engagement, Your Majesty. There was a great deal of confusion at the time. I only meant to illustrate the good intentions of Lord Herra's son—though he may have made a small error during an already stressful time on his return to Vessa."

During the duke's evasive defense, Alina had settled back down, but her heart raced with her ire.

"You brought up an unconfirmed rumor in order to cast additional doubt on Lady Katarina's honor when it was already insulted without reason in the first place. At this rate, Duke Icarus, I may order *you* on your knees before her to apologize beside Sir Herra."

The duke met Alina's stare, the hatred between them potent, but she wasn't through with him.

"Two kings gave Lady Katarina their blessings to learn swordsmanship. She accurately relayed that information and was mocked and disparaged by a man of lesser station. It is not uncommon to demand Sir Seth Herra's life as penance in this circumstance. Which leads me to believe that you are challenging the hierarchy of this court, Duke Icarus." The queen all but hissed the words.

Katarina almost smiled when she noticed many of the noblemen recoil and look away uncomfortably in the face of Alina's wrath. She knew it was only a matter of time before the former Daxarian princess brought the Troivackian court to their knees.

Yet once again, Duke Icarus refused to be put in place so easily.

"My counterarguments were made in the interest of giving a loyal vassal the benefit of the doubt."

"Then leave Lady Katarina's honor out of it." Alina seethed.

Duke Icarus barely stopped a sneer from spreading on his face, instead managing to wrestle it down to a gloating half smile.

He had already accomplished what he had meant to anyway . . .

He had brought into question Lady Katarina's and the queen's reputations as well as caused unease and displeasure amongst the nobles directed at the two women.

And if that . . . *strange* mercenary leader was right . . . then he also had just driven a potential wedge between the queen and Lady Katarina, though Duke Icarus didn't know precisely how . . .

A knock on the council room doors interrupted the tense silence.

"Your Majesty, Sir Seth Herra has arrived," the guard on the other side of the door called out, unaware of the heated discussion taking place.

"Enter," Brendan returned, though he was fighting the very potent, and recurrent urge to draw his sword and decapitate the duke right then and there.

The door opened and shut, and Katarina didn't bother looking over her shoulder as she heard the heavy boots belonging to the one and only Sir Seth Herra approach.

She kept her back straight and masked any emotion she had in that moment.

"Your Majesty." The elite knight greeted and bowed to the king.

"Sir Herra, I have just been informed of a disappointing exchange that occurred between you and Lady Katarina on your journey here to Vessa."

The knight, who stood in a casual tunic and pants with his hands clasped behind his back and his feet braced apart, stiffened. He resisted looking at the redhead that stood to his left in a near identical stance.

"Yes, Your Majesty?"

"I am given to understand that you owe her an apology."

Sir Herra's complexion became tinted with green.

"I . . . I called into question her claims that she would be learning to fight with a sword."

Brendan's stare didn't waver.

"I'm aware of the discussion. You will apologize now instead of in a formal court as per Leader Faucher's order at the time. I have dismissed this offense being punished as severely as it normally would, and we will not speak of this matter after the conclusion of this meeting."

Sir Herra swallowed with difficulty.

The king and queen stared at the man as they waited.

The first person to move was Katarina as she turned toward Sir Herra's profile, her hands still clasped behind her back, her eyes burning into the side of his face.

She knew that she had earned dozens more enemies during that meeting, but this only made her want to savor the knight's apology all the more.

Sir Herra rounded toward Kat. He looked like he was considering killing her right then and there.

She didn't give him the satisfaction of reacting to his obvious animosity.

Instead, she waited with an unnatural serenity for the insincere words she knew she was ripping from his throat.

Slowly, he lowered himself to his knees.

Many men in the council room looked away from the shameful display that made them nauseated.

"I . . ." Seth Herra's voice came out a grumble as his left cheek twitched. "I apologize for not believing that you had permission from my king to learn swordsmanship."

"And for insulting my integrity."

Katarina's prompt made the knight's furious eyes snap up to hers, but he flinched when he found that they were glowing. She looked like she was a triumphant beast about to consume her kill . . .

"I apologize for questioning your integrity," he parroted back, his breaths becoming rapid.

Katarina peered down at him without saying anything. Instead, she simply allowed the occupants of the room to stew in the discomfort.

Until she surprised everyone and offered her hand to him.

He stared at her gloved palm with a mixture of bewilderment and anger.

"We now bow our heads to the same teachers, Sir Herra. Let us begin anew and work to improve ourselves. Can we agree on this?"

No one, including Sir Herra, knew how to feel or react to her gesture.

On the one hand, she wasn't dragging out the ordeal and instead was offering to let the matter rest after receiving what they all knew was a subpar apology. However, for Sir Herra, it placed him with two difficult options. The first, to reject her gesture, which would put him back in a position of needing to apologize. The second . . . be forced to publicly acknowledge her as a fellow soldier. If he ever tried to renege on it, his own honor would be put into question, meaning if he wished to avoid such a fate, he would forever be forced to treat her akin to other knights.

The council wondered if Lady Katarina knew the dilemma she had placed him in as he struggled with the matter.

Duke Icarus secretly raged, and Brendan lifted an impressed eyebrow, though Faucher, Alina, and Eric knew she had planned the move . . .

And once Sir Herra begrudgingly reached up and clasped her hand, he, too, realized she had intended for it as well, as her devilish smile lit her features, and she gripped his palm with impressive strength. The elite Troivackian knight knew then that he had been ensnared. As he rose to his feet, he came to the conclusion that if he didn't do something to get rid of the wretched woman soon, she was going to bring about far more chaos than anyone was capable of withstanding.

CHAPTER 35

KATARINA'S CALLOUT

I feel like that went well!" Katarina stretched her arms above her head as she traipsed into the solar that was empty save for Alina.

She cracked her neck side to side and relished in the ability to move freely instead of standing at attention for what felt like eternity. As she shook free her stiff limbs and gradually released the faintest beginning of her magitch, Kat eventually realized that Alina hadn't said anything. The Troivackian queen had summoned her to the solar when the council had been filing out of the room, the noblemen had all been shooting her dirty looks or avoiding looking at her altogether. However Alina hadn't looked all that pleased herself.

Kat had simply assumed that her friend was putting on her *queen face* so to say, but when she realized they were alone and Alina was looking at her stonily . . . she recognized that something was amiss . . .

"What's wrong? I know that Duke Icarus is being a prime arsehat, but we'll shut him up when—"

"Why didn't you tell me about your fight with Sir Herra?"

Kat balked for a moment, then faced her friend squarely. "I sincerely mean this when I say I had completely forgotten about it by the time I first got here. I only remembered it when I got to know Sir Herra's younger brother while I was away. Hello to you too, by the way."

Alina frowned at Katarina's wry tone at the end. "Kat, after what happened with my mother-in-law, I thought you would be more forthcoming about telling me these things!"

The redhead threw her hands in the air defensively. "I genuinely forgot! It happened ages ago! It just came up now because I figured I'd nip it in the bud before I started training around the men."

"Is there anything else I should know then?" the queen asked, folding her arms.

Kat observed the movement, her eyes dropping to Alina's middle and noting that her friend was doing a magnificent job of hiding her motherly condition thanks to her thick dark emerald winter dress paired with a black cloak.

"Well, I'm guessing you heard about my incident with Lord Miller's younger son . . . ?" Kat cast her mind back.

"I did, thanks to Lord Miller. I didn't even get a letter from you about the incident until after *he* told me!"

Kat let out an aggravated breath. "I was a little preoccupied recovering—sorry if after having someone shove me into a gorge, I didn't fly to my writing desk!"

"What about your spar with Sir Herra's younger brother, where you knocked him unconscious?"

"Good gods, I spar with the men regularly. Do you want me to tell you about every time I bruise someone?"

"You didn't render a man nearly twice your size unconscious each of those times," Alina pointed out angrily.

The redhead felt herself grow more than a little annoyed at being accosted.

"I just get back from months of training, and instead of asking me how it went, or telling me how your pregnancy is going—"

"Shh!" Alina interrupted, her eyes flashing urgently. "For the love of the Gods, Kat, aside from my husband and handmaidens, only you and my brother know. We are going to announce it after you win the duels."

"See, *that's* something we could be having a pleasant discussion about! Instead, you're all shout-y! I've heard some women get testy when expecting . . ." the redhead added on more as a mumble.

Though by her next breath, she wished she had kept her mouth shut.

Alina descended upon her, her finger pointed in Kat's face, her hazel eyes wide in fury.

"How *dare* you try to dismiss me using that! You are no better than those men in there we just faced. They, too, were attempting to pretend and diminish our claims just to give themselves the advantage!"

Katarina responded to her friend's rage unexpectedly then.

She dropped her hands that had still been raised and stared down at the queen in an eerie calm.

"I'm not your enemy, Alina. I'm not trying to deceive or harm you. I have been working hard the entire time I've been away, and if you feel I wasn't communicating enough with you, I'm sorry, but you've always known I am not one to sit and write lengthy correspondence. As for sharing with you the times that I've been slighted or harmed? It happens often, and I don't always like to talk about it." Kat's expression grew shuttered.

"There's liking privacy, and then there is lying and keeping secrets, Kat." Alina breathed, only slightly calmer than she was before, her hands drifting down to her sides.

"Then what are you going to do once I tell you? Are you going to fight my battles for me?" Kat could feel a foreign steeliness in her voice, making Alina give a small flinch that became a frown. "If it's just for the sake of knowing, there are things I don't like sharing with anyone. Embarrassing things, terrifying things, hurtful things . . . I don't talk about them because I'd rather just forget them and move on. There is no need to dwell on them."

Alina's expression shifted, and the way she looked at Kat made her stomach twist.

"Gods, Kat. Just what in the world has made you so frightened of being vulnerable?"

"I'm not frightened of being vulnerable! I—"

"Yes, you are."

"NO!" Kat shouted and took a step back, but she instantly closed her eyes and took a steadying breath. She knew her aura was beginning to wave off her skin. "I don't want pity, condolences, affirmations, encouragement . . . None of it. I don't want my problems being solved by someone else either."

"Then just tell me so I know what's going on!" Alina insisted, a tint of color appearing in her cheeks.

Kat looked to the ceiling, her hand subconsciously drifting to the hilt of her sword as she sifted through appropriate responses in her mind.

Alina gave a small laugh of disbelief.

"Gods . . . I always thought you were different from other Daxarian noblewomen, but I never realized how much like a Troivackian man you are."

"Alright, that is entirely unfair. I smile and am at least moderately better-looking than most of those ale barrels with legs," Kat blustered with a snort.

"You won't even properly face me during this conversation! I knew after our time being kidnapped together you didn't feel fear the same way as normal people, but do you not feel other things normally as well?" Alina drew herself straighter, her question sincere.

Kat's gaze fell to her friend, deep hurt and a hint of anger bright in her golden eyes.

"I prefer keeping things to myself; there is nothing wrong with that."

"It's not normal to force yourself to struggle or face things alone, Kat. It's not normal to hide your troubles from other people to the extent you do, nor to not trust them to listen to you when you say you don't wish them to interfere."

"Well, I'm not Godsdamn normal, am I? Didn't our little adventure with our kidnapping prove that?" Kat's voice had lowered, and her stare sharpened.

Alina hesitated for a moment, but she was far from being through with her friend. "Aside from being a stubborn woman who lacks any ability to sit still, I thought you were at least—"

"At least what? Human?" Kat's aura flickered aggressively with red streaks running through it that stunned Alina with their vividness. "I'm going to repeat what I have been saying to just about every Godsdamn person. I. Am. NOT. Human!"

Katarina moved toward Alina, making her flinch.

"That's right. See? I'm not. You want to know why I don't share things with you? Because you'd find out just how much of a monster I am. You want to know more about me? Fine. Fine! You have very nearly ordered me to, so I may as well try and save what little free will I have."

Kat's aura was rising higher, and her eyes were growing brighter. Alina felt her mind go blank as fear crept into her blood.

"I felt relieved after killing Roscoe. I felt fantastic for weeks, and I was actually able to sleep at night because for once my magic wasn't demanding I drain the life from someone. Didn't you think it was strange that I never got soldier's spells after the ordeal, but you did?"

"Kat, I—"

"I snapped the neck of a coyote while traveling here to Vessa, and I did it so that I wouldn't do it to a person who was around me. I got stabbed again, and it honestly made my magitch significantly better. In Daxaria, I've punched noblewomen in the face. I tried to kill Broghan Miller and would've been successful if I hadn't been grazed by an arrow. I tried to gouge the eyes out of the *devil*."

Kat had been steadily advancing toward Alina, who backed away on shaking legs until her back hit the wall of the solar. As Kat bore down on the queen, her aura lapping at the air like hungry flames, her golden eyes shining, Alina couldn't control the tears rising in her eyes. If the redhead had growled like a beast, it would not have been surprising.

"I'm a monster, Alina, and it's a lot better and easier for us all if everyone just accepts what I give them because, if I'm pushed I don't know what I'll do or where I'll stop."

"Kat, I-I know you aren't like this. I know you aren't a monster, I—"

"This *is* what I'm like. This is what I don't tell you. Even if Mr. Kraft says all I feed off of is intentions, if I don't consume anything? Part of me gets hungry, and I don't know what will happen if I have nothing to take." Kat's voice reverberated around the room ethereally.

Tears spilled from Alina's eyes as she beheld the terrifying, glowing, magical beast before her.

Dropping her chin to her chest as she continued to cry, Alina failed to see the anguished expression that flashed across Katarina's face.

Turning from the Troivackian queen who had begun to tremble, Katarina stalked away and took her leave, slamming the door shut behind herself.

Clasping her hand to her mouth, Alina tried to calm herself down, but she couldn't deny she was rattled to her core. She raised a protective hand to her subtly swollen middle and gripped her dress, unable to properly process the wealth of emotions that overcame her in the wake of her friend's departure.

As Katarina made her way through the castle, she knew the pairing of her glowing aura with her uniform was igniting the whispers that trailed after her.

She should've gone back to her chamber until summoned by Faucher or the king again, but she needed to calm down first.

She shouldn't have shown Alina her true nature.

The poor woman had enough to deal with. The queen didn't need to find out that people like Katarina were what sparked the hunting of witches, when she was trying to restore the Troivackian people's faith in magic and those who wielded it . . .

The redhead had just reached the first floor of the castle and sent a trio of maids scurrying away fearfully when Faucher appeared before her.

Kat's eyes had been fixed blindly ahead, but when her teacher filled her vision, she hesitated.

"We need to talk," he informed her, his voice low.

"Not now. I need to hit something." She tried to sidestep him, but he mirrored her and once again blocked her path.

"Faucher, I need to get outside. Soon." Katarina's hand curled around the hilt of her sword and held tight.

The military man took stock of her aura, her glinting eyes, the hoarseness in her voice . . .

Taking a deep, calming breath in, he acquiesced that she did in fact seem far too agitated to properly receive his lecture regarding her actions during the council meeting.

"You aren't going to be training in the courtyard with the knights."

Kat raised an eyebrow but didn't bother asking the obvious question.

"There is a separate area designated for your training, and we need to discuss its details," her teacher explained intently.

"Faucher." The snarl that left Katarina's mouth echoed unnaturally around the corridor. "I need to brawl."

With his expression turning stony, Faucher reached out and seized the back of Katarina's leather vest, his grip ironclad as he proceeded to stride down the corridor while hauling the redhead along with him without bothering to restrain his strength.

He could tell she was not in a state to be treated lightly.

They had experimented with methods to help maintain her magic during their weeks of training under the helpful observations of Mr. Kraft. They had tried combinations of lack of sleep, lack of food, more exercise, being around only calm individuals whose intentions weren't antagonistic toward her—many things.

However, Mr. Kraft had still warned them all that should Kat get aggravated enough, an outlet for her magic would still be required. If Katarina's emotions were under control, rough handling actually helped her from time to time.

Faucher's mind raced as he considered a way of diffusing her magic while also weighing the political benefits if he was seen hauling her through the castle.

"Don't bother hiding your aura. This will help us in the long run. I'll explain everything to you once we reach the gardens."

"Can we spar while you talk?" Kat asked as she gradually stopped resisting being dragged like a kitten by its mother and instead fell into step beside her teacher until he released her. Enough nobility and servants had already witnessed the shocking display though. Which would help make Kat seem less threatening if Faucher seemed to overpower her at times when her aura was noticeable.

"Yes, we can spar. Keep it together or you won't be seeing breakfast for a very long time."

Kat huffed but didn't argue.

Out of the corner of his eye, Faucher was pleased to see that her aura was starting to dim and she wasn't moving as quickly as before.

He nearly patted her on the back for managing to control herself, though he caught himself in time. It helped when he reminded himself of the events during the council meeting that day. However, he still clapped his hand on her shoulder.

Resisting a grunt of agitation and trepidation, Faucher leaned closer to her ear.

"Anyone ever tell you you're a bloody nuisance?"

"At least once in my life," Kat countered with the start of a smirk.

"If that number isn't in the double digits, I'll shave my beard."

"Are you better-looking without a beard?"

"Are you better-looking without your eyebrows?"

"Well, see, that's not fair. Perhaps you have a handsome jawline."

Faucher shot her a sardonic glance. "A jaw is good for forming words and eating. There is nothing handsome about it."

"Oh dear, it's that bad? Do you not have a proper chin? Is it as weak as your tolerance to spicy food?"

Faucher shoved her playfully, making her laugh and also making her golden eyes cease their unnatural glowing.

Shaking his head, the military man responded to her jibe with, "Gods, you're a pain in the arse, girl."

"And you're far too grumpy a person to be a grandfather," Kat chortled while darting ahead and turning to face Faucher, who briefly rolled his eyes while she jogged backward with her familiar, mischievous expression.

He briefly wondered what about the meeting with the queen had upset Kat to her breaking point, but he decided it was a conversation that could perhaps be saved until after she had worked off more of her energy and magic.

So, Faucher settled for scowling at her bobbing red ponytail as she alternated between attempting to annoy him and racing ahead toward the gardens. The stoic Troivackian was completely unaware, however, that despite his best efforts to look disapproving of her undignified antics, he happened to be smiling a little.

CHAPTER 36

FALTERING FOOTING

S o here on out I'm *not* supposed to train properly?" Kat caught Faucher's downward strike at the last moment, the heel of her boot skidding over the gravel and making her form unsteady.

"Correct. During the day, you will train *poorly* in your designated space. On the other side of the castle. Far from the other knights."

"Really? I can't imagine why," Katarina remarked glibly after throwing off Faucher's sword.

The Troivackian military leader ignored her sarcasm and swung his sword low at an angle, forcing her to awkwardly block him, the strength of her stance tenuous at best.

"At night, we will train properly. You said you can stay awake for days at a time, and we are going to rely on that heavily to ensure our victory," Faucher explained in his usual gruff voice before sliding his own blade down Kat's sword and swiping back to strike again toward her right knee.

Kat barely managed to stumble away from the attack. "Godsdamn gravel," she muttered while widening the berth between herself and her teacher.

"We haven't trained enough on unstable terrain," Faucher noted more to himself than his protégé as he shifted the sword in his hand.

The castle gardens that had been abandoned prior to their impromptu spar were gradually becoming busier with nobles, who feigned interest in a walk amongst the dreary shrubbery in the winter chill in order to better ogle the spectacle of a woman wielding a sword.

"I can stay awake for days, but I'm more likely to show my magic randomly, and . . . well . . . you think I eat a lot *now*?" Kat took a risk and leapt toward Faucher, her sword raised as she flew through the air before dropping it at the last second, his inner left thigh revealing itself to be her target.

Faucher deflected her sword and crashed his elbow into her right shoulder, sending her tumbling over his knee and knocking her on her arse. Faucher lifted the tip of his sword and tapped Kat under the chin, signaling his win.

The redhead let out a huff of annoyance, but when Faucher offered his hand to help her up, was relieved to notice her aura that had temporarily flared up again during their sparring had at last disappeared.

"If you're going to eat like a beast and reveal your magic, we'll have to be even more thorough hiding you this month." Faucher sighed while glowering at a noble couple that dared to draw close enough to almost be within earshot. The pair in question jolted, then made a show of pointing at the sky as though there was something of interest above that took them farther away from Faucher and Katarina.

"Great," Kat grumbled while kicking the gravel idly and pointedly avoiding the curious and judgmental looks she was receiving from several other nearby nobles.

"Come, we'll spar a few more times before midday for good measure. It's good you're clumsy on this new ground, it'll help convince Captain Orion that I oversold your capabilities."

"You mean more than you already did?" Kat asked while rotating her left shoulder and vaguely noting the scrape on her elbow that was starting to sting as a result from her fall.

"I didn't oversell anything." Faucher raised an eyebrow at her. "I am not a man who boasts."

Katarina froze in surprise. "You honestly think that I'd be qualified to pass the knight's test with three more months of training?"

At this question, Faucher allowed a rueful smile to climb up his face. "No."

Kat felt her brightened expression fall flat.

"You're already ready for the knight's test."

Kat balked, then struggled with every fiber of her being not to smile. "Really? Honestly? Even though I've only just begun fighting with a real sword?"

She couldn't hide her excitement.

Faucher tilted his head, his own wry grin softening to something that revealed an ounce of the fondness he had slowly developed for the redhead. "I don't boast, and in war, I bet safely. I want them to be wholly unprepared for the soldier I've trained."

Kat beamed.

She hadn't felt so pleased, proud, or happy in . . .

She failed to think of any recent times, though her mind did guiltily flit back to Alina's crying face earlier, which succeeded in dampening her sunny expression. She shouldn't be feeling so wonderful so soon after that confrontation . . .

"How are we going to protect Caleb and Joshua from their brothers?" Kat wondered aloud in an effort to pull her mind free of the guilt of her fight with the queen.

"We are moving their chambers every night, and on occasion, we will have them stay at an inn in the city so that neither of their brothers can corner them easily. Your peers have their own orders on their conduct and practices for our time here. Similar to you, they will not be training near the other knights," Faucher explained with a small nod.

"Sounds exhausting."

"War is exhausting."

Katarina's gaze fell to the ground as she felt the antagonistic atmosphere of Troivack's court settle heavily on her shoulders. In Faucher's keep, she had had a taste of her old home. A family that was loyal and loved one another . . . Sure they could be arses, but they were good people, and they weren't actively trying to betray, trick, or dominate one another.

When the redhead looked up at the imposing castle, she felt her gloved fingers curl uneasily, her sword in her hand feeling cumbersome . . .

"I don't lose the wars I lead, Ashowan. Just do as I say and all will turn in our favor," Faucher's voice rumbled assuredly to her side.

"Really? Even against Duke Icarus or, I don't know, the devil?"

Faucher looked at the redhead's profile.

It was rare to see her so stoic, and as her golden eyes peered up at the castle and the stray wisps of her fiery hair fluttered around her ears and cheek, Faucher discovered an uncertain side to the witch.

"Duke Icarus, I suspect, will be dealt with by the king or another . . . *invested* party. As for the devil, you nearly bested him without any formal training, and furthermore, you returned from that confrontation without a scratch. I'd say our odds are more than fair, and I've overcome significantly worse chances in the past."

Katarina chewed the inside of her cheek while staring off blindly into the distance. She seemed far from convinced.

Faucher shook his head and raised his sword.

"Aren't you the one always saying your father's cat is more powerful than anyone knows? Isn't that thing coming with Duke Ashowan?"

At last, a small smile returned to Katarina's face. "True. Once Kraken gets here, I'll probably feel loads better. I wonder if he'll like Pina . . . Oh! It'll be exciting to hear what Pina has to say once Kraken and my father interpret for her!" The redhead perked back up.

Faucher chuckled. "If it weren't for that impulsive nature and notable dowry of yours, I'd say you've the makings of a spinster ladened with cats."

"Pfft! Of course I'm going to be a spinster!" Kat flipped her sword and faced her teacher once more. "I just have to avoid pissing off my brother, and I'll live alone happily for the rest of my days being supported by his coffers."

Faucher rolled his eyes, which of course was when Katarina lunged forward to attack.

The seasoned military man didn't even flinch as he parried her blow and swiped toward her middle, but she had been prepared for it and so leaned away nimbly while bringing her sword back up to force Faucher to defend himself.

The two continued sparring wordlessly, but Katarina was yet again losing her footing as Faucher pressed her back over and over until she was going in a small circle.

"I'm going to have you stand on a rope if you're this awful dealing with such an insignificant change in the ground," Faucher barked irritably.

Katarina didn't bother arguing. She knew she was fumbling like a newborn fawn. The shifts beneath her feet as well as the weight of wielding an actual sword was throwing her off balance horribly.

"Sounds good to me. Maybe soak the rope in oil for good measure," she added seriously.

Faucher raised an eyebrow but gave a small nod with an approving glimmer in his eyes. Whatever direction he gave — no matter how difficult or seemingly impossible — Katarina never asked why or how, but instead she would suggest how to make it even more grueling and difficult.

It was one of her traits that reminded Faucher she was, in fact, half Troivackian.

"To be honest, I'm a little worried that it's taking my da so long to get here . . . I thought he would've been here a month ago at the latest," Kat confided abruptly, catching Faucher off guard.

The Troivackian stared at her, momentarily baffled. She wasn't usually so open with him . . .

Whatever had happened between her and the queen had really made the redhead's normally infallible confidence waver.

"The weather is unusual this year. I imagine the Alcide Sea is rough, meaning not a lot of ships are willing to risk the journey—and your father accepted a dukedom shortly before we sent the missive. It would not be an easy time for him or his heir to leave." Faucher cleared his throat. He was never good at consoling women. He'd make a point of asking his wife to speak with Katarina later to avoid having similar talks in the future.

"That's true, but it bothers me more because of what Eric said about the devil's explanation about the strings of fate."

Faucher hesitated lifting up his sword to resume sparring. "What about the strings of fate?"

"Well . . . it makes me wonder if things are so knotted up that my da won't be able to come for a lot longer. And am I still tied to the devil? Does that mean he always knows where I am? Will more magical beasts try to find me here in the castle? Everything seems strange."

"We are dealing with the offspring of the Gods. It *is* strange, Ashowan."

Kat grimaced and reluctantly lifted her sword back up. "I have a bad gut feeling, is what I was getting at."

Faucher openly scowled.

It was Kat's turn to look unimpressed. "Good Gods, are you still a stick in the mud about that? I'll have you know, I haven't heard any women discuss their *dream visions* as you said they would, and I swear I will never talk to you about my womanly times. Ever. Even if you beg me to."

Using brute force, Faucher rushed Kat, making her step back while snapping up her blade just in time to stop her teacher from cutting her from hip to breast. She gritted her teeth against his strength and then with a small flare of her aura thrust him back.

Faucher instantly lowered his sword and moved closer. "Do not throw me off using your power. Only draw upon your skill. Save your power for emergencies. You aren't to use it in daylight until the challenge. Understood?"

Kat's brow furrowed but she nodded once. "Is this for another element of surprise?"

"This is so a petition to have you burned at the stake isn't brought up."

Kat drew back in alarm. "What? But everyone already knows that I'm a witch!"

"That may be, but you made a fine number of enemies this morning. They will use anything they can to strip you of power or bury you." Faucher's earlier black mood began to creep back as he recalled her conduct at the council meeting.

"They can't kill me. Besides, I'm not even going to stay in Troivack for that much longer, and aren't I a high ranking noble now?"

"You're shaking too many cages, Ashowan," Faucher warned, his stare intense. "If they made your death appear as an accident, it is doubtful your Daxarian king will wage a full battle against his beloved daughter's new kingdom."

Kat stilled.

The weighty truth of her teacher's words further sank her spirits.

"This all leads me to the next piece of advice I intended to give to you today." Faucher glanced around them once more and leaned closer when he ensured no one was anywhere near them. "Mend any and all bridges you can. No one, no matter how powerful, can win when divided amongst their allies."

Kat swallowed with difficulty. "Things are fine with my friends and me; they are just small conflicts—"

"Small cracks can make everything prone to shattering with one expert blow. Make peace with the queen, court the prince or don't, but don't waver in whichever decision it is, and lastly . . . talk to Dana." Faucher cleared his throat uncomfortably, his eyes shifting away from his student. "She's calmed down from the dog and sword incident. When she found out the sword had originally had a scabbard on, she felt significantly better about the ordeal."

Kat pressed her lips together before clasping her hands behind her back and sliding forward with a mischievous grin. "Are you saying your daughter is my ally?"

Faucher growled. "She, for whatever reason . . . favors you. She's been upset since the incident."

"Ah, and we can't have beloved Dana upset, of course." Kat nodded, her smile bordering on smug.

Faucher glared.

She held up her hand in surrender, though she still looked a little too good-humored for his liking.

"I want to make up with her as well. I feel genuinely bad about what happened. Though, I do hope you admit how impressive she is with her dogs. Pork Chop got the drop on a mystical being, thanks to her tutelage."

Faucher closed his eyes with a sigh. "Don't bring up Pork Chop to Dana. We haven't been able to find him since that creature made him disappear."

Kat frowned. "Gods . . . that's horrible . . . She really had the highest of hopes for him. She worked the hardest with Pork Chop to show off what dogs are capable of."

"Are you going to ignore what I said about the queen and prince?" Faucher changed the subject seamlessly.

The redhead didn't show any reaction to her teacher as she turned and strode a short way from him. When she did round back to face Faucher, she did so while raising her sword in wait for another sparring round.

"I'm loyal to Alina until the day I die, but we might be becoming a little too . . . different is all."

"I didn't ask for details." Faucher recoiled at the threat of her voicing anything akin to feelings.

"Then don't comment on my personal relationships," Katarina countered with a raised eyebrow before she shuffled forward and gave a half-hearted swipe aimed at Faucher's middle.

He knocked away her sword with a disapproving grimace at her blatant lack of effort.

Kat recovered and swung back to knock his sword away from her while throwing her elbow up by his face, forcing him to take a step back in defense.

"I wasn't commenting. I was giving advice. I know how enemies in this court will try to destroy you and the queen. Ignore me if you wish. My life might become peaceful again if you're sent back to Daxaria early," Faucher informed her glibly.

Kat didn't bother responding. Instead, she focused on quelling the uneasiness that filled her mind and stomach with little else aside from bleakness. Despite her efforts, her sparring didn't improve much. Faucher observed her distractedness but since it served his objective in making their enemies underestimate her, he chose not to lecture her then and there. Though given what he had come to learn about Katarina Ashowan, he would be lying if he said he wasn't concerned with her current state . . .

The woman was prone to hiding her true self and thoughts, and she seemed to become destructive when anyone drew too close to her . . . In other words, she had all the makings of a doomed hero. Faucher had seen it time and time again, and for every one of those times, they usually ended up dying young.

The military leader felt his insides clench.

I will teach her what I know and offer my insights when it is absolutely necessary. If she chooses to sink herself, that is her own business.

Regardless of his efforts to repeat those thoughts, Faucher found himself troubled for the rest of the day and even well into the night at the notion of such a grim fate for his student, though he would never admit it.

CHAPTER 37

A FAULTLESS FORFEIT

Ansar and the imp stood with their hands clasped behind their backs and their heads lowered.

"So, you failed to bind her?"

"Yes, ma'am. Our sincerest apologies." The two bowed toward the woman clad in black seated behind the massive ornate mahogany desk.

The sound of ticking filled the silence.

"Not only that, but you lost my valuable ribbon. Do you know how difficult it is to acquire that piece? You can only create a binding ribbon in the Forest of the Afterlife." The quiet voice of their mistress made the imp's three pupils spin in each eye.

"I offer my life to you, ma'am, as penance," the imp implored desperately.

She regarded him briefly before sighing. "What use would that be? Besides, I didn't really believe you'd be successful. Not when Katarina Ashowan has so many destinies tied to her and her powers. I just wanted her forced back to the castle."

Their mistress leaned back in her dark leather chair. "What you can do as penance, is to weasel out where the devil has hidden. He let his boredom get the better of him as per usual and is now bound to Lady Katarina through fate. It is only a matter of time before the two meet again, but the more information we have, the better. The devil and his followers have run with their tails between their legs, so he's bound to have made mistakes along the way."

Her two subordinates straightened only to bow their heads once more to signify their acceptance of her order.

"Is there anything else I should know about?" their mistress asked, her mild irritation with them pronounced.

The assistant and imp looked at each other briefly.

She leaned forward with the beginnings of a glare forming. "What?"

"Well, ma'am, you see . . . Lady Katarina mentioned that her father was coming," the imp started nervously.

"The house witch?" She hesitated, then raised her eyebrows. "Other than being curious to meet him, I don't see the issue. He'll be powerless once here anyway. Last I heard, the sirins were delaying his arrival."

"He's bringing his familiar, ma'am." Ansar managed to appear calm when he said the words, but his throat bobbed nervously.

The figure had been resting her chin on her fingers as she listened, but her hand then fell away.

Pressing her fingertips into the polished top of the desk, she pushed herself up to her feet and stared down her subordinates.

"Kraken? The familiar who brought about the downfall of Troivack during the Tri-War? The one who successfully strategized the killing of an ancient beast? He is coming here?" her voice rang out in the narrow stone hall.

"Yes, ma'am. That is what Lady Katarina indicated," Ansar confirmed.

Closing her eyes, their mistress took a deep breath in.

"The familiar has never traveled outside of Daxaria before. It could be that with Finlay Ashowan losing his magic, Kraken will also lose his power, but it is good that we know sooner than later."

The imp's eyes darted to the assistant, then back to the woman anxiously. "My brethren will not be pleased with the news."

She gave the imp a hard stare. "There is no need to tell them anything yet. We first gather more information before we raise any kind of alarm."

The otherworldly being did not look convinced, but the perspiration that beaded along his brow signified she had successfully stopped him from arguing the matter any further.

"For now, the plan continues as I originally conceived. We unleash the beings we have brought from the Forest of the Afterlife and solidify the condemnation of magic once and for all in Troivack. We will send Katarina Ashowan back to Daxaria, and our new queen will focus on developing Troivack in more beneficial ways that avoid further bloodshed. If we time it closely with the birth of her first child, our victory should be swift."

Ansar and the imp bowed.

Sure, there were a couple bumps that had arisen in their mistress's grand design. Rarely did any plan proceed without the slightest of hiccups, but they knew she would win one way or another.

Especially if she managed to use Lady Katarina Ashowan's infamous recklessness to her advantage.

Kat stepped out of her chamber while cracking her neck.

It was her second night at the castle, and already she was going to her designated training spot to work with Sir Cas without any prying eyes.

Faucher was required to attend a late-night meeting with the king, and so he would resume being her primary instructor the following night.

The halls were quiet, and a dry chill was barely combated by the lit torches along the marble walls.

Kat loved it.

She had been forced to more or less hide in her chamber after her spar with Faucher in the gardens earlier that day, and she had only managed to entertain herself by playing with Pina and sharpening the fresh nicks out of her sword. To finally be able to move freely without oppressive eyes following her and feel the fresh air on her face bolstered her spirits instantly, and so she rotated her shoulders happily to loosen them in preparation for a long night of training.

A shift in the shadows, however, had her hand flying to her sword hilt.

Eric stepped into the faint light of the torches, revealing his serious expression, while his right hand was pressed, as usual, into his pocket. He wore a snowy white tunic left loosened at his throat, black pants, and his hair appeared as tidy as the day of Alina's coronation.

The last detail made Kat feel even more nauseated upon seeing him, as the unwelcome thought of how he was keeping himself better groomed in order to appeal to the noblewomen he was pursuing occurred to her.

She turned away from his direct, sober stare, dropping her hand from the weapon at her side and wishing that the fluttering in her stomach would cease.

Katarina continued on her original path toward the northeast servants' stairwell that would take her to a small, secluded courtyard on the opposite side of the castle from where the knights trained. Her previously lifted mood was already plummeting.

She was then further agitated to hear Eric's footsteps fall side by side with hers.

"Are you planning on talking to me at some point?" the prince wondered softly, though he kept his face turned forward as they walked.

"Maybe."

Eric raised an eyebrow and tilted his head over his shoulder as they continued.

"Are you going to tell me what's bothering you?"

"There's no need."

"I disagree."

"That's a pity," Kat retorted flippantly.

Eric glanced at her from the corner of his eye and observed the stiffness in her face and posture. He felt his hand grip into a fist in his pocket, and his stomach continued somersaulting, alerting him that his feelings for the redhead had definitely not changed during her time away from the castle.

Letting out a breath he hoped would settle his nerves at least a little, Eric stopped and grasped the sleeve of her tunic, making Kat stop in her tracks.

Unbeknownst to the prince, the gesture made the redhead's heart do the opposite, as it raced onward with no intention of slowing down.

"Kat, are we going to agree that some things are best left unsaid and get along again? Or are we going to talk about this?"

She still had yet to look at the prince properly as she instead focused on sorting out the chaos in her mind and body that stemmed from being alone with Eric . . .

Why did she have to feel drawn to him more than ever? Or feel an agonizing mix of thrill and fury at seeing him again?

"When have we ever truly gotten along?" she responded at last, risking only a quick moment of locking eyes with Eric's, which proved to be a terrible mistake, as her aura briefly flared to life when another impulse to move closer to him surged through her.

"Kat, you and I both know what this is." He sighed, his hand leaving his pocket. "Someone recently made a great point that things are precarious enough in this castle without us acting like awkward children. Unfortunately, I think . . . I think we've hit a point where we can't keep whatever this is up."

Kat felt her emotions cloud her mind, the strength of them briefly rendering her speechless as she fidgeted.

"There's nothing between us that needs to be discussed. It's just . . . just—"

"Godsdamnit, Kat. Stop being like your father for a moment. Let's just try to resolve this situation before it gets worse," the prince interrupted, the barest of hitches in his voice.

"Face what, Eric?" she snapped, but instantly regretted it.

Kat then had the very sudden and clear understanding that if he replied to her honestly, she would have to *hear* his answer, and she would no longer be able to continue avoiding the matter . . .

She could no longer dance around what everyone had been saying.

Not if he himself—

"Kat, do you know what I am to you?"

She smiled.

It was a derisive smile, but it gave her the ability to stare directly at Eric's annoyingly composed face.

"You're just baiting me here to talk to you again. Well played. You've gotten a lot more cunning since coming to Troivack." Kat scoffed and shook her head.

Eric closed his eyes as she turned from him, already bracing himself for what came next.

"I'm in love with you, Kat. Everyone knows it."

Kat froze.

Her aura burst from her body as a rush of tingles and excitement flooded her being.

"And you feel some measure of something for me in return, or you wouldn't be in a twist about my courting other women."

With her cheeks burning, Kat didn't fully look back at Eric. It felt like her heart was choking her . . .

"The reason I've avoided admitting it—and my guess is you have a similar reason, is that I'm crawling toward death's carriage, and you don't need that pain. I'm not capable of being the husband you deserve, and I will only bring you disappointment."

"You . . . You . . ." Kat continued to struggle over the bluntness of Eric's words.

There was no room to hide from them. No vagueness, no sarcasm . . .

"I'm not asking you to tell me your feelings. I'm clearing the air because things are dangerous here and there is no margin for error." Eric said the words and knew he sounded calm and in control, but in actuality, he was seriously debating casually stepping off the nearest window ledge.

He knew whatever Katarina Ashowan did manage to say to him after his admittance, no matter what, it would not bring a simple or easy resolution.

"Will you ever change your mind?" Kat's voice was far quieter than normal.

Eric felt as though he were being gutted. He knew he should have been on his knees before her begging for forgiveness. He didn't even need her to clarify what she meant by her question.

"It isn't about changing my mind; it's about the honest to Gods truth and making wise decisions. I will not always be sober. I will not be strong enough to have a wife I love more than life itself while also ruling a kingdom, and I will not *ever* wish to burden you with my shortcomings as a man."

Kat lifted her eyes to the ceiling, and Eric fought the urge to be sick when he noticed the sheen of tears in her eyes.

"I'd destroy the world to keep you safe and happy, but you want to protect it, and it's just one of the many reasons we are going to do nothing but hurt each other."

"Stop it." Kat looked away from him. She didn't want him to see her crying even harder than before.

"Don't love me back. Please, Kat. You don't . . . You don't need that suffering in your life. You are everything . . ." Eric's voice broke, and it was then he realized that the sight of Katarina's tears drew out his own. "You are everything that is right, and I'll only love you wrong."

Eric looked away from her.

He needed to end the conversation.

He needed to drag himself as far as possible from her soon or else he wasn't sure what he'd do.

"I'm sorry, Kat."

Lowering his head, tears falling from his face, Eric walked in the opposite direction Kat had been heading, leaving her alone once again in the corridor.

When the sound of his steps had disappeared into the night, Katarina let out the gasping sob she had fought with all her might to contain in Eric's presence.

Covering her face, she stumbled back until her shoulders hit the wall and allowed herself to succumb to her grief.

He was right. He was absolutely right about it all. It was horribly fair and candid of him, and it was one of the many reasons she had wanted to avoid the matter and pretend it didn't exist.

The only detail he had perhaps purposefully omitted, most likely for her benefit, was that she would have hurt him one day just as badly.

Somehow, someway . . . she would have let him down. Be it as a queen, a wife, or a mother . . . It was her way.

At the very least, he had given her the great gift and mercy of not insisting to know how she felt about him in return.

Katarina sank to the floor, her tears still running with no end in sight as she permitted herself to, at the very least, think the words he hadn't asked for or hoped to hear in response to his own confession.

I love him. I love him so Godsdamn much, and I should never tell him, or we'll really be ruined.

CHAPTER 38

EFFICACIOUS EVASION

Sir Vohn let out a long sigh as he marched down the darkened castle corridor while closing his eyes and briefly wondering if he would be able to go to bed at a decent hour.

Ever since he had been placed back under the prince's command, he had been bombarded with endless work that kept him awake late into the night and up early in the morning. He barely had time to train . . . though he couldn't deny the nature of the work was wildly interesting.

Discovering more and more about Duke Sebastian Icarus's dealings and the full extent of his reach had been both shocking and disturbing to Sir Vohn. Even if the nobleman was assassinated, he had set up his younger brother to take over his work, and then there were cousins to factor in . . .

Meaning the only way to properly eradicate the family would be to cut off its biggest supporters or make the key figures turn on each other by fueling the entire family's greed.

A feat easier said than done, but . . .

Eric Reyes had already begun a plot of his own.

Its details weren't even known in their entirety to Sir Vohn, despite him doing most of the legwork for the prince, as the future king spent his days dallying with Troivackian noblewomen and visiting the thriving businesses of Vessa under the pretense of pleasure seeking.

Sir Vohn was deep in thought as he made his way down the covered walkway that overlooked the knights' training yard, when he saw a familiar glint of dirty blond hair.

Stopping in his tracks, he looked down to see the Daxarian prince half slumped against one of the training dummies, his face turned toward the shadows of the night and away from the castle.

Frowning, Sir Vohn waited for Eric to notice him, but the prince seemed completely oblivious to the world around him. The knight glanced around the courtyard to see if there was anyone else present but only confirmed his earlier guess that it was empty.

"Your Highness?" he called out while carefully making his way over to Eric. The prince turned and half slid, half stumbled off the dummy.

"Ah, hey," he greeted dumbly while seizing the burlap of the dummy to help steady himself.

Sir Vohn grinned. "Aah. Letting off a bit of steam? Good on you."

Eric released the dummy and managed to stand on his own, albeit with a bit of a sway.

"Yeah." He slipped one hand into his pocket while the other rubbed his eyes.

"Everything alright?" Sir Vohn noticed that the prince hadn't looked at him properly yet.

"Everything's fine," Eric uttered before stumbling past the knight toward the castle.

Sir Vohn raised a curious eyebrow after the royal, then eyed the training dummy and spotted the mostly finished bottle of Troivackian moonshine sitting at its base. Plucking up the forgotten libation, he turned and jogged to catch up to Eric.

"I don't mean to pry, Your Highness, but you don't seem all that fine," Sir Vohn murmured once he fell into step beside the prince in the quiet castle corridor.

"Just had to do something unpleasant," Eric explained blearily.

"Ah . . ." A strong premonition presented itself to the knight. "Does this have something to do with Lady Katarina?"

Eric faltered only for a moment, but it was enough of a reaction that Sir Vohn knew he had guessed correctly.

"What happ—"

"Have you received word from Rozek's harbor master?" The prince's interruption pointedly changed the subject.

"I did. His letter answers a load of nothing. He danced around every question," Sir Vohn relayed while moving his gaze forward.

He knew better than to press Eric in his current state.

"About how we expected. The duke is rewarding his loyalty sufficiently, it seems. I'd like to go in person and see if we can learn more. How long of a journey would you say it is?" The prince began to swerve drunkenly off his trajectory as he spoke.

"I would say if we traveled with only a few knights, it'd be a week and a half give or take."

"I'll make the request to the king." Eric nearly bumped into Sir Vohn as he readjusted his direction.

The two men had reached the prince's chamber and entered the darkened room to find Thomas Julian asleep on the sofa before the crackling hearth, a thick stack of papers still in hand that he had been reviewing for his superior.

Eric and Sir Vohn eyed the youth with small smiles.

"Poor lad is really working hard," Sir Vohn chortled quietly.

Eric stepped over to one of the unlit lanterns on his desk and set to lighting it with a spill. "Mm."

"Should I wake him?" the knight asked while noticing the prince already resuming his own work at his desk.

"Leave him be. I don't think he slept at all last night."

"Neither did you," Sir Vohn pointed out while seating himself in one of the chairs in front of the desk.

"I don't sleep much anyway," Eric replied shortly. "How close is Duke Icarus's primary residence to Rozek?"

Sir Vohn sighed.

It didn't seem as though he were going to have a restful night after all.

"His residence is between three of Troivack's cities. Just on the northern side of the vineyard belt but south of Biern."

Eric nodded pensively. "The vineyards . . . I want to stop and see those as well on our way up to Rozek. I think a surprise tour might be illuminating."

Sir Vohn raised an eyebrow. "Are you intending to miss Lady Katarina's match?"

Eric tensed, but his eyes didn't leave the paperwork in front of himself. "If I miss it, it won't be the end of the world. Besides, I might be able to make it back if we leave in the morning."

Sir Vohn hesitated. "Eric, I think you should be here. Even if it's uncomfortable, there are a lot of people angry with Lady Katarina."

The pages Eric had been poring over slipped from his hands. They instead gently clasped into fists atop the desk, and he finally raised his bloodshot eyes.

"What can I do about it?"

Sir Vohn flinched at the hardness in the prince's gaze. "Try to keep protecting her."

"Investigating a way to destroy Duke Icarus is protecting her as well. Being her bodyguard isn't going to help anything long term," Eric countered evenly.

"That's true, but—"

"Gabe, this isn't a discussion. I need that dukedom buried before I leave for Daxaria, and I'm going to try and accomplish that before the spring."

The knight grimaced and lowered his eyes, but he could tell that the discussion was going nowhere. So after a moment of letting the heavy quiet rest between them, he rose to his feet.

"I'll start packing and working on the request for an escort party to join us from Captain Orion once the king gives his permission."

"Thank you." Eric gave his friend a small nod, a hint of an apology crossing his face.

As the knight turned to the door, he recalled something he had heard earlier that day that perhaps wasn't the best idea to share, but he knew it was important.

"Ah, the queen and Lady Katarina were said to have had an argument of sorts today. Her Majesty is said to have been quite upset . . . Perhaps speak with the queen to see if she's alright before we depart?"

Eric hesitated. The tension in his face was indicative of the urge to dismiss the suggestion, but reticent acceptance prompted him to nod once more.

"I'll check on Alina before we leave. Thank you for informing me about this."

Sir Vohn bowed.

At the very least, during his time in Troivack, the prince seemed to have rediscovered some sense of responsibility and duty . . .

It was something Sir Vohn had noticed mysteriously disappear throughout the years, and he had been all too happy to see its return—despite its coming with the headache of incessant work.

Letting out a breath, the knight left the bedchamber, pondering the prince's poor state and decisions . . .

Who knows. Maybe some time apart will help Eric and Lady Katarina figure out their frustrating situation.

Eric knocked on Alina's chamber door impatiently.

He had wanted to have left for Rozek already, but apparently his sister hadn't been in a state to see him yet.

She did mention a little while ago that her morning sickness was getting to be awful . . .

"Enter." Alina's soft voice reached her brother's ears, drawing him from his thoughts.

Nodding to her two guards, Eric pressed open the door, its hinges giving the barest of squeaks in the frosty morning air. Slipping into the chamber, the prince was only mildly surprised to see Brendan present.

The Troivackian king must have attended the meeting with him earlier and returned immediately after to his wife's side.

Eric's brother-in-law was seated beside Alina, looking over some papers, his tunic loosened and his legs crossed toward the crackling fire as Alina sat with her head in hand and her eyes closed.

She looked more green than pale, indicating that Eric's earlier suspicion about her morning sickness was accurate.

He closed the door behind himself. "Sorry to interrupt, Lina. Just came to say goodbye."

The queen's eyes fluttered open as she turned to look at Eric with a weak smile. "I heard you're going to investigate that nasty duke. Thank you for doing this."

The prince bobbed his head while moving past his sister's chair so that he was standing in front of her. "No problem. It gives me a chance to stretch my legs; I haven't been in one place for so long in years."

Alina's smile drifted away then. "You'll come back, right?"

Eric winced. His prevailing guilt over abandoning his family was alive and well. "I will. I promise."

She nodded but wasn't able to maintain eye contact with her brother, as her gaze momentarily fell back to the fire, the emeralds in her ears glittering in the pale light of day from the window behind Eric.

"I heard you had a fight with Kat," the prince began, his voice quieting.

Alina stiffened and Brendan's eyes snapped up from his papers.

Eric watched as his sister's brows crashed into a frown, her eyes hardening when she looked back to him.

"You knew she got stabbed on the way to Vessa."

The prince wasn't fast enough at hiding his reaction.

"I see." Alina studied her brother thoughtfully. "So that's what you were getting at when you said she would hide things."

Eric briefly lowered his chin to his chest, unable to think of an appropriate response.

"I understand it wasn't your business to tell me, but given that my husband also knew, I can't say I'm all too happy about it."

The prince squinted awkwardly. "Sorry about that, Lina. If I'm being honest, I'm surprised you aren't angrier with me about it."

The queen shook her head, her expression gentling. "I'm too tired to be angry. Besides . . . I have other things to be worried about." She shifted uncomfortably in her chair, which subconsciously drew Eric's attention to the small bump that could have been a trick of the eye to most, but he knew better.

"Will you make up with Kat?" the prince asked, which prompted the king to look to his wife expectantly.

Alina's lips pursed, and she tentatively picked at her left thumbnail. "I . . . I don't think I'm ready for that. Not for a while."

"She was just trying to protect you, Lina," the prince defended.

"To a point." The note of anger in Alina's voice made even her husband look up in faint surprise. "Tell me. Do you also know about the coyote?"

Eric faltered. "Alina . . . how much did Kat tell you about those times?"

Despite her earlier claim that she didn't have the energy to be upset, new fury emerged in Alina.

"So you did know! Gods, to think that you just return to court and you already know everything before anyone else." The queen adjusted herself so that she was sitting up straighter.

"It was a unique circumstance. Between the two poisonings and two attacks—"

"There were *two* attacks?!"

Eric balked.

Apparently, Kat *hadn't* told his sister everything.

"I know she had told me there had been three or four attempts her first day here in the castle, but I thought she was exaggerating! Because I naïvely thought she would tell me about important things like that!"

The prince dropped his head to his hand.

Brendan almost felt sorry for him.

"Yes. The first attack was what made her magic surge to the point she needed to kill a coyote. She was perfectly fine though. I was nearly kidnapped during the second time, and she was stabbed during that one as well. Did you also hear about the incident with the ship?" Eric looked at his brother-in-law, whose eyes had gone wide as though silently ordering the prince to shut up.

Alina stood. She stared at her husband, then at her brother.

"What is the Godsdamn matter with everyone thinking they need to protect me?! What happened on the ship?"

Brendan watched his wife bear down on the prince while remaining perfectly still. He was all too aware it wouldn't take much for her to redirect her anger his way.

"Without being tied to the boat during the storm, she dove off the rat-lines in order to tie our loose headsail." Eric was responding remarkably well given the murderous aura around his sister.

The queen threw her hands in the air and stalked toward her chamber door.

"Alina, I truly think Kat just doesn't see those things as a big deal. She probably forgot—" The prince started to explain but didn't get the chance to finish before the door slammed behind his baby sister.

Eric looked to the king, who was staring at him incredulously.

"How was I supposed to know how much was said?!"

"You should've spoke to Lady Katarina first; that's how," Brendan declared exasperatedly.

Eric closed his eyes for a brief moment, then shook his head and followed his sister's trajectory.

"I'll see you in a few weeks, Your Majesty."

Once the prince had exited the chamber, Brendan let out a grunt of irritation.

"I wonder how long before my wife remembers to be angry with me . . ."

The king closed his eyes wearily as he reached the unfortunate conclusion that the answer wasn't a comforting one.

CHAPTER 39

A ROBUST REVIEW

She poked his face.

He turned with his mouth open.

She stuck her tongue out at him.

He stuck his out at her.

She narrowed her eyes.

His remained crossed.

"You're sure he's not blind?"

Kezia laughed in her usual melodical way. "That is the way newborns are, *ryshka*."

Kat tilted her head as she continued staring at Henry and Kezia's newborn son, Elio. He had a patch of thin, straight black hair atop his head, and from the looks of his slightly creased nose, a close resemblance to his father.

Kezia sat in a gold upholstered armchair in front of the hearth, wearing only her shift and a pale blue silk robe loosely tied, while Kat sat on the couch, peering down at Elio in his cradle and donning her official uniform from Faucher save for the chest plate. She had been permitted a brief visit to Kezia and the new baby over her luncheon break.

"Thank you, by the way, for your gift," Kezia added while watching the redhead's careful examination of her newborn.

"Ah, no problem." Kat didn't bother looking up from the babe.

"He is a little young to appreciate a bottle of moonshine, but I'll be sure to save it for him."

Kat nodded as she tried to poke Elio's face again but was thwarted when his tiny hand clasped her index finger.

"What a spectacular grip he has," Kat announced with a grin and at last looked at Kezia.

She smiled. "Thank you, *ryshka*. I'm sure he will take after the Devark's and grow to be a sturdy warrior."

"Or he could be lovely like you, who knows." Kat shrugged.

Kezia laughed again, her blue eyes twinkling. "Ah, *ryshka*. How I've missed you."

Meeting the stunning gaze of her fellow handmaiden, Kat tried to keep the smile on her face, but she wasn't entirely successful.

The new mother noticed this and was beginning to part her lips to ask the obvious question, when the redhead turned back to the baby.

"I heard Lady Wynonna is supposed to join us today."

Leaning forward to look closer upon her son who still had yet to relinquish his hold on Katarina's finger, Kezia replied, "Ah, yes. She should be here soon. I feel badly that she has been left alone with Lady Sarah to manage Her Majesty's schedule and notes. Particularly, as Lady Sarah has not been shy about expressing her disapproval over our queen's attendance of the council meetings."

Kat grimaced. "No wonder Lady Wynonna's drinking habits are becoming so well-known . . . I'm not sure I'd be able to be discreet if I had to deal with Lady Sarah all the time either."

Kezia sighed and leaned back in her seat as Elio's eyes slowly closed. She was about to respond to the redhead's comment when the chamber door flew open and in stalked Alina with Lady Wynonna following closely behind, looking bewildered.

When Kat registered both Alina's presence and furious expression, her good mood disappeared. Her shoulders slumped forward, and she looked toward the fire for a moment with the same countenance of a weary soldier before she stood and bowed to her friend.

"Good day, Your Majesty."

Alina's storm cloud of an expression only darkened. "You know what I just heard?"

Kat straightened, clasped her hands behind her back, and broadened her stance like a knight receiving orders.

"No, Your Majesty."

Alina's eyes narrowed. "I heard on your voyage here from Daxaria that you recklessly tied off a headsail during that abysmal storm without being tied to the ship, and you survived *two* attacks. The first of which caused a magical outburst. Not just the one where you were stabbed."

Both Lady Wynonna and Kezia gaped at Kat, who didn't so much as blink in response.

"Yes, Your Majesty, that is correct."

Seeing that Kat wasn't eliciting any emotional reaction made Alina fold her arms slowly across her chest.

Behind her, Lady Wynonna nervously sidled over to Lady Kezia.

"Why was this not relayed to me?"

"It was reported to His Majesty to investigate. I have been working to keep my more useful magical abilities hidden to use the element of surprise and better defend against those who are seeking to do you harm." Kat's golden eyes remained fixed on the floor.

Taking a step closer to her friend, Alina barely resisted the urge to start shouting.

"As a friend, I care about you and want to know when dangerous situations appear," Alina announced with a notable hitch in her voice.

"I believe I communicated yesterday, Your Majesty, that our definitions of what is dangerous is varied and harder for me to discern."

"Bullshit."

Lady Wynonna let out a small gasp, and Kezia snatched her arm to stop her from making another sound.

"You listen to me, Katarina Ashowan. I know you. You are *not* a monster. And I know you are smarter than what you are pretending to be. And I know you are more frightened than you like anyone knowing. And do you know how I know?" Alina drew even closer to Kat, who still hadn't budged a muscle. "Because I once listened to you rant for an hour about the first time you got your menses. You do not spare details of anything no matter how unpleasant or unwanted they are. For you to conveniently omit having been in danger, I know it isn't for my benefit or because you *forgot*—it's because you are scared, and you keep trying to push me away so you don't have to face that."

The redhead's eyes at last lifted to meet her friend's.

"I told you the story about the first time I got my menses because it was a humorous story, Your Majesty. Not to make you uncomfortable."

"What in the world could be funny about that?!" Lady Wynonna exclaimed before she could stop herself.

Alina's ferocious expression fell flat, and Kat couldn't resist sliding her gaze over to her fellow handmaidens with a wry twitching of her mouth.

"I happened to accidentally eat rancid meat the night before and was in the midst of dealing with that when my first course started."

Both Wynonna and Kezia recoiled in disgust as they put two and two together.

Alina rolled her eyes to the ceiling. "Lady Katarina is especially proud of when she screamed at her brother and father that she was 'literally dealing with a bloody shit show,' and made them both bolt for her mother."

"Oh . . . Gods."

"Ugh."

Kezia and Wynonna reacted at the same time, prompting Alina to peer over her shoulder.

"See? She tells me about *that* and not about getting attacked in a foreign kingdom."

Lady Wynonna nodded along, still cringing in repulsion at the story.

When the queen looked back to Kat, the redhead's smile was already disappearing. She sensed Alina wasn't through with her.

"Why did my brother know about everything, but you didn't want to tell me?"

A subtle jolt ran through Kat at the mention of the prince, and her face turned pale.

"Eric's the one who told you all this?"

Alina's anger was momentarily hampered by her concern over the sudden look of pain from her friend.

"He thought I knew after I asked him about the coyote. That doesn't answer the question—in fact, that reminds me of another mystery. What the hell has been going on between the two of you? Ever since Daxaria, things have been strange, and while we all have a small sense of what is happening in your present relationship, you have been hiding something ever since my wedding."

Kat looked to Kezia for help but only received an apologetic wince in response.

"I need to go back to my training. I really shouldn't have taken so long of a break." Kat cleared her throat and bowed, then began moving expediently toward the door.

Alina opened her mouth to furiously call her back, when Kezia stood and drew her attention. "Your Majesty, she hasn't seemed herself today. Perhaps we let Lady Katarina have a bit of a reprieve."

The queen barely resisted the urge to argue as she turned and stared after her friend, who had essentially bolted from her. Her wrath and hurt was swiftly replaced with concern and curiosity as she reluctantly turned away from the door and instead made her way over to Kezia's sofa which Kat had recently vacated. Though before she busied herself with greeting her nephew, she found herself thinking, *I wonder if she knows that Eric left this morning . . .*

Sebastian closed the old leather tome in defeat and leaned back in the hard wooden chair with his eyes closed, hoping to stretch some of the kinks out of his spine.

"I take it there was nothing in that book either?" Mr. Kraft asked with a yawn from his place between two towering stacks of paper in the corner of the mage's office.

The room was overflowing with papers and books, magnifying glasses, maps, brass tools, and little else. A small round weathered rug of faded colors took up the center of the office in a halfhearted attempt to add some measure of comfort. The circular room was lined with bookshelves, and aside from that, held two cabinets, a desk, and two chairs for the unlikely duo to continue their fruitless endeavor of finding answers to the magical happenings in Troivack.

"Nothing of significant use here either. The author simply went on tangents about witches and how they were the true demons to walk the earth."

Mr. Kraft closed his own book and nudged his glasses farther down his nose in order to rub his eyes.

"All we know right now is that there are creatures that aren't supposed to be visible or interact with people in this world," Sebastian continued while sliding the book onto the desk to his left.

"Correct. I can see small beings. Pixies, small magic fey of the Forest of the Afterlife, but they don't do much aside from cause small mischief that can be written off. I once had a pixie hide my glasses for the better part of a day . . . but nothing worse than that. Now we have ancient beings from the realm of the Gods that haven't roamed the earth in centuries . . . Imps, dragons, golems . . . All we're missing are sirins."

Sebastian stared blindly at the bookshelf across from him, lost in thought before looking back to the coven leader.

"Four beasts for each element. The ancient text said that they remained loyal to the devil as they, too, believed that the earth should have remained theirs. The first witch barely placated them for centuries, and when the humans started distancing themselves from the ancient beasts and declaring war on them, the devil and witch fought, and he won . . . But the Gods were angered and sided with their deceased daughter, condemning the devil to roam the earth for eternity."

It was an ancient story . . . one that the two men had carefully reassembled during their research.

"It makes sense that the devil would help Duke Icarus villainize witches if the history accounts are correct," Mr. Kraft reasoned.

Sebastian looked at the leader with a frown. "What is strange, however, is what happened with Aidan Helmer all those years ago when he found the dragon in the mountains here in Troivack. If the dragon was loyal to the devil, why did it serve a witch? And why did it serve a witch who sought to put other witches in control over humans? That seems counterintuitive to the devil's motivations."

Mr. Kraft's expression hardened.

He never enjoyed recalling his former superior . . .

Meanwhile, Sebastian continued his musings. "Aidan Helmer was reportedly secretive about the details of the dragon. He claimed he found it by fate while traveling through the northern mountains, but that can't be the entire story."

"No, it wasn't." Mr. Kraft shook his head idly. "He claimed it was his familiar, but while a familiar bond is a very unique relationship a witch can share with a beast, it still seemed too far-fetched."

The coven leader rose from his seat with a grunt and peered aimlessly around the room.

"If I were to hypothesize . . . I think we *will* see the final ancient beast unaccounted for. I think one of these days a sirin will appear. Though admittedly, I fear a dragon more than a sirin."

Sebastian nodded along. "Perhaps given that the imp and golem failed in binding Lady Katarina, it may be sooner than later."

"That is another interesting thing . . . Lady Katarina's report on their attempt indicated that the imp and the golem were not aligned with the devil. They were trying to bind her to *stop* the devil from returning to find her. I had wondered if this was still under his orchestration and he was merely trying to confuse her, but the more I think about it, the more I wonder if there is another being that's a part of this mess."

"The first witch was slaughtered, so it isn't her," Sebastian reminded while he joined the coven leader in standing. "Who else would have the power to summon beasts from the Forest of the Afterlife?"

"What if there was another witch . . . a mutated witch, who *could* summon the ancient beasts." Mr. Kraft turned to Sebastian, his eyes brightening.

"They would have to be older given that they summoned the dragon for Aidan Helmer decades ago . . . Wait . . . Didn't the prince say that during his time with the devil he had mentioned someone had created Witch's Brew and it gave humans the ability to see creatures that weren't of this realm?"

"Then . . . we need to find the witch who is able to call these creatures here . . . And the best way to find her would be—"

"To find out where Witch's Brew is coming from, and who made it."

The two men finished the thought in unison, and they wasted no time in bolting to the door.

Their new theory needed to be relayed to the king, and hopefully, it was the missing key to the mystery of where the ancient creatures were coming from and why they had begun appearing in their realm once more.

CHAPTER 40

MAKING HEADWAY

I f we continue with your line of thinking . . ." Brendan Devark began slowly, his right hand touching his bearded chin while Mr. Kraft and Mage Sebastian stood before his desk.

The pair had just relayed to the king their theory regarding how the ancient magical beasts were appearing and terrorizing them.

"We will have to figure out where the first reports of Witch's Brew originated." Brendan's eyes squinted at his desk in deep thought.

Their assessment of the how and why were not far-fetched.

After all, if there was a witch who was opening portals, perhaps that meant Witch's Brew was from the Forest of the Afterlife . . .

Brendan began nodding to himself. "This might make sense. Alright. I've had physicians and poison testers attempt to run studies of the drug in the past, but there wasn't much they could learn about it. I'll talk to the queen to find out if Daxaria had started testing it at all for more information. Mage Sebastian, please go speak with my assistant, Mr. Levin, and ask him to find the report where Witch's Brew first appeared."

The mage bowed.

"Sire, would it be possible for Mage Sebastian and me to study Witch's Brew ourselves? While the physicians may have made their own observations of it, it'd be interesting to see if we as magic users would be able to find anything different." Mr. Kraft lowered his head as he made the request.

Brendan gave careful thought before responding.

It needed to be done, that much was a guarantee, but he also knew if anyone found out about a witch being a part of running tests on the drug, it would lead to massive headaches and chaos amongst his council . . .

"Mr. Kraft, I believe this is a good idea, however, is there perhaps a place you know of outside the castle that you could use for your testing location?"

The coven leader stilled, his expression becoming unreadable.

"I do . . . yes. Though I ask that the details of the location remain as guarded and private as possible."

Brendan raised a black eyebrow.

Well, the remaining coven members must have had some sort of hideout . . . It only made sense that they try to preserve their haven.

"Very well."

Mr. Kraft bowed gratefully, then with Mage Sebastian at his side, the two exited the king's office to continue with the next step of their plan.

Brendan, meanwhile, kept pondering why both the devil and this other mysterious witch seemed interested in Katarina Ashowan. He understood about as much as a mere mortal man was able to understand about the workings of the Gods—that the devil was concerned about becoming entangled with Lady Katarina . . . But why? What about her was so problematic?

Aside from her propensity to aggravate people and get into trouble.

Releasing a long exhale, the king thought back to what they had come to learn about the redhead noblewoman's magical abilities as well as the dialogue the prince had reported having had with the devil several months ago.

The devil, who called himself Sam, had asked if she had killed before . . . if she could kill a deity . . .

Brendan's first inclination was to think the devil was worried Katarina would try to kill him, but what if that wasn't the case? What if he was more worried about a God-like witch opening portals to the Forest of the Afterlife? Though wouldn't the devil be more powerful than a mere witch?

The king's mind was humming. He was close to realizing something; there just was a piece of information he was missing . . .

He squeezed his eyes shut. *Katarina Ashowan can be stronger and faster than regular humans. She can see in the dark. She can stay awake for days on end and eat enough to put a kingdom in debt. She can consume deadly poison and only requires a few hours of rest to heal . . .*

The king recounted the details of her powers, feeling a fluttering in his gut that told him he was getting closer.

Her magic consumes other magic directed at her, but it also consumes intentions directed at her. The devil asked if she could consume the entirety of another witch's powers, and if she could consume a curse, or if she would take on more power . . . Wait.

Brendan stood from his seat, then hastily exited his chamber. He needed to ask Lady Katarina a question . . .

What he was thinking didn't answer everything, but depending on her answer, it would be an important piece of the puzzle all the same.

"You need to throw him off his game. Dante fought him yesterday morning before he had to go check on his wife, and he lost horribly. You don't stand a chance," Sir Cas murmured in Kat's ear as she observed Piers roll his shoulders casually.

"I've sparred with him before," the redhead pointed out while rotating her right wrist.

"This is different; he's going to try to enrage you today. The knights that you spar against are going to insult you because during a fight, all is deemed fair," Sir Cas explained while he, too, stared at Piers, who waited for her in the center of their small makeshift training area.

"Most people in Troivack say annoying things to me. I think I'm immune at this point," Kat replied flatly while peering around her new training ground.

Normally, the space they were using was where the guests of the castle balls would park their carriages. It was on the opposite side of the castle from the proper training grounds for the knights, and while it may have been awkward in shape and lacking the nearby amenities of the training grounds, it did have one very important feature . . .

Privacy.

The first-floor windows were nonexistent, and thanks to one of the tower bases starting at the second floor, that corner of the castle grounds was quite hard to see.

Kat faced Sir Cas more directly while plucking up the sword she had left leaning against the castle wall while performing her warmup.

"So your advice is to annoy Piers before he can annoy me?" she asked with a halfhearted smile.

Sir Cas eyed her for a moment before replying. Kat had been off the entire morning and into the afternoon following her meeting with Lady Kezia and her new son. Even Faucher had looked a little disgruntled when they'd crossed paths to trade off training Lady Katarina . . . as though he, too, was bothered by her pale face and somber attitude.

"Yes. If you can manage it," the Daxarian knight confirmed with a serious nod while forcing himself to be present once more.

"Oh, don't you worry. I'll throw him off his game. Just like how my da taught me."

"You're not going to tell him he has broccoli in his teeth, are you? Lord Ashowan used to do that to a lot of the new problematic knights back in Austice," Sir Cas said with a teasing smile.

He was heartened to see color rise in Kat's face as she momentarily balked before becoming indignant.

"N-No! Of course I have something completely different in mind!"

Sir Cas patted her shoulder with a chuckle while also pressing her toward Piers, who had his hands on his slim hips as he waited impatiently for the redhead to join him.

"Besides, aren't I supposed to look awful while training during the day?" she asked under her breath to the Daxarian knight.

"True, but the bottoms of your boots are still slick from standing on the oiled rope last night. I think keeping calm while minding your footwork is going to be more difficult than you realize."

As if on cue, Kat slipped and barely caught herself as her left heel glided off one of the stones. Sir Cas let his hand rest on her back after making sure she wasn't going to fall on her arse.

"Good luck."

Piers smirked at her, flipped his dagger in one hand, and clasped his sword in the other while setting his feet apart to prepare for the spar. "Well, well. If it isn't the woman who thinks she can be a knight," he crowed at her.

"And if it isn't the boy who doesn't know how to be a man," Kat bit back.

Piers stared at her, blinking rapidly. "You thought of that way too quickly."

Kat lunged forward with her sword, forcing Piers to parry and attempt to stab her exposed side, only to have Kat step closer to him as she dodged and bashed her forehead against his nose.

"Holy sh—" Sir Cas's words were cut off as Piers stumbled back and Kat lifted her sword again, half expecting him to be too caught off guard to defend himself.

But Piers had been trained under the keen eye of his father, and so he blocked her attack but realized belatedly that he had dropped his dagger.

"A brutal type of attack that would make any Troivackian teacher proud . . . but did you have to break my nose? You know I make my living with my looks," Piers asked as he and Kat began to casually clash swords together.

"I didn't realize you lived in poverty. I'll be sure to give you some coin later." Kat followed through on her strike, forcing Piers to use both his hands on his sword hilt to cast her off and draw their locked weapons in a circle that eventually sent Kat stumbling after her boot slipped on the stone.

She recovered just in time to block Piers's lazy follow-up attack after he picked up his dagger.

"Alright, Ashowan, I was going to ease into the insults, but you're coming at me like I just bedded your mother, so I guess there's nothing I can do." Piers jabbed his dagger toward her stomach, and when she leapt back out of the way, she stumbled again as she then also had to duck under the arc of his sword.

"Wonderful, let's see if you know any big words." Kat flipped her sword in her hand and swept up toward Piers's face. When he was occupied defending her with his own sword and knife (else his left bicep be cut), she sunk a punch into his exposed right side, partially winding him.

Piers began to double over, his face still bloodstained from her earlier headbutt, but as he did so, he reared back, recognizing that she was about to do it again. "Were you honestly going to smash my nose into my skull just now?!" he demanded, incensed.

"Is this part of your insults?" Kat's smile was menacing.

"Good Gods, it really was a disservice to your parents that you were born a woman. You would've been an incredible brawler." Piers disengaged from her and accepted a clean towel from Sir Cas to mop up the blood from his face, while she, too, accepted a towel to wipe the droplets that had splattered on her own cheeks.

"It's alright; I was born a witch. So that makes up for it."

"Alright, remember Ashowan, in case someone is watching, you're supposed to look dainty. I know it's a foreign skill to you, but think you can try?"

Kat raised an eyebrow and readjusted the grip on her sword in silent approval.

Piers eyed her for an extra moment before looking at Sir Cas, who grimaced in response.

She was definitely worked up about something . . .

The youngest son of the Faucher family decided to take a stab at what it could be.

The two crossed swords once, then twice, more as a means of making the steel of their weapons ring pleasantly, but by the third time, both had thrown their full strength into the exchange, and Piers decided it was time to test Kat's control.

She had just parried another attack and kicked his blade from his hand. Their swords were once again locked together, with her teeth clenched and bared.

"Tell me, are you just bedding the prince to get favors? Or do you have some delusion about being the queen of Daxaria?"

All color drained from Kat's face, and for a fleeting moment, Piers wondered if she was going to try to kill him the same way she had Broghan Miller . . .

She cast off his sword and bore down on him, her eyes gleaming with magic.

Kat swiped her sword by his middle, forcing Piers to leap back. Using the extra breath of time, Kat scooped up his dropped dagger and continued advancing on him.

"Words are all you have to distract people from the fact that you struggled to measure up as a son in the Faucher family," she called out, her voice ice.

Piers stiffened, then gave a humorless half smile. "You have a knack for destroying relationships, it seems." He thrust the point of his sword forward, which Kat deflected easily, then spun and jabbed the knife toward his side, but Piers kneed her in her back and sent her tumbling to the ground before she could complete the attack as her boots failed to grip the stones beneath her feet.

He stood over her, eyeing her dispassionately while she slowly rose back to her feet.

As Piers and Kat stared at each other, their expressions hardened and the courtyard quiet as their breaths rose in puffs in the faint light of yet another cloudy day, they were interrupted by Sir Cas.

"Perhaps we start with milder insults! I can't tell if you two are genuinely trying to kill each other or not!"

At this, Kat and Piers blinked, then broke out grinning at each other.

"I think we made the innocent one uncomfortable." Piers laughed while relaxing his stance and seizing Kat's head in his hand, mussing her hair and making her squawk.

Kat flailed around under Piers's grasp at first, then cracked an eye open to look at Sir Cas, who was letting out a sigh of relief.

"Jeez, Sir Cas, you were the one to tell me to bother him first!"

"I said *annoy*, not start a bloodbath!" the Daxarian knight hollered helplessly.

"Pfft, this is far from a bloodbath." Kat snorted.

"Speak for yourself." Piers half flung Kat's head back as they walked over to where Sir Cas stood.

The redhead eyed Piers's nose that still had blood staining its sides. "Oh, please. That was a scratch at best. The way you're whining, you'd think I'd maimed you."

"Mm-hmm, and when I mentioned the prince, it was almost as though you were going to cry," Piers fired back while reaching for his water flagon.

"Yeah, well . . . You've got . . . teeth!" Kat managed awkwardly while reaching for her own water.

Piers half laughed, half choked. "What?"

Even Sir Cas looked amused.

Kat drank from her flagon, allowing water to dribble down the sides of her mouth and ignoring the looks she was receiving from the two men at her side. She hadn't been as prepared for a follow-up insult as she usually was.

"Alright, shall we try that again? Kat, this time try to rely less on your fists; it makes it too obvious that your strength isn't normal if someone happens to pass by," Sir Cas noted quietly while glancing toward the nearest corner of the castle.

Kat didn't respond, as her cheeks were filled to bursting with water, but she nodded while turning around. Though she ended up spitting out a small amount when the three of them all discovered Brendan Devark had appeared behind them.

No one knew when or where he had come from, and it was a little disturbing to say the least.

Brendan stared at Katarina's puffed out cheeks flatly. "Lady Katarina, I need a word with you."

The redhead carefully gulped the rest of her drink and bowed. "Yes, Your Majesty, is everything alright?"

The king didn't respond to her query and instead gestured around the corner, indicating he wanted them to step away together.

Kat frowned. She had the sneaking suspicion that whatever had brought him to see her that morning wasn't going to improve her mood, and it made her wonder if she could get her hands on another bottle of Troivackian moonshine that night from Lady Wynonna . . .

CHAPTER 41

AN OPTIMAL OUTLET

Kat stared at Brendan Devark expectantly. She had a bad feeling about whatever had brought him to see her. She silently wondered if he was going to lecture her about her conduct during the council meeting where she wrangled an apology out of Sir Herra or about her fight with Alina . . .

"After you killed Roscoe, did you notice your powers grow stronger?"

It felt as though Kat had been dropped in an ice bath.

The redhead felt her insides harden as she stared at the king's stern features.

Why the hell was he asking such a question . . . ?

"You know, Your Majesty, I had just started thinking the queen was having a positive influence on your communication skills . . ."

"This is a serious question, Lady Katarina." Brendan's gaze didn't waver.

Feeling herself growing nauseated, Kat took her time regaining her composure before answering, and for once, the king didn't look annoyed.

"I did notice . . . that my magitch didn't occur as frequently, and . . . other abilities did become stronger, yes."

Brendan nodded to himself, his eyes intent as they fell to the ground, his mind working through some notion that had prompted the question in the first place.

"Your Majesty, what is going on?" Kat asked while her stomach continued to twist.

The king had already begun to turn away from the noblewoman, an urgency in his face that did little to soothe Kat's anxiety.

"I need to speak with Mage Sebastian and Mr. Kraft. I will inform you of our findings perhaps by this evening. Good day, Lady Katarina."

Then just as silently and swiftly as he arrived, Brendan Devark left, marching along the east wall of the castle amongst the manicured shrubbery to his left and a span of gardens to his right.

Reluctantly, Kat turned away and trudged back to where Sir Cas and Piers were supposed to be waiting to continue her training. Though upon nearing the corner of the castle again, she heard different voices that didn't sound all too friendly . . .

Sure enough, when she returned to her training space, she found four knights snickering at Sir Cas, who was smiling pleasantly at them in his usual affable way, while Piers was in the process of executing an impressive eyeroll.

"What's happening here?" Kat called out as she approached the group.

The four Troivackian knights turned and stared at the redhead, their hostility bared like teeth at the sight of her face. But after a moment, they remembered that regardless of the fact that she wore trousers, she was still the daughter of a duke.

They all executed sloppy bows, during which Katarina looked at Piers, who was shaking his head in silent warning.

Kat closed her eyes for all of a breath.

Why must today be so Godsdamn awful?

Still, she remembered Faucher's strategy and advice . . .

To act as ladylike as possible to make it seem a far-fetched notion that she even knew which end of a sword was pointy.

Then she also remembered how fun it could be to torment arsehats . . .

"Good day, sirs. How can we be of help to you today?" she greeted while pitching her voice higher.

Though she didn't realize she had subconsciously gripped the hilt of her sword.

A move that was not lost on the unwelcome visitors.

"We were just asking Sir Cas and Mr. Faucher here where we might find Joshua Ball. He doesn't seem to be in the castle anywhere." One of the knights, who had shaved the sides of his head leaving a mop of black curls to dangle in front of his forehead, responded while his comrades behind him smirked.

Katarina made a show of looking to the sky and squinting as though thinking long and hard about where she last recalled seeing her fellow student.

"Can't say . . . that I've seen him since I got here. Maybe he went to help back at Faucher's keep?" She shrugged.

"It's *Leader* Faucher," one of the men behind the first speaker barked. He was a shorter, stouter type with everything but his mustache and eyebrows shaved.

Kat leaned to the side and tilted her head to stare more directly at the knight who at least had the self-awareness to lower his gaze.

"I was told by him to call him Faucher unless he was giving me an order, to which I'm to respond with *sir*."

None of the knights could think of a retort to that, so instead the ringleader of the knights decided to take back control of the discussion.

"So the bastard of the Ball family ran back to the keep with his tail between his legs?" He laughed. "Sounds about right."

"Pardon me, Sir . . . ?" Sir Cas strolled leisurely around the men until he stood to their sides, scratching his pale blond hair idly as he did so.

"Kochek," the ringleader retorted, openly sneering at the Daxarian.

"Right, Sir Kochek, we are in the middle of training Lady Katarina, so I'm afraid I must ask you to continue your search elsewhere."

The four knights rounded on Sir Cas, all smiling coldly.

"You can't order us to do anything. You're a foreign knight here. You have less rights and say than a serving wench." Sir Kochek leaned his head down, his smile snakelike.

Kat looked to Piers, who met her questioning look and answered with a small shake of his head.

They had to remain as inconspicuous as possible. They had to appear weak until it was their moment to strike . . . even if right at that moment she wanted to beat the breakfasts out of their stomachs.

"Well, given that I am following the orders of both Leader Faucher and His Majesty, I'd say it's more with their authority in mind that I made the request." Sir Cas smiled charmingly at them, his eyes wide and innocent.

It then occurred to Kat . . . that while she had seen Sir Cas spar and demonstrate with her and her fellow students, she had never seen him in a real fight . . .

"Won't do the lady any good no matter how hard she practices. So it won't matter if we take our time looking for Joshua the whelp, will it?"

"You know I can hear you, right?" Kat asked while making her way over to Sir Cas's side and earning herself another round of glares. Behind the group, Piers was placing his hand over his eyes.

He could tell things were not going to be resolved peacefully.

"It's a fact, my lady. It doesn't need to be an insult. I'm not sure you understand how all of us have been training since before we could read.

There is no chance someone who just began their lessons in the autumn could be anywhere near ready for the knight's test," one of the men on the right spoke. He was the least antagonistic in appearance with his hair trimmed close to his head and his beard tidy. He had a long face, and one front tooth pushed slightly in front of the other.

"Well, that doesn't narrow down when you started at all! How am I supposed to know if you can read? You can't even understand a request to take your disrespectful attitudes back to your captain." Kat leaned forward with a devilish grin of her own.

The men collectively looked murderous.

"Play with your sword all you want, Lady Katarina. You won't like the result of the match, that's a promise," Sir Kochek growled at the redhead.

"What if I *want* to lose? Will I like it then? I mean, I'm sure it'd earn me all kinds of sympathy. Right, Sir Cas?"

"Absolutely." The Daxarian knight nodded along with a smile.

"You dare take this lightly? You dare disrespect Leader Faucher and our tradition of honor?" Sir Kochek seethed openly.

"I'm just asking you hypothetically—aren't you trying to make me resign myself to losing? You're a very confusing person." Kat sighed exasperatedly.

Sir Kochek raised his hand as though about to backhand Kat across the cheek.

"What's going on here?"

Startled, the band of knights jumped and turned around to see Conrad Faucher standing beside his brother Piers, who was clamping his hand down on his mouth so tightly that it stretched the skin around his eyes, as he continued watching the scene before him unfold.

"Nothing." Sir Kochek's hand curled into a fist and fell to his side.

Conrad stared at the knights levelly before glancing at Kat, who smiled and waved.

"Lady Katarina, is everything alright?" the middle Faucher son asked carefully while eyeing the knights, who shifted awkwardly around the noblewoman.

"I'm trying really hard not to strangle a knight, so I've been better!" she replied cheerily.

The knights in question tensed, but they didn't look back at the redhead.

"Your father's student is being disrespectful and belligerent," Sir Kochek informed Conrad darkly.

"Well, how else am I supposed to treat trespassers who won't leave when you ask them nicely?" Kat wondered loudly.

Piers raked his hand through his hair while staring at Kat, angry exasperation etched into his normally cool expression.

"Are you *trying* to get into a fight?!"

Kat gave a single shoulder shrug. "Couldn't hurt."

"No, see"—Sir Kochek whirled around, brandishing his finger in her face—"it *will* hurt, Lady Katarina. When I teach a lesson, I make an impression."

Kat chewed the inside of her cheek and stared at the knight with her eyes narrowed.

"Piiieeers?" she called out in a near whine.

The youngest Faucher son threw his hands in the air while looking to his brother. "Unbelievable," he muttered before looking back at the redhead, who hadn't budged an inch despite Sir Kochek looming menacingly close to her face.

"Fine! But only because he *did* start it and they'll never believe him without more witnesses," the youngest Faucher son acquiesced, though he had a demented glint in his eyes as he did.

"More like he won't want to admit he gets his ass handed to him by a woman," Conrad mumbled under his breath.

The knights didn't have time to wonder why Faucher's sons were so cavalier about the danger Kat was placing herself in, nor did they get the chance in the moments that followed.

Kat's foot came up to crush Sir Kochek's groin, but he backhanded it away easily. What he hadn't known was that the redheaded noblewoman had been expecting him to do just that. With the added benefit of her forehead aligning beautifully with the bridge of his nose, he cast off her knee, and she used her forward falling momentum to bash her head against his face, making Sir Kochek stumble back into his comrades.

"What is with the headbutting this morning?!" Piers shouted from the sidelines.

Kat was cracking her neck as she faced the men, her forehead spattered with Kochek's blood. When she smiled at the antagonizing Troivackian knights, her eyes began to glow.

"What can I say? I'm a Daxarian who's been having a *very* bad day."

When the four knights stumbled back to their training grounds, they all sported various bruises and cuts, and they were already searching for their captain amongst the men.

Only the courtyard wasn't filled with knights training, or talking, or even just milling about . . . No, they were all huddled around something to the left.

Sir Kochek gestured his friends forward, though he limped as he made his way over to the group.

"Men! That Ashowan witch isn't human! She's a demon! You all need to—"

The man's words died in his throat as all the knights turned with eerie synchronicity to stare at them. They looked . . . angry.

"W-What? We went asking about where Joshua Ball was, and—"

"UGH! They woke her up!"

The men broke out in furious shouts, and some even cursed.

"W-What?" Sir Kochek stared at them in confusion. Why weren't they asking why they were in such terrible states? Furthermore, who was asleep? He didn't see a woman or child anywhere near them.

That is, until Sir Cleophus Miller, the most bloodthirsty man of them all, was revealed in the middle of the crowd. The most *terrifying* man they'd ever known . . . The strongest . . . The one that with a single glance could inspire nightmares in a man for years . . .

He loomed as large as ever amongst them with a small kitten on his shoulder. Her paws were tucked under her body primly, her green eyes slowly blinking awake, and her freckled nose twitching in the wind.

Sir Miller stalked over toward Sir Kochek, who until that day had casually avoided the infamous warrior.

When the beast that called himself human stood before the four battered knights, his beady eyes glaring down at them in the silent, cold winter day, Kochek found himself wishing Lady Katarina had killed him and saved him from the visage of hell he was facing.

He swallowed. No! *Perhaps Sir Miller is the one who can stop that Daxarian witch!*

"S-Sir Miller! As I was saying, Lady Katarina, that redheaded bitch, isn't—"

Sir Kochek didn't get to finish what he was saying before Sir Miller's beefy hand that was bigger than most men's faces came up and wrapped around his throat and hoisted him in the air.

"Speak ill of the woman who brought us the only perfect creature to ever walk the earth again, and I will cook your remains for her to eat at her leisure." Sir Miller's rumble sent several men shuffling back, though even more frighteningly to the four knights, they appeared to be doing so not out of fear, but to give the man room to carry out the threat.

Sir Miller dropped Sir Kochek in a heap on the ground and turned back to the throng of knights.

For a very still breath, no one moved . . . until Pina leaned forward and nuzzled against Sir Miller's cheek, eliciting a uniform bout of *aawws* from the men.

Sir Miller kissed her furry cheek tenderly before whispering, "Thank you for forgiving me, princess. I'll make sure no one ever upsets you again."

That was all the kitten needed to ignite a pleased purr in her belly.

CHAPTER 42

A SMALL SCUFFLE

Kat, Sir Cas, Piers, and Conrad strolled into the castle for the dining hour, sweaty, tired, and with random splatters of blood on their clothes. All of them were in brighter spirits than they had been at the start of the day. The entrance they came through was usually designated to footmen and the occasional laundry maid, but at that time of day, the narrow hall was empty . . .

Save for Leader Faucher, who stood with his arms folded and glowering at the group as they came in.

Piers was the first to notice his father as he finished remarking on something that had Sir Cas laughing.

They stopped short as Faucher straightened, dropped his arms to his sides, and stalked over to stand directly in front of the group.

"I heard an interesting rumor about four knights who had received a beating today from a supposed demon," he started, his eyes resting on Katarina, who was staring ahead blankly.

"Though one was blathering on about how one of my sons punched their groin," Faucher growled while turning to Piers.

"I slipped," Conrad announced casually, making his father's head snap toward him.

Faucher was momentarily taken aback that it was his most docile of sons who had been the one to join the brawl.

After absorbing that piece of information, he looked to Sir Cas. "Was I unclear on the plan?"

The blond knight stepped forward. "I apologize, Faucher. They were becoming aggressive and weren't leaving when we dismissed them."

"Then you should have handled them without Lady Katarina's involvement. We can't tip off Captain Orion," he reminded furiously.

Sir Cas bowed his head.

Still displeased with the situation, Faucher looked to his sons, who also had their heads lowered.

Katarina was the only one not offering an apology, though she did at least have the good sense to keep her eyes downcast.

Faucher watched her wordlessly. When they'd been training the previous night, she had arrived with her eyes red and her cheeks blotchy. He hadn't asked any questions, but during their time together, he could tell her mind was far from their practice.

Something had happened. And given that the prince had left not only the castle but Vessa first thing that morning, he could take an educated guess that the two had had a *discussion* of sorts.

If they decided to stop their ridiculous avoidance of their relationship, then regardless of how it ended, it's for the better.

"All of you, go eat dinner. You should count yourselves lucky that the knights were distracted by Sir Miller and Ashowan's familiar."

At this, Kat couldn't stop herself from looking up in confusion. "What did Pina do?"

Faucher raised an eyebrow. "It would seem the knights are quite taken with her. Captain Orion had to ask her to leave, as none of them were getting any training done."

The redhead blinked. "She got kicked out of the training courtyard for being too cute?"

Unable to resist, everyone lifted their faces to gaze at Faucher imploringly. That couldn't have been what happened . . .

"She was distracting the men . . . so . . . Captain Orion allowed her to nap in his office."

No one spoke.

Until a burst of laughter escaped from none other than Conrad.

Having rarely heard his son speak let alone laugh, Faucher was unable to hide his surprise, nor was he able to fight off the slight upward turning of the corners of his mouth.

Next thing they knew, everyone was laughing or chuckling, or in Kat and Faucher's case . . . smiling.

"Come on, you bunch of mutts. Ashowan, you—"

"Eat alone in my room as usual."

"Yes." Faucher had already turned and was leading them back into the depths of the castle, but when he heard her dull response, he glanced over his shoulder at her somber expression.

He noticed both his sons and Sir Cas exchanging worried and curious glances at one another over her lackluster response.

"By the way"—Faucher cleared his throat—"His Highness Prince Eric has left with a small entourage to tour the northeast of Troivack for the next few weeks."

The military leader continued walking as though nothing of consequence had happened. If he were honest with himself, he wasn't sure why he bothered telling Katarina about the prince's whereabouts. She didn't need to be aware of his every move . . .

Meanwhile, behind his swishing cape, Sir Cas, Piers, and Conrad bore witness to the redhead's reaction to the news.

She stilled . . . grew concerningly pale . . . and then continued making her way laboriously down the corridor. A beleaguered air surrounded her as her golden eyes dimmed and she proceeded to pass the group without bothering to bid farewell for the evening.

In her thoughts, she became resolute to enact her previous plan of urging Lady Wynonna to send her a bottle of moonshine. She wasn't supposed to resume training with Faucher for another four hours . . . which gave her plenty of time to consume enough to numb her emotions.

However, her thoughts were interrupted when Piers threw his arm around her neck, and with his other hand he mussed her hair.

"Lighten up, Ashowan. You've got a cute cat and you beat the mutton out of those knights today with only a bit of our help."

Kat proceeded to reach up and seize Piers's curly black hair and yanked hard, making the two reduce themselves to squabbling like children, while Conrad and Sir Cas left them behind on their journey toward the servants' dining hall.

The Daxarian knight shared a knowing look with Faucher's middle son, but neither of them said anything.

Thanks to Faucher's declaration, everyone was able to deduce what had made the redheaded witch so out of sorts that day.

"Oyy! No biting!"

Piers's sudden shout from behind them succeeded in making Conrad snort in laughter yet again.

"I'm glad those two get along so well," Sir Cas announced with a grin of his own.

"She's like the little brother Piers always needed," Conrad agreed, his smile remaining fixed in place.

Sir Cas laughed. "Well, I guess we can leave it to him to cheer her up."

Conrad nodded, his eyes becoming thoughtful. "I wonder if she and the prince will ever sort out their problems."

The Daxarian knight hesitated as he cast his mind back to his memories of the prince, which included everything from his drunken behavior to his more recent bout of ambition. He concluded that . . . if he were in Eric's shoes . . . he'd probably avoid a commitment that could hurt another person when he was so unsettled.

But then again, if it meant he'd lose someone he felt for so strongly . . .

"WOULD EITHER OF YOU MIND *HELPING* ME?!"

Piers's urgent plea made Sir Cas and Conrad swing back around in time to see Katarina dangling from behind Piers with her arms around his neck, him clawing at her grip and turning a deep purple.

Without another word, they went to lend a hand.

Their thoughts returning to the safer topic of violence and training, both Sir Cas and Conrad proceeded to advise Kat on how better to strangle someone in the future, much to Piers's dismay.

Eric drank gratefully from the flagon of water Sir Vohn had handed to him and wiped his mouth with the back of his hand before handing it back to the knight.

"Thanks for that."

"Not a problem, Your Highness. I have to admit, I haven't seen you like this in quite some time. It brings me back to the old days." Sir Vohn eyed the prince, who was shielding his eyes against the sun and stared out over the leagues of vineyards before them.

"Like what?" Eric asked idly. During the entire journey, his mind had been somewhere far from his present.

The Daxarian knight glanced around to make sure that none of the Troivackians escorting them were within earshot. "Cleaning out the moonshine stashes while also completing our work at the same time. Brings me back to your mercenary days."

Eric eyed Sir Vohn emptily. "It's how I am. I relax to excess, but when it is required, I'll then work to excess."

The knight grinned and fell into step beside Eric as he made his way back to their camp. He had taken a short walk upon waking up that morning in an effort to sober up again.

The prince had spent the first two weeks of traveling in a drunken haze . . . There wasn't much to do besides playing cards in the carriage while sharing cups anyway . . . but they now had officially crossed into Duke

Icarus's territory. They had left the carriage at the last town they'd passed through for the sake of discretion, and so the time of overindulgence was once again coming to a close.

"I'm surprised that there aren't guards or patrols out in these fields. Doesn't the duke know with a couple of torches his vineyards could be gone in the span of a night?"

Eric's gaze thoughtfully moved over the picturesque scene before them. The rising sun had cast the sky in a pale light, and the wind rustled the leaves of the grapevines and trees that grew more avidly along the northeast of Troivack. Unlike the southeast, the land they traveled wasn't flat desert but instead was filled with rolling hills, valleys, and streams . . . It was beautiful.

They had passed through small towns with quaint shops and pleasant people that made Eric think about how much Kat would enjoy traveling to such places . . .

A figure in the distance moved, drawing the prince from the threat of more painful thoughts pertaining to a certain redhead.

"I think I see their patrolmen coming." He nodded northward and noticed in their camp that several members of the entourage were already clipping weapons onto their belts.

"Whatever happened to the sword Captain Antonio gave you?"

Sir Vohn's sudden question made Eric's stomach roil. No one had asked him that before . . . and he'd preferred it that way.

"The foot soldiers' swords are just as sharp, and I don't feel bad if I dent them."

The Daxarian knight opened his mouth to say more but didn't get the chance to, as riders bearing down on their camp neared.

"Your Highness! I swear I sent a letter alerting the dukedom that you were arriving, so there shouldn't be any issues!" Mr. Julian rushed up to the prince, his hands clenched together.

Eric nodded, appearing entirely nonplussed. "It's fine. They probably just weren't expecting us to come in through the vineyards."

The lad looked at the riders drawing nearer and observed their murderous expressions with a gulp.

"Thomas Julian, we will be fine. You have my word." Eric's quiet voice succeeded in making his assistant lock eyes with him, and the prince could tell that the young man did feel some measure of reassurance from his words.

It was excellent timing, as five men had arrived atop massive black steeds and were leering down at the entourage.

One of the Troivackians tasked with Eric's safety stepped forward. "We are escorting His Highness the prince of Daxaria Eric Reyes to Duke Sebastian Icarus's estate. There was notice sent!"

The riders didn't say anything.

Instead, they drew their swords.

In an instant, everyone in the entourage freed their own weapons and began to take a defensive position in front of Eric, who continued watching the newcomers calmly.

"Sir, you are in the presence of royalty traveling with the blessing of King Brendan Devark himself. Sheath your weapons *now*," the Troivackian knight roared.

The leader of the five mounted men spurred his horse forward. Dressed in black and steel armor, his black hair long and his beard scruffy, he glared down at them.

"The prince rides at the front. We ride from the back," came the gruff reply. The man revealed he also had several missing teeth as he spoke.

Eric strolled between the knights, who were standing at the ready to protect him, until he was mere feet from the patrolman.

"That's fine with me. We'll take down our camp and be on our way, Sir . . . ?"

The Troivackian straightened in his saddle while staring appraisingly down at the Daxarian royal.

A move that Eric would see him executed for if he wanted to ensure he was going to be taken seriously.

While coming to this conclusion, something had shifted in Eric's eyes that prompted the Troivackian to raise an eyebrow, his derisive expression faltering.

"I'm a hired mercenary. Name's Hoff."

Eric didn't react to Hoff's unabashed disrespect as he casually made his way around toward the side of the man's horse.

Hoff watched him without saying a word, eyeing the prince's hand that lay on the hilt of his sword.

However, he was so preoccupied with the calloused hand on that hilt that when Eric casually plucked his concealed dagger from under his tunic and plunged it into the man's thigh, he hadn't been anticipating it.

Hoff roared, but Eric twisted the blade, cutting the femoral artery before ducking to dodge Hoff's swinging sword.

He missed.

The fight exploded, and the Troivackian knights displayed their prowess and proceeded to cut down the men one by one alongside Eric, who did most of the work without a second thought.

By the time he was finished, there were three unharmed horses standing and five lifeless bodies on the ground.

Eric turned to the nearest Troivackian knight, who was in the process of wiping his blade clean, and distantly recalled his name to be Sir Levi.

"Is it because they looked down on Daxaria, or do you think the duke will try to use this information to turn people against my kingdom?"

Sir Levi regarded Eric with respect before bowing to him. "He cannot use this against you. Not with all of us as witnesses."

The prince pondered this point briefly before facing the man more squarely. "One of the knights should ride back with my assistant and inform His Majesty what has happened here. There's a chance they kill all of us at his estate and silence the whole thing."

The knight didn't mask his surprise. "Your Highness, should that happen, it would mean Duke Icarus is treasonous, and—"

Eric held up his hand, stopping the knight from continuing. "If I'm wrong, then I merely lose one knight serving in an entourage for the journey. If I'm right, however . . . then that means we may have saved His Majesty King Brendan Devark from a member of his court."

Sir Levi's mouth clamped shut, admiration shining in his eyes.

The prince was risking his own life to confirm whether the duke was a threat to their beloved king.

Perhaps he was a drunk . . . but he was a master swordsman, deadly in battle, and honorable.

While the Troivackian knight turned to shout orders to his men, Eric made his way back over to where Sir Vohn and his assistant remained. Thomas Julian was only fifteen years old . . . and having just witnessed the brutality of an up close battle, he was in the midst of vomiting profusely while Sir Vohn patted his back.

"There, there. Yes, I know. Rough go when it's your first time seeing this kind of thing . . ."

When Eric reached them, he locked eyes with his old friend and gestured with his head a short distance away.

He'd communicate the new plan with Sir Vohn, and then . . . well, then he'd do what he did best: walk into a deadly situation and gamble whether it was his time to board death's carriage.

CHAPTER 43

FRIEND OR FOE

The entourage that remained with Eric left him with approximately fourteen knights including Sir Vohn, and all were collectively grim as they rode through the duke's vineyards.

As beautiful as the day and scenery were, the terrible scenes in the fields made the world seem dark.

As they passed by the workers in the vineyards, they soon discovered that the predominant force behind the duke's successful business . . . was enslavement.

Eric eyed their dirtied clothes stained in grime, their borderline starved figures, and the thin wire around their necks with telltale loops used to tie them together in a line.

"His Majesty does not condone slavery," Sir Levi informed the prince, his expression one of disgust as he eyed the patrolmen, who rode their horses back and forth with whips at their hips. Surprisingly, none of the senior workers seemed to take exception to Eric's presence, which only put everyone even more on edge . . .

"I imagine the duke keeps this hidden. Most of these enslaved people are of mixed birth. Half Daxarians and Troivackians . . . some Zinferans . . . even one or two Lobahlans. If Lobahl or Daxaria found out about this, I know it could spark a war."

Sir Levi nodded. "I never would have thought His Grace was doing such a thing . . . though he can argue he had ownership of these people for years. It's harder to condemn the noble families that have had lifelong servants, given that it was only recently that the laws against slavery came to be. But he shouldn't have acquired any people within the past five years. It is a finable offense, but I don't know that it would be so simple, given the magnitude of people we're seeing here . . ."

"I'm guessing condemning slavery was something that only came about because of Daxaria's insistence a few years ago . . . ?"

Sir Levi shook his head. "His Majesty was already investigating the matter when Daxaria started discussing trade restrictions if slavery persisted. Lobahlan delegates had come two years earlier to make similar demands."

That certainly grabbed Eric's attention. "Lobahl sent a delegation? They never interact with other courts or kingdoms!"

Sir Levi nodded. "It's true. However, Troivack has had our own private dealings with them throughout the decades. Particularly with the coffee trade."

At the mention of the coffee business, Eric was fully invested in the discussion.

Finlay Ashowan and his wife owned a large amount of the trading ships for the bean brew . . . What did Lobahl have to do with it all?

"I can't say I know all the details, Your Highness," Sir Levi added as he noted the prince's attention homing in on him. "It is a matter the Troivackian courtiers keep private."

Eric frowned.

He would need to investigate this tidbit of information further once he returned to Vessa . . .

However, at that time, they were approaching the side of Duke Sebastian Icarus's estate.

The building was essentially a small castle with its rounded walls and towers made from red slate.

It was a magnificent holding for times of war, Eric observed, as the windows were small and it was difficult to discern where the front of the keep was.

The moment their horses' hooves touched the courtyard, the small group was descended upon by knights and guards, all wearing black trousers and tunics under pieces of armor. Dual swords were on the hips of the knights, and for the mercenaries and common soldiers, spears sharpened to deadly points were in hand. There were seven of them that the group could count at a glance as they approached.

"Trespassers, cease or we will gut you on these stones!" One of the knights shouted while striding toward them from the side door of the keep. His head was shaved bald, his goatee was long, and he wore silver earrings in each of his earlobes. He did not appear any friendlier than the last men from the estate they had encountered.

Eric stared down at the newcomer as he drew near, his expression cold.

"This is Prince Eric Reyes of Daxaria. We have already been accosted by hired men of the Icarus household. If you wish to avoid persecution yourself, I suggest you mind your tone," Sir Levi hollered ferociously down at the man.

Sir Levi was in his early forties and kept his long black hair streaked with gray tied in a bun atop his head. His beard was long, and his stare keen.

Duke Icarus's knight raised an eyebrow, a glint of condescension entering his gaze.

Eric didn't blink as he peered down at him.

Several of the men around their greeter shifted uncomfortably.

"I see. I suppose we did receive notice of the prince's arrival, though we expected you to come by the road and perhaps in a carriage. My name is Sir Cardoso. I oversee this keep's safety while His Grace is absent." After his introduction, Sir Cardoso bowed.

Eric didn't say anything as he continued staring at the man steadily. It was beginning to make the guards unbearably uncomfortable . . .

Sir Cardoso even became inclined to lower his gaze after a moment of awkwardness, then he turned slightly toward the keep and suddenly roared, "BOY! COME HERE!"

A slender lad perhaps only sixteen years of age stumbled out of the keep.

Another unfortunate soul who had been enslaved.

His head was bowed, revealing short oily black hair.

Eric stiffened.

"Boy, see to arranging the prince of Daxaria's quarters." Sir Cardoso looked back to Sir Levi. "It might be a wait. It isn't common for visitors to come while the master of the house is away, you see."

"Duke Icarus consented happily to His Highness's visit," Sir Levi growled in return, his eyes narrowing.

The two knights were staring at each other menacingly, but they were distracted when Eric dismounted his horse and stepped past the duke's men toward the boy.

He squinted at the lad, who remained rooted to the spot, still bowed with his hands clasped in front of him.

When he stood only a couple feet away, realization and recognition filled the prince's face along with incredulousness.

"Eli?!"

The enslaved boy's head snapped up, his slanted eyes widening. "Eric?!"

"Good Gods! What the hell are you doing here?!" the prince exclaimed in shock.

"I thought *you'd* be dead by now!" the boy spluttered in equal astonishment.

"Thanks!" Eric managed while faltering back a step. "Holy antlers . . . I thought you *were* dead!"

As the realization sunk in, the prince clasped the lad in a clumsy embrace. "Son of a mage, Eli. This is . . . Gods." He couldn't finish the sentence as he clapped the boy's bony back once and then leaned back while clasping his shoulders.

"How did you get off Insodam?!" the boy asked, his brown eyes fixed in disbelief on Eric's face.

"I commandeered a—" Eric stopped himself from finishing his reply as he belatedly remembered they were not alone.

Turning to stare around himself, the prince regarded the knights and guards dazedly before blinking. Realization shadowed his face.

"Sir Cardoso, was it?" He turned and walked over to the knight, whose lips were already curling. He knew where this was going, and his eyes were widening fractionally in panic.

"This boy was with me nearly two years ago on a ship traveling from Zinfera. Care to explain how he is *enslaved* in Troivack today?"

Sir Cardoso's hand inched toward the hilt of his sword.

"If you're thinking about fighting us and claiming ignorance, you should know missives reporting what we have seen in these fields as well as witnesses to the earlier attack within the duke's borders have already been sent to His Majesty's court in Vessa." Sir Levi's sharp voice succeeded in drawing the knight's glare.

"I'm going to make you a deal." Eric's soft voice startled Sir Cardoso. He hadn't heard him come closer. "Take the men loyal to you and run. This dukedom is at most a month away from crumbling from what we learned during our investigation. If you are incriminated, you will be put to death."

Sir Cardoso bared his teeth, his eyes wide as he visibly debated his best option.

"I won't chase you. It's already been established the duke has illegal dealings with the slave trade and is even taking part in the rebellions and attacks breaking out all over this kingdom. So, either stay and wait for the king's army to come and slaughter you or run while I'm being merciful."

"You're a foreign noble, you—"

"I am the brother to the queen of Troivack." Eric moved closer still, filling Sir Cardoso's line of vision. "If you think I'm here of my own volition, think again. Daxaria's ties to Troivack are stronger than ever.

Decide now. Are you condemning yourself, or are you going to save your hide?"

Sir Cardoso's throat bobbed.

He eyed his men around him, who already were inching away from the prince.

Had it been another pompous fool wielding his nobility in front of his nose like a shield to bash through obstacles without spilling blood, perhaps Eric's pressuring wouldn't have worked.

But a hardened knight knew eyes like the prince's. That paired with his blood-splattered tunic from the morning's previous fight convinced Sir Cardoso that defending an empty keep wasn't worth the hassle.

Without another word, he backed away from the prince and strode toward the front of the keep with the guards following suit shortly after while exchanging looks amongst themselves, everyone occasionally glancing over their shoulders nervously at the prince's entourage.

"That just confirmed the duke's involvement in the rebellions," Sir Levi said breathily while staring after the retreating men. The disbelief was written all over his face.

"That's right, but my guess is he's going to gather help to have us slaughtered while at the same time alerting the duke. We'll send four extra missives using the duke's birds, grab as much evidence as we can carry, and leave before nightfall. Understood?" Eric gave the orders while also addressing the Troivackian knights behind Sir Levi.

The men let out a single unanimous "Hoh" and sheathed their swords.

"Move as quickly as possible while on high alert. Duke Icarus wouldn't have left this keep only with a flimsy defenseman like Sir Cardoso."

The knights once again acknowledged Eric's order and began filing into the keep.

Eric then rounded back over to Eli, who was staring at him wide-eyed.

"Are you . . ." the lad began with a whisper while glancing at Sir Vohn, who hung back and waited for the prince. "Are you impersonating *royalty* for a job?"

"Ah . . . about that . . ." Eric slipped his right hand into his pocket while shifting his boots uncomfortably. "I . . . never *did* actually tell you my background . . ."

Eli blinked, color draining from his face as his eyes darted to Sir Vohn and back to him.

"Are you saying that you . . . you are Prince Eric Reyes of Daxaria?! Are you jesting?!" Eli's voice exploded, his eyes round.

Eric winced in confirmation.

The young lad threw his hands into the air before allowing them to fall back, his left hand landing atop his head, seizing his thick straight black hair in bafflement.

Meanwhile, Sir Vohn observed the young man with a raised eyebrow.

He was Zinferan as was evident by his slanted eyes and black hair, but his paler skin indicated that he may have a Daxarian parent . . .

"I saw your ship burn in the attack . . . How did you survive?" Eric asked quietly while also looking over Eli's head when he heard shrieks and hollers from within the duke's residence.

"The ship that attacked us belonged to Duke Icarus. Apparently, that merchant vessel I'd boarded had a few crates of illegally acquired moonshine that belonged to him."

"He burned an entire ship for a couple of stolen crates?" Eric's brow furrowed. He knew the duke was a despicable man, but . . . all that trouble for negligible cargo . . . ?

He paused. Then looked pensively at Eli.

The lad faltered when he realized what was happening.

"Alright, it would seem we *both* weren't entirely honest with each other during our time together." Eli cleared his throat.

Eric raised an eyebrow and waited expectantly.

"The thing is . . . Er . . . Well . . ." the boy scratched his dirty hair awkwardly while gnawing the inside of his cheek. "I'm . . . I'm the duke's insurance plan. For keeping this place secured . . ."

Straightening, the prince barely resisted putting a hand on the hilt of his sword.

He had traveled with Eli for nearly a year, and the unfortunate lad had been nothing but kind when he wasn't faced with horrible life-or-death situations.

He risked his former friend taking the opportunity to attack and waited.

Sir Vohn wasn't feeling as generous with his trust and stepped forward while gripping his weapon readily.

Eli backed up and put his hands in the air. "N-No! T-The duke made me! I don't want to—He blackmailed and threatened me, a-and I had no way to escape, but you're here now, and . . . It's unfair of me to assume you can help me, but—"

"Eli . . . why are you the duke's insurance plan?" Eric's voice was hushed, but the underlying tension was still audible.

The boy fidgeted and fearfully glanced to where the duke's men had disappeared around the corner.

"Hey." Eric clasped Eli's shoulder, drawing his attention back to him. "I can help you. I can get you out of here and back home or give you a new life in Daxaria. I owe you. And I know you wouldn't get involved with Duke Icarus lightly."

Eli dropped his chin, and Eric could feel his thin shoulders begin to tremble.

"T-The thing is . . ." The boy closed his eyes as though he couldn't bear to see the prince's reaction to what he was about to say. "I-I'm a witch, a-and I'm supposed to guard the keep. I . . . I was supposed to k-kill you when you arrived, and then . . . then I was going to be given to the devil."

CHAPTER 44

AROUND AND BACK

Eric sat on the steps of the keep as the men collected the last of the evidence they were able to find against Duke Icarus, though sadly it wasn't as incriminating as they'd hoped . . .

However, the prince didn't have time to dwell on the matter, as his attention was entirely focused on Eli, who was wiping tears of frustration from his face.

"I s-swear he hasn't made me kill anyone before . . . He wanted me to be a secret last resort," Eli repeated, his voice rasping as he stared out over the vineyards.

"I believe you."

"He took me from the water after the ship exploded and—"

"How is it he knew you were a witch?" Eric asked while gradually leaning forward to rest his forearms on his thighs.

Eli flinched and began to subconsciously shift away. "I-I'm not sure."

His expression hardening, Eric fixed his unwavering stare on the side of the young man's face. "Given the situation I just found you in, I need you to be more forthcoming, Eli."

The boy hunched his shoulders, his lower lip beginning to quiver again.

"It . . . It's just . . . Do you swear you won't drag me into everything if I tell you?"

Eric let out a small huff with a frown. Just what in the world had a boy as young as Eli gotten embroiled in . . . ?

"Alright. If it's within my power, I will keep you as far from whatever it is you fear as I can, *but*"—the prince paused, drawing Eli's watery gaze to him—"if I ask you to tell someone what you've told me, I need you to trust me that it's for a very good reason."

"You and your negotiations," Eli blurted before he was able to stop himself.

Eric grinned but held out his hand.

"I want something else."

The prince dropped his hand and stared at Eli incredulously. "I give you immunity despite being a part of an assassination plot and finding you with a traitor, and you have the audacity to ask for more? Gods, where did the sweet, compliant child, who—"

"Please never ask me to show my magic."

Eric blinked and tilted his head. He was pensive for a moment. "I will add this to our deal, but you have to tell me why that's the case."

Eli's nose scrunched before he reached up and furiously scratched his hair.

"Fine. It's just . . . it only seems to bring me trouble, and the ones who sold me into slavery might find me and try to come after me again if it becomes known where I am."

Eric considered this point quietly for a moment, then gave a slow nod.

"Your Highness! We've finished going through the duke's study!" Sir Levi's call from behind the prince had him turning around.

"Good. Once the horses are retrieved from the troughs, we'll depart."

The Troivackian knight bowed and wasted no time enacting the prince's orders.

"Well, this explains why you were always comfortable bossing people around," Eli noted wryly. "I can't believe the man who fell off a balcony after three days of drinking is the future king of Daxaria."

Eric's eyes widened as he glanced around them hurriedly. "Right. Maybe keep those kinds of details about our time together quiet, hm?"

Eli snorted.

"Back to my earlier question, how was it the duke was able to find you, and what was it that made you such an important target?" The prince met the lad's eyes with a small smile, hoping it would help make him less fearful.

Unfortunately, regardless of this move, Eli's hands began to tremble.

"W-Well . . . the truth is . . . that I'm . . . I'm one of the Zinferan emperor's adopted children. The emperor found out about my magic and thought it was something akin to a party trick, and my father . . . well . . . he wanted the power of me becoming a member of royalty."

Eric gaped. Whatever he had been anticipating, it hadn't been that.

"Eli . . . you're a prince?!"

"I'm one of fifty-four; there's no reason to get carried away . . . though most of my fellow adopted siblings have likely been killed off at this point. I don't know how many are left. The slave traders . . . They were supposed to kill me and throw me overboard as well, but . . . I used my magic to try and escape and failed. Once they learned what I could do, they at least let me live, but . . . it was because they had all sorts of uses for me." The boy swallowed with difficulty, his gaze lost to terrible memories.

Eric watched his friend, who suddenly looked older than his sixteen years and clasped his shoulder.

"I don't ever want to go back to Zinfera. I just want . . . to live and work in peace." Eli faced Eric, at least looking a little calmer now.

"Well . . . I won't lie to you. Things aren't exactly the safest right now with me here in Troivack, but once it all settles down again, I will take you back to Daxaria with me and find you work. Deal?"

Eli nodded with a tight lipped smile.

"Fantastic. Now, please tell me that as a prince of the Zinferan emperor you were taught to ride a horse." Pushing himself up onto his feet, Eric began to rotate his shoulders in preparation for the hard ride back to Vessa.

"I can." The younger boy rose as well, his posture notably straighter than when the two had first reunited. "By the way, what were you doing traveling as a mercenary and hanging around Insodam all that time if you're a prince?"

"Ah, here are the horses!" Eric declared loudly while striding over to where Sirs Levi and Vohn reappeared from around the keep. "Eli, I'll give you the horse I was riding before, and I'll take one of the stallions from the patrolmen yesterday—they're too big for you."

Eli didn't repeat his question, already sensing that just like his own torrid past, Eric's was not a simple one to explain.

So instead of bearing all their secrets to each other, the reunited friends set to returning to Vessa with the hopes of reaching the city before any of the duke's men or members of the rebellion could catch up with them.

Once mounted on his horse, Sir Levi sidled up to the Daxarian royal, his eyes already fixed on their new young charge.

"If you hadn't known that boy, things would've been far messier and prolonged . . . It seems the Gods don't wish us to be away from Vessa."

Eric felt his heart thud and his hands grow cold.

Things *had* gone a little too smoothly . . .

Looking around, he half expected to find the devil standing on the courtyard stones behind him. Watching him, his dark eyes drawing him closer, pulling forth emotions and shadows that Eric didn't want to face again . . .

"Your Highness? Is everything alright?"

Sir Vohn's concerned tone snapped Eric's attention back to the vineyard before him.

"Yes, just thinking about the best route to Vessa. We can't go the way we came, so let's risk cutting to the west and taking the long way down. We might run into one of the rebellion groups, but if we don't, there'll be no chance they can catch up to us."

His shouted commands had the knights mounting their steeds and gathering around him, and with his fist then punching into the air signaling them, the entourage set their horses into motion, leaving behind the keep they thought they'd be staying in for at least two weeks.

As the group rode, Sir Vohn glanced again at Eli and found himself shaking his head.

There was something about the boy he couldn't put his finger on . . . but . . . if Eric trusted him, that was all there was to it.

At least until they got to Vessa.

"Ashowan! You have a visitor!"

Katarina halted her attack midstrike at Sir Cas's announcement.

Turning to look over her shoulder, she found Dante striding toward her, frowning.

"Haven't seen you in ages, Dante. How're the children doing?" Kat then turned and resumed her training on the dummy.

"Why didn't you need to punish me?"

Kat fumbled her attack and looked over her shoulder to stare in bewilderment at Dante.

She noticed he appeared quite tired, and he was scowling at her fiercely.

"Pardon?"

"You said before you walked into that meeting our first day here that you didn't need to punish me. Why?"

Kat blinked. "Has this been bothering you all this time . . . ?"

"I want an answer," Dante insisted irritably.

Visibly fighting off a smile, Kat slowly squared herself with the large Troivackian man.

"What will you give me if I tell you?"

Dante growled.

"Alright, then I won't tell you if you're going to be that way." Kat turned back to her dummy and hefted her sword back up to attack.

"What do you want?" The words were strangled.

Kat grinned and slid her gaze back over her shoulder. "I want a night out in Vessa, drinking with my peers."

"No." Dante turned on his heel and proceeded back toward the castle.

Kat jogged after him. "Come on! It's the Winter Solstice in a few days, and all I've been doing the past few months is training endlessly! Please!"

"Not a chance."

"You know it's bad for me to have no fun; I might just find mischief to get into!"

Dante rounded so quickly on Kat that she almost collided face first into his chest.

"Do not jeopardize *everything* with such childishness. You are better than that, Lady Katarina."

Kat glared up at Dante wordlessly for a moment, then walked back to her dummy as the snow started to fall on the courtyard for the second time that morning.

"There is such a thing as training too hard." Sir Cas's quiet voice drew Dante's hardened gaze to him. The Daxarian knight had been taking a drink of water by the castle door when the eldest Faucher son had arrived.

"We cannot have her fail during the final test," Dante argued back vehemently.

"She might if we don't give her a moment to breathe. She's remarkable, don't get me wrong, but for the past three weeks, she's trained nonstop. I think she has maybe only slept an hour or two here or there—she's even *looking* tired. Yesterday I actually caught her yawning . . . She's more than ready, so can't we let her have some fun?"

Dante stared at the redhead's back, his expression unreadable as he listened to Sir Cas's words.

However, he still resumed his journey back toward the castle all the same. "We'll arrange something celebratory for her after the sparring. Nothing until then. Oh"—he hesitated, then handed a missive to the Daxarian knight—"a blacksmith that worked on Lady Katarina's sword has been pestering my mother. He keeps saying he wants to talk about the sword with her. Says that he had wanted to meet with her sooner. Do you know anything about this?"

Sir Cas raised an eyebrow while accepting the rolled up piece of parchment and shaking his head. "I knew she had the sword she found repaired, but I haven't heard the details other than the fact that it is a true Theodore Phendor piece."

"Right, well see that she reads that. The man has come by once every fortnight, and my mother has enough on her plate with trying to oversee the keep's repair."

Sir Cas bowed his head.

Casting one final look toward Kat, Dante climbed the steps into the castle. He hadn't worn his winter cloak, not knowing how bitterly cold it was outside, and he had to get back to helping manage his father's work. Though as he made his way back down the corridor, a small shadow flit by, stopping him in his tracks.

"Pina?" Dante peered down into the wide eyes of Katarina's familiar. "Are you on your way to see your mistress?"

Her purrs became audible as the familiar pressed her cheek against Dante's calf.

His entire face relaxed as he bent down and scooped the kitten up so that he could feel her whiskers tickling his ear.

"You're being treated well, I hear," Dante murmured while idly scratching the downy fur behind her ears. "Apparently Captain Orion had to ban the knights that are to fight against Lady Katarina from meeting you."

Pina pressed her freckled nose to Dante's cheek, making him chuckle.

"It seems anyone who meets you doesn't want you to be upset . . . and so they don't want to fight your witch." Unbeknownst to Dante, his voice was becoming higher pitched as he spoke dotingly to the feline.

"That, and Sir Miller will go on a warpath for you, won't he?" Dante cooed as he continued walking farther into the castle, completely unaware that he was smiling blissfully while cuddling and talking with the feline. "You're such a sweet girl. Your little paws feel cold! Don't worry, I'll get you in front of the fire, and you'll be able to have a warm nap."

Whatever Dante had been stressed about before had melted away. He had no grim thoughts or feelings of trepidation . . .

No, all that remained was Pina with her soothing purrs, her soft fur, and of course her adorably freckled nose.

"Pina, do you want anything for the Winter Solstice this year?"

In the years to come, Dante would look back on that day and have a little bit of regret for not listening to Sir Cas and letting Katarina have a rest . . . Though he would mostly remember how delightful Pina was. Nonetheless, that day would be burned into his memory.

CHAPTER 45

AN OVERDUE OVERTURE

W ell, Ashowan, are you ready?"
Kat sat on the steps to the castle and drank deeply from her flagon of water, her golden gaze staring blindly ahead, dark bags under her eyes, and her face paler than normal.

"Ashowan," Faucher attempted to growl at his student in the dark, his breath coming out in a puff, but he failed. Since the night Katarina had come to train in tears, his worry for the redhead had only increased.

She had trained . . . and trained . . . made one feeble attempt to get her hands on Troivackian moonshine, took his chastising stone-faced, and continued to train. She no longer prattled on at great length, or tried to infuriate him, and recently no longer even smiled . . .

By the night before her spar against the Troivackian knights, she looked tired and broken.

It angered Faucher, and he had no way of finding an appropriate means of handling that feeling.

Dante had told him about her request to have a night out with her comrades, but he had agreed with his son that she needed to focus on her training more than ever and not risk any slipups.

However, he found himself second-guessing that decision when he took stock of her poor state.

Regardless of her obvious exhaustion, Kat was still remarkable with a sword—there was no doubt about that—but after teaching and observing her closely for months, Faucher knew there wasn't the same energy or quickness there had been since they first returned to the castle.

"Ashowan," he repeated.

When Katarina still didn't answer, Faucher tapped her shoulder.

"Hm? Yeah. Sure thing," she replied before rubbing her eyes.

"You should go to bed tonight. We covered what we needed to," Faucher advised while nodding toward nothing in particular.

"It's fine. I want to make sure I didn't twist my ankle when I threw you off last time." Kat stood stiffly, and Faucher could see from the way she moved that her limbs were heavy with fatigue.

That month, she had performed an inhuman amount of practice and training, and while she still ate voraciously, Faucher could tell she was reaching her limits.

"No, Ashowan. You need a good rest before something important like tomorrow."

"I'm fine. Come on, old man. Let's do a final push, and—"

The distant clattering of hooves echoed up to them in the darkness.

Both Katarina and Faucher fell silent and turned toward the west wing of the castle by the knights' barracks and stables.

While the Troivackian military leader had only turned toward the sound, Katarina was already striding hastily toward it.

It didn't take long for it to occur to Faucher as to why that was . . .

Godsdamnit, she thinks it's the prince.

Faucher followed her expediently, catching up and matching her quick pace.

"You shouldn't reveal to people you're up and about now. It might clue them in that you've been training at night."

"They'll just think I'm doing a last-ditch training effort with you before the spar. It's fine," she dismissed easily, her eyes glowing in the night, as they rounded the castle corner away from any lit torches or braziers.

"Ashowan, it could just be another messenger from the prince's entourage. It doesn't—"

"What messenger?"

Faucher clamped his mouth shut with a grimace. He had decided not to tell her the news about the prince being accosted at the duke's manner, or that he was on the run from the rebellious groups in Troivack. He hadn't wanted to distract her more than she already was.

Kat's eyes narrowed as she glanced briefly at Faucher. She could guess that information had been withheld from her and why, but she didn't bother pestering her teacher about it as they approached the doorway to the castle that would take them across a corridor to the knights' training courtyard.

When she heard voices, however, she increased her pace to a near jog.

Faucher let out a grunt as he watched her gleaming ponytail bob in front of him.

He had a bad feeling in his gut . . .

When Kat stepped onto the covered walkway that wrapped around the training ground, she stopped. Her eyes fixed on the group of horses with men standing around them.

Faucher was able to catch up to her, but he needed to squint at the shadows to discern if it was the prince's entourage.

"Wait here," he murmured while moving toward the side steps to the courtyard.

As he descended onto the stones, two of the men turned toward him, and Faucher felt a small knot of unease in his belly loosen.

"Sir Levi, glad to see you all made it back safely," he greeted while continuing forward, his eyes casually roving over the horses and men in search of the prince.

"Leader Faucher! What are you doing awake this time of night?" Sir Levi's surprise was evident in his tone as he held out his hand and clasped Faucher's once he'd reached them.

"I had a few matters to take care of when I heard the horses. Weren't you traveling with a carriage for His Highness?"

"Ah, we had to abandon the vehicle even before being attacked, which turned out to be for the best. We needed to move expediently given our pursuers." Sir Levin leaned closer. "I couldn't believe it. I saw it with my own two eyes . . . Duke Icarus is definitely taking part in treason and helping the rebellion. We were being pursued heavily until three leagues before Vessa . . . Honestly, if we hadn't hurried like the prince urged us to, we would've been overwhelmed and slaughtered."

Faucher's brow furrowed. "Did you collect evidence?"

"As much as we could, plus we have a witness who apparently knew the crown prince from years before . . ."

Straightening, Faucher didn't bother hiding his search for the prince. "A witness can be helpful, but where is His Highness?"

"Glad to see you missed me, Faucher."

Relief flooded the Troivackian's body as he turned and regarded Eric Reyes, who had appeared from the other side of the group and stood unscathed if more than a little travel weary and a mite ungroomed.

"Your Highness," Faucher greeted with a bow. "It is good you have returned safely."

Eric nearly smiled, but his eyes suddenly darted over Faucher's shoulder, and the military leader didn't need to guess at what had drawn his attention, as the prince then looked as though he'd been punched in the gut.

Faucher squared his shoulders and blocked Sir Levi's view of the covered walk. "You must be tired from your journey. You should report to His Majesty and then rest."

"Of course." Sir Levi bowed and began to lean around Faucher to stare at the prince as though to ask him to come along, but Faucher clasped a hand on Sir Levi's shoulder and propelled him back into the throng of knights and horses. "I shall come with you. I would like to speak with this witness you brought as well."

"Ah, yes. Sir Vohn, would you mind escorting the boy? This here is Eli . . ."

While the rest of the entourage gradually shifted away and back toward the main entrance to the castle and some of the knights tended to the horses, Eric and Kat stared at each other from a distance.

His fingers were already trembling from the damnable pull toward her that had tripled in strength while he was gone. Running low on sense and restraint, Eric was unable to stop himself from casually making his way over to the side stairs of the walkway, slipping into the shadows along the wall as Katarina sidled over to meet him there.

When she reached him and Eric could make out the details of her face by the faint glow of her eyes, he felt his heart trip over itself.

She looked terrible.

"So . . . you're back," Kat greeted, her breathing markedly faster.

"Yeah . . . Yeah, I am. Hey, are you alright?" Eric's brow furrowed, and his hand began to rise as though about to clasp her arm, but he stopped himself and instead slipped it into his pocket.

"Fine. Just been busy. The spar is tomorrow." Kat's voice was already a croak. She felt like she was going to be sick, standing there staring at him.

"Oh, I'm . . . I'm glad I didn't miss it," Eric managed to say sincerely, though it was a struggle.

Every inch of him wanted to touch her. Hold her. His blood was screaming at him, and the trembling in his hands spread to his legs.

"Would've been nice to know that you . . . you were leaving." Kat forced herself to look away. Tears were coming to her eyes, and she was furious about it.

"I'm sorry. I just . . . I needed to try and get evidence on the duke, and after our . . . after our talk, I figured we may need space and time away from each other."

Kat nodded as though she agreed, but she still couldn't look at him.

She wanted him to hug her. She wanted to hear him say he loved her again . . . The need had become urgent ever since she had admitted to herself that she felt the same for him.

Kat felt like she was falling apart every breath she spent in his presence.

"I was drunk the first half of the journey. I killed a bunch of people again, too," Eric informed her without thinking.

He had no idea why; there was no point. Was he just trying to remind her the reasoning behind his decision about their relationship?

Whatever his halfhearted, ill-conceived ploy was, it did not have a reaction he could have anticipated.

Katarina looked at him, blinking back tears as she glared at him.

"And? Are you telling me that to hurt me? Or is it that you're an idiot and think I fell in love with you during the two days you spent not being an arse around me? I already know what you're like."

Eric nearly collapsed to his knees.

Did she know she'd just admitted to loving him?

Did she know she was breaking him?

"Gods know when it happened or why. It probably all started because of our time in the garden at Alina's wedding, or when you came and got me the night of the coyote." She shook her head furiously, her toes beginning to turn away as though about to storm off, but then her hands found her hips, and she looked back at his stricken expression.

"Eric, I am well aware of your problems, so it doesn't matter what you did. I already love you despite knowing all the awful details about you."

"Kat, stop saying it." Eric could barely speak.

"Saying what?" she demanded irately.

"Stop saying that you love me."

Kat stilled, but only for a moment before she took another step closer to Eric. His hazel eyes were intense, and when they locked with her golden ones, he was unable to look anywhere else.

"It doesn't matter if I do or don't, does it? You've made up your mind. It doesn't matter if I tell you that I don't care if how you love me is wrong. Or that it doesn't matter to me that you're a mess, as long as you love me back the best you can. Right? *None* of that matters."

She was inches from his face, and he was already past the point of thinking clearly.

"Kat, leave."

"Why the hell should I?"

"Because if I move at all right now, things will get worse."

Eric was attempting to take slow breaths, but they weren't helping, and Kat could see that.

"Leave," he repeated, his vision starting to spin.

"No."

There was a single moment after her defiance. A single moment where there was quiet nothingness, but they stood upon that peak for only that small gap of time . . .

"Godsdamnit," Eric rasped before grabbing Kat by the back of her neck and kissing her with overflowing mind-numbing emotion and satisfaction.

Pressing him back into the castle wall, her hands cupping his face, Kat felt her aura flicker to life as it flooded her body with happiness, and relief as she at last collided with the man she had been pulled to for months. Fiery heat scorched her from the inside out, and it was utterly intoxicating.

Holding her close, Eric didn't realize that Kat had reached for the handle of a nearby door behind him . . . a door to a storage closet.

"Kat." His voice was hoarse, his fingers gently grasping the hair at the back of her neck, his mouth still a breath away from hers. "Kat, what are you—"

"Shut up." Her voice had come out an angry plea, and when Eric's eyes fluttered open and he saw the desperation, desire, and love in the gaze that stared back, he found himself unable to say anything else.

He allowed Kat to push him back into the closet, and he allowed her to close the door behind them, but thereafter, he was the one to grab her again and kiss her. Which just so happened to be exactly what she wanted.

As a result, neither Eric nor Kat were seen again that night, as neither one of them happened to leave the storage closet.

CHAPTER 46

A DISMAL DISCOVERY

F aucher!" Sir Cas knocked desperately on the military leader's chamber door. "Godsdamnit," the Daxarian knight muttered frantically under his breath as he kept glancing around.

He continued to pound the door, this time without bothering to be quiet, as he confirmed no one else was nearby.

At last, the door opened to reveal a bedraggled Faucher, his eyes bloodshot and his hair sporting random curls springing high above the others.

"Sir Cas, there better be a Godsdamn good reason for this." Faucher's eyes flit with a squint toward the window behind the Daxarian knight, revealing that the sun had not yet risen.

"Faucher, do you know where Lady Katarina is?"

The military leader's face paled around the two scars that ran along his face as he poked his head out and double-checked that no one was around the corridor.

"What do you mean? I went to hear the report from Sir Levi, and she went to bed. Is she training without you? I had told her not to train anymore last night, but she still might have—"

"No. I checked the training yard, and she isn't there, and her maid says she never returned to her chamber last night."

Faucher was completely awake.

He turned, snatched his vest, and threw it over his wrinkled tunic, then seized his boots and thrust them on.

"Get my daughter to bring me her dog Boots and meet me by Lady Katarina's chamber."

Sir Cas nodded and set off quickly toward Dana's chamber.

"Greg? What's wrong?" Nathalie's soft voice behind her husband barely registered in the man's ears as his mind was already racing.

Had the prince said something else to Katarina that upset her? Had she run off to a pub to drink her sorrows away?

Then another horrible notion entered his mind . . .

One that made Faucher feel sick to his stomach.

"Nattie, go with Sir Cas to Dana's chamber, right now. I'm going to meet you all in front of Lady Katarina's chamber. Hurry."

Lady Nathalie had never seen her husband so panicked in all her life. It was to the point where all pretense of hiding his emotions was abandoned.

As soon as the door closed behind him, she proceeded to get ready as quickly as possible, wondering what new chaos had released itself the day of the spar . . .

"Did he say why . . . ?" Lady Nathalie stood outside Lady Katarina's chamber, facing Sir Cas. Her daughter was by her side with sleep still caked in the corners of her eyes, her dog Boots sitting and panting happily at her side.

"He didn't, but I'm worried someone tried or succeeded in abducting Lady Katarina to prevent her from participating in the spar today," Sir Cas explained in hushed tones.

"Oyy, is our champion fighter still getting her beauty sleep on a day like today?"

Both Sir Cas and Lady Nathalie jumped at the sudden call, but upon finding that it was only Piers and Conrad making their way over to them, settled back down.

When the two men had reached the small huddle, Piers reached up and attempted to ruffle his sister's hair only to have Boots give a warning growl that had him dropping his hand away swiftly.

"What's this party about?" Piers asked while peering at his mother's and Sir Cas's tensed expressions.

No one got the chance to answer him before Faucher darted around the corner and bolted straight to the group, the terror and fury in his expression alarming everyone.

"Get Poppy to retrieve something of Ashowan's."

"Father, what—" Piers had never seen his father in such a state, and it was deeply unsettling, but he wasn't able to finish the question before his mother was knocking on the door.

Poppy opened it a crack, her wide brown eyes surveying the group before she let out a small sigh and opened the door a little wider.

"Poppy, dear, could you please get us something Lady Katarina has worn recently? A tunic? A sleep shirt?" Nathalie asked kindly.

The maid nodded hastily before darting back into the room and returning with what appeared to be a dirty tunic.

"Thank you, and remember, anyone who comes by, tell them she is sleeping in before the spar," Faucher ordered while snatching the garment, the edge in his voice making the young maid flinch.

"Y-Yes, sir."

"Good. Now close the door."

Poppy didn't need to be told twice.

"What's going on?" Conrad felt his own gut begin to flutter worriedly as he watched his father press the shirt to Boots's nose.

"Dana, tell him to search." Faucher ignored his son and instead addressed his daughter.

Blinking in confusion but sensing it wasn't the time for questions, Dana bent down. "Boots, search! Search, Boots!"

The chocolate-colored mutt gave a small bark before eagerly sniffing the tunic in Faucher's hand.

Then the dog took off at a steady trot back up the corridor toward the servants' stairwell with the crowd in tow.

Boots continued pulling Dana along, his nose lowered close to the ground as he guided them down the stairs. Once they touched down by the kitchens, he moved them toward the official training courtyard . . .

"Gods, did the knights pick a fight with her this morning?" Piers wondered aloud, anger sparking in his eyes.

"Stop talking." Faucher's voice was low and dangerous. His heart was in his throat.

He sincerely *wished* all that happened was that the knights had picked a fight with her. He wished with all his might it had nothing to do with the fact that when he had gone and checked with the prince's sleepy-eyed assistant, he discovered that the prince hadn't returned to his own chamber the previous night either . . .

Boots hesitated when he led them out onto the covered walkway surrounding the training yard. During that time, Faucher scanned the area desperately.

But aside from the muddy stones, the braziers weren't even lit in the early chill of the day.

Then, Boots continued to pull them to the right . . . then down by where Faucher had left Katarina standing the night before . . . then around the corner to the left, until . . . the dog stopped in front of a storage closet and sat down.

He then looked up at Dana and gave a soft woof.

"Good boy, Boots. Very good boy." Dana bent down and gave a loving scratch behind her dog's ears that had his stub of a tail wagging happily.

Faucher stared at the door, the horrible gut feeling he'd had since the night before tripling.

"Why in the world would Ashowan be in there?" Piers scoffed while reaching for the door handle.

Faucher's hand snapped out and seized his son's wrist in a death grip.

"Nathalie . . ." Faucher couldn't take his eyes off the door. "Nathalie, I need you to look inside."

He felt like he was trapped in a nightmare.

Frowning and concerned over her husband's state, Lady Nathalie wondered what had him looking as though he had just heard mortally bad news . . . But she obeyed, quietly lifted the latch open, and slipped inside.

"Piers, Conrad, Sir Cas, stand over there and keep your backs to the door," Faucher ordered while pointing toward the arched opening that overlooked the courtyard. "Block it from sight."

"Father, could you tell us what—"

Nathalie stumbled out of the room, her eyes wide and her face void of all color.

"Greg . . . Oh Gods, Greg . . ." she said breathily.

Faucher observed the violent shaking in his wife's hands and how her knees were buckled, and then the pair locked eyes.

"She's there?"

"Yes," Nathalie whispered.

"And . . . ?"

"Yes."

Faucher dropped his face to his hands.

At that moment, he couldn't think straight, he couldn't hear or see anything . . .

"Gods-fucking-damnit," his voice was broken and angry.

"Father . . . ?" Dana asked fearfully.

Faucher barely managed to swallow without being sick. "Dana . . . you and your mother are going to walk Lady Katarina back to her chamber. Don't ask her any questions. Just get her to her chamber, and your mother will see to the rest."

He looked to his wife, who nodded in complete understanding. Turning back to the door, her hand on its handle, Nathalie took a fortifying breath and entered again.

Faucher regarded his sons and the Daxarian knight, who were all waiting expectantly and frowning.

What had happened? Conrad and Piers had rarely ever heard their father swear so crudely in front of their sister, and *never* had they seen him so . . . unnerved.

"Turn your backs and block the view," Faucher repeated with a rasp.

Hesitantly, Conrad, Sir Cas, and Piers all did as he ordered.

They stood in silence. Faucher couldn't hear anything, but perhaps it was because his heart thundered in his ears. His stomach roared with terror and nausea . . .

The door opened.

Nathalie exited first, and then . . . out stepped Kat.

Her long red hair was free from its ponytail and mussed. Her face pale, and her eyes . . . fixed to the ground.

Faucher saw the awkwardness of her movements, saw how her tunic was untucked, and the way she clutched the bunched training vest she had worn the previous night to her middle.

He felt his eyes grow warm.

Kat didn't look at him and merely allowed herself to be slowly guided away by his wife, his daughter staring perplexedly at the redhead while ushering her dog back with them by his lead. Dana was obviously unaware of what was happening, and it was the smallest of mercies to the military leader's mental state.

Faucher remained in the cold winter wind long after Katarina had left his sight. His heart was still hammering, and rage coursed through him as he continued staring at the door.

"Piers . . . stand guard outside this door. No one comes in no matter what sounds come out," he heard himself say the words. "Sir Cas, Conrad . . . you will come with me in that room, and you will make sure I don't take things too far."

"Faucher, what the hell has happened?" Sir Cas had held his tongue long enough as he turned back around and stepped toward the military leader. "Did she steal the king's moonshine or something?"

When Faucher moved his head toward the Daxarian knight, it took visible effort for him to meet Sir Cas's gaze. His sons were equally invested in hearing the answer.

"Last night . . ." Faucher's voice was hoarse, but he plundered on, determined to finish his sentence without shouting. "Late last night, the prince's entourage returned."

Sir Cas blinked, caught off guard and momentarily unclear what Faucher meant.

Piers, however, was the first to realize just what had transpired.

"I'm going to kill him."

Faucher barely managed to catch his youngest son by the front of his tunic, stopping him from barging into the storage closet.

"Guard. The. Door," he rumbled powerfully before thrusting Piers back, though he sympathized with the bloodthirsty look in his son's eyes.

But then, because Faucher had been preoccupied with preventing his son from entering the room, he wasn't quick enough to stop Sir Cas, who seized the door handle and flew inside.

"Shit."

Faucher and Conrad also darted into the room, closing the door behind them in time to block the sound of Sir Cas, who already had his hand around Eric's throat and had the prince hauled up onto his feet from his place on the floor and slammed against an armoire filled with foot soldiers' uniforms.

"What the hell did you do? Are you Godsdamn insane? *How* could you have done that?! Don't you know everything she's worked for?!"

Eric apparently had been sleeping until that very moment, and so when his eyes fluttered open, his hands flew to Sir Cas's wrists. He was just about to proceed with bashing his head into the knight's face, when he registered Faucher standing just behind Sir Cas, staring at the rumpled sheet on the floor that had at one point been covering a piece of furniture in the room that was filled with stacked benches and other odds and ends. A single small round window let in the barest amount of light near the ceiling, allowing the exchange to proceed in private.

The prince went mostly limp, allowing Sir Cas to continue throttling him without a fight, while Faucher crouched and shifted the sheet on the ground.

Sure enough . . . he found the telltale sign of what he had dreaded.

Turning the sheet over to hide the evidence from his son, Faucher rose and straightened his shoulders.

"Sir Cas, release him."

The blond knight did not obey.

Faucher reached out, grasped the back of Sir Cas's tunic, and yanked him back. Though the Daxarian knight was panting, he looked more fearsome than anyone could've imagined.

Eric remained on his feet, half slumped against the armoire, wearing his trousers but nothing else. His tunic and boots were discarded elsewhere in the room.

Faucher stepped forward, his dark eyes deeply foreboding.

"Do you know what you've done?" The roar in his voice was barely contained.

Eric's tired, mortified eyes told the military leader that the prince did, indeed, realize the gravity of the situation.

Faucher pummeled his fist into Eric's gut, sending him to his knees on the floor.

He breathed hard, staring down at the Daxarian royal.

"At least you weren't drunk." Faucher seethed. "Or that would've made you sick all over my boots. Not that I'm all that comforted." He bent down and grabbed Eric by the front of his throat. The prince didn't resist in the slightest.

"If she loses today because of this oversight of sense, you've doomed us all." Conrad's quiet voice near the door was no less fierce than his father's.

"Damn the match today. Do you know what will happen to *her*? She's now compromised, and her father, a duke in your kingdom, will arrive one of these days. What do you think will happen to *our* king when the duke discovers his daughter has been bedded out of wedlock and might be carrying a bastard when His Majesty was tasked with ensuring her safety?!" Faucher demanded while shaking Eric once before releasing him and standing.

"Godsdamnit." Faucher closed his eyes and took a fortifying breath. Behind him, Eric gradually brought himself to a seated position, his back against the armoire.

The prince had nothing to say.

Faucher rounded on him again, coldness filling his gaze.

"Well, Your Highness. Prepare yourself. After today's spar, where my student will beat everyone regardless of the foolish behavior that took place last night, you two are going to be wed, and there isn't a Godsdamn thing you can say to stop it from happening."

CHAPTER 47

SOOTHING A SCANDAL

Outside, there was a flurry of activity as servants and squires worked together to clear the dummies from the corner of the training courtyard that was to host the official sparring between Katarina Ashowan and the Troivackian squires and knight.

Inside, there was an energetic fervor amongst the nobility as some speculated the fight being remarkable entertainment, while others dreaded the mockery it would invoke for their esteemed men-at-arms. The women who had been ordered to witness the event ranged similarly . . . Some didn't wish to see such brutality and violence, while others were secretly excited for the matches, their curiosities getting the better of them.

However, there was a small group of people in the Troivackian king's castle that, unlike everyone else, weren't thinking about the match at all.

"Are you . . . Are you certain?" Brendan fumbled his words.

A sure sign he was shaken to his very core.

He sat behind the desk in his office, staring down at Faucher.

"Yes, Your Majesty. I offer my deepest apologies. This is entirely my fault. I knew that His Highness had hung back to have a few words with Lady Katarina, but I hadn't anticipated this outcome." Faucher was on his knees, his head lowered before Brendan, his voice gravelly.

"You left them unsupervised in the middle of the night?!" The king rose to his feet, his eyes wide.

"I should have realized when His Highness did not join us in our discussions about the duke's keep . . . but I had assumed he'd gone straight to bed instead."

Brendan looked around his office as though trying to find some magical being floating there, telling him he was simply in a bad dream.

"Gods . . . do you realize her father could choose to start a war with us over this? Everything we've worked for could go up in flames." While his tone was incensed, it wasn't accusatory toward Faucher. "Godsdamnit . . ."

"If we can convince Lady Katarina to marry the prince, it will negate much of the damage. Though there of course will be talk of how quickly it took place."

Brendan leaned heavily on the edge of his desk. "Did the prince really say he'd abide by whatever she wished? If he only said that after you beat it out of him, it could lead to even *more* issues . . . Hell, it might already be enough to start a war just because you assaulted him."

Faucher had nothing else he could say.

Eric *had* said that whatever Katarina wanted to do about the situation, he would obey, but that declaration was made while the prince had stared at the ground, unable to stand as he faced the blade of consequence for his decision . . . as well as an actual blade.

Conrad had bided his time well and almost got the better of Eric before Sir Cas stopped him, albeit the Daxarian knight had been a little reluctant to do so.

"At least Duke Ashowan won't have his magic here in Troivack, otherwise he would most likely kill us on the spot when he discovers what's happened," Brendan muttered half to himself while collapsing back into his chair. "Then again, he could take over completely if he declares this kingdom his new home . . ."

"Your Majesty, might I suggest we get through the match today before there are any decisions as to what will be done."

Brendan's attention snapped to his former teacher. "Can Lady Katarina even fight in her state? She may need a physician . . . Gods. If she becomes with child, and we find out in a fortnight before her father arrives . . ." Brendan dropped his head to his hand.

Faucher felt his rage from earlier begin to bubble forward . . . but it was because he found himself thinking about Katarina's future.

She was beyond gifted with the sword.

Teaching her and watching her learn . . . It was as though she had been remembering a skill she had once been a master of years ago, and as much as Faucher hadn't wanted to admit it . . . she was born for it.

She could have carved herself an admirable career as a knight back in Daxaria. She could have lived freely as she always claimed to have wished.

"Faucher, it isn't your fault. Not really. I did not mean to place the blame entirely on you. The Daxarians are of course responsible for their reckless behavior—particularly His Highness." Brendan sighed while finally regaining enough of his strength to stand again.

Faucher raised his face to his king, his expression still burdened and unconvinced by the king's assurance.

"Go talk to Lady Nathalie and find out what condition Lady Katarina is in. We'll go from there. I'll speak with the prince."

Faucher stood up and bowed. "Yes, Your Majesty."

Once alone in his study, Brendan looked to the ceiling, shaking his head. "Gods almighty, maybe everyone in Daxaria aside from Alina *are* fools."

Then, staring at his door, he crossed the room, his mind turning to his troublesome brother-in-law, but just as he reached the handle of the door, he froze as a realization dawned on him.

If Katarina Ashowan decides to marry him . . . she'll be the next queen of Daxaria and my sister-in-law.

Brendan's hand fell from the handle.

Turning back around, he strode over to his desk where a bottle of moonshine sat barely touched, uncorked it, and proceeded to take several mouthfuls of the liquor.

"Lady Katarina, would you perhaps like to talk about what happened?"

Nathalie stood off to the side away from Kat, her hands clasped in front of her skirts as the young woman finished fastening on the clean uniform that identified her as Faucher's student. Poppy had already disappeared from Kat's chamber to the kitchens to bring her mistresses a hearty breakfast before her match, leaving the two alone.

Despite the conversation being able to take place in private, Kat didn't respond to Lady Nathalie's gentle suggestion.

"You might feel a little sore today, and the bleeding is perfectly normal—"

"I'm fine," Kat interrupted, her voice deceptively calm.

Nathalie lowered her eyes thoughtfully as she considered what might be the best thing to say to the young woman in that moment.

Then she remembered who Katarina Ashowan's mother was, and it suddenly became perfectly clear to her.

"Drink a painkiller tea an hour before the match, and if anyone asks where you were, claim you spent the night with Dana. She and I will corroborate."

At last Katarina's gaze lifted and locked with the Troivackian noblewoman's. She nodded seriously.

"Thank you. I greatly appreciate that, Lady Nathalie. Apologies for you having to deal with my embarrassing display."

Lady Nathalie waved her hand. "It isn't the first time in history to happen." She was lying.

It *absolutely* was the first time in history a swordswoman almost couldn't make her first official match because she'd been bedded while unwed—by a crown prince, no less . . .

But Nathalie decided that pointing that fact out was not going to be helpful to the redhead, who, she could tell, was doing her best to remain as composed and controlled as possible.

Kat turned to face Nathalie, her expression unreadable . . . At the very least, she looked better rested than she had in weeks.

"Is my uniform up to par?"

Smiling a little to herself, the Troivackian noblewoman nodded. "It is. You remind me a lot of your mother right now, if I'm honest."

Kat stiffened in shock. "You know my mother?"

Nathalie stepped forward and gently tugged the soft blue leather vest Katarina had just finished fastening, even though it didn't require any straightening.

"I do, yes. In fact, we used to know each other quite well."

"Why didn't you say anything?" Kat questioned with a frown.

Nathalie smiled and peered up into Kat's eyes while her hands floated to her upper arms. "Because your mother wouldn't want me to. But today . . . I thought it might help you to know."

"So I can remember how she's going to kill me even if I survive the sparring?" Kat asked with a raised eyebrow.

Caught between a laugh and wanting to lecture the redhead, the Troivackian noblewoman stepped back and once again held her hands in front of her skirts.

"You remind me of her today because you aren't hiding from your responsibilities. Regardless of how you might be feeling, you are facing your life and all that may not be easy about it."

It was brief, but for a quiet moment, Katarina revealed her emotions.

Her vulnerability, her determination, her somber awareness of the coming consequences, and yet at the same time . . . there was a peace in her that surprised Nathalie deeply.

She saw that Katarina didn't regret what had transpired, but . . . she also saw that the future was still uncertain.

Kat turned and looked out the window. "Looks like it'll snow again today. That'll be to my advantage."

Nathalie nodded, then leaned forward and drew Katarina's eyes back to her.

"Remember. Troivackians fight dirty."

Kat gave a small derisive laugh. "Oh, I know. It'll be fun."

Nathalie smiled. "Exactly like your mother again."

At this observation of similarity, Kat frowned. She knew her mother had learned to wield knives in self-defense, but when had she ever been in an actual fight?

She didn't get to ask any clarifying questions, however, as Poppy returned with a heaping tray of food. Kat's serious mood resumed.

After she ate, she'd be going down to the courtyard where the nobility would be starting to gather around to watch the spar. However, what was even more frightening to the redhead was that she'd be facing Faucher, and the idea of him looking at her with any kind of disappointment was something she wasn't sure she could bear.

Brendan looked at Eric blankly as his assistant, Mr. Julian, finished trimming his hair that had grown unruly again while he'd been away. Once that task had been finished, the lad hastily dusted off the prince's shoulders. Without bothering to grab his own winter cloak, he scurried from the room.

He hadn't wanted to even bother finishing the haircut to begin with, but the king had insisted.

Once the two were freed from their audience, Brendan waited, his arms folded.

Eric stared ahead, his eyes deadened and his shoulders slumped in defeat.

"If you were going to regret it so much, why did you do this?" Brendan barked, snapping the silence in half.

Eric closed his eyes and stood laboriously. As he did so, Brendan noted the bruising around his throat from where he had been strangled by two different men and felt an ounce of satisfaction.

"Wasn't thinking clearly."

"Faucher told me you were sober."

"Was tired and . . . No. Never mind. There's no excuse. Don't make her marry me." Eric turned to stare at Brendan, and the king could see it then. The fear in his eyes for Katarina's sake . . . Not his own.

"I imagine she was complicit in what happened, Your Highness. You both must accept what comes next. Or can you promise that she isn't carrying your offspring?" Brendan asked matter-of-factly with a small shrug, though his dark eyes never left the prince's face.

Eric held his brother-in-law's gaze only for a moment before he recoiled in guilt while nausea boiled in his belly, prompting him to rub his forehead.

"I'm normally careful . . ."

Brendan didn't have any sympathy to spare.

"You'll marry her."

"Only if she wants to. If that's what she says has to happen, then fine, but if she refuses, don't push the matter. She always said that she never wanted to marry." Eric shook his head and looked toward the window.

The king felt his teeth clench. "I will not allow the wrath of her father to break over my people."

"Fin will be even more furious if he finds out she married because she was pressured to. He's a powerful man in Daxaria, so even in this situation, she does have options. She'll have to leave immediately with the duke once he arrives, but that's for the better anyway with the devil interested in her," Eric mused aloud, his hand once again finding his pocket.

"How convenient for you."

Eric turned around to stare at Brendan when he heard the acid in his voice.

"You know I'm not saying this to run from her. You know I could destroy her with how I am."

"Then put in the Godsdamn work so that you don't." Brendan descended upon his brother-in-law, his teeth bared. "You're lucky enough that you care for each other at the very least. You think I relish in the idea of her becoming related to me?!"

The king turned away furiously, his arms falling to his sides, but he wasn't finished.

Looking back at Eric, he forced himself to a more tolerable level of calm.

"If you say to her that you'll simply do as she wishes, she'll think you don't want her. And knowing how Lady Katarina is, her pride will prevent her from saying she wants to marry you. She won't force you to do something that you do not wish to do. So you're going to ask for her hand yourself, and you will be damn convincing about it. If she says no after that? Then fine. I won't force her. Agreed?"

Eric met Brendan's eyes and bowed his head in acceptance.

Satisfied, the king took his leave to return to his wife—Katarina's best friend—who had no idea what was transpiring. The stress of the day was already high enough . . .

Not to mention Brendan already feared his wife's mood lately when something as small as the saurkraut bowl ran empty during dinner. He didn't want to inform her that on top of it all her brother was having a rushed wedding to her best friend because of a scandal.

CHAPTER 48

FORGIVING FOLLIES

The din of the courtyard was rising to a deafening roar as Katarina made her way down the shadowed corridor. The sword at her side gently nudged her leg as she walked, and a royal blue cape was clipped to her shoulder over her uniform. Her steps, despite the clamor outside, echoed loudly in the hall.

Should I look at everyone when I go out, or keep my eyes down and only look at Faucher? No . . . Eric might be out there somewhere. I need to look demure and composed until fighting. Faucher mentioned catching them off guard and rattling them time and time again, so I really should—

The rambling in Katarina's mind was momentarily silenced as she exited the castle, and the sheer energy of the crowd sent an electric tingle rushing through her. She hesitated in her journey to gape, as the packed covered walkway around the training courtyard was filled with nobility and even the occasional servant. Above, more people were crammed in the windows of the several floors of the castle, eager to watch. Some people were even leaning out of the windows, craning their necks to get a better look of what was transpiring below.

Swallowing, Kat was barely able to stop her aura from surging forward.

Ignoring the looks of disgust, disapproval, and curiosity from the throng on either side of the courtyard exit, Kat threw her shoulders back, but kept her eyes downturned.

Once she descended the steps and took a sharp left, she proceeded down the cleared patch toward a roped off section where she knew Faucher and his sons awaited her.

Though she had to pass benches filled with Troivackian knights, and despite avoiding looking in their direction, she could feel a steady stream of hatred . . . at first. For whatever reason, as she walked, it faded into vague interest.

Kat's eyebrows twitched, and she risked a small side-glance to her right and found the knights staring at her whispering amongst themselves, but she shrugged as she passed, feigning passivity.

That's odd . . .

Once she entered the roped off section, Kat lifted her face and felt her stomach roil as she laid eyes on the Faucher family.

During her walk, she had forgotten why she was nervous to see her teacher that morning . . .

Faucher wore his official uniform and chest plate with his maroon cape attached at his shoulders. His curly hair tidy and his beard trimmed, he had his arms crossed as he gazed ahead at the square of courtyard that had been kept cleared for the spar.

Dante stood on his left, while Piers and Conrad sat on one of the two benches that had been set to the side for their personal use.

Under the covered walkway overlooking the sparring ring, Alina and Brendan sat in two ornate high-back chairs, their heads adorned with their crowns. Brendan wore his usual all-black attire, and Alina donned a deep red dress that was close in color to Faucher's cape and a black fur-lined cloak around her shoulders.

On her left . . . sat Eric.

His eyes remained fixed straight ahead on the ring, his face pale. He wore a navy blue tunic covered by a long black coat.

Kat didn't let her gaze linger.

As she looked back over to the men in her corner, she found Piers and Conrad staring at her.

Another unpleasant jolt rocked through her stomach, nearly making her flinch under their somber attention. She struggled to force herself to approach her teacher but somehow managed to.

"Leader Faucher," she greeted with a stiff bow.

Faucher didn't look at her. "Sit. Miller, Herra, and Ball will be joining us shortly."

Kat's right hand closed into a fist as she tried to remain in control. "Yes, sir."

She turned to take a seat on the bench, but the way Piers and Conrad couldn't meet her eyes again made her boots stick to the stones under them. Dante didn't even turn in her direction from his place on his father's left side.

Faucher, sensing she hadn't moved any farther, glanced over his shoulder at his sons, then at Kat's profile . . .

His heart squeezed in agony.

"You are a soldier before anything else, am I clear?" he barked abruptly, startling Kat into looking into his firm, brown eyes. "Nothing takes away from that. I'm livid, and many other things, Ashowan, but we can talk about that later, because that isn't as important as a soldier's duty. You fight for your honor, your kingdom, and until I say otherwise, you fight for me. And if you fight for me, you fight proudly. Understood?"

A look of pain, guilt, apology, gratitude, and . . . love. Faucher saw it all in Kat's eyes before she donned her impressive mask of infallible confidence.

In turn, Piers and Conrad finally locked eyes with the redhead as she straightened her spine and lifted her chin.

With a long sigh, Piers stood, moved closer, and clapped a hand on Katarina's shoulder, then leaned down so that only she might hear what he had to say.

"You're a part of the Faucher household now. Regardless of your bad decisions, that is not going to change. Just make better choices here on out."

Kat stiffened, and in the heavy silence that followed as Piers drew himself back up and peered down at her, he was not prepared for her face to remain stony as she proceeded to casually lift her arm and flick him between the eyes with great force.

"W-What the—"

Conrad snorted behind him.

It was Kat's turn to bow forward and speak her piece to the youngest Faucher son.

"Listen you, what happened last night isn't your business, but . . . thank you."

Kat fixed a very level stare on Piers, who reared back at first. But after a moment, he succumbed to a half smile.

"Alright, you pain in the arse . . . Father, should we review the strategy with this *nishka*?"

Kat put her hands on her hips, narrowed her eyes, and informed Piers: "*Jebi esh nishka, toora dondo.*"

Faucher rounded on the redhead in alarm, and even Conrad's gaze snapped up in shock.

"You speak the old Troivackian tongue?!" Faucher asked, unable to hide his awe or recall that he was still angry with her.

"I'm certain I told you about that." Kat waved her hand dismissively.

"No, you did not," Faucher insisted incredulously. "There are even members of the higher nobility that don't know that language! How in the world—"

"*Faucher, jebi toor gockla teir ba deshdum povarkus jeshi pa povark? Menna toor ka gebdi ashiyet.*"

"Lady Katarina, are you having a stroke?" Sir Cas had entered the sectioned off area during Katarina's addressing of Faucher, and with him came Ladies Nathalie and Dana with the faithful Boots panting at Dana's side.

Faucher looked at his wife, then back to Kat, still too shocked to speak.

"Erm . . . even my old Troivackian's not *that* good. What did she say?" Piers asked Faucher.

"I more or less told him if he's going to be distracted today of all days, maybe he should take a seat," Kat clarified with a smile before looking back at Piers. "Do you know what I called you?"

Piers's eyes narrowed, and he folded his arms irritably.

"Dumbass."

Everyone's eyes flew to Faucher, who was wearing a mystifying smile as he stared at Katarina.

"Wait, Father, are *you* calling me a dumbass? Or did she—"

"Does it matter?" Conrad interjected while barely staving off a grin of his own while seating himself beside his sister.

Piers rounded on his brother while Kat cackled, but her reprieve from the seriousness of the day ended when Duke Sebastian Icarus stepped into the sparring space in front of everyone.

Many people cheered—including the knights—but after a simple bow of his chin, he turned toward Faucher's corner where Lady Katarina stood.

"Good day, everyone. I thank you for coming to this event. To those of you who are unaware of how today is to proceed, I will explain it briefly so we do not delay. Some of us are busy men of His Majesty's court."

While he didn't look at anyone in particular, Duke Icarus's words struck those it meant to all the same.

"There are to be three rounds per opponent; no magic use will be permitted," he added while casting a cool side-glance at Katarina.

She smiled coyly and waved.

Meanwhile, Faucher glowered but nodded.

The duke ignored both of their reactions and instead turned to the Troivackian knights.

"You are the blood of our kingdom. I know you will not let our faith in you be for nothing."

His icy stare made some men gulp, while the older knights more familiar with him bowed their heads wearily.

The duke strode back to the stairs to take his seat in the first row of chairs to view the matches.

Kat leaned over to Faucher and through clenched teeth whispered, "I thought it was one round per person."

"It was, but if we dispute it, it'll make us look desperate."

"Isn't His Majesty pissed off that he changed rules without permission?"

"Ashowan," Faucher's rumble issued a warning in response to her harsh language, but he found himself emotionally unable to be mad at the red-head any more than he already was. "His Majesty banked on this. It'll only make you more impressive when you win."

"Oh lovely, you knew about it, too, and just didn't feel it was worth mentioning?" Kat asked, her voice rising a pitch.

Faucher looked at her irritably.

"A soldier should be able to trust their teacher and leader," she countered with surprising solemnity.

The Troivackian military leader sighed and closed his eyes wearily.

"I didn't tell you because it doesn't matter. You can beat their best squires repeatedly for at least an entire day before your aura shows."

"Half a day."

"What?" Faucher's head snapped back around, his eyes wide in alarm.

Kat's expression did not show any indication that she was jesting. "Faucher, I've not properly slept for a month. My magic is barely suppressed. If I had a few days of decent sleep, I could easily fight them for days without my magic coming through."

"Ashowan, they could draw out these duels. Why didn't you mention it?"

"Are you serious right now? You're trying to lecture me about transparency? Really?"

Both student and teacher looked away from each other, rolling their eyes in unison.

"Alright. That doesn't change much. Just make sure your first opponent can't fight after the first round. I want you to be as quick as possible. Remember: quick doesn't mean sloppy. Then smile at the knights. Insult them in the old tongue. It'll enrage them."

"How severely do you want the squire's leg to be broken?"

Faucher pondered the question.

"As clean a break as possible, but if he tries something dirty after the fact, break his nondominant wrist."

Kat nodded in agreement, her golden gaze fixed on the sparring ring as her opponent entered with cheers and applause from the knights at his back.

"Ah, they chose Praum. That's a shame. He would've been a fantastic knight," Dante observed with a sad shake of his head.

Faucher bobbed his head in sympathy.

Kat eyed her opponent, almost bored. "Alright, well. Wish me luck."

"You have talent and the proper education. There is no need for luck, Ashowan," Dante reminded her hotly.

"Pfft. Says the guy who doesn't even know how I punished him for being a prick when we first met."

"WHAT DID YOU DO TO ME?!" Dante roared while launching himself toward the redhead, only for Faucher, Sir Cas, and Piers to successfully hold him back.

"Oyy! You had your chance to find out! Now don't distract me! Apparently, we all suffer if I mess this up." Kat tossed her nose in the air and strode out of their waiting area.

Dante seethed behind her in his father's arms, but once Kat had reached the center of the sparring space, the Faucher heir allowed himself to go limp before straightening himself again.

"Is there any chance she will lose, Father?" he mused after clearing his throat and resuming his composure, all too aware of his wife's and daughters' gazes observing his strange behavior from above . . .

At this question, Faucher turned sternly toward his eldest son. "Faucher men don't make bets unless we plan on winning by a landslide."

Pleased, Dante nodded back to his father, feeling completely reassured.

"Have you honestly forgiven her for what she did?" Piers queried, his normal haughty expression fading as he stared at Katarina's ponytail fluttering in the gentle winter breeze that smelled of coming snow.

Faucher turned and regarded not only Piers, but also Conrad, who had risen and joined him at his side, then Sir Cas, whose eyes were once again disconcertingly steely. He had hidden such a look when Kat had been present.

"She is still my student. Nothing changes that or takes precedence over it unless I say so."

Behind Faucher and his sons stood his wife and daughter.

While Dana still had no idea what had transpired, his wife gazed at her husband's back with the utmost adoration and respect.

Only Conrad glanced over his shoulder and noticed this.

Without bothering to comment on the exchange, he leaned forward. "Admit it, Father. She's your favorite student. If one of us weren't married, you'd want her in the family."

Faucher didn't answer. He merely cleared his throat and stared at Katarina Ashowan's back. Though he did glance over his shoulder at Dana and . . .

He smiled.

It was a smile of such tender love and openness that Dana felt her breath be stolen from her throat.

Somehow, she knew everything her father wanted to say to her, and she had no idea why he had chosen that moment to show her such a thing . . . but there was zero doubt in her heart about its meaning.

Katarina Ashowan is incredible, and yes, I love her like a son, but you, Dana . . . are my only daughter, and I love you more than life itself.

CHAPTER 49

SPECULATIONS
WHILE SPARRING

Katarina stared at the squire known as Praum, who stood before her with a measure of sympathy. He looked strong and as though he could already be old enough to be a knight with his worn face and stubbled chin. He was impressively tall and had thick biceps and straight black hair that looked a little oily . . .

He jeered at Kat and eradicated her momentary pity.

With all her might, Kat fought the urge to smile at the man right then and there.

Instead she went to draw her sword, only to have the irritating Duke Icarus stand up from his seat.

"Ah, Captain Orion, perhaps for safety purposes we should use wooden swords for Lady Katarina. Oh, and if you wouldn't mind introducing who the lady will be fighting as well as her opponent's skill level, that would be greatly appreciated."

Again, the redhead had to resist showing an expression that was not the one designated to her by Faucher.

Praum laughed with the rest of the knights as Captain Orion made his way from his own chair along the row of noble observers and down the steps.

The young military leader did not look happy at all about what was transpiring.

He seized two wooden swords from a barrel he passed, and once in the sparring ring, handed the wooden sword to Praum while he tossed the sword at Kat, who made a point of not even bothering to try catching it and instead merely stared eerily at Captain Orion.

For a moment no one breathed.

Faucher stalked into the ring behind her, his murderous presence looming over Captain Orion, who flinched before his former teacher.

"You disrespect my student like that again and you will answer to me, Nathaniel Orion. Am I clear?"

Faucher spoke quietly, but even Praum's face paled as a result of his words.

"Pick up her sword and hand it to her," Captain Orion snapped to the squire.

The young man opened his mouth in surprise, but after taking stock of his superior's face, obeyed.

Kat accepted the crude weapon without a word of thanks and continued staring in her disconcerting manner at her opponent. Captain Orion turned toward the nobility and spectators. "This here is Squire Jase Praum. He was set to become a knight years ago but only just returned to training three months ago, as he had been tending to family matters."

The squire bowed to the nobility.

"He is my top student, and we expect him to pass the knight's exam with flying colors. When I call, the spar shall commence."

Kat passively observed that the squire in question was most likely only a year or two younger than Captain Orion. She was supposed to spar against someone who was as "inexperienced" as she was.

The captain and duke were cheating left, right, and center . . .

Ah well. It wouldn't matter either way.

The nobility proceeded to clap politely.

Then, without any further pomp, the Troivackian captain made his way back to his seat, leaving Kat standing in the ring with Faucher at her back.

While Praum waved to the knights, who were resuming their whoops, laughs, and hollers, Faucher bent down to Kat's ear and whispered.

"Break whichever wrist you want. I don't take insults lightly. Show them."

Kat couldn't resist; she smiled.

Faucher strode back to the benches, his cape swishing behind him.

When Praum managed to stop basking in the cheers of his peers, he finally looked at his opponent and was momentarily taken aback by the hungry, vicious smile on her face.

But just as soon as he saw it, it disappeared in the blink of an eye, making him wonder if it had been his imagination . . .

Collecting his composure and swagger, Praum raised his wooden sword and took his starting stance facing the redhead.

"Don't worry. I'll go slow for you." He laughed as Kat raised her own wooden sword.

She didn't say anything.

"FIGHT!" Captain Orion roared from his chair, spittle flying from his mouth.

Praum raised his arm back, but Katarina stepped closer, and in a blur of movement, his wrist was suddenly in blinding pain, his wooden sword already on the ground. Nausea from the agony racked his body, but he didn't have time to draw a single clean breath before there was a knee to his groin, a hand seizing the hair at the back of his head yanking him to the side over Kat's knee, and then a loud crack from his leg as her other foot gave a sharp blow.

By his next breath, Katarina had dropped him in a heap on the ground and was already striding back to the benches by Faucher. She handed her wooden sword to Sir Cas, who nodded in approval and respect before she rounded to face the training ring while standing at attention at Faucher's side.

The only interruptions in the shocked silence were the grunts and whimperings from Praum on the ground in the ring.

Kat stared with feigned disinterest at the faces of the knights across from her.

The younger ones were pale, some cringing around their middles as they stared sympathetically at Praum. However, the older knights were sitting up straighter, with new seriousness and a glint of interest appearing in their eyes.

Faucher addressed Kat quietly. "You didn't smile or swear at them."

"Are you mad because I didn't?"

"More so concerned."

"He was too easy an opponent. Just felt petty at that point."

Faucher grunted in agreement.

Meanwhile, the spectators were too stunned to know what to do.

Save for the Troivackian king and queen.

Alina turned and locked eyes with Duke Icarus, who sat on the other side of her brother, and she raised an eyebrow. "Perhaps remind Captain Orion that he is supposed to announce the winner of the match."

The duke fought off a twitch under his right eye as he turned to the captain, who was sitting on his left staring in open horror at the state of his squire.

"Announce the winner. Then bring out Sir Marin. If she bests him, I'll make sure Sir Herra has his chance," Duke Icarus hissed so that only the young man might hear.

Captain Orion clenched his teeth but rose from his seat while Praum was carried out of the ring.

Upon locking eyes with Sir Herra, the elite knight nodded in understanding.

The captain then looked over at Faucher and felt a trickle of cold sweat run down his back despite the air starting to turn bitingly frigid . . .

"The winner . . . is Lady Katarina Ashowan of Daxaria."

The only ones to clap were Eric, Alina, Brendan, Sir Cas, and of course the Faucher family.

However, while Captain Orion descended from his seat to give his men advice, Eric Reyes turned to look at the duke. His deceptively bored expression regarded the reedy man with a lazy eyebrow raise.

"It's odd how it feels as though your friend *Sam* hasn't been offering you much help as of late."

The duke met Eric's hardened stare coolly. "I haven't a clue what you are talking about, Your Highness."

"Hm. How odd . . . Eli had quite a bit to say about your time spent together."

The duke sneered. "Your search and seizure at my home will not go unpunished. You will soon feel my wrath, and I will take that child back one way or another. Even if I have to give you an entire crate of Witch's Brew."

Eric tensed, and the duke smiled gloatingly. "That's right. I know all about your troubles with the drug. Tell me, does your father know about that?"

The prince was saved having to answer as Captain Orion led Katarina's new opponent into the ring.

"This is Sir Esteve Marin. He was knighted last spring."

And that concluded the introduction.

Captain Orion was making it painfully obvious how nervous he was becoming about the imminent match.

The audience broke out in murmurs.

"Why was it Leader Faucher was asked to step aside as captain again?"

"With these magical beast attacks, shouldn't he be the one teaching and leading the men?"

"Captain Orion was only knighted a few years ago."

"Goodness, that woman really just destroyed his student in less time than it took me to finish my mouthful of moonshine . . ."

Brendan and Alina shared knowing glances as such sentiments fluttered around the crowds.

Katarina once again entered the ring, this time there was no mention of her using the wooden sword, and the knight she faced bowed to her respectfully.

She returned the gesture.

Captain Orion did not return to his chair beside the duke on the sidelines, and instead he stood with his arms crossed amongst his men.

"FIGHT!" he roared, his eyes flitting briefly to Faucher.

He flinched when he saw the smile on his former teacher's face.

The knight stepped forward and executed his first two strikes politely and with moderate strength.

Then in a blur, his left hand left the hilt of his broadsword, and using the heel of his palm, he shoved Kat back a step.

She didn't have time to be winded, however, before he rushed at her, forcing her to deflect his attacks one right after the other. He was merciless in how swiftly he pressed her back, and she couldn't find the timing to bring her sword up for an attack of her own. Overhead, underhand, to the side; his swings were too powerful and required all of her strength to hold against them.

Then she stumbled, and she felt a firm hand behind her grab her shoulder to stop her falling flat on her arse.

"SIR MARIN IS THE WINNER OF ROUND ONE!" Captain Orion's jubilant cry sent a chorus of cheers through the crowds.

Kat felt her hand grip her sword more tightly. She didn't have to look behind herself to know that it had been Faucher to catch her.

"He used your tactic against you. He rushed you first. Don't let him catch you off guard again. Make it like you intend to lunge and dance away, make him chase you. And just because he's polite, don't forget he wants to kill you in a real fight."

Kat gritted her teeth and steadied herself on her feet once more.

She then stalked back to the middle of the ring and locked eyes with the knight.

Sir Marin looked . . . calm.

He wasn't looking at her in disgust or like she was tiresome . . . He looked at her as though she were a *real* opponent. Given that it was the first time Kat had seen that look in someone's eyes, she found herself feeling uncomfortably nervous.

She shifted her hold on the hilt of her sword.

"FIGHT!"

Just as Faucher had ordered her to, Kat pretended to lunge. Sir Marin swung his sword with impressive speed toward where her predicted attack would land, but Kat was already launching herself off to his side, then ducking low and swiping her blade toward his exposed middle.

She was certain she'd won . . .

But that was when she felt a stinging near her ear.

She looked over her shoulder and saw Sir Marin's blade plunged into the ground behind her head, its edge having nicked her flesh. He would've slit her throat in a real fight just as she would've gutted him.

"DRAW!"

Kat's golden eyes slid upward toward Sir Marin's face, her breaths coming out in puffs. She could feel her increased temperature as the steam rolled off her skin, and she felt sweat prickle along her hairline.

He stared down at her, his breaths coming out a little faster, but he appeared as composed as before.

Kat hesitantly stood and started to walk back to her position, when four figures approaching the benches with Faucher drew her attention.

Broghan Miller, Caleb Herra, and Joshua Ball were walking toward her side of the ring, and while their backs held themselves strong and straight, their pale, gaunt, tensed faces spoke of the stress of the past month.

Caleb Herra had been the biggest meathead of them. Gruff, blunt, and always frustrated with how his ability with the sword was slow in returning to him. He had lost weight during the month outside of Faucher's keep, and he kept his gaze fixed blindly ahead.

Joshua Ball had dark bags under his eyes, his thumb already curled behind his fingers as he nervously fought fidgeting . . . He knew his brother was in the crowd watching him. Kat had been so preoccupied with her own training and woes the past month she hadn't properly considered how torturous and dangerous a time it had been for the young man.

Joshua had never been able to shine or even look up without fear of his brother's wrath, so to face a crowd of angry people . . .

Broghan Miller was the only one of them who marched confidently as he lead them to the ring. For good reason too.

No one would risk offending the brother of Cleophus Miller, the largest man in all of Troivack, who also happened to be following the line of Faucher's students . . . with Pina on his shoulder.

Kat lowered her eyes to the ground.

She wanted to look at Eric.

She wanted to share a whole conversation with him in a single look . . . But something in her also wanted to independently reconcile something that had been bothering her for some time.

So instead, she peered up at the crowd.

Kat saw the noblemen, most of them staring at her disdainfully, though a surprising amount with inoffensive interest . . . But the noblewomen and their daughters . . . They were the most spellbound.

They stared at her as though their lives depended on her every action.

The storm in Kat fell quiet then.

She wanted to win the sparring.

Not for fun.

Or to gloat.

Or even for Alina . . .

She wanted to win to show that the lowly could be the strong. That the undermined possessed undiscovered talents. That the beaten were not the defeated.

She had once said to Eric she wanted to protect people and that she felt it was her destiny, but the truth was, that wasn't all she wanted.

She wanted to lead.

She wanted to help people who were good but oppressed become strong.

Kat rounded back and stared at Sir Marin. She battled down her aura, but she felt potent emotion well up inside of her.

She would win.

And it was because the results meant more to her than ever before.

CHAPTER 50

CLASHING AND
CONSEQUENCES

The leather of her sword's handle creaked beneath her shifting grip as Kat let out a slow, steady breath while eyeing Sir Marin.

In the few spare moments she had before the spar resumed, she did something she had rarely felt the need to before . . . She evaluated her opponent carefully.

Faucher had barked countless times that she should know how to do so. However, she had always been able to rely on her magic, and when sparring with Faucher at night at the castle, she had already become accustomed to his style of fighting.

Her golden eyes roved over Sir Marin.

Given his age, he had been knighted during Faucher's time acting as Troivack's military captain, meaning he was efficient and less prone to flourished moves. He was practical. He also must have significant faith in his former teacher, as he was treating Katarina as an equal.

Sir Marin was a man of loyalty and respect, but that didn't mean he wouldn't fight dirty if necessary.

Gods, he is a tricky bastard . . . I'll have to surprise him. I'll have to use something that wouldn't be a technique Faucher would've shown him . . .

The solution appeared in Kat's mind like a ray of light from the heavens.

And in her gut, she *knew* it was what would determine she'd win.

"FIGHT!"

Kat rushed Sir Marin, feigning desperation in her shuffling steps as she swung her sword down toward his left thigh.

He blocked the attack and cast off Kat's sword, exposing her left side.

The crowd could see the opening, and some of the women closed their eyes, unable to watch.

Sure enough, he threw back his elbow into her side, making her crunch down over her bruised ribs. Sir Marin swept his sword back down toward Kat's head, which she managed to block, but with a turn of his wrist and a drop of his arm he had her weapon on the ground.

Everyone braced themselves for the winning strike from Sir Marin . . .

He drew his sword back . . .

Katarina suddenly smirked.

From her hunched position, she burst upward in a jump, her right arm wrapping around his neck and wrenching him down. Using him to hold herself up, Kat's foot shot out, kicking his sword from his grasp. However, what most people didn't see was her left hand had reached under the back of her vest during her kick and produced a thin dagger that she brought right to Sir Marin's throat.

Even though there was silence, the air hummed.

Then shrieking cheers broke out.

Kat's heart was racing, and she watched Sir Marin's eyes widen a fraction as he realized what had just transpired.

Patting his shoulder while offering a brilliant smile, Kat released the knight from her hold and backed up a few steps. She basked in his stunned reaction and swept a bow to him before picking up and sheathing both her sword and dagger. She looked over her shoulder toward Faucher, who was smiling proudly, while everyone in her corner was jumping up and down and clapping and hollering. Kat then turned her exuberant expression toward the nobility, though she was momentarily distracted by the sight of the hundred some women in attendance screaming and cheering at the top of their lungs.

Pride surged in Kat's veins as she watched many of the noblemen stare in open shock, while others were trying to no avail to get their womenfolk to settle back down.

When the redhead finally did look toward Alina and Brendan, her eyes were again drawn away . . . to Eric.

He was beaming and standing on his feet while applauding. He lifted his right hand to his mouth and let out a shrill whistle.

Kat blushed, then at last succeeded in facing Alina and Brendan.

The queen applauded with a triumphant smile of her own. While the king didn't outwardly smile, Kat could see the approval in his eyes.

She bowed to them.

The crowd grew even louder, and so Kat looked at the many Troivackian faces and waved.

She spotted Ladies Sarah and Wynonna both clapping. Though only Wynonna was smiling, Sarah did have a look of begrudging respect.

Then she noticed Lady Kezia pressing through the crowd with her husband, Prince Henry, at her side. Her breathtaking blue eyes were filled with tears as she celebrated with everyone around them.

Kat knew without a shadow of a doubt then that this was the proudest moment in her entire life.

However, the ruckus died down rather quickly, and out of the corner of her eye, Kat could see Captain Orion striding toward her, his face pale and his brows lowered.

He couldn't bring himself to look at her.

"Lady Katarina has won." His displeasure over the announcement was profound, and barely heard over the din that hardly quieted in his presence. "Therefore, I ask you, Your Majesty, to test the true limits of Lady Katarina's prowess . . . that she spar with one of our *elite* knights."

Fresh, fervid chatter burst from the crowd.

Brendan frowned.

He lowered his eyes briefly, though under his lashes, they slid toward Duke Icarus.

Alina turned to her husband, her true thoughts and feelings hidden.

He considered this request as many of the noblemen around him cast questioning and uncertain glances at the duke.

Then the Troivackian king locked eyes with Katarina Ashowan.

She in turn looked at Eric, whose previous good mood was replaced with darkness as he stared at the young captain.

Dropping her gaze briefly in deep thought, she decided to take a small risk . . .

"Your Majesty, I am fine to spar against the elite knight that is selected, but I ask that I be permitted to use my magic at least once during the match."

Her request sent waves of discussion through the onlookers until the king raised his hand and silenced them all.

Brendan looked disapprovingly at Captain Orion, who audibly gulped.

It didn't take a brilliant scholar to deduce that the young man had just signed and sealed the king's disapproval.

After all, the naïve young man had just revealed his loyalty to Duke Icarus over his king.

"Very well, Captain. However, for Lady Katarina to be declared the overall winner, she will only be required to win *one* out of the three rounds, and I am approving her request for a single use of her magic during the match."

Exclamations of surprise were heard throughout the courtyard.

However, Katarina wasn't finished. She raised her hand in silent request.

"Yes, Lady Katarina?" Brendan asked with a regal bob of his head.

"Your Majesty, given that this changes the terms of our initial agreement, may I ask for an additional reward should I win?"

Everyone save for the king leaned forward eagerly.

Brendan arched a dark eyebrow, but after a moment of careful thought, nodded.

"Then I ask that any woman, regardless of status, who wishes to learn the sword be permitted."

The uproar was ungodly.

The king's eyes widened amidst the chaos that erupted around them before once again holding up his hand and calming down the outrage instantly as if by magic.

"Lady Katarina, as impressive as your development and talent with the sword is, I am well aware that it is because of your magical lineage that you are on par with my men." The noblemen in the audience all nodded in relief. "That being said, I am willing to *discuss* with my council the possibility that women be trained in self-defense. I believe at the very least, such a change could be beneficial, and if anything, you *have* proved the fairer sex is capable of stomaching violence."

The notion was so alarming to everyone present that no one knew how to react.

Without needing to placate anyone in that instant however, Brendan gestured to the captain, who was beginning to turn a shade of olive green as he pointedly ignored the foreboding attention coming from Duke Sebastian Icarus.

Haltingly, the captain bowed, then made his way back over to the sidelines. But as he moved, Kat stared after him and noticed none other than Sir Seth Herra rising from his seat.

Her gut clenched, prompting her to turn and walk back to Faucher and gesture for some water, though that hadn't been the true purpose of her visit.

Kat accepted the flagon he passed to her while murmuring, "I have a bad feeling about this."

Faucher gave an almost imperceptible nod. "As do I. It's too planned."

Caleb Herra surprised everyone then by stepping forward.

"My brother is not above punching a woman in the face. Keep your guard up and mind his boots. He sometimes has his squires sew razors in his seams."

Kat recoiled slightly. "Gods, he is a prick."

For once, no one chastened her crude language.

Caleb Herra tilted his head in agreement, while Piers, Conrad, and Dante shared telling glances.

Cleophus Miller joined the discussion with Pina still asleep on his shoulder, which in turn drew more eyes to the group.

"He recently had his right shoulder put back in its socket. Hit there as many times as you can."

Kat blinked. She never had gotten used to the terrifying man's adoration of her familiar, nor his loyalty to her that came from their relationship . . .

"Thank you," she managed before locking eyes with Faucher.

"Do your best not to use your magic at all. If it's an emergency, so be it."

Kat nodded sternly while handing back the water flagon.

Piers leaned forward then, his own expression uncharacteristically grim. "Beat him no matter what. No one thinks this is a fair decision. Even the nobles who dislike you; you can tell almost all of them have at least a shred of decency." He nodded toward the audience, though Kat had decided she didn't want to rattle her nerves any worse and chose not to spare them any attention.

She looked at Sir Herra's profile as he bowed toward the king and queen.

Unlike Sir Marin, I can at least irritate him while we fight . . .

Kat made her way back to the center of the sparring space and waited for Herra to do the same.

When he finally met her gaze, she saw the hardness in his face.

He didn't look smug anymore . . . and for some reason, he even looked a little nervous . . .

Kat's instincts screamed at her.

Had she known she was fighting against him sooner, she would've considered rejecting the challenge.

Kat drew her sword; Sir Seth Herra drew his.

"FIGHT!"

Seth exploded in movement similar to how Sir Marin had charged her, only Kat was ready for it that time. She leapt to the right, forcing him to change his direction and, therefore, lose part of the momentum behind his attack.

She was able to cast off his first strike by ensuring her footwork was faster than his.

He easily had more than a hundred pounds on her, and so she knew her best defense out of the gate was to keep him chasing her.

Sure enough, Kat led him around the ring, deflecting his strikes and feigning lunges. Though she had yet to execute any of her own attacks.

At this rate, I need to best him in a single blow.

Snow began to gently fall from the sky as she moved. She gritted her teeth and hoped that Seth's footwork training had lagged behind. A single slip from him was all she needed . . .

The knight was rapidly becoming breathless, and sweat beaded around his brow as he tried to keep up with the nimble redhead.

"Running away won't save you," he panted.

"I'd say this is more like taking the dog for a walk," Kat responded evenly, which revealed to Seth that she wasn't nearly as winded as he was.

He glowered, then took a risk and half leapt into his next attack. This succeeded in both blocking Kat's path and forcing her to defend at the same time. He then landed a firm uppercut into her gut before headbutting her to the ground.

Eric was standing in less time than it would've taken most to blink, but Alina seized his arm, stopping him from speaking out.

Flat on her back, her head throbbing but sword still in her hand, Kat scooted back barely in time to avoid what would have been Seth's finishing blow. But she knew she wouldn't be able to dodge from her position for long.

Sure enough, his sword was already being drawn back.

"KAT! KICK HIS ARSE!"

The hoarse shout from Eric distracted Seth from his next attack . . .

And that was when Kat decided she was tired of the duke's sly, conniving means of besting her—first with the number of rounds, and then by casting a third opponent at her.

She would show him what it meant to challenge her.

The first matches were fought for those who felt weak in Troivack, but this? This was to show she was not going to suffer injustice in silence.

Besides . . . she said she'd use her magic only once, but she had never said for how long.

She hadn't intended to fight quite so dirty, but then again . . . they'd started it.

The light in Kat's eyes ignited, her aura burst from her body, and when it met with her sword, the blade itself was suddenly burning with ribbons of glimmering red magic weaving in the air around it.

Kat thrust her sword in the ground and rose to her knee before pushing herself up to standing, causing Seth to stumble back fearfully.

She plucked up her sword, and with a single hand at its hilt, swept the blade toward the knight's middle. He blocked the attack, but the clang of the swords meeting rang out and echoed around the castle walls like thunder. The force of her single-handed attack shouldn't have had that amount of power . . .

She flipped the sword in her hand, swiped the weapon backward, and even though Seth once again countered her, the strength behind her strike jarred the knight's wounded shoulder, making his right knee buckle. Kat punched his exposed side, and the crack could be heard from those nearest the ring.

He let out a yelp but impressively still attempted, despite the pain, a counterattack by grasping his sword with his left hand and twisting to stab Kat's belly that had turned toward him during her punch.

Her own blade came crashing back down onto his with enough inertia that the weapon fell from his hand.

Then she thrust the point of her blade under his chin while her left hand seized his tunic, pinning him in place.

He trembled beneath her grasp as he beheld the blazing aura around her, her golden eyes aglow and filled with determination . . . He could feel it in his blood . . . In that moment, he knew she had killed before, and this revelation made her infinitely more terrifying.

No one cheered.

Slowly, Kat released his tunic and moved a step backward. With a deep, careful breath in, she closed her eyes. When she breathed out again, her aura shrank smaller and smaller until it reabsorbed into her body entirely and her eyes were no longer two small suns.

When she opened her eyes, she grinned at Sir Seth Herra.

His face twitched, then he was drawing something out of his pocket with incredible swiftness. He loosened the top of whatever it was, dove forward, and drew his hand back as though he were about to punch her in the face.

There were shrieks and shouts of outrage from the women in the crowd. Kat belatedly saw something powdery flying toward her face when, midair, the dust froze in place, and Kat easily dodged Seth's fist.

She was saved having to fight him further by Cleophus Miller, who, with impressive speed from the sidelines, descended upon the knight. Pina was awake on his shoulder, and her pupils were thin as slits as she stared down at Seth. One bone-crushing punch to the knight's face from Cleophus sent him flying across the ring.

He lay unconscious, splayed across the stones like a broken doll.

"Aah . . . thank you," Kat managed to Cleophus while still reeling from what had just happened.

She then noticed that whatever Seth Herra had been trying to throw in her face was still floating in the air along with the old leather pouch it had come from.

She looked to Cleophus, but he appeared every bit as confused as she was, and so she turned to the crowd and found that they were all gaping with their mouths hanging open at the nobility under the covered walkway.

Following their eyes, Kat found herself staring at . . . Kezia.

Her hand was outstretched, and her mouth moving softly while the silver oval pendant she always wore around her neck on a black ribbon glowed.

Kat's sword fell to the ground.

Kezia Devark . . . the most beautiful woman the redhead had ever met . . . her friend . . . the only woman that had made Kat question whether she had any preference to women over men . . . was a mage.

CHAPTER 51

A PROMISING PROPOSAL

Ryshka, I promise I did not want to hide it from you!" Kezia half pleaded, half laughed as she and Kat walked down the castle corridor.

"But . . . But . . . why?! Gods, Kezia, I just . . . This is too much."

The new mother smiled up at Kat and gently reached out to pinch her side as they walked.

"I was supposed to guard Her Majesty in secret. My magic was to be a last resort, but with Mage Sebastian away with Mr. Kraft, there was no choice." She chuckled musically.

Kat couldn't bring herself to look at Kezia as they walked away from the clamoring courtyard.

Brendan had Sir Seth Herra detained and was in the midst of questioning Captain Orion while the royal physician examined the powder.

Most of the nobility had stayed behind to find out what had transpired, but, sensing that the topic of magic could get dragged into the conversation while everyone was in a state of heightened emotions, the two women were hastily excused.

Ladies Nathalie and Dana had escorted Kat inside with Sir Cas, but Lady Kezia had met them in front of the redhead's chamber door and asked for a walk in order to explain herself.

With a sigh, Kat dropped her chin down and finally mustered up enough courage to give her friend a small side-glance.

As usual, she looked stunning, and her dark red dress only made her more enticing to marvel at.

"You're too damn beautiful," Kat muttered irritably.

Kezia laughed heartily. "Thank you, ryshka. Though, can you honestly tell me you hold all those terrible old biases against mages?"

Kat grumbled while pouting, prompting Kezia to stop and face her.

"I like you better than most humans," the redhead admitted at last.

"Then that settles it." Kezia leaned forward and brushed her lips against Kat's cheek. "We are still destined to be lifelong friends."

Blushing, Kat's hand came up to touch her cheek, her eyes finally locking with Kezia's.

"Godsdamnit, woman, that isn't even fair!"

Kezia reached up and squeezed Kat's upper arms. "I'm desperate for your forgiveness. Do I have it?"

Dropping her head back with a loud groan, Kat looked at the Troivackian woman with a half smile. "Of course. Besides, now I can gloat to Sebastian that you're a better mage than him, and that makes me happy . . ."

Kezia laughed once more before dropping her hands to the front of her skirts where she clasped them, then looked over her shoulder at the door they stood before.

"I must get back to my son. He'll need to eat before I am pulled in for questioning, and . . . I'm given to understand you have something you need to face before the end of today as well, *ryshka*."

Kat frowned, then followed Kezia's gaze and realized they were in front of the solar.

Her eyes narrowed. "Did you only want to walk with me to make me come here?"

Kezia, still smiling, shook her head. "Of course not. I just thought we might save time talking and walking."

Still unable to hold a grudge against the Troivackian woman, Kat nodded reluctantly, though she did face her friend more seriously once more.

"Do you think what happened today will be enough to arrest Duke Icarus?"

Her good-humored expression fading, Kezia shook her head. "I have my doubts, but hopefully that powder we were able to save will lead the investigation toward that end . . . But you have had enough trials for today. I'm sure all will be disclosed later."

Though Kat still had lingering feelings of foreboding pertaining to the event, she agreed with Kezia. She knew she had to tackle her problems one at a time to not become overburdened.

Staring at the solar door, she gently bit the side of her tongue while working through her nerves.

"Go on, *ryshka*. We will speak more soon. Your exile will be lifted, and so we will be in each other's company every day once again."

Kat nodded and even managed to give a halfhearted smile.

She wasn't looking forward to what would come next.

Stepping forward, she wondered if she might face the storm behind the door and ask it to wait until the following morning. She *had* just made Troivackian history . . .

Kat didn't notice the sneaky smile Kezia wore behind her back, however, and instead she pushed open the door while her friend took her leave.

When the redhead entered the solar, she had fully expected to see Alina ready to descend upon her, already plotting about what they were going to do, and how, with regards to her night with Eric, as well as asking for an ungodly amount of details. Instead, she found that her best friend wasn't present at all . . .

Eric stood with his navy blue tunic unlaced at his throat, his hand balled into a fist against his leg while his other was rested against the window ledge of the solar.

Kat blinked, and her heart plummeted to her stomach, prompting her to subconsciously shuffle backward.

But then he looked at her, and a rush of heat and magic coursed through her, holding her in place, making her aura briefly flicker to life.

"Hi, Kat."

"Hi."

Eric turned from the window, his fist nervously tapping his leg. "Don't worry about that snake of a duke. We'll get him."

Tight-lipped, Kat smiled and bobbed her head.

Eric struggled to hold her gaze, but he did find himself capable of giving a small smile. "Your sparring was incredible. It was absolutely unbelievable how you were able to get so good in such a short amount of time; I'd be curious to see what more you could do with a dagger added into your fighting styles."

Kat beamed, instantly forgetting her awkwardness. "Really? That would be fun to learn! Faucher might go for it too! He did say normally at this point in my studies I'd learn to wield dual swords, but the broadsword wouldn't feel natural for me given my size, unless it was my only weapon, but I don't like cumbersome fighting. Would you teach me some of your dagger techniques you used when sparring with His Majesty a while ago?"

Eric gave a half smile at the end of the redhead's rant. "Sure."

Kat's grin brightened, but it didn't last, as she noticed the tension around Eric's eyes and the frozen line of his mouth.

"So . . . we got caught," she started haltingly with a wince.

Eric cleared his throat and nodded while dropping his gaze briefly before looking back up at her.

"Are you feeling alright?"

She attempted to laugh flippantly, but it wasn't as convincing as she'd hoped it'd be.

"I swear, you'd think the act involved me getting tossed down three flights of stairs, the way everyone keeps asking me that."

"That isn't what I mean." Eric took a hesitant step closer.

Kat swallowed as the pulse in her throat fluttered.

"Well, I . . . It was . . . You know. You were there."

"That I was." He let out a long breath of air. "Kat, do you regret it?"

She stiffened, but when she saw the nervousness in his face, she couldn't bring herself to be mad . . .

"I don't think so, no."

"You know what comes next then." Eric took another step, and Kat felt her legs grow weak and her eyes widen.

"W-Wait! T-There's the whole courting thing, or just seeing how things go, a-and—"

"We got caught. Even the king knows, and . . . there's the chance of a child. We are past being able to take things slow." Eric stared at her, his hazel eyes anxious yet also gentle.

"I . . . I mean, it might not be the case!"

"Kat, do you want to marry me?"

An overwhelming rush started up from the redhead's stomach, winding her and making her shoulders hunch as though he had just jabbed her in the stomach.

Eric held her gaze and did his best to appear as steady as possible, even though it was a struggle every moment in her presence.

"*You* don't want to get married though!" she reminded him a little too loudly.

"Neither do you," he countered quietly.

"I-I know, but . . . marrying you comes with a whole bloody kingdom! I come with a cat!"

Eric laughed softly. "Don't forget your family."

"My family . . . right . . ." Kat trailed off, remembering her father, mother, and brother . . . and Likon.

Oh Gods.

She had completely forgotten about Likon!

"Kat," Eric called her frantic mind back to the present. "Look, I'm not going to lie to you and say this is an ideal situation—"

The redhead chortled with a crazed glint in her eyes.

"But if I'm going to marry anyone, it's going to be you, and that answer isn't going to change. I'm not going to force you, and if you do decide you want the marriage to end at any point, or I hurt you in some unforgivable way, I will do everything in my power so that you can end it on your terms."

"As lovely as it is that you're already thinking of the end of our marriage, I . . . Eric, you don't really want this, do you?"

There it was.

The direct question he had feared being asked.

Eric's eyes fell to the ground, and Kat felt her heart sink.

Then he reached out and gently grasped her hand.

"What I really don't want is to hurt you or take away what would make you happy. I want you to be free to do as you please."

Kat tore her attention away from his troubled face, her irritability rising once more.

"This is the most depressing proposal ever."

Caught off guard, Eric had no choice but to laugh, and then he kept laughing at the absurd situation they found themselves in until he stumbled back and had to cover his eyes as he doubled over with Kat gradually joining him.

"Godsdamnit, Kat, we really are a disaster." He sighed after getting over the spell of humor while Kat gradually settled back down herself, a partial smile still gracing her lips.

Unable, and perhaps a little unwilling, to avoid the pull of her warmth, Eric drew closer to the redhead.

Cupping her face, he kissed her. Slowly, carefully . . . adoringly.

When they pulled apart and Kat stared up at him with the same maddening combination of love and vulnerability that he had seen in her face the night before, Eric closed his eyes and dropped his forehead to hers.

After a quiet moment of careful consideration, he stepped back again.

Kat was already missing his nearness, when he then proceeded to lower himself down onto one knee.

"You're right. That was a bit too grim, so let me give it another try." He grabbed her hand again and stared up at her, his own gaze loving and captivated. "Kat, I'm a selfish man, who has made a lot of mistakes—"

"This is your idea of being less bleak?"

"Shut up." Eric tugged her hand a little, making Kat smile again. "I'm being selfish again. Kat, I'm going to love you in all the wrong ways, and I'm going to make thousands of more mistakes."

"Alright, your self-esteem can't be *this* bad."

"If you don't quit being a brat, I'm going to stop," Eric informed her flatly.

"Right, right. Carry on."

Eric chuckled, his chin momentarily dropping to his chest with a mite of exasperation.

"Kat, I'm going to love you until the day I die, and if you decide to marry me, I'm never going to want to let you go. I'm going to be yours, and if you let yourself be mine . . . Gods, you're going to see that I love you beyond what is considered reasonable every day."

Kat didn't say anything as Eric peered up at her, his sincerity bright in his eyes.

"Kat, you don't try to fix me or make me a better man; you love me as I am, which makes you absolutely mad, but . . . you're the only one who I want to share my life with in all my forms, whether it be my good or bad days." Once finished, the prince stared up at her expectantly, waiting.

Kat blinked at Eric, then crouched to be eye level with him.

Pulling his hand to her lips, she kissed his knuckles.

"Eric, I know you're scared as hell of what happens to me, just like I'm terrified of what happens to you, but you promised to fight at my back. So I'm going to fight at yours. I'm going to be the most chaotic wife you could imagine, but at least I know I don't have to pretend that I'm not someone or something else if you're my husband. All my life . . . one of the main reasons I didn't want to get married was I was certain no one could really be happy with who I am with all my . . . eccentricities."

"Eccentricities? Really?"

"Okay, now it's your turn to shut it."

Eric held up his free hand in surrender, then gestured for her to continue.

"I was scared that a husband would expect me to tone down my antics or to . . . to be a version of myself that'd smother me. To make me feel I wasn't enough. You're the only one who doesn't expect or want that, and you're even offering to throw a kingdom into uncertainty if I decide I want to bugger off and do my own thing. I'm going to be a terrible wife in every traditional sense, and I'm going to want to keep learning sword fighting and doing troublesome things, but . . . I also want to be what you need as well."

Eric considered her words, then nodded with a shrug. "Sounds like you won't be boring. That's good enough for me."

Kat blinked at his glib, underwhelming response to her heartfelt declaration, and then shoved him.

Subsequently, Eric toppled over onto his back, but he had not relinquished her hand yet, so she found herself being pulled on top of him.

Staring up at Kat from his position on the floor beneath her, Eric felt his breath catch in his throat when she looked up at him from his chest where she'd landed, suddenly looking shy.

Closing his eyes, he allowed his head to fall back onto the stones beneath him.

Did he really deserve happiness like this?

Wasn't he going to bring Kat misery like the devil said?

"Eric? Are you ready to see the look on the Troivackian king's face when we tell him I'm going to be a part of his family?"

Eric's eyes flew open.

"I don't think I've ever been more ready for anything in my life."

Kat laughed and pushed herself up to kiss her betrothed again. "Shall we do it now?"

"Woman, if you keep lying on top of me like this, we aren't going anywhere for a long while."

Blushing bright scarlet, Kat sprung up onto her feet, leaving Eric to sit up with a groan.

He regarded her from the floor, and she noted the tired bags under his eyes . . . It had been a stressful morning.

Eric held his hand out to her. "Help your elderly husband up."

"Oh Gods, I'm marrying a grandfather. Should I buy you a cane as a wedding present?" Kat grasped his hand and pulled him to his feet.

"You do that, and I'm buying you a ball and chain with my initials on it to slow you down."

"Pfft, I can easily run with one of those if I use my magic."

Kat clasped her hands behind her back and began to skip toward the door, when Eric seized her arm, making her turn back around to face him.

"Kat, you do truly understand you're going to be crowned a queen, right?"

The redhead balked, her expression growing stricken as *that* reality dawned on her . . .

"Oh Gods . . . the paperwork . . . the meetings . . . Can I change my answer? Can I cancel the engagement?"

Eric raised an eyebrow. "So much for fighting at my back."

"Can't I just oversee the knights? I could see that being fun."

"You could make trousers a trend for women in your position of power," Eric suggested as they continued walking out of the solar.

"You raise a great point! Oh, my mother might kill me if I did, but it'd be worth it . . ."

The two continued talking as they always had as they made their way to the king's study where he was most likely handling the residual matter of Sir Seth Herra's illegal attack. A glow of happiness that had nothing to do with Kat's magic hung brightly around the pair.

The couple were in such fine moods as a result of their conversation, however, that they had promptly forgotten one other important detail until they arrived at their destination and Eric raised his hand to knock.

"KAT AND MY BROTHER DID WHAT?!"

Eric's hand froze as Alina's shriek reached them effortlessly in the corridor.

Both the prince and Kat stared at the door wide-eyed, then looked at each other.

"Would you like an early dinner first maybe?" Kat asked, her voice pitched higher than usual.

"That sounds like a fantastic idea." Eric nodded energetically.

The two swiftly rounded back the way they had come, both more than willing to delay facing the wrath of the queen of Troivack, Eric's sister and Katarina's best friend.

CHAPTER 52

FATES OF FRIENDS

Kat had her forehead in hand as she laughed, while Eric proceeded to flick a glob of goat cheese at her.

"Why do you always throw food at me?!"

"When have I ever tossed food at you?" Eric challenged indignantly.

Kat shoved the food in her mouth to her cheek to avoid choking. "When you made me pancakes!"

The prince scoffed. "Who do you think I learned to do such a thing from? My father or yours?"

Kat ended up laughing all the more.

The couple sat in the vacant corner of the outdoor area where Kat had trained the past month, plates of food in their laps, and hot cups of moonshine between them in the cold.

"Wait, so . . . when you fell in love with me, you threw butter at me?" the redhead asked between gasps.

"What about your father or me makes you think my reaction would be more mature? Honestly, I saw Fin twice as much as I saw my own father from the time I was sixteen years old!"

"Oh Gods . . . well, I can't even say how ridiculous it is because, apparently, it bloody well worked!" Kat was sent into fresh peals of side-splitting laughter, while even Eric succumbed to the point of watering eyes.

"Oh, Gods. It's fantastic being able to speak like this," the redhead admitted with a relieved sigh.

"For now, anyway . . . In a few months, we'll see how quickly we've become sick of each other," Eric noted casually.

Kat gently smacked the back of her hand against his chest. "Oyy. Don't go scaring me off the nuptials now that I have no choice."

The prince chuckled and shook his head, but the look in his eyes made Kat grow wary.

"Do you think Alina will forgive us?" he wondered with his gaze remaining fixed on the ground.

The instinct to lie nearly overcame Kat's knowledge that she needed to be truthful.

"I . . . don't know. She and I have drifted apart since coming here."

Eric looked to his betrothed with a mixture of concern and alarm. "Why so?"

"Honestly . . . ? She's . . . She's doing, feeling, and thinking too differently from me now. Before, when we first met, she was timid, but she wanted a bit of adventure and fun. She was forthright with her feelings even though it took a bit of goading. She was still figuring life out . . . but now . . ."

Kat trailed off, feeling emotions clutch her throat. "She's a queen, and . . . and it's wonderful, but I don't feel like we have anything in common anymore. She's married, pregnant, leading a hostile nation, rewriting laws, plotting . . . I'm just swinging a sword around and beating people up like I always wanted to, but now it just seems like I could be doing better."

"Does it help if I remind you that you are about to be married and also possibly pregnant?" Eric asked with a raised eyebrow.

Kat looked at him flatly. "No. No it does not. And you know why."

The prince let out a small sigh while leaning back and crossing his arms thoughtfully.

"You know . . . your father said this to me once." He paused, pain mixed with fondness in his voice. "'Best friends might drift apart in life as everyone grows and changes, but you know you're best friends when you have faith that you'll come back to each other one day.'"

"I feel like this is a great time to remind you how much of a hypocrite you are," Kat replied glibly.

Letting out a groan with a half smile, Eric looked up to the sky while his breath clouded in front of his face.

"Now that we're . . . we're getting married, are you going to make amends with my da?"

Eric's expression fell, and his eyes wandered as he lost himself in thought.

"Can you tell me now what exactly the fight was between the two of you?" the redhead pressed gently.

Eric set his dinner plate down, then rested his elbows against his knees while rubbing his hands slowly in the cold.

Kat waited.

"When Fin . . . When Fin found me and found out about . . . about the Witch's Brew . . . His first reaction once I'd sobered up was to apologize for not being there for me enough after my mother passed. He hugged me and told me to come home to be with my father and sister. Told me that sharing in our grief together would be helpful."

Kat didn't interrupt with her usual smart-ass remarks, sensing that this was one of the rare times it was best to hold her tongue.

"I agreed to go with him. Then the morning I was to leave with him, I asked if he was able to take over some of my father's and my duties while we tried to recover. I trusted him more than just about anyone in the court— aside from Lord Fuks, but I also knew more instability would've broken out if I'd appointed additional duties to the earl."

The redhead allowed herself to give a small smile at the mention of the delightfully demented Lord Dick Fuks.

"Your father said he would be able to stay with us for a few weeks, but after that would need to return to his duties . . ." Eric paused, and while Kat couldn't see his face, she could hear the sadness in his voice. "I told him a few weeks weren't enough. I told him too much had happened in a year. I needed time, and I wasn't . . . I knew I'd fall apart with more responsibilities on me, only if it happened at court, then all the nobility would see it. I told him I'd better not go home if he couldn't stay longer to help."

Kat frowned, but she cast her own memory back to the time Eric was recounting . . . She remembered shortly after the queen died, her mother shut up in her chamber, barely eating or sleeping . . .

She remembered how she herself had avoided being at home as much as possible . . . She had been getting into even more trouble than usual. It was the year she had really become renowned for her reckless behavior.

Her gut twisted guiltily.

"He argued saying it was part of my duty, and that when life got hard, we had to try and persevere the best we could. He tried to promise that the courtiers would give me all the grace in the world . . . I knew better." Eric sat straight again, then leaned back while crossing his arms. "I told him he was welcome to become the next king, and I was serious about it. I was trying to convince him that I was . . . I was not right in the head. I was having soldier's spells regularly and barely knew whether it was day or night."

Kat felt her own agitation at her father's handling of the situation.

"He told me that he was going to retire. Once I became king, he didn't want me relying on him . . . He was angry when he said it, but that was all I needed to hear to take off again."

"Eric, I am so sorry—"

"That wasn't the end of it, and . . . I didn't want to be the one to tell you about this kind of thing, but . . . given how things are going to be with us and your family, I think it's better everything is on the table between us."

Kat felt nervousness brew wretchedly in her gut.

"I followed Fin. Our fight made me wonder if he wasn't as great as I'd always thought him to be." Looking to the ground, the prince frowned. "Kat, are you aware that your family is not only growing schools and branches of government for the Coven of Wittica, but they also have shares in just about *all* brothels in Daxaria? Including here in Troivack? They have their hands in several . . . *questionable* establishments."

Recoiling slightly, Kat's mind leapt back to what she knew of her family. "W-Well, we keep the brothels safe with a union for the prostitutes so that—"

"And generally, that is true in all the brothels, yes. The women and staff are always treated well, but . . . there are a lot of drugs that still come and go in those places, and from what I started to learn, there wasn't a ban on those drugs. Your family was permitting them to be sold and consumed, though I did recognize that they were careful about them . . . It wasn't at all what I expected. I then discovered that your mother has been making deals with my father to take talented criminals under her employment for years. She's a powerful woman, Kat, and many people are afraid of her for good reason. She hides herself well, and I was only able to learn as much as I did because of my status and connections. But it only makes her more fearsome to me." Eric finally looked at his betrothed, his expression apologetic. "I didn't want to be the one to tell you about this. When I returned to Daxaria this summer, I found out your brother has not only been aware of these business dealings, but he is starting to learn how to lead them, though it didn't take me long to figure out you had no part in any of this. Am I right? You had no idea, did you?"

Kat shook her head, her face drained of color.

She remembered certain oddities about her mother that others had observed as being peculiar: the fact that Annika Ashowan knew how to wield knives, that she knew how to hunt and survive in the wilderness, that she was so involved in the various brothels . . .

"Listen, I never brought this up with your father. There could be more to this than I know, but . . . I have been wary of your parents for quite some time. Back then, when I realized how far their reach went, I traveled to Zinfera—those stories, I'd like to leave for another time though."

Kat swallowed with difficulty, then gratefully recalled she had a cup of moonshine at her side.

She took a mouthful, and once she had accomplished swallowing it, faced Eric squarely. "I think . . . when I ask my father about all this . . . I want you there with me."

"You don't have to, Kat. If this is something you want to keep in the family—"

"You are now part of the family. Isn't that why you told me all this?" Kat pointed out sternly.

Eric hesitated in answering. "I did it so you might understand my behavior around your father. Gods know I don't need to look like I'm acting any more irrational."

"Agreed."

Kat and Eric locked eyes, then after a beat, both laughed. Neither of them wanted to dwell on unpleasant topics when they'd only just been granted some measure of happiness.

A sudden look of bashfulness overcame Kat, however, making her duck her head and hide her cheeks that had reddened. "By the way, I . . . er . . . When the wedding does happen . . . would you . . . er . . . would you mind if I wore my uniform?"

Eric blinked in surprise, then laughed. "Why the hell would I mind?"

Kat sighed in relief then, wearing a brilliant smile, she leaned forward and kissed his cheek.

Looking equal parts startled and pleased, Eric wrapped an arm around her and pulled her close, pressing a kiss of his own to her forehead.

When they pulled apart, Kat stared up at him in that enticing way that was making the prince want to kiss her more profoundly, when the couple was interrupted.

"OYY! YOU TWO!"

Both Kat and Eric looked up and over to find Faucher with his sons all standing at the exit of the castle.

Piers had been the one to shout, and he stared while looking irate at the prince, whose arm was still around Kat's shoulders. Conrad was frowning beside a scowling Dante, who had Pina on his shoulder, and he was presently scratching her cheek while staring at Kat disapprovingly.

"Er . . . Hi, Piers," Kat called over, feeling instantly self-conscious as she pulled away from Eric and stood.

The youngest Faucher son stalked over to the couple. "Just because we decided we still accept and care for the redhead doesn't mean we like you." Piers brandished a threatening finger into Eric's face.

"Aw! Piers!" Kat smiled up at the Troivackian.

"Shut up!" Piers moved his finger over to her face as he continued glaring at Eric, who rose to his feet while holding the man's gaze steadily.

He could tell Piers was still considering attacking him.

Faucher approached them next. "Your Highness," he greeted with a rumble before turning to Kat. "The two of you have been summoned to see our king and queen."

Kat's eyes rounded. "Is Alina still angry?"

Faucher stared at her levelly without offering an answer.

The redhead cringed. "That isn't good."

"I take it you two agreed to marry?" Faucher asked instead. While the question had been aimed at both of them, he still only stared at Kat.

She looked over her shoulder at Eric, who risked taking his eyes off Piers to return her gaze. "We have."

"Good. Your wedding is taking place before the midnight hour."

"I . . . Wh-What?!"

"Her Majesty ordered this if you two had reached an agreement."

Kat's jaw dropped, and her hands found her hips as she stared at Faucher incensed. "That woman and her plotting! Just what—"

Faucher looked to Eric while Kat continued with her tirade.

The prince's face had paled, but he met Faucher's stare head on, then dropped his eyes to the back of Kat's head as it bobbed aggressively during her tangent.

His wide, anxious gaze softened, and he let out an almost imperceptible breath with the right corner of his mouth twitching upward.

The expression told the Faucher men everything they needed to know . . . And so, with Kat still speaking at great length about how the Troivackian queen had become addicted to elaborate schemes, they all herded her toward the castle for her wedding.

CHAPTER 53

ROUNDING UP

With her eyes the size of saucers, Kat stared down at the furious queen of Troivack, Alina Devark.

Behind her in the solar stood Ladies Kezia, Wynonna, and even Sarah . . . though only Lady Kezia and the queen knew what was going on.

"Hi, Alina, did you enjoy the sparring match?" Kat asked faintly with a smile.

"It was spectacular! I absolutely loved how fast you broke the first man's leg! I almost laughed out loud!" Wynonna crowed excitedly before Lady Kezia shot her a warning look and shook her head with a small wince and kind smile.

The widow in her black turban grew perplexed and raised an eyebrow, then looked at Lady Sarah who, for once, was in a similar state of confusion.

"Katarina Ashowan, just what the hell have you gotten yourself into?! You're marrying my brother?!"

"What?!" Lady Sarah exploded in alarm.

"Congratulations!" Lady Wynonna cheered behind Alina.

Kezia dropped her forehead to her hand. She had tried to tell the queen that it wasn't wise to have this discussion in the presence of the other handmaidens . . .

Kat barely resisted making a jest, but when she saw the deadliness in the queen's eyes, dropped her chin to her chest, then met Alina's stare directly.

"Yes. I'm marrying your brother."

"Because you made a stupid error in judgment? Were you drunk?"

"What did she do?" Lady Wynonna whispered to Lady Sarah who was, leaning forward in equal interest.

Kat recoiled, not liking the accusatory tone of her friend's voice. But when she stared down into Alina's hazel eyes that were so very much like her brother's, she had to make the humbling admission that she hadn't confided in Alina about her personal affairs in a long time, and so to the queen, it very much would look like she *had* simply done something careless and foolish.

"No. It happened because Eric and I love each other, and . . . then . . . you know . . . we had a bit of a fight, and well. *That* happened . . ."

"What happened?" Lady Wynonna asked eagerly with Lady Sarah nodding beside her.

Alina looked over her shoulder, her gaze shooting daggers, but Lady Kezia raised her eyebrows with a look that clearly said *I told you not to bring them here.*

The queen returned her attention to her friend and folded her arms over her middle while leaning back.

"You love each other? Why? When? What the hell have you two been doing behind my back?"

"It wasn't behind your back, Alina. I have my own life separate from yours, and to be perfectly honest, no one is surprised. No one but you."

"I beg to differ! How could anyone—"

"Oh, no. Pardon me, Your Majesty, but just about everyone near them knew. All the knights, the entire Faucher family, all of us—Wait, Lady Sarah?" Lady Wynonna jumped in while listing people on her fingers.

"Well, to say I *knew* wouldn't be right, but . . . I'm not . . . *exactly* surprised," the Troivackian woman bristled a little.

"Then why did you go out on three separate courting dates with him?" Alina demanded accusatorily.

"He's a prince!" Lady Sarah snapped with her cheeks blazing red.

Alina turned back to Kat. "Wonderful. So everyone knew but me."

The redhead stared at her friend with an uncharacteristic calm. "You've been busy, Alina. You are accomplishing so many great and wonderful things, and you're going to be a mother soon. Eric and I just have a peculiar relationship, and it wasn't easy to talk about."

Alina gripped the sleeves of her red dress and closed her eyes before taking in a deep breath. "You were at each other's throats from what I heard. I could see there was a measure of attraction brewing, but . . . when did this all change?"

"Well . . . you see . . . at your wedding . . . we—"

"What about my wedding?! What have you both been hiding from me about that day?! I knew there was something . . ." Alina's eyes popped open, and her arms fell to her side.

"Well, that was when we first spoke and kissed and then—"

"This type of relationship has been going on since my wedding?! Wait, you kissed at my wedding and didn't tell me?! Why did you throw him bare-arsed into the pigpen?!"

"I beg your pardon?"

"You did what?"

"Did he already have his pants off, or did you have to do that bit?"

The three noblewomen burst out behind Alina at the same time. Lady Wynonna, of course, was the one to ask the strange question.

"Well, after we kissed, I saw him with another woman, and . . . I may have been a little upset about it . . . Then he thought it was because my father had said something to me, but it wasn't, and so we fought back and forth. Then I had a magical episode in the desert, and he was kind to me, and then he was an arse, then I was stabbed, and he was there for me . . . Then he helped hide my stab wound when he led me up the castle steps. After that, we kept getting to know each other, and when I saved him from being kidnapped, he made me pancakes. We danced together and agreed to team up, then we went together to get my sword fixed, and he stopped me from killing Broghan Miller. Then I avoided and ignored him because he was courting other women, then he told me he loved me and that we shouldn't be together and he left for his trip. When he returned and I told him he was an arse and I loved him, then we . . . talked . . . and now we're apparently getting married."

The room was dead silent.

"I think that's everything."

"You tried to kill my brother?" Lady Sarah asked, visibly confused.

Kat looked at her in alarm. "I completely forgot you two are related."

Alina held up her hand and blinked. She opened her mouth to speak once. Twice. The third time when nothing came out, she looked behind her at her handmaidens, who, aside from Lady Sarah, were squinting and thinking through the onslaught of information they'd just received. Lady Wynonna pulled a flask from her skirts and took a gulp before offering it to Lady Sarah. The woman accepted it and proceeded to chug the contents for an impressive amount of time.

"Why is it you are saying Eric and I have to get married tonight of all nights after the sparring match?" Kat queried, trying to get the conversation away from the possibility of any uncomfortable questions.

Alina licked her lips. "Well . . . tomorrow is the Winter Solstice, and . . . and I was going to announce my pregnancy."

Kat smiled. "That sounds great."

"I was thinking we could also declare you wedded my brother, as it would seem like you two planned it purposely to avoid a big fuss. It would add a lot of chaos, and people wouldn't be able to spend their entire time at the festivities obsessing about my pregnancy, or the details of your marriage."

"Either way though . . . the wedding will feel rushed. None of my family is here, and Eric is the next king of Daxaria. We should be getting married there."

"We can't wait that long, now, can we?" Alina pointed out dryly.

"Oh!" Lady Wynonna burst out in understanding with Lady Sarah grasping the widow's arm in both shock and fascination at the drama.

"They slept together!" Lady Sarah had most likely meant to whisper the discovery, but apparently the moonshine had encumbered her senses rather quickly.

"Congratulations on having a baby, Lady Katarina!" Lady Wynonna waved at Kat, who was looking at the ceiling as though she were wishing it would collapse down on her.

"I'm not . . . We don't . . . Never mind. It probably isn't happening like that."

"Yes, but we aren't risking a war breaking out over *probably* if we can avoid it," Alina reminded sternly. "We are going to say that the prince waited as long as he could for your father's arrival to marry you, but he made an agreement with His Majesty that if after the sparring match he had not arrived, for the solstice, you two could be married privately. A proper ceremony and coronation will take place, of course, back in Daxaria. You two will most likely be returning to the kingdom with your father once he arrives." Alina paused to sigh. "If we had any idea of when he was going to get here we could maybe wait, but his last missive was weeks ago, and I think this timing is better."

"It'll still be strange that we get married here. People are going to talk about it," Kat concluded, her expression uncharacteristically serious.

"That's easy to explain away." Alina announced, her cheeks turning pink. "You two wanted to get married here because you both love me and didn't want to make me travel with a newborn."

Kat couldn't help but break into a tentative smile. "Well . . . you're right there *is* that factor, too . . . but what about his courting dates with other women? Won't the courtiers find that suspicious as well?"

By this point, the redhead already knew that Alina had crafted an explanation for everything, but she was still curious to hear the answers.

"We're going to say that you asked Eric to be certain he wanted to marry you. As far as I'm aware, none of the noblewomen thought he seemed all that interested in them."

"One of Duke Icarus's daughter thought he was," Lady Sarah reminded while swaying where she stood.

Kat winced.

"Well . . . even so, it's a good enough reason. Though the nobles will have some conflicting thoughts about you, at least it won't be the kind to destroy your reputation." Alina concluded while at last turning to address everyone in the room and not just her friend.

"I'll be honest, I'm surprised I still *have* a reputation to destroy," Kat muttered more to herself.

The queen looked back at the redhead, a small frown returning to her face. "So . . . you really weren't kidding about wanting to be my sister-in-law, hm?"

Kat grinned. "I don't joke about stuff like that. Though at the time, I had completely forgotten that you also had a brother."

"Wait, so . . . so Lady Katarina, *you're* going to be the next queen of Daxaria?" Lady Sarah asked while looking openly mortified.

"That would be correct, Lady Sarah!" Kat responded delightedly as she watched the Troivackian seize Lady Wynonna's sleeve and tug it twice, prompting the widow to wordlessly hand her back the flask.

"Oh Gods . . . I'm trying to imagine you surviving the paperwork . . ." Alina mused with a ruthless smile.

Kat's good-humored expression dwindled then. "Isn't this my wedding day? Can't we only talk about happy things? Try to imagine your husband's reaction when I get to call him my brother-in-law. That's already cheered both Eric and me considerably!"

It was Alina's turn to have the coy look on her face be wiped clear, as she stared at her friend flatly.

Kat waggled her eyebrows.

Alina continued to stare.

Kat's smile deepened as she leaned closer, then nudged her friend gently in the ribs.

At last, Alina broke and laughed. "Oh Gods, fine. I admit it's funny, and I won't lie to you, I would part with nearly all the gold I possess to see, my father's assistant, Mr. Howard's expression when you tell him. Do you think you could get your father to break the news to him? Because . . . Gods, I might send a painter to Daxaria with you to capture the moment."

Next thing the two women knew, they were howling together, clasping on to each other.

When the pair eventually calmed down, their eyes watering, they stared at each other.

Understanding and warmth passing between them.

"I can't say I'm surprised you of all people would be getting married in such an unorthodox manner, Lady Katarina." Lady Sarah stepped forward with a sniff, though she stumbled as she did.

"What can I say? I find a predictable life boring."

Alina, still smiling, reached out and clasped her best friend's hand.

Eric's words came back to Kat then . . .

Even though she and Alina were fundamentally different people . . . they did agree on the bigger things, and while they may drift apart every now and again . . .

Kat knew they'd find their way back to each other one way or another.

While the inhabitants of the Troivackian castle were quiet, Katarina Ashowan was wide awake.

Fresh from a bath, her hair combed thoroughly and dried, she glanced out a window she walked past in the castle corridor.

Snow gently fell outside, blanketing the world in a quiet embrace.

Despite the results of the match rocking the courtiers and staff to their core, along with the suspicious attack from Sir Herra, the evening of the Winter Solstice brought with it a peacefulness that was replete with a magical quiet and awe.

Children somehow managed to fall asleep as they waited for the mystical Osik to come and leave them blessings or presents, and their wonder tended to be infectious even to the grown-ups.

Kat felt like a child again.

She was giddy and excited and knew something wonderful was about to happen as she walked down the corridor with Alina by her side, followed by Lady Kezia, Lady Sarah, and Lady Wynonna.

She had donned her uniform that identified her as one of Faucher's students but conceded in leaving her hair down in its soft gleaming waves. Kezia had seen to magically producing small white flowers that Lady Sarah had pinned into Kat's hair.

She was the most unorthodox bride in all of Troivack, but . . .

"It's perfect for you," Alina had declared with a tearful smile.

Kat had cleared her throat and pretended to be nodding her thanks to Lady Sarah instead of hiding her own emotions.

When the entourage of women arrived at the throne room doors, Kat found Sir Cas, Lady Nathalie, Lady Dana, Faucher, and all his sons standing waiting.

Alina squeezed Kat's hand and stepped forward to address the group.

"We'll all go in first. Lady Kezia is going to magically create some music for Kat to enter with. I believe His Majesty, Prince Henry, and Prince Eric are already inside."

Everyone bowed or curtsied to the queen in response.

But as they moved to file into the throne room, Kat took a nervous step. "Er . . . Faucher?"

The military leader faltered, but Lady Nathalie had a knowing smile on her face as she ushered Dana in.

"What is it, Ashowan?"

"My . . . My da isn't here . . . and . . . I know I don't need to . . . to have someone give me away, but I . . . well—"

"You want me to walk you down the aisle?" Faucher was stunned.

Kat blushed and looked everywhere but directly at him. "Well, you're . . . you're father-ish. You have a beard with gray in it, and you stand in my corner. You're my teacher, and you've been there for me and . . . you mean . . . You are . . . You're special to me," she finished awkwardly.

Faucher was grateful she wasn't looking at him because emotions were welling up in his chest and there was an irritating wetness in his eyes.

"Well of . . . of course. You're my student, and you're under my command. It . . . It only makes sense."

He had never had so much trouble speaking in his life.

Kat peered up at him, her golden gaze aglow.

Faucher blinked rapidly and wiped his eyes with a grunt.

The soft notes of music wafted out to them from within the dimly lit throne room.

"Well, come now, Ashowan. You've made a mess, time to make the best of it as usual." He offered her his arm which she gingerly took.

"Yes, sir, and . . . thank you." Kat smiled, feeling her throat ache as she couldn't help but miss her family, but she also felt immensely grateful for her new loved ones being present.

She knew that she would have more hell to pay for what she and Eric had done, but at the very least for that night, she chose to bask in the fine company and wonder of the evening ahead.

With neither Kat nor Faucher needing to say another word, the doors opened.

CHAPTER 54

DECLARATIVE DUES

That woman attacked Lady Katarina with a golem?" The devil rose from his seat, the shadows along the walls flickering menacingly as Leo delivered the news in the small, cramped room of the cottage the two of them had grown up in together.

"Yes. She also sent her assistant and an imp to try and bind her. Which explains why, about a month ago, you woke up with those chest pains, master." Leo bowed, his expression serious, his left hand touching the hilt of his sword that hung at his side.

"Godsdamnit. If she had only kept coming after me directly, then that would be one matter, but she's striking at those tied to me . . . It's been ages since she's cut so close." Sam's dark eyes slid to the narrow, peaked window that overlooked the solstice evening's cloudy sky.

While Leo couldn't see it, the red string that had woven itself amongst the devil's heart had tightened to the point of it causing significant pain day in and day out . . . but Sam would never admit to the fact.

"Duke Icarus has stopped responding to us as well. I'm given to understand he may have sided with that woman and is taking her advice. It's hard to predict what *she* is after right now. If she used the golem attack to try and block the connection you have with Lady Katarina, perhaps she is trying to protect the Daxarian witch."

Sam shook his head. "Lady Katarina doesn't need *her* protection, and that wench already knows it." He frowned, his thoughts whirling deeper and deeper . . . "Perhaps she is trying to draw me out to unite all of Troivack and its witches against me."

"Didn't she try to use Aidan Helmer to that end?" Leo recalled with a frown.

The devil nodded, his eyes still fixed on the wall. "She did, and that blew up in her face magnificently. Though I wished a dragon hadn't had to die along with that fool." He paused.

His frown melted away to an expression of alarm. "Or . . . had that been on purpose? Had she pushed Aidan Helmer while expecting him to fail? Was it possible she already knew about the house witch? Had she already learned of the will of the Gods?" The devil shook his head.

It didn't seem likely.

A sudden pain gripped Sam's chest, making him close his eyes with a small flinch.

He could feel himself drawing closer to his wit's end.

The devil had known it would be annoying, but . . . the string of fate that connected him to Lady Katarina was much like the redheaded witch's powers: burning and intense.

Striding toward the window, Sam rested his palm against the windowsill.

"I don't know what that cur of a woman is up to, so I may have no other choice but to reveal myself to the world. Leo, are you prepared for what will follow?"

Sam looked over his shoulder and found his subordinate had grown stressed and wary.

"You'll die."

The devil scoffed. "Yes, yes. Rest assured I'll be back again as always. My curse won't break if—"

He stopped.

"Master?" Leo stepped forward tentatively.

Sam turned, his eyes wide with realization. "If she figured out that Katarina Ashowan's magic is capable of consuming my curse and freeing me, she would want me to stay far apart from Lady Katarina. This explains why she would try and interfere with Katarina's fated connection to me. Then, knowing her . . . she will arrange Lady Katarina's death to take place in a *very* particular way . . . It would be in a style that would make her a sacrifice for Troivack, which in turn would cause . . ."

"Witches to be deemed as . . . heroes."

The devil nodded, then . . . a faint smile spread over his lips. "I suppose that trifling woman is becoming a little more ruthless as she ages. Very well. Tell the men to prepare themselves, Leo. I will go and handle this myself. Consequences be damned."

* * *

Well aware of how last-minute her wedding was, Kat did not have any expectations for the throne room when she entered with Faucher.

However, she should have known the abilities and determination of both Alina and Kezia combined were not to be underestimated.

Before her was the aisle to the thrones, only the carpet had been removed some time ago, and candles lighting the way to the stairs now flanked either side outlining where it used to be. Brendan stood in place of where, in Daxaria, a magistrate typically was positioned to wed couples.

To Brendan's left stood Eric, Prince Henry, Sir Cas, and the Faucher sons.

To his right stood Alina, followed by Ladies Nathalie, Kezia, Wynonna, Sarah, and Dana.

A soft white light from Kezia's necklace was glowing and emitting gentle yet enchanting music from around her neck. It was a melody that called Kat and Faucher forward, and unlike the grim percussive music that the redhead had become used to during her stay in Troivack, it was beautifully uplifting.

However, after she looked to Kezia, she then noticed whom the occupants of the room were focused on . . . Kat felt her cheeks flame red as everyone stared at her.

She'd never liked being the center of attention with matters that showed any of her vulnerabilities.

So she fixed her attention on one person only.

Eric.

He looked nervous, and Kat couldn't help but smile when she saw he looked at her as though she were the only person in the room . . .

And as though Piers, Conrad, and Dante weren't staring daggers into his back.

Kat felt Faucher stiffen beside her, and it took her a moment to realize that it was because she had started to glow . . .

"It's just because I haven't had much rest, don't worry," she murmured to her teacher with a small chuckle.

"His Majesty wasted candles," Faucher grumbled beside her, making her bite her lip so as to not laugh any louder.

She knew he was feeling a bit out of his element.

It was nice to know she wasn't the only one.

At last, Kat reached the head of the aisle. She heard a suspicious sniffle from Alina directly behind her.

Brendan regarded the couple before him as Eric carefully reached out and took both of Kat's hands in his own.

Faucher gave a small bow to Brendan, then retreated, his cape billowing as he made his way over to the side with his sons.

Eric was staring at Kat, his face pale and terrified, but she clasped his hand and his shoulders visibly relaxed as he continued looking into her brilliant golden eyes.

"Today, we have all come to witness the exchanging of vows and commitment to the joint ruling of the kingdom of Daxaria between Lady Katarina Ashowan of Duke House Ashowan Viscount House Jenoure, and His Highness Crown Prince and knight Eric Reyes of Daxaria." Brendan's voice for once did not fill the room, but it reached the ears present all the same.

Eric's grip on Kat's hands tightened.

She shifted forward and let out a small shuddering breath.

They felt like complete fools and wholly unprepared, but when the two discovered that they were *both* shaking in their boots, Kat gave a nervous smile, while Eric's stiff half smile grew more assured.

"Do you, Lady Katarina Ashowan, vow your loyalty and commitment to His Highness Crown Prince Eric Reyes? To live at his side as his wife from this day forward, regardless of health, adversities, or wealth, and to care for him to the best of your ability with honesty and trust?"

Kat's aura flickered higher as her heart felt as though it were expanding in her chest beyond its limits.

"I do."

"Do you vow to uphold both the pride of your family as well as the pride of your husband's family that, from this day forth, shall be your own?"

"I do."

Brendan cleared his throat. "His Highness has requested a slight altering to the traditional Troivackian vows, and so I will also ask you, Lady Katarina . . . Do you vow to fight at your husband's back through every battle one or both of you shall face, be it large or small, and celebrate the good, be it large or small, for the rest of your days together?"

Kat's eyes began to water.

She had never felt happier than she had in that moment.

"I do."

Brendan cleared his throat, then looked to Eric.

"Do you, Crown Prince Eric Reyes of Daxaria, vow your loyalty and commitment to Lady Katarina Ashowan of Duke House Ashowan Viscount House Jenoure? To live at her side as her husband from this day forward, regardless of health, adversities, or wealth, and to care for her to the best of your ability with honesty and trust?"

"I do." Eric's voice was hoarse, and his stare intent on Kat.

"Do you vow to uphold both the pride of your family as well as the pride of your wife's family, that from this day forth, shall be your own?"

"I do," his voice hitched.

Kat's hands twitched in Eric's grasp.

Oh Gods. This is really happening. It's actually real. This is not a dream. This is not some strange plot. Eric and I are getting married. MARRIED!

"Do you vow to fight at your wife's back through every battle one or both of you shall face, be it large or small, and celebrate the good, be it large or small, for the rest of your days together?"

"I do." Eric's thumb stroked the back of Kat's hand.

Alina gave a soft, watery gasp behind her friend.

"You will sign the appropriate paperwork with Her Majesty Queen Alina Devark and Sir Hugo Cas as witnesses to this union," Brendan informed them sternly. He nodded to a small round table with a lantern already lit where the paperwork sat waiting.

"Your Highness, Lady Katarina, please come this way." Prince Henry's soft voice broke the momentary trance that had the newly wedded couple pulling away from each other.

With Kat blushing brightly, and Eric gingerly rubbing the bottom of his lip with his thumb, they both avoided meeting anyone's eyes. They then followed the Troivackian prince over to the table to complete the paperwork that would make their wedding legally sound.

It took only a few moments, and by the end . . . Kat was grateful that her hand once again found Eric's. Her mind was racing too quickly to hold on to any of the details in that moment, but the warmth of Eric's slightly damp, calloused palm helped settled her nerves.

When they returned to stand in front of the king, he nodded to them, and they bowed in return.

"I send you both off with my blessings and well-wishes. I anoint you with peppermint oil as a reminder of the touch of sanctity that the Goddess and Green Man bestow upon couples such as yourselves." Brendan accepted a bowl of oil from Henry.

He touched his thumb to Eric's forehead and then Kat's.

"I now pronounce you . . . officially wedded to each other. You . . . may kiss the bride."

It wasn't like the Troivackian king to struggle to express himself, but fortunately nobody paid it much mind, as they were too engrossed with watching the actual couple.

His hand flying up to cup her face, his fingers grazing the back of her neck, Eric kissed Kat. His nerves and intensity created a kiss that had Kat's aura flickering around her as she seized the front of his navy blue tunic and allowed him to pull her close.

Their audience gave a loud echoing round of applause, and when the kiss ended, Eric and Kat stared at each other, still holding the other close. For an instant, time around them stopped, and in that moment, Kat saw Eric in his entirety. She saw the broken, the dark, the uncertain, the afraid parts . . . but also the unfathomable amount of love for her he had. She saw passion, she saw a gleam of life . . . she saw his goodness, and she also saw that, while their future was far from simple, he wanted it with her.

Kat turned a brilliant smile toward Brendan, who spared her a rare smile of congratulations.

"Thank you, Your Majesty. I will do my best to be the most doting sister-in-law you could envision!"

The room fell silent.

Brendan's good-humored expression dropped as did the color in his face.

Alina snorted behind the redhead, her peals of laughter were the only sound as Kat's smile toward the Troivackian king became dazzling. Kezia and Nathalie were forced to delicately cover their mouths, while Dana's shoulders shook violently.

With his face red as a beet, Prince Henry, however, was the one who broke the dam as he let out a loud "HA!" before succumbing to full-blown hysterics.

The entire throne room save for Brendan Devark and Lady Katarina were laughing to the point of tears. Kat winked at the king, and he looked to the heavens despairingly before closing his eyes with a wince and dropping his chin to his chest in defeat.

It was done.

From then on, no matter what . . .

Katarina Ashowan had officially become . . . a *distant* relative to the Troivackian King Brendan Devark.

CHAPTER 55

THE KING'S CONSTERNATION

Alina rested her head wearily against her husband's shoulder as she watched Kat talk and joke with the Faucher sons while everyone else enjoyed a glass of heated moonshine.

Eric was standing quietly beside his new wife, nodding along to whatever she said, his gaze warm whenever his attention drifted over to her animated face.

"How did I never see it? I mean . . . really see it."

Brendan turned to look at his wife, his eyes crinkling in their corners as he smiled. "You've been busy."

"I know . . . but . . . Kat always picks up on anything I'm feeling almost instantly. I thought I was the same way with her."

Raising an eyebrow, Brendan looked over to the redhead he had begrudgingly come to respect.

"Being the daughter of a hero with dangerous abilities comes with its own burdens. Especially when her abilities are tied to her emotions."

"It's just that it seems like . . . like I've only ever known the surface of her, and I actually have no idea of her actual depths . . . But when I see her with Eric . . ." Alina trailed off and shook her head, longing touched with sadness in her darkened hazel eyes. "They *know* each other."

Brendan stared at his brother-in-law and observed the way Kat was subtly leaning back into him.

It was true.

The pair had found some kind of understanding in each other that no one else could fathom reaching with them.

"Are you ready for her to keep teasing you about being her brother-in-law?"

"They might divorce at some point. All hope is not lost."

Alina laughed and gave her husband a gentle nudge. "Glad to see you're working on developing your sense of humor."

Brendan took a moment to enjoy the scene before him. His subjects and family members were happy as they quietly celebrated the Winter Solstice Eve . . . Eventually, the king turned back to face his wife.

"I'm proud of you."

Taken aback by the abrupt declaration, Alina straightened in her seat and regarded her husband in open wonder.

"You have grown stronger and bolder. You are known as no easy adversary in the court here in Troivack, and that says a great deal."

Alina laughed, albeit with a note of bitterness. "Honestly, I'm not doing anything all that revolutionary. I'm just hard to pin down because they've never dealt with women in an official setting."

"Do not underestimate yourself. That alone is difficult to manage amongst the nobility. While things with my mother did not go the way I had wished, I do know she would be equally impressed with how you have taken to creating a place for yourself here."

Alina nodded slowly. Despite her husband's words containing the highest degree of praise, her hand subconsciously rose to her swollen middle that was hidden under the layers of her winter garb.

"She was strong in her own right. I feel bad for her in a way because she probably could have been an even better and revolutionary queen than I am if your father had been anything like you."

The queen's words had a profound effect on her husband. Brendan's eyes filled with pain but also appreciation for the implied compliment from his wife.

The two fell back into silence in time to see Kat slap her hand over her mouth, double over in laughter, then stumble. Eric caught her instantly, and when she struggled to remain balanced, he set to picking her up in his arms.

"Pardon us, everyone, but I think . . . due to her lack of rest the past month, Lady Katarina is . . . indisposed," Eric explained as Kat's initial squeak over her new husband carrying her quieted down.

"Wait!" Alina sprung to her feet excitedly and rushed over to her brother as her friend began clumsily wrapping her arms around the prince's neck.

Eric looked at Alina while hoisting Kat up in his arms a bit higher to steady himself. "If you need to speak with me, I can come back down once I put her in the carriage."

"No! That isn't it! I've never seen this woman drunk before! How can you be putting her to bed?!"

Caught off guard by the queen's declaration, everyone turned with interest toward the redhead, who was grinning in Eric's arms, her head slumped against his shoulder.

Realizing that he was not going to be able to whisk Kat out of their impromptu reception as quickly as he'd planned, the prince set her back down carefully while still holding up most of her weight.

The redhead swayed on the spot, her eyelids fluttering.

"Kat! I have so many questions to ask you!"

"MMyeah? What's uuh . . . What's up?" She tried to force her eyes to look straight ahead at Alina, but instead wound up going a little cross-eyed.

Eric couldn't help but let out a small snort of laughter.

"When did you know for sure that you were in love with my brother?"

"Mmm . . . Mm . . . Not sure . . . maybe when he . . . when *he* said he loved me?" Kat managed while closing and opening her eyes one at a time experimentally as the room spun around her.

"Pardon me, Your Majesty, but I have a much more pressing matter," Dante interrupted the queen and Kat, striding forward urgently.

Blinking in surprise, Alina stepped back to allow the man to bend down to attempt to meet Kat's gaze head on. "Why did you punish my brothers back when they first met you but not me?"

The redhead laughed and staggered again, forcing Eric to catch her to stop her from falling on the floor.

Dante leaned closer to her face. "Ashowan. You need to tell me."

Kat opened one eye that still struggled to focus and regarded the eldest Faucher son with a groan. "Thas . . . Thas cuz of Pina."

"What? What do you mean? What did Pina do? How is—"

"Dante, come now, you've had your turn." Piers shoved his brother out of the way and crouched down to eye level with Kat. "Now, Ashowan, admit it. I'm your favorite in my family, right?"

"Ooh. Piers-y. Piers. Piiiiiiers." Kat reached out and pinched Piers's cheek, then tugged it back and forth while he raised his eyebrows at her. "Dana's my favorite. Mmkay? She's . . . She's got puppies . . . an' . . . an' . . . you? You're . . . I mean you're ssshhfine! But, like . . . you don't have puppies."

Piers straightened himself with a sigh. "Damn. I *did* forget about the puppies."

Conrad approached next, and Eric was starting to wonder if he should take exception on behalf of Kat . . . However, Conrad rarely ever spoke, and so the Daxarian prince resigned himself to allowing one more question before he let Kat get a well-deserved night of undisturbed rest.

"Um . . . I was wondering if it would be alright if we visit you in Daxaria." Both of Kat's eyes flew open.

She blinked at Conrad, her face serious, and then she threw her arms around his neck, bawling her eyes out.

"Conrad! Of course! Jus' . . . You should live with uus! Come live in Daxaria!" She pleaded while Conrad awkwardly hugged her back.

Eric watched at first in surprise, and then with a half smile before he cast a glance toward Faucher, who shifted uncomfortably. He could have been blushing, but the dim lighting from the candles was making it difficult to discern, though the prince could tell he had wanted to know the answer just as much.

"Alright, I think that is enough for tonight." Eric gently touched Kat's shoulder as she continued to cling to Conrad. She appeared to already be half asleep.

Conrad looked apologetically at the prince, but he waved off the unspoken sentiment before he turned his back and crouched.

"It's embarrassing to say, but carrying her on my back will be significantly easier."

"I had wondered why you had started working on weight training with Sir Cleophus Miller," Henry observed wryly from where he stood with his arms around his wife.

Eric cleared his throat. "I had just wanted to get a bit stronger. In Daxaria, I only needed to be fast."

No one bought his excuse.

Even if the prince may have taken a long time verbally admitting to how much he had wanted Kat, his actions had always said everything for him.

With the redhead loaded onto the prince's back, the pair set off out of the Troivackian throne room. The king had graciously arranged for a private room for them at an inn in Vessa to avoid any prying eyes, and so all Eric had to do was successfully slip out of the already cleared corridor, through the servant exit, and to an inconspicuous carriage that awaited them.

Eric would return to the castle first thing the following morning, and Kat would arrive later under the pretense that she was recovering from her sparring matches the day before.

Which is exactly how everything went, though the prince hadn't known he'd be hauling Kat into the vehicle while she was more or less unconscious, but he made do.

Once safely stowed inside the black carriage, snow falling outside peacefully, Eric closed the door and plunked himself down beside Kat. He knocked the roof three times and felt them lurch into motion.

It had been a very long day that had felt like it had been three.

He turned to stare at Kat while regaining his breath.

They'd been caught together that morning.

He'd been threatened, pummeled, talked to . . . Kat had won her sparring matches, then he had proposed, and then . . . they were married.

All in a day.

"And here I thought Fin's wedding was excessive with getting knighted, ennobled twice, and married," he murmured with a laugh as he reached over and gently laid Kat's head to rest on his shoulder.

As the quiet nestled around him, Eric could at last explore his thoughts regarding everything.

I truly don't think I'm ready to be a husband, but . . . I don't think she's ready to be a wife either.

An electric jolt ran through Eric's being.

She's . . . Kat's . . . Kat's my wife.

He blinked as the realization settled in.

Earlier, he had jested with her about being married, but teasing about it and the reality of the situation were two very different things.

Eric stared at her sleeping profile.

Her long nose. The wisps of her red hair that had come free from the pins and framed her face, her slackened mouth with her lips still turned up ever so slightly in the corners as though the instant she awoke she was prepared to smile . . .

"You . . . You're my wife. Mine . . . With me . . . forever . . . or until you get rid of me." Eric attempted to make a joke to himself, but there was a lump in his throat that stopped him from getting away with it.

"Gods, let's be honest . . . the second you said you loved me back, there wasn't a chance in hell you could get rid of me. You're stuck with me now, Kat." Eric kissed her forehead and rested his cheek against her head.

She smelled of amber and spices . . .

He smiled.

For the first time in a long time, the broken prince of Daxaria had the sense that everything was exactly right. Everything was as it should be . . .

And he was lucky enough that where Katarina Ashowan was supposed to be was by his side on this wintry solstice night in Troivack.

* * *

Alina and Brendan awoke the morning of the Winter Solstice unceremoni-
ously thanks to the relentless knocking on their chamber door.

Brendan let out a grumble.

The knocking only grew heavier until he let out a dull roar and crossed
the room in only a loose fitting white tunic and comfortable trousers.

Throwing open his chamber door, he scowled down at whoever dared
wake him in such an unholy way, when he found himself staring down at
his assistant, Mr. Levin.

"What is it?" Brendan demanded furiously.

"Y-Your Majesty, I beg your pardon, however . . . His Grace Duke Finlay
Ashowan of Daxaria has arrived and is asking to see his daughter."

The Troivackian king felt his ire drain from his being.

"He isn't supposed to—I didn't even know that he—" Brendan stopped
and stared down at the ground, attempting to gather his sleep-addled wits as
he heard Alina rise and pull on a robe behind him.

"Have Duke Ashowan escorted to my office and alert Prince Henry.
Send Lady Kezia to rouse Lady Katarina."

Mr. Levin nodded and left swiftly. Though the man had no idea that
Lady Katarina wasn't even in the castle, Brendan knew his brother and
Kezia would know what to do.

After relaying the news to Alina, who was then prompted to vomit thanks
to the combined efforts of her morning sickness and fresh anxiety, Brendan
splashed some icy water on his face and dressed himself in a great hurry.

He passed by garlands and holly that had been used to decorate the
castle in the previous weeks for the solstice. He passed smiling servants and
nobility alike, already excited for the day's festivities.

He could barely hear their greetings and well-wishes over the sound of
his blood roaring in his ears.

He reached his office, and with his heart in his throat, he pressed the
latch open, still clinging onto the hope that it was all a very bad dream.
However, when he looked into his office, he found Finlay Ashowan, donning a fine navy blue wool coat trimmed in gold, a snowy white tunic, and
tan trousers. His blue eyes as piercing and magical as ever, even though
Brendan knew that he shouldn't have any magical abilities outside of
Daxaria . . .

"Happy Winter Solstice, Your Majesty." Finlay bowed and straightened.

As he did this, Brendan closed the door behind him and noticed that the
house witch had not come alone.

Sitting at his feet, with his chest fur as fluffy and regal as ever, was Kraken.

When Fin had righted himself, he stared at the Troivackian king coolly.

"Now, would you care to tell me why it is so difficult for my daughter to come and see me this morning?"

Brendan swallowed.

While he had thought the prospect of dealing with the devil unsettling . . . He had grossly underestimated the sheer magnitude of stress he felt having to tell Finlay Ashowan, the infamous house witch, that his daughter had been bedded and wedded to the future king of Daxaria, all while on his watch. And all of that had to be said before any mention of the assassination attempts.

The Troivackian king did his best to brace himself, but he knew deep down that there was nothing he could do that would sufficiently prepare him for what was to come.

ABOUT THE AUTHOR

Delemhach is the author of the House Witch series, which they started in order to share with readers some of the warmth, fun, and love of food they experienced while growing up. Born and raised in Canada, Delemhach discovered their love of fantasy and magic at a young age, and the affair has carried on well into their adulthood. Currently, they work multiple jobs, but the one they most enjoy, aside from writing, is privately teaching music to people of all ages.

Get whiskered away

with updates on your favorite
magical hijinks, the coziest
content, and all things
Delemhach!

Visit

mailchi.mp/podiumaudio/delemhach

*to sign up for
Delemhach's newsletter!*

Podium

DISCOVER MORE

STORIES UNBOUND

PodiumEntertainment.com

www.ingramcontent.com/pod-product-compliance
Lightning Source LLC
Chambersburg PA
CBHW031340180325
23662CB00026B/65